Wildwood
Exit

Wildwood Exit

Joel E. Turner

LEVEL
BEST BOOKS

To Anne

Praise for Wildwood Exit

"Hard-boiled, heartfelt, and hilarious, *Wildwood Exit* combines reluctant gangsters, goofy romance, and small crimes with life-or-death stakes in an expertly crafted story that's so Jersey you can practically smell the refineries…or whatever that is." — Jon McGoran, author of *The Price of Everything*

"When John McGinty agrees to manage a Jersey shore restaurant owned by his friend Lou Scolletta, Ginty finds himself in a precarious position, navigating Lou's business and personal problems. Just how connected is Lou Scolletta? Funny when it's supposed to be funny and nasty when it's supposed to be nasty, Joel E. Turner gives the reader a fresh take on crime at the Jersey shore in his debut mystery, *Wildwood Exit*." — Jeff Markowitz, author of *The Other*

"The 1980s are getting started as John McGinty stumbles onto the seedier side of life at the Jersey Shore. If the Philadelphia Irishman doesn't know the easy way to survive among small-time criminals and their volatile family situations, he certainly knows how to spin an entertaining tale. You'll want to yell at Ginty to stop but he doesn't, and therein lies the fun. A great read whether or not you are familiar with the Jersey Shore location." — Jane Kelly, author of the Meg Daniels Mysteries

This old world may never change
The way it's been...
I've been searchin'
For the dolphins in the sea
And sometimes I wonder
Do you ever think of me?

—Fred Neil

Chapter One

The car bumped hard, the undercarriage hitting the edge of the shoulder, as it careened off the Garden State Parkway, heading for a stand of trees. The bump woke me up, and I jammed on the brakes and fought the steering wheel, cutting it hard left, but it was too late. The car fishtailed as the front smashed into a tree, the rear swinging right as the brakes took hold and crashing into another tree. I was flung forward, my hands coming off the wheel and banging against the console.

My hands were cut and bleeding as I sat staring at the road, the car twisted at a forty-five-degree angle. Pain throbbed from my right temple, and I realized I must have hit the windshield or the roof. A heaviness pressed down inside my head above my eyes, and I felt an urge to close them and go to sleep.

I forced myself to stay awake and get out of the car. I knew I was still technically drunk, but the crash had pumped enough adrenaline into my veins that I was hyper-aware, despite the likely concussion. I tried to open the trunk, but it was stuck shut, the right fender crunched in and bent on the top where it met the hatch.

A car passed going north on the other side of the Parkway. I looked back up the south-bound lane and saw no traffic. I stepped onto the road and half-jogged across, stepping over the median and across the north-bound lane. I glanced back at the car, slanted cock-eyed in the grass just past the Exit 6 sign for North Wildwood, then hurried through the grassy stretch alongside the road and into the woods that bordered it.

My only thought now was to avoid getting a DUI. I could deal with the car later. What a disaster. I had just bought the damn thing yesterday afternoon from a guy in Buena with a badly running nose and a burning desire to take my cash and go meet someone to make him well. That's what I got for taking a lead on a cheap car from a guy holding up the end of the bar at a beer-and-a-shot place down the street from my house. I could have asked Lou to hook me up, but the price was right, and I just wanted something to get me through the summer. So I hitched a ride to Buena from a buddy who was headed to Margate, where I met Drew, the guy with the dripping nose. Drew had that pressing business to attend to, so he was fine with giving me the uncompleted paperwork.

Drew said, "Just see Mitch at the title place here next week, he'll handle it."

I trudged through the patch of woods, distancing myself from the Parkway. I came to a two-lane road and ran across that into deeper woods on the other side. I was about ready to just sleep under a tree there, when through a gap in the branches I saw an open field.

I pushed forward to the perimeter of the woods and stopped, trying to make out where I was. If it was somebody's back yard, I would have to be careful. But there were no lights, just a dark field spreading out before me. I looked to my left and saw a brighter patch on the ground and a hundred yards beyond that a low building, maybe a garage?

I walked through tall grass to shorter grass, and as I got closer to the bright patch, I realized what it was: a sand trap.

I was on a fairway of Wildwood Country Club, the home course of my friend Lou Scolletta, whose house I was supposed to have been at four hours ago. There was probably a caddie shack I could hide out in, but I opted for a makeshift bed in the grass of a hollow a few fairways over. I lay down and, in the brief period before I passed out, wondered if this was the best way to prepare for the first day on my new job.

* * *

There was no way I wanted a full-time job working for Lou. I knew just enough about Lou to know not knowing anything more was the prudent path. The fact that he had just fired the prior manager for dipping in the till did not make the opportunity more appealing.

But there was a crazy part of me that thought running a place—a restaurant, not McNabb's Tavern, the decrepit neighborhood tappie in Southwest Philly where until last year I humped kegs, mopped up fluids, breathed a lot of smoke and told myself I was the "manager"—might be something I could do. Because I was nowhere right now. No degree, no trade—just fifteen years of bartending that had ended when the last McNabb standing decided—wisely—that this was no way to make a living. The new owners didn't need a mug like me in the fern bar that McNabb's was to become.

I knew The Seabreeze, the quintessential Jersey Shore restaurant. When Lou bought it six years ago, I helped out a few weekends bartending when some of the corner boys he had hired just disappeared on him. It wasn't hard finding someone to cover for me at McNabb's. Our weekends were slower in the summer anyway, with a lot of folks going to the shore.

Lou and I hung out more back then. He bought the place in 1977 when I was thirty and Lou maybe thirty-seven. It was sort of a vanity project for him; his main business was a Cadillac dealership in South Philly. The following summer, he showed up at my bar with his son Davy—guess the kid was sixteen. He wanted Davy to get a summer job. Could we take him on, washing dishes, whatever? I wondered why he didn't hire him at the dealership, but I guess he wanted him to work for someone else.

So I hired him, and he was okay, typical teenager, hardly said a word. There really wasn't that much to do—we had a kitchen and did some sandwiches, but it wasn't much to keep a dishwasher busy.

I guess that was the first favor I did for Lou. And I did owe him big, seeing as how his dad got me out of the draft back in 1967. Plus, Lou got me my first restaurant job, which was really a pretty good gig at a nice South Philly restaurant. But with Lou, you never felt like he was looking for payback. He just came off as a great guy, not like he was some connected dude that you had to say yes to. I'm sure he sold a lot of cars seeming like a great guy.

I used to give Davy a ride home sometimes, which often led to Concetta—

Lou's wife—asking me in to eat. There was always food, loads of food. She'd give me a plate of pasta, red wine out of a jug—might be ten o'clock in the evening, but so what? Then Lou would show up, and he wouldn't bat an eyelash that I was there. Then he had me down to a little mom-and-pop restaurant near his dealership for dinner, and I met some of his friends. They were mostly older and had gone to Bishop Neumann or Southern, but a few knew guys from Kingsessing, my old neighborhood in Southwest Philly.

I thought about that pasta and how a mick like me was going to run a real restaurant, and, as I passed out in the wet grass at 3:30 AM, whether Davy was still having the same nose-dripping problems as Drew from Buena, a path I saw him starting down two and a half years ago.

* * *

The sound of a mower woke me up. The guy running it looked like he had seen worse. He pointed me to the caddy shack and gave me some coins for the payphone. Thank God Lou picked up, but then that's Lou, he's not surprised if some fuckup calls him at dawn. I washed up as best I could with cold water and no soap in the filthy sink in the shack's bathroom, then waited outside the locker room, not wanting to meet up with anyone, until Lou arrived.

What a night. Blitzed out of my mind, drinking stingers like I was twenty in Somers Point, dancing with those crazy chicks, trying to teach me to moonwalk like Michael Jackson on that Motown show a couple of months ago. It was the Friday after a Monday Fourth of July, and it felt like the bar itself was stumbling under the strain of a week-long bender.

I had just stopped in for something to eat, then met these girls, three of them, late teens, which led to my dancing lesson. As it got late and the stingers took their toll, I figured maybe I'd just crash in the back seat for a couple of hours, then get breakfast somewhere, rather than roll in drunk at four in the morning and freak out Concetta.

Then two of the girls disappeared and the last one, Sharon, became glued to a chair at my table—that is, her butt was glued to the chair, but her face ended up stuck to the table itself, her long brown hair straggling out into the sticky remains of many ungodly drinks. At closing time, I struggled her to her feet and managed to get her to moan out where she was staying in Sea Isle City, a couple of towns south. After she vomited in the parking lot, I got her into the back seat and drove as carefully as I could, taking Route 9 to avoid the faster traffic.

I got the girl out of the car at her shabby rental duplex, leaving her sprawled on a chaise lounge in the screened porch. I banged on the door until one of her roommates appeared in a long t-shirt. We got her into bed and I talked the roommate through how to make sure Sharon didn't choke on her own vomit.

I sat in my car, worrying about the girl. I was old enough to be her father, but being plastered in a Somers Point bar at closing time didn't exactly qualify me to be *in loco parentis*. I was just a more experienced wastrel, a thirty-six-year-old failed bartender who would have been a disappointment to someone, if there was anyone left to fill that role.

When I left the girl's rental, I figured it wasn't much farther to Wildwood, and what the hell, why not take the Parkway? But of course, that's what impaired judgment is all about. So fatigue and drunkenness once more exacted their toll on a stupid Irishman, and here I was creeping around at dawn like an escaped convict

The door to the club's locker room opened, and the attendant poked his head out.

"Lou's here."

I pushed myself up off the asphalt where I had been avoiding the stream of Saturday dawn patrol golfers passing in and out of the locker room. There was an ugly smile of a cut on the side of my palm. I had washed the dried blood off, but the wound was still bruised and weeping, ragged scraps of a paper towel embedded within it.

Lou was on a bench between a row of lockers, close to the cinderblock wall, two Styrofoam cups of coffee next to him.

"You look great," he said.

I sat astride the bench, my back to the open end of the row. I pulled the paper towel off my hand and blotted the cut.

"Lucky I'm alive," I answered.

Lou asked, "How did you get here?"

"I walked."

"Right." He took the top off his coffee. "From the Parkway?"

"Yeah."

He pulled the tab off a mini-moo and poured it into his cup. "And the car's still there?"

"I was pretty wasted. If I stuck around, I'd be in jail right now."

"You gotta get it towed. You'll get a fine for abandoning the vehicle."

I had been thinking about the not-quite-completed title transfer and thought I'd try out my logic on Lou.

"It's not my car."

"I thought you bought it from some guy in Buena."

"I did. He was in a hurry, and the tag joint wasn't open. It was pretty late, maybe nine o'clock."

"So…"

"So he had the forms—the title and shit—he signed them and gave them to me. Said the tag guy was cool, he'd accept his signature without him being there. I said I'd stop by sometime this week and get it all taken care of." I lifted my hands. "So, it's still his car."

A loud voice hailed me. "Yo, Ginty."

A big guy in a golf shirt and shorts was opening a locker behind me. He took a sleeve of balls out and came over. He shook hands with Lou, then turned to me. His hands went up.

"You're a mess, man. Better get cleaned up or Minnie won't let you out on the course."

I opened my hands in front of me. Besides the one major wound, they were covered with scrape marks and dried blood. Then there were my clothes.

"Been working on my piece of shit car—exhaust is falling apart." I folded my hands up. "Don't worry, I'm not playing."

Lou cut in. "Yeah, Frank, Ginty's just here for the canasta."

Frank laughed.

"The girls'll clean you out good."

Frank hovered like he wasn't planning to leave. Lou gave him a little nod.

"I'll catch you later, Frank."

He lumbered off, slamming his locker shut and tugging a bucket hat on top of his sunburnt head.

"Nosy fuck." Lou stood. "You gotta get cleaned up. That dick will be telling everyone on the tee that he saw you in here."

"My shit was all in the trunk. I couldn't get it open."

Lou looked at me. "Your bag was in the trunk?"

"Yeah."

"Anything…?"

"Nah, nah. Just clothes, shaving kit."

He made a little gesture with his index finger.

"No prescription bottles… receipts?"

"No, man, nothing. And I got the title and old registration."

"Okay." It seemed settled to Lou. "I'll get you some stuff in the pro shop. You can put your shit in here."

I stuffed my clothes into his locker and took a shower. The cut on the side of my palm hurt pretty bad. The attendant got me some gauze and tape, and I covered it up.

I was combing my hair in front of a mirror when Lou popped in.

"What, you about a 36?"

"Yeah, that's good."

I wandered out and stood in front of the television in the corner, away from the lockers, with a towel cinched around my waist. A few guys came in, but nobody I knew.

"Hey."

Lou was back. He held up a pair of plaid pants and a blue golf shirt.

I pointed at the pants. "What, I'm fucking Rodney Dangerfield?"

"They were in the lost and found. You wouldn't believe what a pair of pants costs here."

He pulled a pair of socks out of his pocket.

"Get dressed, we'll go back to my place, figure it out from there."

Lou's house was in Wildwood Crest, back toward the bay, a half dozen blocks or so south of Wildwood proper. We went upstairs to the kitchen, got coffee, and walked out onto the deck. Concetta was lying on a chaise lounge beside the tiny pool below us.

Lou called out, "Yo, babe."

She pulled her sunglasses down and looked up. I waved.

"Ginty?"

"Hey, how you doin'?"

Concetta wore a black bikini and had a late August tan in early July.

"What happened? We missed you last night. I would have gone to Potito's and got some pastries."

Lou turned his collar up against the wind.

"Something came up." He gave me a smirk. "He took a little detour."

"Yeah?" Concetta pulled her legs up and hugged them. I tried not to look at her too hard.

"Yeah, Ginty was just coming down the Parkway and decided to get off at Exit 7."

"7?" Concetta took her sunglasses off. "You mean 6, right?"

"No, 7."

"There isn't an Exit 7."

Lou looked at me. "Ginty created his own personal exit, brand new."

"Whatever." Concetta went back to her tanning.

Lou said, "Come on, I got something I want you to do."

We went inside. Lou washed up a few wine glasses.

"Can't be bothered cleaning up after her friends."

I looked out the kitchen window at the street.

"How far you to the beach?"

"What the fuck does it matter, she never goes."

Lou sat at the kitchen table and pulled out a money clip. He counted out a sheaf of bills and tossed them on the table.

I held my hands up. "That's alright, man, I got some cash."

"Yeah, well, I got a favor to ask."

I put the cash in my pocket. I felt really tired and rubbed my head.

"Long fuckin' night, you know."

"Take a nap, you can use the kids' room."

"Yeah, think I might. So, what's this favor?"

Lou put his hands on the table and twisted the big college ring he wore.

"There's a guy in Rio Grande, he's got some parts for me."

"Parts?"

"Yeah, he's got…I don't know, bunch of things, electronics, belts, rotors, batteries. I need to get them today, but I got…." He nodded toward the sliding door. "She's got some… open house or something, she wants me to help."

"She's doin' real estate now?"

"Yeah. You can take the Bronco. Stop by the Garden and pick Pinto up. You know him?"

"He at that tailgate, back in the fall? Kinda short but solid?"

"Yeah. He stays down here most of the summer. Comes up to the dealership sometimes when we're busy. His old man and mine were tight. Anyway, he knows the guy."

He got up and went to a cabinet that had china and crystal on its shelves. He knelt and opened a door at the bottom. Inside was a safe. He flipped the dial around, then opened it and took out an envelope. He did a quick riffle check of the cash and handed it to me.

"Twenty grand."

I nodded.

"Save me some time going back tomorrow. Plus, the guy wants to do it today."

"No problem."

Lou was making himself a Bloody Mary. He held the bottle up.

"You want something?"

"Just a little."

He poured some vodka into a short glass and slid it over to me.

"Help you sleep."

* * *

When I got up, Lou and Concetta were gone. There was a note on the kitchen table with Lou's keys. "Get there by three. Don't worry about locking up."

I went back to the bedroom to get my wallet. There was a picture of Davy on top of the bureau, high school days, a big smile on his face, his arm around Concetta. He looked like he did the second summer he worked for me. He had just finished up his junior year at Bishop Newman. He was getting a little more gabby then, wise-cracking—he had this little mustache, like kids have, barely there, took his whole life to grow it.

I had a problem with him one night. It was busy, don't know why, maybe there were a lot of guys watching the Phillies, so I had all I could do to sling out beers and shots. No one was eating anything, so I had Davy clearing bottles and glasses off the bar and the handful of tables.

A cop came in. Of course I knew the guy, McMenamin. He was okay, calm, and not about to cite us on anything like underage drinking or staying open too late, as long as there was no trouble. He stood at the end of the bar, waiting for me to come down, his cap off, wiping sweat off his red forehead.

He gave me an irritated look. "Got a little problem."

I nodded. "Kinda busy—is it—?"

He cut me off. "See you out back."

He put his cap on and walked out. I had one guy covering the bar. "Chick, can you...?"

Chick looked irritated, too. "Get that punk Davy out here, would you?"

I walked through the kitchen and storage area to the back door, which was open. I figured Davy was out back smoking. Down the steps, there was a sort of driveway/loading area with a garage that fronted on an alley. McMenamin was at the bottom of the steps, and as I came down, he looked over toward the garage where there was another officer standing next to three kids arrayed against the garage door like a lineup at the precinct.

One of them was Davy. The other two I recognized from the neighborhood—kids, maybe fifteen. We walked over, and McMenamin pointed at a couple of six-packs of beer at the feet of the other officer.

I looked at McMenamin. "So…?"

"Do I gotta draw you a picture? What do you want me to do?"

The other cop, a tough-looking black guy, held out his hand. There was a couple of bucks and some change in it.

"I got this from your loyal employee here."

Davy stepped out from the door. "Hey, how do you know that wasn't mine to begin with?"

The cop took a quick step and grabbed Davy by his t-shirt and lifted him up. "Shut the fuck up."

He pushed him back against the door with a bang.

McMenamin came over to Davy. "So…if you didn't take any money, then you're just fucking stealing from your boss here and sharing with your friends…who just told Officer Taggart here that they paid you."

The two kids were scared shitless. Davy just looked pissed that he had gotten caught. McMenamin took the money from Taggart and moved toward the kids.

He gestured at the bigger one. "Put your hand out."

The kid stuck his hand out like he was going to shake with the cop. McMenamin grabbed his wrist and twisted it so his palm was flat, facing up. Then he put the bills and coins in it.

He stepped back. "I know you guys. I know your parents. So get the fuck out of here before I change my mind."

The kids were frozen to the spot. McMenamin jutted his head out at them, and they scrambled away down the alley.

He turned to me. "Now, Mr. McGinty, I assume you're not in on this little deal?"

I shook my head. The other cop picked up the six-packs. McMenamin gave him a nod.

"How 'bout we take that for evidence?"

The two cops sauntered off. Davy stepped away from the garage door and started to walk past me. I put my hand up and stopped him, pushing him back against the garage. His back bumped hard against it, and I pressed him there for a few seconds, feeling the bones of his narrow frame. His eyes flashed anger at me, then shifted down.

I let go, and he sagged into himself. "What the fuck are you doing?"

He stared down, avoiding my eyes. I bent down so my face was looking up at him.

"Don't I pay you?" I lifted his chin up, not rough, just to make him look at me. "Hey, what would your dad think?'

It was like I had stuck his finger in a socket. "You're not gonna tell my old man, are you?"

Now he was scared. If he wasn't Lou's kid, I'd fire him on the spot.

"Just get the fuck back to work."

I didn't have kids, but I knew from experience about angry dads, so I never said anything to Lou. It was just a couple of six packs.

He kept his nose clean the rest of the summer. He stopped working in August, heading to the shore for the last month before school started. The last day, I asked him about college. There was no question his parents expected it.

He was putting dirty glasses on a tray. "Whatever. Probably go to Temple."

"It's a good school. What are you going to study?"

"I don't know. Criminal justice?" He smirked to himself.

He was supposed to work until eight, but at four, I told him to take off. "You gotta pack for the shore, right?"

When I gave him his pay packet, he shook my hand and looked sheepish. "Hey, I'm sorry about the stuff with the beer. It was stupid."

I held his hand and grabbed his shoulder. "Don't worry. I did a lot of stupid stuff when I was a teenager."

Which was true, but it was a pretty poor imitation of parenting.

* * *

It was 1:30. It took me a few minutes to get the Bronco's seat and mirrors adjusted—it was like a chariot compared to the dinky sedans I drove. I felt like the Marlboro Man driving it.

The Garden was a diner. Pinto was sitting in a booth in the window. He waved to me from inside. I went in and slid into the other side of the booth.

He smiled and patted my hand. "How's yer Irish ass?"

He laughed an old-guy laugh, though he was late forties, best I could tell. He was one of those guys who was always happy. Brown to a crisp with greying hair combed straight back in a fifties' pompadour.

We went out to the wagon. Pinto grabbed my arm.

"I need a smoke. Lou don't like it if I smoke in his car. Says it hurts the resale."

There was a bench outside the diner, so we sat there while Pinto smoked. He talked steadily about the shore and the pain-in-the-ass nephew whose house he was living in.

"Kid won't fix nothin'. Hot water heater went out. I did it myself, got a new coil, put it in."

He lit another cigarette, rubbing out the old one on the sidewalk and setting it next to him on the bench.

"Says, hey thanks, Unkie, how much was the part?" He shook his head. "I said don't worry about it. Went out to dinner with his whole family, kids and shit. Bill comes—I offer to pay, just to be polite you know—he's like 'Wow, thanks'. So I pay for that too."

"That's unbelievable," I said.

Pinto echoed me. "That's what I said, fucking unbelievable."

"What did he say?"

"What did he say, what?"

"Well, when you said it was—"

"I didn't say fuckin' nothin'."

An old couple going into the diner looked over. Pinto waved at them.

"What am I supposed to fuckin' say? The kid doesn't have a clue."

I stood up. "Come on."

Pinto took his cigarette butts over to the receptacle by the door and put them in.

"I try to keep it clean out here. They're good people."

We got into the wagon, and I started it up and pulled out.

It wasn't far, maybe ten-fifteen minutes once we got on Route 9. We turned onto a little road by a produce stand, and after a mile or so, Pinto waved me toward a rundown garage. One of the bays was open, and a guy in dirty overalls came out with a wrench in his hand. He had long hair and a beard. He made me feel respectable.

Pinto bounced out of the car. "Hey, champ, ¿que pasa?"

The guy shook Pinto's hand, but didn't look too thrilled.

"Lou was supposed to come," he said.

He had a funny accent, half Mexican, half country. Get on the other side of Route 9, and it's like you're in Virginia or the Baja sometimes.

Pinto shrugged. "He's a busy guy, Ramon."

Ramon led us through the garage and into a storage room. There were stacks of boxes of different sizes. Pinto rocked on his heels and dragged on a cigarette that I hadn't even seen him light.

"You got a hand truck or something?" he asked.

Ramon went back into the garage and returned in a minute with a hand truck. He nodded at the Bronco.

"Why don't you pull that over here?"

I backed the Bronco up to the garage. It took us a while to get everything loaded. I was taking the hand truck back into the garage when Pinto pulled me aside.

"You got the cash?"

I got the envelope out of the glove compartment. Pinto put his hand out. I hesitated for a second. He gave me a look that made me think maybe he wasn't always such a happy guy.

"Come on, I do this for Lou all the time."

I gave him the envelope. He pulled out the cash, licked his thumb, counted out ten bills, and held them out to me. He gave me the look again, and I took the cash. He counted out another ten and put them in his pocket.

Ramon came out of the garage all smiles. Pinto closed the tailgate and handed him the envelope. Ramon took the wad out and started counting it.

Pinto jutted his chin out. "Eighteen."

Ramon stopped counting for a second, then continued. When he was finished, he held the envelope out.

"Lou said twenty."

Pinto shook his head. "No, man, he told us eighteen."

"He told me twenty."

"Eighteen, that's what he gave us." Pinto shrugged. "Sounds like a pretty good price for this stuff."

Ramon went back through the garage and into the office without saying a word. We followed him in and watched as he picked up the phone. Pinto acted insulted.

"You think we're fucking lying?"

Ramon took the wrench off a loop on the back of his overalls.

"No, man, just a misunderstanding."

Pinto's back was to me, and there was a bulky something just above where his waistband would be, under his shiny jacket. Ramon didn't seem threatened by Pinto. He held the phone up to his ear for half a minute, then put it down.

"No answer."

"He had to go to an open house with Concetta." I offered this to prove I could speak.

Ramon nodded. "I'll talk to him later."

Pinto clapped the guy on the shoulder. "Hey, I understand, you gotta make sure."

Ramon smiled, but it wasn't a smile that made you feel good. We went out and got in the wagon, and I turned it around. As I pulled out, I saw Ramon watching us, twisting the wrench around in his hand.

We stopped at a light on Route 9. I turned to Pinto, who had the window down and was banging his hand on the outside of the door in time to a song on the oldies station.

"What the fuck did you have to do that for?" I asked.

"What?"

I turned the radio down. "Shorting that guy. He's gonna call Lou."

"Let him call. That's way too much for those parts, anyway." He turned the radio back up. "Man, I like that song, come on."

There was a 7-11 just past the light. I pulled in.

"I wanna get some coffee."

"Good idea."

I got coffee and joined Pinto at the counter. I could see he had one of the hundreds out.

I nudged his shoulder. "I got it."

I put my coffee down next to his. He had a little blueberry pie.

Pinto smiled at the girl behind the counter. "And Camels, soft pack."

I gave her a five. Pinto was already out the door. He was standing by the driver's side when I got to the car.

"Hey, let me drive, will ya?"

I was beginning to understand him better. Everything was going to be a fight, or the promise of a fight if you didn't agree with him. Maybe that's why he was so happy. I gave him the keys.

As we headed back to the island, he turned onto the northbound ramp of the Parkway.

"Where the fuck are you goin'?" I asked.

He bounced his hands on the steering wheel. "I love drivin' these things. We'll take it up to Stone Harbor and back, won't take a few minutes."

I started to say something, then settled back in the seat, looking out the window. Pinto raced past a car in the right lane to get on.

"Fucking prick, why doesn't he move over?"

"You could have gone behind him if you weren't going a hundred."

"Fuck you, too."

I shook my head. Pinto punched my arm hard.

"Hey, man, I'm just kiddin'. Loosen up."

We were at Stone Harbor in maybe two minutes, it seemed. I saw my car on the way but didn't say anything. We got to the light for Stone Harbor Boulevard, and Pinto started driving up the causeway into town.

I looked at him. "Thought we were going right back."

"You got a curfew or something? I wanna see the ocean."

We drove into town and cruised around, checking out the people going to the beach.

"Shoulda brought my trunks." He stopped at an intersection and waved a bunch of girls through like he was a crossing guard. "That's some high-price pussy."

"They're teenagers, Pinto."

"So?"

He drove up to the beachfront and parked the Bronco at the edge of the dunes. We walked up the wooden ramp that led to the beach. A girl in a lifeguard helmet was sitting by the end of the ramp on a camp chair, reading a book.

"Do you guys got tags?"

Pinto ignored her and kept walking.

"You have to buy a tag, sir."

"I just wanna get my feet wet."

He stepped out of his moccasins and ran down to the water like he was a marine. The girl looked at me.

I offered, "We're not staying."

The beach was pretty crowded, but we could see Pinto striding up to the water, puffing his chest out.

"If he's not back in two minutes, I'm getting the lifeguards to radio the cops."

I gave her a bill. "Give me a couple of tags."

She handed them to me and I took off my shoes, rolled up my pants, and hopped through the blankets and umbrellas. Pinto was talking to a woman with a toddler at the water's edge. I handed him a badge.

He held it between two fingers like it was a sand crab. "You didn't fuckin' pay for this?"

"What, you got to prove you can get over on a teenage girl?"

"These tags are bullshit. Nobody owns the beach."

The woman had moved away, picking up her kid and heading toward the lifeguard stand. I turned the other way.

"Come on, we're here, let's take a walk."

We went a few blocks until we came to a jetty. Some guys were fishing there and we watched them for a few minutes, but they didn't land anything.

Pinto kicked my ankle. "Nice pants."

"Got them in the pro shop at Lou's club."

"Yeah?"

I told him about the car, which I realized as I was talking was a dumb idea.

"So your shit is still in the trunk?"

"Yeah. It got banged up and I couldn't get it open."

We went back up the beach and then up to the ramp. When we passed the girl, Pinto made a show of tossing his badge in the trash can.

"See ya around, honey."

She didn't look up from her book. Pinto was quiet as we drove back down and got on the Parkway. After a couple of miles, we got to my car. Pinto pulled off on the shoulder.

I put my hands up. "What are you doin'?

He opened the door. "We'll get your shit out of the trunk." He got out and slammed the door.

"Jesus Christ."

I got out and ran around to the back of the Bronco, where Pinto was shifting boxes around.

I grabbed his arm. "Just leave it, man."

"Why?"

"The cops could come along any minute."

"So?"

"I told you—I'm ditchin' this car. I don't want to be caught anywhere near it."

"So you're just gonna leave it there?"

"Are you fuckin' listening? It's totaled. It's a clunker, it ain't worth fixin'."

"Is it locked?"

"The trunk is."

"You got the key?"

"Not here. It's jammed anyway."

Pinto pulled a crowbar from under the mat.

I put my hands up again. "I am not breaking into it."

"Don't worry." He held the crowbar in front of my face. "That's my job."

The car was facing halfway toward the road, its right front end smashed against one tree, and the back right fender crunched against another. Pinto approached the trunk and looked at it with a professional eye.

"There's an easier way."

Pinto trotted around to the front door, opened it, unlocked the back, then squeezed into the space in front of the back bench.

"Move the seat up, give me some room to work."

I moved the seat up as Pinto wrenched at the seat bench. There was a metallic ripping sound, and he fell back.

"Okay, now…"

He went to work on the backrest. He was a strong dude, I'll give him that. He yelled as he strained to pull it out.

"Get on the other side."

I climbed in through the other door, and we pulled.

"One, two…"

We yanked it up together, and the back came off on one side, his side. He shooed me away.

"Let me do that."

A couple of solid pulls and he had the seat out.

"Give me the crowbar."

He used the bar to bang through the plastic barrier, then put his head and shoulders through the gaping hole and reached around. In a few seconds, he pulled back, dropping my bag on the floor.

"Anything else?"

"No, that's it."

I came around and got the bag. "Fuckin' A, that's crazy…"

"Get the fuck down!" Pinto flattened himself on the floor of the car. I ducked behind the car as a State Trooper flew by at high speed.

I stood back up. "Fuck, he had to see the Bronco."

"Yeah, you're right." Pinto got out of the car and looked down the road. "Come on."

We could see the trooper slowing down as he got to a turnaround a half mile down.

"Let's get the seat back in."

We got the bench and backrest in real fast. The car had been in a crash, so it made sense the seat might have been jostled.

The trooper was paused in the turnaround, waiting for traffic to slow. We hustled up and got the bag under the back seat of the Bronco. The trooper had pulled out and passed by us slow on the other side with his hand out.

"We gotta wait now," I cautioned.

"Yeah."

"We were driving by, saw the wreck, and wanted to make sure no one was hurt."

It took a few minutes for the trooper to go up to the next exit and get on the southbound side. As he came down the road with his flashers on, Pinto was on the shoulder, waving crazily until he pulled up behind the Bronco.

The trooper sat in his car for a minute, then got out real slow, like they do. He had the big hat with the badge, sunglasses, boots, bulky holster, the whole bit. Pinto pointed at the wrecked car.

"You seen this, officer?"

The trooper didn't say anything. I'm thinking, of course, he's seen it, he drove right by, and it's been there since three AM. But then maybe acting stupid was a good idea.

"You guys alright?"

I nodded. Pinto shook his head.

"Yeah, we're okay, we were just—jeez, that car's all mangled up. We thought—we thought maybe there was somebody in it."

A car zoomed past. The trooper gestured, and we moved on the other side of the Bronco, away from the traffic. Pinto kept babbling.

"Yeah, like I said, we were worried—"

The trooper cut him off. "License and registration."

Pinto looked at me. I figured it was a good bet he didn't have a license, or didn't want the trooper running a check on him.

"Sure." I handed him my license then opened the door of the Bronco and searched through the crap in the glove compartment and finally found the registration and insurance card. I gave them to the trooper.

"It's my friend's car."

The trooper pulled the registration out of the sleeve.

I said, "You can call him if you want."

He handed the cards back to me. "Not a problem."

Pinto was digging at the gravel with his toe. "Was the guy alright?"

The trooper turned to him. "What guy?"

"The guy driving the car."

"How do you know it was a guy?" The trooper's stance stiffened just a little, and he put his hand on his belt near his gun. I stared at Pinto, thinking why the fuck can't this guy just keep his mouth shut?

Pinto held his hands out, palms up. "Hey, I dunno, I'm just..."

The trooper laughed. "It's alright, I'm just messin wit' you."

That was weird. I hadn't met too many troopers who liked to joke around. And with that jokey dago accent? Now he looked at me.

"You sure you're okay?" He pointed at my sloppily bandaged hand, the dressing red and ragged.

"Yeah, I'm okay. Banged my hand up working on my car."

"You got a place down here?"

"No, no—I'm staying with my friend—the guy who owns the car."

The trooper walked to the edge of the road, looking at the wreck. He knelt down, and I could see him rubbing his hand over skid marks on the asphalt.

"There wasn't anybody," he said.

The trooper got up and moved back as more traffic approached.

Pinto came up next to him. "Yeah?"

"No, no one in the car. Someone called it in—maybe five this morning. Our guys came out here. The car was empty."

"That's crazy." Pinto seemed to want the conversation to go on, which I did not think was a good idea. "So...hey?" Pinto put his finger to his lips. "Did you check the local hospitals, maybe the guy—or whoever, the driver, you know—woulda—"

I tried to look interested, thinking, would you just shut the fuck up?

The trooper shook his head. "We did that."

Pinto kept going. "I guess you ran the plates and all..."

"Right, but we haven't been able to locate the guy. Maybe he had somebody come pick him up. We figured maybe he was drunk and didn't want to risk a DUI."

Pinto nodded seriously. "Right, hadn't thought of that."

"Or maybe the car's stolen." The trooper had sauntered over to the Bronco and was looking through the rear windows, staring long enough to make me nervous. The squawk box in his car crackled, and some words came through. "You guys should move along." He started back to his car. I got into the Bronco as fast as I could.

Pinto waved like the trooper was his best friend. "Hey, anything we can do."

The trooper stopped and seemed to think for a second, then pulled out his pad and pen.

"You know, let me get your names, a number we can reach you at. Just in case..."

"Sure, sure."

I gave him Lou's number. Pinto gave him a number that ended in two zeros, which I guessed was the diner.

"Thanks, guys."

The trooper went back to his car. Pinto turned to me. "Maybe you should drive."

"Maybe you should just shut the fuck up."

We switched around, and I pulled the wagon out onto the Parkway. The trooper remained on the shoulder.

"What the fuck is wrong with you?"

"What?"

"Fuck...a fuckin' State Trooper? You answer his questions, not try to solve his fucking crime."

"It's not a fuckin' crime. It was an accident—somebody coulda been killed there."

"You fuckin' moron, somebody is me. Now he's got my name—when they finally find that junkie I bought it from, he'll tell them he sold it to me."

"Hey man, you said they couldn't prove it was yours."

"You—" I banged my hands on the steering wheel. "They'll know I was fuckin' lyin'."

"You worry too much, man. That cop was alright."

"Alright? Why do you think he decided to take our names?"

"Just calm down, man."

"And we got all this shit in the back? He could have asked a million questions about that."

"So?"

"Ramon look like a Mopar dealer to you?"

"Don't be such a nervous Nellie. I acted like a stupid fuckin' dago, runnin' my mouth. What's wrong with that? What, you wanted me to take the fifth?"

"You weren't actin'—you are a stupid fucking dago."

Pinto got quiet. I looked up, and flashing lights were coming up behind me fast. I pulled over, and the trooper whizzed by us. He hit the siren a blast and waved.

I pulled back onto the road. Pinto laughed.

"Wanna go home and change your underwear?"

* * *

I dropped Pinto at the diner and went back to Lou's. He wasn't home yet. I got a beer and laid out in a lounge chair by the pool. I read the newspaper Concetta had left, and fell asleep. I woke up to Lou calling me from the deck.

"I got Ramon on the phone."

He waved me up and went inside. I hurried up to the kitchen, where Lou was on the phone.

"Nah, I haven't talked to Pinto. Yeah, the other guy's here. What? Alright, lemme talk to him." He pressed the phone against his chest and looked at me like he had a toothache.

"How much did Pinto take?"

"What?"

"Don't fuck around, he always does this. How much?"

"Two grand."

He nodded like that was normal.

"Ramon, it's a misunderstanding. I'll drop by on my way back to the city tomorrow. What?" He looked at me while Ramon was talking. "Fuck me." He laughed. "Yeah, that's what we should do. Serve the little fucker right." More talk from Ramon. Lou held his hand up in an okay sign and winked. "Yeah, cool."

He hung up. "He give you any?"

"A grand."

Lou held his hand out. I went in the bedroom and got the cash. He put it in the safe.

"I was going to tell you."

Lou stood up. "Don't worry. I could have told you he might do that, but I figured better if you didn't know." He chuckled. "Ramon said I should give him fifteen hundred dollars and he'd get the rest from Pinto."

I shook my head. "Probably be fine with Pinto. Guy's always looking for trouble. You gonna get the cash from him?"

Lou waved his hand. "I'll deal with him."

"Hey, I got my shit from the car."

"What, you went back out—it was still there?"

"Yeah. Pinto insisted." I hesitated. "A trooper came along while we were there."

"You're fucking kidding me."

"Yeah, but it was alright—we already had the stuff out of the car. We said we just stopped 'cause we thought somebody might be hurt."

"What'd he say?"

"Just asked for license and registration, you know, the usual. He seemed to believe us."

He had a little canvas cooler bag and was putting cans of beer in it. He stopped for a second and looked at me.

"He didn't wonder why the Bronco wasn't in your name?"

"I just told him the truth, said you were a friend."

Lou zipped the bag shut. "Come on—cocktail hour on the beach."

* * *

When we got back, Concetta was in the kitchen, in a bathing suit with a big t-shirt over it. Thank God.

"You're staying for dinner, right?" she asked.

Lou came up the steps, a towel wrapped around his waist, wet from the outdoor shower.

"He's stayin' period." He jerked his head to the side, shaking water out of his ears. "He's my new manager."

"Oh." She held up the wooden spoon that she was stirring the gravy with. "Congratulations."

That meant Lou hadn't told her.

"Just helping out," I offered.

She resumed stirring, other hand on her hip. "Lou always needs help."

It was a nice dinner, the first home-cooked meal I had had in six months, if you don't count Marie's in the neighborhood, where they say it's "Just Like Momma Cooked". I tried to help with the dishes, but Concetta wouldn't hear it.

"Go, go."

Lou nodded me out to the deck. He had a bottle of red in his hand and a couple of cigars. He shut the slider, and we sat down.

"Great dinner." I finally got the cigar lit in the wind. "Man, how does she do it? She was out all day."

"Gets the sauce from her ma. Dump it in the pot and—presto, smells likea robusto." He slid an ashtray across to me. "So we'll go over to the Seabreeze in the morning."

I was having second thoughts. "Lou, I don't know, I'm just a bartender."

"What, what's to know?"

"I can't run a kitchen or anything."

"Kitchen? We got a cook, a chef, whatever. Robert, just hired him this spring, he's good."

"So what do you need me for?"

He rubbed his fingers together. "Watch the cash register. Not like the last guy."

"Yeah, you told me."

The manager had been there a couple of years. Sheila, the bookkeeper, figured out what he was doing. I'd been down a couple of times since he was running the place, but had never met him.

"Make sure no one's dipping in the till. I don't think he was doing it alone, know what I'm saying?" He frowned at his cigar. "Maybe you can figure that out too, right?"

"Yeah, but you gotta order food, do the waitress schedules—"

"See, you know it all already." Lou took the cigar out of his mouth. "Just give me a month. If you like it, finish out the summer." Lou beckoned for the ashtray. I pushed it over, and he tipped the ash into it. "A special favor for a friend—*capisce*?"

I knew then I couldn't say no.

"Alright." My cigar had gone out. I laid it in the ashtray. "But I gotta find someplace to stay."

"What?" Lou was insulted. "You stay here, my friend."

"I don't know, Lou. Concetta's here all the time, won't your daughter be down?"

"They ain't coming until Labor Day. Anyway," he filled our glasses, "you can keep an eye on Concetta for me."

I tried to make a joke. "What, make sure she eats her vegetables?"

Lou didn't laugh. "Kevin told me he saw her down in Cape May, back around Memorial Day."

"Who's Kevin?"

"Bartender at our joint. You'll meet him."

"Probably some real estate shit."

"Nine o'clock at night? Having a smoke with some slick-looking dude outside a bar on Washington Street?"

Fuck. I didn't say it, but I definitely thought it.

Chapter Two

In the morning, I went to the Garden, just to get out of their hair while Lou packed up for his Sunday return to the city.

Pinto was in his customary booth.

"Hey, top of the mornin' to ya!"

The diner was busy, but the two booths on either side of him were empty. He had a cigarette behind his ear and his permanent cup of coffee in front of him.

I sat down. Pinto lowered his head.

"My partner in crime."

I decided that Lou had not talked to him yet. Maybe he never would. Could be some crazy plan to keep Ramon off-balance. I managed a smile.

Pinto lifted his eyebrows. "How's the beautiful Contessa?"

"You mean Concetta?"

"Yeah, man, she is—"

I held out the laminated menu. "Stop."

"What?"

"Just stop."

"I'm just remarking on her outstanding poise and charm."

I ordered coffee and eggs and ignored him. He went on about his nephew's house. I took his Daily News and spread it out so I could pretend to read the sports.

Pinto asked, "So, what, you going back today?"

"Nah, I'm staying down for a while."

"What, you taking a vacation?"

"I'm helping Lou out."

"You gonna power wash his deck?"

"No, with the restaurant."

"You washing dishes?"

"I don't know, they had to fire some guy, so he just wants me there for a while."

Pinto scrunched forward, clenching his fists. "You mean that fuck Arnie—the manager?" Pinto pressed his lips together and looked around the diner. "I told him I could take care of that."

I thought, "Of course, Pinto, but he wants someone who won't steal more money".

Pinto kept at it. "What, you musta run a restaurant before."

"Yeah, that's right." A lie, but whatever.

"Alright, alright." Pinto accepted the slight, figuring his honor was saved because I had the experience, though, what the fuck, he could do the job standing on his head. My eggs came, and he left me alone for a few minutes while I ate. When I pushed my plate away, he started back in.

"Hey, you heard from the cops?"

He was tilting back toward happiness as he remembered the mess I was in.

"Not yet."

"What you gonna tell them?"

"I'll tell them you were driving."

"What?"

"Yeah, that's why I didn't call it in. I mean, Christ, you were wasted. Plus, your license is suspended."

He looked at me with a truly pissed off expression. Good guess on the license.

"You motherfucker."

I tossed a bill on the table and stood up.

"You are a stupid dago, Pinto."

For a minute, he looked like he was going to come after me. Then he collapsed against the booth, clapping his hands and laughing.

"You got me, you dick."

* * *

When I got back from the diner, there was an old green Cadillac parked out front. Lou stood smiling next to it, which I guess he was pretty good at.

"You need a car."

"What, I mean…"

"Just use it, it's been on Mackey's lot for a year. You have any problems with it, call him."

He picked up a leather gym bag and carried it to the Bronco. I followed him over.

"You wanna drive over together?" I asked.

"Nah, I talked to Sheila, she said better if you come in tomorrow, it'll be slow." He handed me a house key with a little plastic tag on a chain. "She's been there forever, knows everything."

Lou opened the driver-side door and set the bag on the seat. He unzipped it and pulled out an envelope.

"Can you run this over to Ramon for me? I'm supposed to meet a guy for lunch—better if I don't have to make that stop."

"Sure."

Lou tossed the bag in the back and got into the Bronco.

I stuffed the envelope in my pocket. "When'll you be back?"

"Friday—maybe Thursday night, if I can get away."

He pulled out, and I stood in the driveway, feeling like a kid dropped off at camp.

I went inside; the house was empty. I figured Concetta must be off to her real estate job. I had some more coffee and read the paper. I nodded out on the sofa, and decided to go for a walk to kill time. I went all around, checking out the houses, then down to the beach and back, edging north into Wildwood, and finally stopping at the Seabreeze.

The place was quiet. I took a spot at the bar and had a beer. The bartender was a big guy in a black vest, could have been wearing a rug. He didn't seem to want to chat. I turned in my stool so I could see the dining room, but there wasn't much to see. I was halfway through my beer when a skinny lady with red hair came out of the back. She started across the floor, and I called out to her.

"Sheila!"

It took her a couple of seconds to recognize me. It was probably at least a year since she had seen me, when I was down to work a party at Lou's. She came over and gave me a hug.

"Ready to work?" She smiled at the bartender, who tilted his head up for a second, looking at me like I was a sneaky son of a bitch. "Kevin—this is Ginty. Our new manager."

Kevin put down the glass he was polishing and shook my hand. He didn't say anything, but I got the feeling that was normal for him.

Sheila said, "Thought you were coming in tomorrow."

I shrugged. "Yeah, I just was out walking—Lou went up, Concetta's at work—didn't have anything to do. So…"

"You want something to eat?"

"Nah, I don't think so, I oughta get going."

Sheila patted my hand. "I'll get you something. Don't expect Conci's cooking just for you."

She smiled, her face narrowing. It felt like a little shot at Concetta. Sheila went off to the kitchen. Kevin seemed content to fiddle with stuff behind the bar and not talk. I decided I had another day before I was officially boss, so left him alone.

Sheila came back in a bit with a Styrofoam container.

"Chicken parm." She handed it to me, a clear invitation to leave.

* * *

There was a moment as I sat in the Cadillac watching Ramon bang a big wrench against the exhaust of a car on his lift that I thought maybe I should have brought Pinto with me, which had to be one of the stupidest thoughts I had ever had.

I got out, and the slam of the door got Ramon's attention. He squinted in the sunlight as he came out of the garage. I held out the envelope.

"Lou asked me to drop this off."

I figured the less said, the better. He took the cash with one hand, the other holding the wrench like it was surgically attached. I was considering how to politely leave as he walked past me to the Caddy. He reached through the window and under the dash, popping the hood. I came around next to him as he propped it up and studied the engine.

"Nice ride."

"Lou loaned it to me."

"Watch your fingers." He dropped the hood shut. "I rebuilt that. You have a problem, let me know."

"Sure." I was ecstatic that he wanted to talk about the car instead of the two grand we had tried to steal from him.

"Your friend," Ramon took the envelope from his pocket and tapped it against his leg, "this was his idea, no?"

I didn't answer, trying to avoid fingering Pinto and myself at the same time.

"It is okay. He pull shit like this all the time. Thinks he is a smart guy." He gave me a smile that made me think how alone we were. "What about you? You think maybe it is too much for what you picked up?"

I had to say something, which I did with a forced smile. "Hey, I was just doing a favor for Lou. What the fuck do I know about car parts?"

Ramon pushed the envelope into his pocket and pointed at the garage with the wrench.

"You want to see the receipts? I get them from a friend in Michigan—you know where Flint is? Up the road from the Motor City. You get original parts there—cheaper than aftermarket here." He smiled, close to a real one this time. "It's a Chicano express deal, eh?" He sauntered towards the garage. "You want a Coke?"

"Yeah, great." I felt like you did when you were a teenager, just trying to get home, and the older hoods on the corner insisted you have a beer with them. There was a beat-up vending machine in the corner of the garage.

Ramon plugged a few coins in it.

"My treat." The smile was real now.

I drank it down, like I was thirsty, which I was, but not like I was scared, which I also was.

"How long you work for Lou?" Ramon asked.

"I just started—helping him out with the restaurant."

Ramon held the bottle against his cheek, looking out over the fields across the street like he was scouting for Indians—or maybe cowboys would make more sense.

"I wish you luck there. My papa say when you have a job, keep your head down, focus on your work—don't pay attention to things that do not concern you."

"Sounds like good advice." I slipped the bottle into the wooden case, my mouth drier than when I started drinking it. "Thanks for the Coke."

Ramon put out his hand and we shook. He released my hand, and I moved one foot in front of the other to the car. He waved to me as I spun the big Caddy around, dust rising up in a cloud.

It was a little challenging driving with my head down, but by the time I got off Route 9, I was getting pretty good at it.

* * *

When I got back, Concetta was out on the deck with another woman. I looked through the slider at the two of them, both wearing bright tank tops over their deep tans, a big bottle of white on the table.

I pushed open the door and waved.

"Hey, Ginty, come on out."

"Just wanted to let you know I was back."

The friend smiled. "Didn't know you had a boyfriend, Concetta."

"He's one of Lou's buds. Hey, get a glass."

"Let me eat my parm." I held up the package and retreated into the kitchen. I heated up the chicken parm and found myself evaluating its taste and texture, like I actually knew something about cooking. Not bad was my conclusion, though the gravy was bland compared to Concetta's, or Concetta's mom's, I guess.

I got a fruit juice glass from the drain board and went out on the deck. Concetta waved her glass, one of those big ones with the long stem, at her friend.

"Ginty, this is Carol. My boss."

Carol looked at me, not saying anything. It was like she was appraising a property and wasn't impressed. Then she smiled at me like I was a stupid renter and put out her hand.

"Hello."

She was attractive, but not my type—out of my league, really—and I sure wasn't hers. I shook her hand.

I said, "I just stopped by the restaurant for a beer. Talked to Sheila."

Concetta grimaced. "How's she holding up?"

I shrugged. "Seems alright."

"How was your parm?"

"Not bad."

Carol drained her glass and held it out. "My mother goes there for brunch. She likes the bread pudding."

I filled both our glasses. She continued with her appraisal of me.

"So, are you a cook?" Carol asked.

"Nah, I don't know shit about restaurants." I gave her a little smile. "Sorry. I'm just helping Lou out—he fired the manager and needs someone to keep an eye on things."

Concetta picked up a folder.

"Carol, I got some questions about these properties."

I took the hint and went inside. It occurred to me that maybe Concetta would rather Carol not know about Lou's problems at the restaurant. My guess was that there wasn't too much that went on in her patch that Carol didn't know about.

I was cleaning up the remains of the parm when the two of them came inside. Carol set the wine and glasses next to me on the kitchen counter. I watched her walk to the stairs. She was built really well, like she went to

33

the gym. She turned with her hand on the banister and caught me looking at her. She gave me a little finger wave as she went down the steps. I tried not to have a hard-on.

Chapter Three

I could have walked to the restaurant Monday morning, but figured I ought to use the Caddy. You could tell they tried to get the smoke out of it, but it was still there. The engine throbbed when I got it up to forty, like an old man running on the beach when he shouldn't.

Sheila was sitting at the bar with a cup of coffee. There were a few young guys, busboys or waiters, going around, setting tables and yelling to each other across the room.

Sheila looked up. "C'mon in the back, we got an hour before we open."

We squeezed past the service bar, where Kevin was cutting up lemons and putting the wedges into a bowl. The office was tiny with a metal desk covered with stacks of paper. Sheila went behind the desk and started going through the routine.

"Robert orders all the food—he'll be here in a while. I run the cash register for the dining room; bartenders run their own. I settle them both at the end of each shift."

"What if they're under?"

"Comes out of their pay, so they're careful. We do the bartender's drawer together, cuts down on arguments."

"How else can money…leak out?"

Sheila lit a cigarette and pushed her chair back. "Right to the point, huh?"

"Well…"

She talked with the cigarette in her mouth. "There's a million ways. Waiters, bartenders, cooks—they give shit away. With food—eh," she knocked her ash off into an overflowing ashtray, "who cares? Usually, it's just a big sandwich or some clams or something to impress their friends or angling for a tip. The bar, that's a different story. We went to metered bottles five years ago—I don't like it, and there's ways to get around that, but you wouldn't believe how much went out that way."

I thought about some of the dives I went to in South Philly and the generous pours you got there. But, then, often enough, it was the owner.

Sheila picked up a bunch of yellow slips of paper and straightened them out, then stapled them together. "The real money, that's with the vendors."

"Yeah?"

"Of course. That's what happened with Arnie."

"So, he got bogus invoices...jacked-up prices?"

Sheila patted her hair. It was real, but the color, a weird orange-red, wasn't. "Let me count the ways. Buying stuff that was hoisted, paying for prosciutto and getting bologna, ordering top-shelf booze and getting house brands. The vendor takes a cut and kicks back the difference. He did it all. Surprised he got away with it as long as he did."

"And you..."

"I do the books. I'm a bookkeeper. Not an accountant, but I track all the pennies. That's how I figured out what Arnie was doing."

"So who's doing the buying now?"

"Robert does the food, I'm doing the rest, paper products, cleaning stuff."

"What about the booze?"

"That, too."

"Okay, so maybe you can show me...you know, next time you do an order?"

She did a good job of not looking irritated. "Absolutely. And we'll get Robert to do the same with his."

"So who's everybody work for?"

"Kitchen staff all works for Robert. Waitresses, busboys, bartenders, everyone else, works for me." She stubbed out her cigarette. "And I guess I work for you now."

I shrugged. She gave me a look that suggested it was the other way around.

* * *

I spent the rest of the morning sitting at the bar and trying to stay out of the way. Robert was in a rush when he came in. I hung out in the kitchen as he ordered around the prep cooks—two Scottish women—checked inventory and started making soup. He was a young guy, younger than me anyway, and looked like he knew what he was doing.

"We'll get a drink later." He chopped a bunch of onions up with a scary knife and pushed them into a pot. "After we break down."

I could tell he wanted me out, so I went to the bar. Kevin was polishing glasses. He filled me up a glass with club soda from a hose with a black plastic sprayer. He was amiable but quiet.

I tried to get him to talk. "You live here in town?"

"Nah, I'm out in the Villas."

Lunch was starting to get busy. There weren't too many drink orders. Mostly, it was club soda or iced tea that the waitresses got themselves. The waitresses were a mix, two or three old gals who looked like they could do the job in their sleep, and a couple of college girls who were still learning the ropes. I ordered lunch off the menu and ate at the corner of the bar.

I ordered dinner early, and as I was eating, an old couple came in and sat next to me. They were regulars, you could tell. The guy had a martini and the woman a glass of some pink wine. They split a basket of fried clams and looked like the happiest couple in the world. When they left, the guy paid the bill, then carefully set a pile of quarters on the bar and nodded seriously to the bartender, a stocky guy named Ted. He had a flat top and was a PE teacher from Delaware somewhere.

Ted gave the old guy a smile. When the guy was out the door, he swept the coins up and tossed them in a big plastic cup.

"Guys been tipping me fifty, seventy-five cents in quarters for ten years."

I took a walk, killing time until closing. The bars were surprisingly quiet, but then it was a Monday. When I got back, Robert was at the bar, changed out of his whites. He talked to me about the food side of the operation. He was a pretty impressive guy. I wondered what he was doing in this old-fashioned shore dining room. But I decided it didn't make sense to pry, so early on.

Robert finished his VO and left. Sheila came over, like she had been waiting for him to leave. She leaned over the bar.

"Ted, let's do your Z-out."

I looked out at the floor to see if everyone was gone. My experience was not to open the register and start dealing with cash unless all the customers were out and the doors were locked. There was still one table with two loud couples near the front.

"You want to wait until they're gone?" I asked.

Sheila shook her head. "Don't worry, bar's closed. Come on."

Ted pulled the cash drawer out and nodded with his head toward the back. I followed him to the office. He set the drawer on Sheila's desk and sat in her chair. It took him about five minutes to count the cash, checks, and credit card receipts and record the totals on an accounting sheet. Sheila came in with a slip of paper.

"Here's the register numbers."

She handed him the paper. He wrote down a few of the numbers, and used a calculator to figure out totals and differences. He put some of the cash back into the drawer and the rest in an envelope.

"Three bucks over." He stood and moved away from the desk. "And change. Think I put some tips in."

Sheila sat down and went through the same process, a little quicker, checking his numbers. When she was done, she initialed the accounting sheet, and Ted did the same. Sheila took a few bills out of the envelope and dropped them on the desk.

"There's your over."

She went over and squatted down by a safe in the corner, opened it, and put the cash in.

I looked at Ted. "So you guys share a single cash drawer?"

Ted nodded. Sheila stood and brushed some crumbs off her pants. "They have separate codes, so we know who sold what. But, yeah, they're in there together." She gave Ted a narrow smile. "Keep each other honest."

"Very professional."

"Thanks." The same smile. It had been a long day for her. I saluted them and went out to the bar and finished my beer. Some of the waitresses were sitting at a table, gabbing. Two of the older ones looked over at me—the kind of look you get when you're a stranger in a neighborhood bar.

It was enough for one night.

Chapter Four

Tuesday morning, I lay in bed, looking at the cheap artwork on the walls and wondering how long it would be before I wouldn't owe Lou for what he—that is, his dad—did for me over fifteen years ago. I had just finished two years at a junior college, halfway to a degree, but didn't have the money—or interest—to find a four-year program. It was all business stuff at the JC, which bored the shit out of me, though I did get to take a film course. That was crazy—a beatnik professor with a projector and film canisters showed us classics of European cinema. An eye-opener for a guy like me, whose idea of a great movie was *Von Ryan's Express*.

Anyway, there I was, June 1967, my 2S deferment gone, now 1A and staring at a foreboding notice from my local draft board. One of the guys in the apartment had gone to this doctor in South Philly and gotten a letter saying he wasn't fit to serve. Spine issue or something. He was like, didn't you fuck your knee up playing ball, go see this guy.

So I went to see him. Dr. Scolletta, nice guy, really serious. He did an X-ray of my leg and wrote me this long letter to take to the draft board. When I reported for induction, I had no idea what would happen. But the guy just looked at the letter for thirty seconds, scribbled something on my form, and next thing you know, I'm back on Broad Street, 4F.

My dad was pissed of course, thinking I should serve my country and all that shit, but we weren't talking too much by then. I went back to see Dr. Scolletta to thank him. We had a long talk about the war, which he thought was a huge mistake. He was an educated, thoughtful guy—I mean, he was a doctor, so of course he was smart, but he knew about stuff going on in the world. Opposite of my old man.

He asked me what I was doing for a job, and you could tell he was disappointed that I was tending bar at McNabb's. He told me to talk to his son, who worked at a car dealership. He seemed to think that profession was kind of amusing, but better than slinging beers and shots.

Almost as a favor to him, I went to see his son. Lou was in his late twenties then and already sales manager at a Cadillac dealership in South Philly that he bought a few years later. We hit it off great—I guess most people hit it off well with Lou, that's how he's sold so many cars. He could tell I wasn't going to be a car salesman, but he had a friend who ran a nice restaurant, needed someone to tend bar. So I took that job, was there for eight years, then the guy sold the business—none of his kids wanted to keep it going.

Looking back, eight years seems like a long time to stand behind the same bar, even if it was a good restaurant with a respectable clientele. But it just seemed to happen. There were phases. Like the first two-three years, I was still basically a snot-nose kid, learning to show up on time and look presentable. I wasn't even twenty-one yet, so it was six months before they even let me pour a drink in front of customers.

Then one of the older guys quit, and I was—you can't say promoted—but given more responsibility. So I did some ordering of liquor and supplies, set the schedule for help, and coached the new hires in how to be worthy of the red vest that we all had to wear.

That went on for maybe three years. More of my friends were getting married and working for real: wearing ties and carrying briefcases, even if they were just assistant mortgage bankers; or getting entrenched in trades and unions—carpenters, bricklayers, Teamsters of assorted stripes. I was making enough to buy a row house in Southwest Philly, and if I needed a little extra, there were always catering jobs I could latch on to.

Then there were the last few years. Guys who were married were having kids now. My social life was getting weird: guys' wives were always trying to set me up, which was just embarrassing. Everyone seemed to be either moving on to respectability, or getting stuck in a reenactment of their father's life. I alternated between going to the neighborhood bars, just out of boredom, and double dates or dinner parties where I was matched up with girls antsy to find someone to latch on to for life.

I started to wonder if I was going to wear that red vest for the rest of my life. So, in a way, I was relieved when the restaurant closed.

That's when I went back to McNabb's. After a year, I took over ordering booze and supplies, and hiring bartenders for an extra buck an hour. It was still less than I had made in my red vest days, but let me fool myself into thinking I was advancing my career.

My McNabb run lasted nearly seven years, and then it got sold and made over into a yuppie bistro. It was close enough to University City that there were professors and students who wanted something more sedate. The new owners needed someone who "understood" wine, so they said. Welcome to the 1980s.

From there…nobody seemed to be hiring, or they were lousy jobs I didn't want to take. So for the last year, I had been doing catering jobs, which could be good, but not regular. I even did parking at some events, like at the Spectrum or Palestra.

The last couple of years, I hadn't seen Lou as much. He was busy with the dealership and the Seabreeze, which he had bought from a friend of his father's. It wasn't a fancy place, but Lou liked being the big cheese there. And he knew a ton of folks—relatives and just people from the neighborhood—who were in the food biz, so it was familiar to him.

So, between the draft thing and that good job I had for a while, you had to say I owed him. And I could use the work; plus being at the shore for the summer, what was not to like?

Concetta was having her morning coffee on the deck. She had a stack of listings and was making notes with a gold pen. I scraped a chair back and sat down.

She spoke without looking up. "How's things at Le Bec Fin?"

"They treat me like I'm a cop or something. Sheila, anyway."

"The lovely Sheila."

That was an unfair shot coming from her. Sheila had to be sixty-plus. Of course, she probably always looked the way she did.

"She's alright. Tough old gal."

Concetta recapped her pen—a fountain pen?—and put the papers in her briefcase. I looked at the seagulls and thought about Davy. They had tried everything, that was what they always said. He had been in and out of rehab the last couple of years, more out, and was always crashing at a friend's dump of an apartment or on the streets.

I had gotten my first glimpse of where he was headed the winter after he finished high school, right around Christmas. College had not happened. Davy seemed to be turning into one of those guys who thinks working is for schmucks.

This time, he was on the other side of the bar. He had grown a few inches, or maybe it was the Cuban heels. The mustache was gone, and he was wearing a leather jacket, holding out a twenty-dollar bill. He was also high as a kite, his eyes glassy and a lazy smile splitting his face.

"A couple of Seven and Sevens." The bill fell from his fingers.

The guy with him was shorter and more compact, with the same leather coat and a pork-pie hat. He didn't look as high, just fidgety, scanning the room in a way I had seen too many times from guys who were looking for someone they could imagine had insulted them.

I put my hands flat on the bar. "ID, please."

Davy spread his arms out. "Hey, come on, it's Christmas."

His friend grunted dismissively, looking around for the fighting partner of his dreams.

I took a glass and scooped it through the ice bin and set it on the bar, then poured a double shot of whiskey into it. I filled it with 7-Up from the soda gun. I pushed the twenty back at Davy.

"On the house. Merry Christmas."

He lifted the drink with a little chuckle. "Yeah, merry fucking Christmas."

His buddy turned to face me, his fingers gripping the edge of the bar. "Hey, what about mine?"

I stared at him, thinking about the baseball bat I kept under the bar. "You got an ID?"

"What the fuck?" He tipped his head toward Davy like he was the tough guy he dreamed of being. "You served him."

I tilted my head and raised my eyebrows. "So you don't got an ID, is that what you're saying?"

He turned away, talking over his shoulder. "Aw, fuck you, man."

I looked at Davy. "Get him out."

Davy looked around like he had no idea what I was talking about, which was entirely possible. "What, hey, I gotta finish my drink."

His friend's face was getting red. He jammed his hands in the pockets of his tough-guy jacket and twisted around. "Fuck this shit, let's get outta this dump."

Davy held his drink out. "Look, Benny, I'm gonna finish this first, just relax."

Their conversation had drawn the attention of Charley, one of our regulars who was trying to enjoy his Rolling Rock and unfiltered Camel a few stools away. Unlike Benny, Charley didn't go looking for trouble, but if it landed in his lap in the form of a belligerent asshole, he wasn't going to ignore it.

Charley turned sideways on his stool. "Hey, didn't he just ask you guys to leave?"

His tone was friendly, but the unblinking eyes, the full beard and brown hair pulled back in a ponytail, the cut-off denim jacket with patches that weren't Boy Scout merit badges, the thick arms—all these would have been signals to a normally observant person that you did not want to mess with this guy. But Benny didn't seem to pick up on these social cues.

Benny pushed out a scoffing breath and said, "Mind your own business, you fucking hippie."

Charley gave me a look that said, I'm sorry, but you know…He stepped off his stool.

Benny's hands came out of his pockets and clenched into fists, like this was the moment he had been waiting for. He didn't seem to understand that while some guys with ponytails and beards were gentle, peace-loving souls who communed with the flowers, other guys with the same hair situation were Viet Nam vets who had seen shit much worse than a back-alley fight in South Philly over a gambling debt, and spent a lot of quiet energy keeping

44

said shit in the back of their minds with beer and the numbing buzz of a sports broadcast in a tappie like ours.

Charley stepped toward Benny, and Davy got between them.

Davy tried to de-escalate the situation. "Yo, Charley, it's cool, man, we're just leaving."

He slopped his glass on the bar. I had my hand on the baseball bat. Charley was staring past Davy at Benny, who rocked back and forth, toe to heel.

Charley smiled in a distant way. "Maybe I'll go with you."

I pulled the bat out and laid it on the bar, with just enough force to make a convincing thock. I looked at Benny but spoke to Charley.

"Charley, how about I buy you a drink?"

Charley's smile disappeared. He didn't move. Davy patted him clumsily on his big shoulders.

"Hey, man, have a good Christmas."

Benny had started toward the door, kicking a chair out of his way to show he wasn't scared of it. Davy's eyes were a little more alert as he leaned over the bar.

"Sorry about this guy, he's just..."

Charley offered, "A punk who better never show his ass here again?"

Benny was out the door, thankfully. I shook my head and watched Davy follow him out, thinking that's one more item for the don't-tell-Lou file.

* * *

Concetta left for the office, and I got more coffee. I thought I'd go in a little later today, not commit to a routine. Already, I was acting like the cop they thought I was.

Getting ready to go, I thought about the car. I couldn't believe I hadn't been contacted yet. Maybe they couldn't find that junkie in Buena. He was the only connection. But how could they not find him? What, was he hiding out?

And when they did find him? He says he sold it to some guy, but he's got no papers to prove it. He gives them my name. And of course, like a stupid gabby mick, I told him all about coming to work for Lou at the Seabreeze.

I took the Caddy out for a spin and tried to forget it all. Which was nice, and lasted for all of about twenty minutes, until I stopped in at the Garden. Already, I was feeling like I shouldn't eat where I worked, though certainly that was stupid, given that I was close to broke.

Pinto was there, of course, but not alone. I could see the back of the other guy's head, and it was that feeling of who is that? When you definitely know who it is, you just can't fucking believe it, you are so disoriented.

Junkie Drew from Buena was sitting across from Pinto, eating pound cake, all the time jiggling, not just his foot, his whole body jiggling. Pinto had the biggest smile I had seen yet, but that was no surprise. Whichever direction this was headed, it was a red-letter day for the Pinto boy.

"Ginty, hey, look who's here!" His cheeriness was unbearable. Drew shifted his eyes up and kept munching.

"Shove over." There was no way I was sitting next to Drew. Pinto almost got surly, then decided to move over for the greater good.

I looked at Drew's grimy face. "How'd you wind up here?"

Drew nodded his head, chewing and wiping his mouth with a napkin.

"I went to the Seabreeze, but they said they didn't know when you'd be in." He took out a cigarette. "They said maybe you'd stop in here, said Lou liked to come here."

"Surprised you didn't just come to Lou's."

"I don't know where he lives. Didn't want to be asking about him."

"Who'd you talk to?"

"Some kid, busboy or something." He put the cigarette in his mouth. "Hey, I don't wanna get the kid fired or nothin'."

He had his lighter poised. I got up.

"Outside."

We all went out, Drew lighting up inside, then exhaling the smoke just as he got out. Pinto was looking serious, which I read as he had already gotten the story out of Drew and was playing his part. Drew sat on the bench like a shoobie enjoying his day off. I stood in front of him.

"How'd you two get acquainted?"

46

Pinto said, "I heard him asking for you at the counter." He smiled. "So, I introduced myself."

I was in no mood for Pinto's sarcasm. I nudged Drew's foot with mine.

"Did the troopers come to see you?"

He nodded. "Yup. They came alright." He squinted up at me. "Told my landlady 'bout the wreck. But they didn't see me."

"What, you hid out 'cause you don't want to pay for the towing?"

"Hey, I didn't know what they wanted. Just standard procedure to avoid Mr. Charlie."

"Well, now you know."

"Yeah, well, it's complicated."

Pinto came in front of Drew and kicked his shoe, the kind of kick that suggested there was lots more where that came from.

"That's for fucking sure. Tell him the story, you piece of shit."

Drew stubbed out his cigarette and, in the same motion, put another in his mouth. He started to toss the butt in the street then stopped, seeing the look on Pinto's face. He put the butt in his shirt pocket.

"No need to get salty, compadre." He turned to me. "I was gonna come see you about the car anyway. We got a situation—the wreck just makes it more...complicated."

"What, don't tell me it was stolen when you sold it to me?"

"No, that would be easy." He lit the cigarette. "There's something in it, and we need to get it out."

"What's that?"

"An eighth."

I looked at him. "An eighth of what? Pot?"

His look was scornful. "What? Pot? What the fuck?" He looked off into the traffic. "H."

"You left an eighth of heroin in the car?" That seemed very unlikely to me.

He tilted his head like, yeah, it's fucking crazy, but it's true.

I kept at him. "Come on, if you had an eighth, you'd be over the fucking moon high, with the rest stuffed up your ass."

He chuckled. "You got the first part right."

Pinto sat down next to him. "Tell him what happened."

Drew spoke. "Day I saw you—a few hours before you came by, I was giving this guy a ride. He's...like my dealer. His car was in the shop, so I was giving him a lift from this cantina where he hangs out. I rolled a stop sign and fuck if there wasn't a cop right there. He pulls me over, writes the ticket. Eduardo—that's the dealer—he's smooth as can be, passing the time with the cop. He sends us on our way, but I can see he's trailing us a block or so back. I figured he knew who we were. We get to Eduardo's house and he pops out, says goodbye like I'm his best friend, cheery as shit, while the cop is hovering back there." He waited while a family walked by us. "Then Eduardo called me that night—after I sold you the car—and said he had to come by, he left something in it."

Pinto was more animated now. "He was real happy when you told him, right?"

"He knew it was his own-ass fault. But he was still pissed."

I tried to think where this was going. Drew was calm now, and Pinto had picked up the jiggling. He nudged Drew with his knee.

"Keep going."

Drew took a drag, absorbing the nicotine as deeply as he could.

"So we gotta get the H."

Pinto laughed. "You hear him, he wants to get the H."

I wanted Pinto to leave, just let me sort this out. But he was already in too far to boot out.

"Eduardo'll let me have a few bumps if I get it." Drew looked up at me. "Figured you could help me."

"Why do you need me?"

"Shit, I ain't got no car, right? I sold it to you."

"What, did you hitchhike down here?"

"Took the bus."

"Why am I going to help you?"

"'Cause otherwise I tell the cops it's your car. They cite you for abandoning a vehicle. Then they find the dope. You're fucked all over."

"How's that help you?"

Drew was on his third cigarette now. "They're gonna find me eventually. If I don't dime you, then I get run in for the H."

"How much is it worth?"

"Maybe a grand."

"What do I get?"

"Like I said…"

Pinto put his hand on Drew's shoulder and squeezed. "We'll work that out, right? How you feeling now, Drew-boy?" He rocked him back and forth like a rag doll. "A little short?"

* * *

Pinto was first out of the car, of course. Drew was cowering in the back seat. Pinto opened the door and jacked him out. I had wanted to leave Drew in town, but Pinto thought otherwise.

"We get run in, he's going with us. We'll say it's his car—we picked him up hitchhiking, trying to get to it."

"On the Parkway?"

"He's a fuckin' junkie, who knows what they do?" Pinto had Drew stood up by the side of the road. "Come on, man, no time to be roadkill."

The car was the same as before, but there was yellow tape around it.

Pinto led Drew to the car. I looked back at the roadway, thinking maybe I could have just waited in the Caddy, or even ditched them. Pinto opened the front passenger door and was pushing Drew's skinny frame into the car like he was a crash test dummy.

"Where'd he put it? He stuff it in the seat?"

Drew had his hand under the seat. "Think he said he put it…" He turned his neck, his face frowning. "Can't reach all the way."

Pinto started to pull him out. "Let me get…"

I held Pinto back. "No, let him do it."

Pinto stepped back. "Yeah, what do we know? He's some crazy guy we…"

Pinto had the solution to every situation that would never happen. Drew's face suddenly flashed a smile. He held up a bag of white powder.

"Party time!"

* * *

We didn't see any troopers on our return trip, thank Christ, and were back in the booth in under an hour, Pinto ebullient, springing for lunch for all. Drew didn't order anything. He had gone from ecstatic to anxious, the jiggling coming on strong.

The waitress walked away, and Drew put a hand on the table.

"Man, I need…"

Pinto said, "You can wait. We got business to talk."

"I…I just…"

"Five hundred."

Drew didn't seem to hear him. He was turning his neck around, like he was trying to crack it.

"Man, just gimme a little…"

Pinto put his face halfway across the table. "Five hundred. We want five hundred. You go back and talk to your friend about it."

Drew gripped his jaw with one hand, the other under his thigh. "Shit, five hundred. Eduardo ain't going to pay you to get his own shit back."

"It's our shit now." Pinto had commandeered the bag, which was fine with me. "I don't care how you dirtbags work it out. Seems like a good deal—five hundred for a grand's worth."

Drew didn't look so good.

"You okay?" I asked.

"I…" He got up from the table. "I gotta hit the head."

Pinto started to get up. I put my hand on his arm.

"He ain't goin' nowhere."

I saw the cashier following Drew back to the men's room with her eyes.

"We gotta get him out of here. Anyway—" I stopped while the waitress brought our sandwiches. "What the fuck are you thinkin'? You want to go all the way to Buena to rip off some punk dealer? What the fuck is wrong with you?"

"Why shouldn't we?"

"We? There's no fucking we here. Anyway, you have no fucking idea who he is or who he runs with. Maybe you get a few hundred bucks. Or maybe he's got some friends with him."

"Let him try."

I ate my sandwich, watching for Drew with one eye. Finally, he emerged, looking like he'd lost ten pounds, loping in slow-motion between the tables.

I stood up. "I'm done."

"What do you mean you're done?" Pinto said it like I was going home early on a big night out.

I put a bill on the table. "I gotta go to work. Maybe I'll call the troopers when I get there."

"Call the what?"

"Sure, why not? I'll come up with some story. Like I said before, I had to cover for you when we were out there."

"Hey, come on."

Drew was sliding back into the booth. I put my head next to Pinto's.

"Give him the fuckin' eight and let it go." I turned to Drew. "I gotta go."

Drew nodded. He seemed to see the situation more clearly than Pinto.

I left the odd couple alone with their thoughts. Time to see Sheila.

* * *

I don't know if it was just a big day for orders or if Sheila had orchestrated the whole thing to impress me. But it was an hour and a half of ticking items off a list, with three different trucks unloading their stuff. The first had cleaning supplies, soap for the bathrooms, coasters, paper towels. Then there was the laundry—napkins, kitchen whites, bar towels, aprons. And finally, the liquor.

The guy looked familiar, fat with a big mustache, wearing a flat cap, the kind with a big button in the middle of the top. He set a case of VO in a corner of the storage room. I asked him where he was from.

"Southwest Philly."

51

"Me too. Where'd you go to school?"

"Went to Mitchell, then Bartram."

"Okay. I went to Catholic school. MBS, then Tommy More."

"MBS—Fifty Sixth and Chester, right?"

"Yeah."

"I knew a lot of guys who went there."

Sheila came in with a bottle of Jameson's and a glass. She poured out a healthy shot and handed it to the guy. She let me tick off the list. I pointed with the little pencil at a line.

"What about the Galliano?"

"Galliano?" The guy ran his finger down the list to the line. "Must have missed that. Shit, can't believe you ran out. People still drink stingers?"

Sheila was taking bottles out of a box and putting them onto a shelf. "Had a bunch of old girls in here last week, think they were reliving their youth."

"I'll have to come back with that."

"Don't worry, bring it next time."

I left her counting bottles and went out to the bar. There was a guy sitting there talking to Kevin, a glass of white wine in front of him. Kevin walked past me as I approached, his eyes opening wide for a moment, then he dropped a towel on the bar and went into the back. I went behind the bar, filled a glass with ice, and sprayed some soda in it. The guy had a pack of cigarettes and a gold lighter stacked next to his glass. He was staring at something, or nothing, on the wall behind the bar. He drained the glass and set it down. I came down to where he was.

"Want another?"

He looked at me for a moment. "You a new bartender?"

"I'm a friend of Lou's, just helping out for a while."

I sorted through the bottles of white Kevin had on ice under the bar and held out two. He pointed at one, and I filled his glass. He was dressed nice, a light-colored sports jacket, blue shirt. When he took the glass, there was a flash of a cufflink, a black stone.

"Hey, let me buy you one." His elbows were on the bar, and I could see the monograms on his cuffs: AG.

I felt something weird about the guy. What was he doing here at the bar in the middle of the afternoon, anyway?

"It's a little early for me," I said.

"Yeah, and I guess you gotta be careful about drinking on the job. I mean," he turned around on the stool, "what if all the waitresses and busboys did that? But, then, you," he tipped his glass toward me, "you ain't no busboy."

I put my hand out. "John McGinty. They call me Ginty."

"Ginty, right, glad to meet you." A cufflink came across the bar. "Arnie. Arnie Goldbaum." He saw me tumbling to who he was. "Right, that Arnie."

"Nice to meet you," I lied.

He held on to my hand a few seconds longer than normal. "My replacement."

I shook my head. "Just helping out."

"Yeah, whatever." His voice became a little depressed, like he had been acting and now was tired of it. There were loud footsteps, and Kevin came up behind me.

He gave a little snort. "You meet our friend here?"

"What's the matter, Kevin, you miss me?"

Kevin was punching keys on the register. He turned and nodded at the bottle on the bar.

"You give him another?"

Arnie slipped off the stool. He was a lot shorter than I had expected. He dropped a bill on the bar. Kevin pushed it back to him.

"I got this. For old times' sake." He did not sound friendly.

"Keep it then. For your service." Arnie cocked his head and looked at me. "Was hoping I might see Conci here. Tell her I was looking for her, will ya?"

Kevin tossed the bill at him. It floated to the floor as Arnie walked away.

"I ain't your servant."

Kevin bent over, filling a bucket with ice from the bin. Arnie was at the door, talking to one of the older waitresses. She kept looking over at us.

I went around the bar and picked up the bill. A twenty. Arnie was stepping away from the waitress, opening the door into the bright sunlight. He pointed a finger at me, the thumb pulled back.

I put the bill in my pocket and turned back to the bar. Sheila was standing in the dark corridor, looking at me, folding a towel and smoothing it against her stomach. I went back to where Arnie had been sitting, reached over the bar, and got a beer glass. I poured some of the white wine in it and sat back to enjoy the afternoon.

* * *

I was looking at the dinner menu when Robert appeared and took it out of my hand. Ted came down and put a bottle of red on the bar. Robert gave him a nod you almost couldn't see. Before I could say anything, Robert spoke.

"Come on."

We went in the kitchen. There were two plates on a high stainless steel table against the wall, stools on either side. He set the bottle down, grabbed a couple of glasses from a shelf, and sat against one of the stools. He wasn't really sitting or standing, just balanced on the edge in his stained whites, looking better than anyone in the dining room.

"Veal piccata, a little pasta," he said.

"I didn't see that on the menu."

"Don't order off the menu, just talk to me." He rolled up a few strands of linguine. "Unless you wanta the meatball."

While we ate, Robert filled me in on who to buy from and who not. The fish he bought himself each day at a dock-side market in Cape May. The meat, usually from a few of Lou's South Philly friends.

"I spread it around."

"That okay with Lou?"

"That's the way it's done."

The wine was more like what Lou would serve at home than the jug stuff that we poured for the shore crowd. I peered at the label on the bottle.

"What's this?"

"Barolo. Pretty much just keep it here for Lou."

"What's it run?"

"If you gotta ask…"

I'm no gourmet, but I knew enough goombas to have had more veal than I really cared for over the years. But this food was outstanding. It was all a little fancy for Wildwood. Maybe in Cape May it would fit.

I said, "Don't take this the wrong way, but how come you're here?"

"I like Lou. He helped me out with the place I had in Philly."

"What happened with that?"

"Divorce. Too complicated not to just sell it."

One of the cooks came over, teenaged guy. Robert talked him through something about green beans. The kid went back to the stove, a ponytail hanging down under the little cap they wear.

"I met Arnie today," I said.

Robert stacked our plates, putting the forks and knives on top. "Good old Arnie."

"Why is he coming back here?"

Robert put the cork in the wine bottle and tucked it under his arm. He slid from the chair.

"Looking for an old friend?"

* * *

Concetta was in fancy jeans and a shiny top.

"Tuesday is oldies night," she said.

I tried to fend her off. "I've heard them all."

"Come on, there's tons of girls there."

"That's okay." I switched channels, finding the Phillies game. "I'll watch the game."

"There's a TV over the bar, you can watch it there."

I thought about Lou. Maybe it would be worse if I didn't go.

We took her little Fiat to the bar. She had a gaggle of friends there, crowded around a spot at the bar. Carol was sitting on a stool with a yellowish drink and a long cigarette.

It was awkward. You couldn't really talk with them; they were eyeing all the guys in the bar, pointing with their chins. The group went out to the dance floor and left Carol. I pointed at her glass.

"Not a stinger, is it?"

"Lillet."

"We just ran out of Galliano—that's why I mentioned stingers."

"Oh."

That's about how I would expect it to go. Not that I was interested in her. She was kind of scary, really.

Carol talked without looking at me. "Getting the Seabreeze in shape?"

"Seems to run itself."

"Wasn't that the problem?"

I got a beer and squeezed in next to her. "You know this Arnie guy?"

"Tsh."

That was a yes, but exactly what kind of yes, I wasn't sure.

"He came in today. Acted weird, didn't tell me who he was at first."

"A clever man."

"I'm wondering if he'll come back."

"Why should you care?" She pushed her glass a few inches in on the bar, and a bartender immediately appeared and refilled it with ice and Lillet. "You're not afraid of him?"

"Nah, I just don't like dealing with wackos."

"Hey, Kemosabe!"

Pinto had appeared, as if on cue. He looked and smelled like he had just come out of the shower and doused himself in Aqua Velva. He wore jeans that looked like Concetta's and had a big gold chain over his black t-shirt.

"Gonna introduce me to your friend?" He bounced back and forth, heel to toe. Carol gave him the same assessing look she had used on me.

"Carol, this is Pinto. He's a friend of Lou's."

Pinto stepped back and put his hand on his chest dramatically. "A friend of Lou's? I'm not a friend of youse?"

He held the pose for a few seconds, then gave me a fake one-two to the chest. "Ahh, I'm just kiddin' ya."

I went to take a leak and give Pinto a chance to work his charms. When

I came back, they were gone, and I spotted them on the dance floor. She was a good six inches taller than him in her sandals. Concetta and crew came back over, and I let her pull me out. The DJ talked incessantly, but the music was pretty good; old-school Motown instead of the usual Michael Jackson. When we came back, Carol had detached herself from Pinto, who had moved down to the end of the bar, leaning up onto it talking to the bartender, his feet barely touching the floor. He gave the guy a little salute and waved me down. He took my arm and walked me toward an alcove where there were a few chairs and a cigarette machine.

"I got it figured out."

I looked back over at the girls. "Good luck, man, that Carol is a tough one."

This punch to my arm was harder. "No, man, forget that *miserable.*" He tugged my arm. "I'm talking about the stuff."

He squeezed a hand into his jeans pocket and pulled a tiny bag filled with white powder up where I could see it. I looked around and slapped his hand.

"Are you fuckin' nuts? What're you doing with that?"

Pinto pushed the bag back down and gave me a pitiful look. "Man, you said it yourself. That junkie doesn't have any money. But this," he started to pull out the bag again, "we can sell these for twenty bucks a pop. Maybe make two, three grand."

"I'm not dealing fucking junk, Pinto."

A woman came out and opened her purse, picking out coins and buying a pack of Salems. She gave us both a wet look as she passed back into the bar.

"What the fuck, Pinto, why didn't you sell her some? Shit, let's put up a sign."

"We don't need a sign, man. They'll find us." Another woman, a real skinny one, was at the cigarette machine now. "You'd be surprised."

Pinto was staring at the girl who had her hand halfway up the inside of the machine. He nudged me.

"Look at this."

The girl reached up with her other hand and pounded the panel where you put the coins in. Her hand was out of the machine now, and she pulled on the toggle, hard.

"God damn machine, took my money!"

She gave it another whack and pulled some more. She was squatting down, blocking our view of the slot at the bottom.

"Wow, there you go!" She stood up, holding a pack of Camels. She was blonde, or at least the bottom five inches of her hair was blonde, and her skin had that really dark tan, with wrinkles around her eyes and mouth, like she spent all her time outdoors. If you told me she slept on the beach, I would believe it.

She turned toward us, holding up the cigarette pack, as if to prove her victory. She tore off the cellophane and dropped it on the floor as she went back into the bar.

"I think I'm in love." Pinto looked a little dewy-eyed. "I haven't seen anyone do that in years."

Chapter Five

Next day, it was Pinto's turn to show up in the bar during the lull after lunch. He was wearing the same clothes as the night before. He rotated back and forth on a barstool, reading the menu like it was the Wall Street Journal. Kevin ignored him in a way that told me he knew him all too well.

"Concetta get you tucked in good and early?" Pinto asked.

I ignored the comment. I was wondering about something else.

"So what happened with Drew?"

"Waddya mean?"

"He just let you keep the stuff and went back to Buena?"

"Nah, nah." Pinto looked up at me over little half-lens glasses he must have got in Woolworth's. "He's still here."

"Here? What, is he staying at the Port Royal?"

"Of course not. He's staying with me."

"What, at your nephew's place?"

"He's fine, he's fine. Nobody's there this week." He held out the menu. "Clams casino any good?"

"Yeah, they're good. So you got a kicking junkie back at your nephew's place? Hope you got everything nailed down."

"He ain't kickin'. What, you think I got no heart?"

Why was I asking him about this stuff? Then again, why was he here?

Kevin brought me an iced tea. Pinto gave him the big wave.

"Yo, Kevvy boy. What's happenin'?"

Kevin ignored the question. "You want anything?"

"Me? World peace, right?" A Pinto laugh. "And clams on the half shell with a beer." He slapped down the menu.

Kevin nodded like he was in pain and went back to the kitchen. Pinto jerked his thumb in Kevin's direction.

"Boss oughta talk to that guy about his attitude."

"I'm the boss, and his attitude is fine. So what do you want anyway? Or are you just here to brag about whoever you fooled into thinking you were a nice guy last night?"

"You know I don't kiss and tell. Let's just say she was a nice Catholic girl. Friend of Concetta's."

"Not Carol?"

"Didn't I just say I don't tell?"

After a bit, Kevin came back with a half dozen clams. Pinto shook dots of Tabasco onto the clams like he was a New York painter.

"It's amazing what these girls get into."

I didn't bite. What would he say if he did kiss and tell?

Pinto held a shell up to his mouth and forked in the clam. "First time someone paid me when…you know."

"Maybe a new career for you."

He considered this philosophically. "She wasn't paying for my *cazzo*." The hand came out of his jeans pocket with a little packet again. "She'd prefer coke, but…" He stuffed it back in his pocket. "Don't worry, I know how you are. Sort of a prude."

Drew hanging around town was not good. Having his dealer pissed and putting the screws on him could go in a bad direction. And Pinto, as my close associate, was the worst part of the story.

I spoke to Kevin, pointing at Pinto's plate.

"That's on me." I slid off the stool. "I got stuff to deal with. Check you out later."

Pinto smiled as he slurped down another clam.

* * *

The woman on the phone was not impressed.

"You want to report what?"

"I was in an accident."

"Where are you now?"

"I'm in Wildwood."

"Are you still with your car?"

"No, no. I'm sorry. The accident was on Friday."

"Friday?"

"Yeah, I crashed on the…the grass, you know, next to the shoulder on the Parkway, maybe three o'clock. Saturday morning, then, not Friday."

"So you were in an accident almost a week ago? Why are you calling?"

"Well, you see, I walked away, just left the car there."

"You walked off the Parkway."

"Yeah."

I figured it was better the cops find out all this from me rather than from Drew. Even better if I could talk to the cop.

"Where's the car now?"

"I-I'm not sure."

"You didn't go back."

"Well, yes, I did go back."

I had decided before the call to tell the truth, except for the visit from Drew and the heroin.

"I went back out Saturday afternoon. To get my stuff, I had a bag in the car."

"Uh-huh." She was writing things down now. "And you just left it there then?"

"The car is totaled."

"You didn't get it towed?"

"No."

She breathed loudly while she wrote. I had the trooper's name, or at least what I remembered from his nameplate, on a scrap of paper.

"I met a trooper then. He stopped when he saw us."

"Yeah?"

"I thought—I thought maybe I should talk to him. Purcell. Didn't get his first name."

"Hang on a minute."

Sheila came in and got a jar of olives. Her look told me she was none too happy about having Pinto occupy the bar.

The lady came back on the line. "They towed the wreck. You're gonna have to pay for that, you know."

"That's fine."

"Plus they may cite you for abandoning the vehicle."

"I...can I talk to Purcell?"

"He's gonna call you."

I gave her the restaurant's number and went back out to the bar. Pinto was by the door talking to one of the busboys. I didn't have any doubt what it was about. I went over and grabbed his arm. He resisted for a second, raising a finger to the kid.

"Hey, man, talk to you later."

He pulled his arm away and went out the front door ahead of me.

"Don't have to bum-rush me."

"Fuck I don't."

He was moving around on the sidewalk. I grabbed his shoulders and leaned down, my face close to his.

"Don't fucking deal dope in the restaurant."

He smiled, and I thought he might hit me in the gut, but he backed off.

"I wouldn't do that to Lou."

"And don't do it to me either."

He shook free. "You the bouncer too?"

"Pinto, what the fuck? You're talking to a busboy, all quiet? He your nephew or something?"

"He might be."

"He's not your fucking nephew. And I'm hoping he's not a freakin' junkie either."

"Nah, man, all's he wants is some weed."

"So you were trying to sell him something."

62

The hands went up. "Hey, don't worry. I won't do nothin' in the restaurant, okay?"

"And don't bring Drew around here. You gotta send him back to Buena."

"I send him back now, that dealer's gonna be all over my ass."

"Not if you just give him the shit like I said."

"We got a deal. He's helping me cut it down into little bags and sell it, I'll make three-four times more that way. I'll give him some cash then and send him home; he can deal with his man however he likes."

A couple came walking over from the parking lot. Pinto gave them a big smile and opened the door for them.

"How you doin', folks?"

They smiled back. Pinto nodded as they stood inside waiting for Sheila to seat them.

"See, that's how you treat customers. Take a lesson."

He walked away like he was the mayor of the town, lighting a cigarette and throwing the match in the street.

* * *

Purcell put his hand up. "Just spaghetti and meatballs."

I acted like a concerned host. "No veal...?"

"Nah, I never get a decent meatball." He drank his beer. "What I get for marrying an Irish girl."

Purcell had shown up right in the middle of the dinner rush, or what passed for a rush on a Wednesday. Normally, a cop was not good business, but he got a lot of admiring looks from all the blue-hairs, and you could tell the guys respected him. I mean, he was a trooper, not a shore cop.

"How's Lou?"

"You know Lou?"

He stabbed at a crouton on his salad plate with a toothpick.

"I been down here for eight years. So, yeah, I know Lou."

I looked at him. "Why didn't you say something out on the Parkway?"

"Just following procedures."

I thought that over. "You weren't worried we'd stolen the Bronco or anything?"

Purcell chuckled through a cherry tomato. "I knew Pinto was one of his guys." He gestured with his fork. "So, Lou…"

"Doing good. He's up in the city now, be back down this weekend."

"You're taking Arnie's place?"

"Yeah. He was in the other day."

I guess it was just an instinct that made me say that. He didn't say anything, but maybe that was standard procedure, too. Sheila stopped at the table.

"Everything alright, officer?"

Her eyes glowed like she was talking to Al Pacino.

"Everything is fine, dear," Purcell answered.

I swear she curtsied before she walked away, an extra wiggle in her walk. Purcell saw me watching her and laughed.

"Some of these gals, they just love the uniform." He leaned back as the waitress set a plate down. "Especially the old ones."

I watched as he tucked in to his meal. I had told him the story already, why I didn't admit it was my car originally, and he had just nodded. Of course, I didn't mention Drew's visit and the H.

"So you going to issue me a…citation or whatever?"

He paused, a big twirl of spaghetti on his fork and spoon. "What for?"

"I dunno—abandoning a vehicle."

"I don't understand—the car belongs to some scumbag junkie in Buena, right?" He put the pasta in his mouth and chewed, then stopped. "Right?"

I hadn't told him Drew was a junkie, but then he was a cop. "Right."

He kept eating, a napkin tucked into his collar. "He hasn't returned our calls, funny thing. I like it, though. We'll pass all this along to the local force out there. They'll get a kick out of it. Good excuse to bring his ass in to the station."

"Hang on for a second."

I went to the bar and got Kevin to give me a bottle of the red Robert had me drinking the other night. I walked back with the bottle and two glasses in my hand like I was Rick in Casablanca sitting down with Victor Laszlo. I filled them up and lifted mine.

"*Salute.*"

Purcell tilted his up and took a quick slurp, then returned to the spaghetti. "You mean 'thanks for picking me over a dirtbag junkie'?"

I laughed. "Yeah, something like that."

Purcell swabbed up gravy with a piece of bread. "What're you hanging 'round with that nutball Pinto for?"

"Lou sort of assigned him to me."

"We've run into him before."

"Yeah?"

"Nothing serious—speeding tickets, a bar fight."

I shrugged.

Purcell said, "I never heard a guy lie as much as he did out there."

"Yeah, you can't get him to shut up."

We shared the wine and relaxed, watching the dinner crowd begin to wander out.

"Hey, I appreciate your coming down." I was wondering why he had come at all.

"A friend of Lou's…"

"Anytime you want to come in—bring your wife, family. Robert is really good, believe it or not."

Purcell poured out the last of the wine into our glasses. "I just might." He drank the wine back like it was beer.

I smiled and nodded like an idiot, wondering if he had made the trip for the free meal or just to meet little old me again.

Chapter Six

Concetta was in shorts and a tank top on the deck when I came out Thursday morning.

I got coffee and joined her. "No work today?"

She put the newspaper down. "Taking the day off. Carol's got me working the weekend."

"Jobs are a bitch."

"How's yours? You seem to be getting into the routine."

"It's different."

"I'm sure."

A seagull landed on the edge of the roof and twitched around.

"I met Arnie this week."

"Yeah, I heard."

"What, Carol tell you?"

She nodded, blowing smoke and stubbing her cigarette out. I looked at the seagull.

"He was asking for you."

She didn't take the bait. I tried some more. "He seems like a slippery character."

"Everybody knows that."

She shifted forward in the chair, leaning against the table. This was too weird. Coffee on the deck with Concetta every morning for the summer? Nothing would ever happen, but still.

"Robert said maybe he was looking for an old friend." I tried to sound jokey. "But who would be friends with that creep?"

Concetta got up and stepped in front of the seagull. "Aren't you supposed to be finding that out?"

* * *

The beach was pretty quiet, mostly families, wives that is, with little kids. I figured I ought to go; I mean, I was at the shore. Concetta laughed at me as I packed a sandwich and a couple of Cokes in a little cooler, putting sunscreen on. I had found a straw hat in the garage and had a towel draped around my shoulders, a folding chair under my arm.

"Bring me back some water ice."

I hadn't been down the shore this long in what, maybe six, seven years. Back then, a bunch of us went in on a house in the Crest. We were still young enough we remembered doing the group rental thing in our early twenties. So we tried to relive our youth, but were already turning into old fucks at thirty. Sweeping the sand up in the kitchen every day, guys sitting around in wet bathing suits watching the Phils. We did hit the bars and some of the guys brought girls back, but more often it was girlfriends from home, wives even, coming down.

Now sitting on the beach, deciding when I would go in to work—this was good, I guessed. I drank my Coke and ate my sandwich down close to the water, throwing a ball back to a little kid scrambling around playing handball on a court drawn in the hard wet sand.

Maybe I had found my calling.

* * *

That afternoon, Concetta filled the guest spot in my daytime talk show. I was actually busy—Robert wasn't in yet, so I was handling deliveries from the produce guy. Boxes of lettuce—lots of them, maybe ten or so.

"You sure this is how much we need?" I asked.

The guy—kid, really, long hair in a ponytail—pulled the hand truck out from under the last stack he had brought in.

"Yeah, we won't be back until Monday."

I flipped the lid off a box and picked out a head of iceberg. I figured I should check something out.

One of the dishwashers helped me get them into the walk-in. When I came out, Concetta was standing next to a steam table. She was dressed up, not like when she went out dancing, but a nice dress, heels. She was twisting a ring on her left hand. Wasn't that supposed to be a sign of something? You saw women do that on TV shows when…

I took a towel off a rack and dried my hands. "What's up?'

She started to put her hand on the steam table, and I jumped forward and grabbed her.

"Careful. That's hot."

She looked at the pot of soup that was bubbling there. "Oh."

I dropped her hand and walked toward the bar. "Come on, it's cooler out here."

I sat at my usual stool. "You want something? Coke, glass of wine?"

"No, no." She looked around like she had never been there before. Sheila was watching us from across the room, where she was giving instructions to a few waitresses. "Have you heard from Lou?"

"Lou? No, he hasn't called here."

"Alright, I thought he might have said something…you know, like when he was coming down."

"He said Friday—or maybe tonight."

Sheila came over, a handful of order pads in her hand. She put them on the bar. Ted appeared just as she sat at the stool on the corner and set an iced tea down. Sheila settled in with little movements and hooked a foot around the rung on the stool.

"Hey, Connie, how's it goin'?"

"Great, Sheila, keeping busy. How's my boy here workin' out?"

"Your boy?" Sheila gave me a look that was meant for Concetta. It was not quite a smile. "He's a good boss."

Connie? I never heard anyone call her Connie. I laughed because I couldn't figure out what else to do. Sheila sat on the stool like it was her personal spy station, which it was. She wasn't going anywhere. It didn't take a genius to see she didn't like Concetta hanging around.

I stood up. "Hey, you got a smoke?"

Sheila gave me a look that said she knew I didn't smoke. But Concetta went with me out the front door. She stood there twisting a toe on the sidewalk.

"You got that smoke?"

She looked startled. "Oh, right." She opened her pocketbook—not the usual straw one—this one was small and a pale blue that matched her shoes. She gave me a cigarette.

"Guess I need a light, too."

She rummaged and brought out a black lighter with silver trim. It had her initials on it and was expensively heavy.

"I gotta go to this thing in Cape May."

"Yeah?" I looked at the cigarette. It was one of those skinny kinds that women smoked.

"Some realtors' group, like a networking thing."

"Right." It was definitely a thing, no doubt about that. Of course, it was in Cape May.

"So, if Lou comes down, can you just let him know where I'm at?"

"Sure, sure." I turned toward the street, smoking like a nervous teenager, which was half true.

"I left him a message, but you know, he doesn't always pick them up."

A couple came up the sidewalk, the guy holding the door open for his wife, looking at Concetta when his wife went in before him, like he couldn't help it.

"Okay, no problem." I stubbed the butt out in the ashtray next to the door. "Cape May, huh? Haven't been down there in years."

"Me neither."

Why did she have to toss that lie in? I was going to ask her where the "thing" was, but thought better of it. She smiled, and I thought maybe she was thanking me for not asking.

I put my hand on the door.

"Gotta get back. Sheila says Thursdays can be busy."

Concetta gave me a little wave and stepped off toward the parking lot. I watched her and wondered what drove someone to fashion such a mangled and unneeded alibi.

* * *

I was hauling in buckets of ice for Kevin and Ted, dumping them out into the bins under the bar, when I realized how much I was enjoying myself. Sheila had said it was like warmups for the weekend, and it did have that pressure-valves-been-released feeling. People stayed at tables long after their meals were gone, and drink orders were non-stop. At first, I was afraid the guys would feel like I was butting in on their world, but by ten o'clock, we were splitting up the work like old hands.

We finally turned out the last of the stragglers around twelve-thirty—an hour after we were supposed to close—and Robert came out to the bar still in his stained whites. I let Ted close out without me looking over his shoulder and shared a bottle with Robert. Sheila appeared at the corner of the bar, signaling with her thumb.

"I got Lou for you."

Robert filled my glass and lifted his to me.

"The boss calleth."

Sheila looked tired. "I'm going home."

The handset of the old-style phone was sitting on the desk. I picked it up.

Lou was chipper. "Hey, Sheila says you had a good night."

"Yeah, I gotta check the numbers, but a lot of people."

"Don't worry about the numbers, we can go over all that tomorrow."

"Right. Yeah, it was definitely busy."

"Good, good."

There was a pause that just made me feel nervous. I filled it in.

"Guess you're not comin' down tonight."

"Nah, nah—I got—there's some stuff I gotta be here for in the morning, so…I'll try to make it out by lunch time, beat the traffic."

"Makes sense."

"Yeah, definitely." There was noise; he was probably in a bar or restaurant himself. "How's Concetta, you see her today?"

Did I see her? "Yeah, I just talked to her late afternoon. She was heading down to Cape May."

There was a moment of silence. Then Lou said, "Cape May?"

"Yeah, you know, some realtor thing. She said she left you a message."

"Right. She didn't mention Cape May, I figured it was somewhere close."

"No, well, whatever, she stopped by the restaurant, then she went down."

Lou laughed. "That's good, she never comes by the restaurant. What, did she go down with Carol?"

"I don't know, she was by herself."

"Alright, whatever. Hey, do me a favor, is Robert still there?"

I went back out and thumbed Robert back to the office. Kevin was drinking a club soda. I hadn't asked him, but he seemed to not drink at all, though you would never have guessed that from his face. He pushed the glass around in wet rings on the bar.

"Another weekend."

That was talkative for Kevin.

"Hopefully not too bad."

"I hope it is, tips are better."

Robert came back out. He stood by his stool and drained the last of his wine.

"Lou wants me to fix up something special for tomorrow, for dinner at his place."

"Something nice for him and Concetta?"

Robert unbuttoned his shirt and turned to go to the kitchen. "He didn't mention her. He said he wanted to give you a break."

"I don't need a break, I've hardly been working."

Robert took off the shirt and slung it over his shoulder. "When the boss says you need a break," he pointed his index finger at me, "you take a break."

I went out and started up the Caddy. I drove home, whistling like Andy Griffith, wondering if it was better or worse if Concetta was there.

Chapter Seven

Concetta was still out when I got home. When I got up around four to take a leak and peeked in the bedroom like an anxious dad, she was asleep under the sheets, the blue sheath of a dress tossed over a chair.

I was up and out before she stirred. I figured I should do an early shift if I was being summoned for dinner. The prep cooks were busy making deviled crab, stirring big pots of soup, cutting up lettuce and dumping it into a grey trashcan with loads of ice, water and potato whitener. Kevin wasn't in yet, so I futzed around behind the bar, checking the bottles that hung upside down with metered dispensers and lining up replacements. When Kevin appeared, I stuck around long enough for him to decide if I had messed up his system, but he seemed okay.

I bought a pack of Camels from the machine—I wasn't planning to really start up again, but I didn't want to keep bumming smokes off everyone, and I was spending a lot of time out back or in the front with whomever was taking a break. It was a good way to figure out what was going on.

Which today was freaking out about the weekend. One of the waitresses quit—didn't show up, anyway; one of the Frialators conked out, burner all clogged up; a toilet was overflowing. All this on top of the usual fuckups that happened as everyone shifted into a higher gear. It seemed like everyone was doing someone else's job. A dishwasher was swabbing the bathroom; a busboy was scrubbing pots in the kitchen; Kevin was clearing tables; I was behind the bar. So when Robert came out at four-thirty—the only relaxed person in the place—and handed me a basket to take back to Lou's, I was glad to get out.

Back at Lou's, I unpacked the basket—plastic containers of salami, cheese, marinated vegetables; a loaf of Italian bread cut into little slices; a bottle of champagne—and cleaned up, putting on a nice shirt. Meanwhile, Concetta had come in and was bent over, staring into the refrigerator.

"What's all this stuff?"

She had her nose in a container of artichokes and red peppers.

"That's for dinner—Robert sent it over," I said

She closed it up and tossed it back in the fridge. Lou must have called her, right? The phone rang. Concetta ignored it, so I picked it up.

"Hey, how we doing?" It was Lou.

"Not bad, I just got back." I pointed at the phone and mouthed "it's Lou". Concetta ignored me and went into the bedroom.

"Is Concetta there?"

"Yeah, let me get her."

"No, no, that's okay. I just stopped to get some stuff, be there soon."

I found a platter in the kitchen, arranged the antipasto on it, and put the bread in a basket with a napkin under it. Concetta came out, dressed down from her real estate clothes. She poured vodka into a glass.

"We got champagne." I pulled the bottle out of the fridge.

She shrugged and belted back the vodka. "I need a cigarette."

I thought better of uncorking the bubbly and got a can of beer instead. I followed her out to the deck and lit up a Camel.

Concetta laughed. "You really are a restaurant worker now."

At least she was laughing. I looked at the burning end of the butt. "Guess I better watch this."

"You and me." She gave me a serious look. "Really, do you like the job?"

"Today, I wasn't so sure. But, yeah, it's fun. There's always something going on."

"If you're really into the food biz, you could do better."

"I don't know about that."

"The Seabreeze—it's pretty run-of-the-mill."

"Don't let Lou hear you say that."

I found myself lighting another Camel, the first one still smoldering in the ashtray. I was just about through my beer when there was a sudden blast of rock music from out front. Concetta got up.

"That'll be hubby."

Lou came up the inside stairway, a huge bouquet in one hand, an overnight bag in the other, a couple of cigars in his shirt pocket. He tossed the bag on the floor and pressed the flowers against Concetta's chest, hugging her with the other hand.

"Hey, how's my little broker?" He squeezed her butt.

Concetta put her hand on his face and gave him a big kiss. "These are so nice."

She sounded sincere. Who the hell knew? She took the flowers to the sink and unwrapped the paper around the stems, then laid them flat on the cutting board and whacked off the ends with a big knife. Lou picked a slice of salami off the tray and bit it in half, looking around the room, patting his stomach.

"Man, it's good to be down."

"How was the traffic?" Concetta put a vase on the table and tweaked the flowers, pulling the stems apart so they weren't all bunched up.

"Okay, till I got to Somers Point. All jammed up there."

I got the champagne out of the fridge. This time, I wasn't going to ask. I popped it open, filled a glass, and handed it to Concetta, then one for Lou. He was already outside, so I got one for myself and brought the bottle along.

This was more like normal, like the Lou and Concetta I knew. She brought out the food and we noshed and drank, Lou telling a funny story about a sale one of the guys had made today. Concetta laughed, sitting next to him, her hand on his leg. We worked through the bottle, the sun heading down over the bay.

Concetta lifted her head, cocking her ear toward the glass doors. "You hear something?"

We all listened. I could hear water running, a few clinking sounds.

"There's someone in there," I said.

Lou got up, looking concerned, stepping quietly over to the door.

Concetta and I followed behind, like two little Indians. Lou slid the door back and put up his hand, holding us back. He stepped in, then waved us along behind him.

There was a woman at the sink. She was short and fat, and was talking to herself while picking apart greens under the running water. She had dark hair puffed up on top of her head and was wearing an apron over a green dress that reached to her calves. Lou went up behind her and, giving us a signal to be quiet, dropped his hands on her shoulders.

"Mrs. Minnucci!"

"Jesus!" She spun around, a knife suddenly in her hand. Lou jumped back. "Hey, it's me, *mia cara!*"

She slumped, still holding the knife. "Louis, I not know…you scared me!"

"Scared you? You're about to cut off my *coglioni* and you're scared?"

"Oh, you." She slapped his chest. "Roberto asked me to do…a…your supper, *capisce?*"

Lou stepped back, and Concetta moved in, hugging Mrs. Minnucci. They talked in Italian, Mrs. Minnucci getting very animated. She kept saying "Concettina" and something like "Daveed". She had moved back from Concetta and was admonishing her, the hand without the knife making little angry movements, thumb and forefinger together, punctuating each word.

Lou looked morose all of a sudden. I knew the look—he was pissed and holding it in. Concetta was nodding her head, like she was agreeing with Mrs. Minnucci, or at least accepting what she was saying. She bowed her head, like a girl being yelled at by a nun for chewing gum during Mass.

"Hey." I walked toward the door to the deck, picking up a bottle of red wine and a corkscrew from the kitchen counter and waving Lou along. He whispered something in Concetta's ear and engaged for just a few seconds with Mrs. Minnucci, talking to her about the pasta she was working on, then retreated, smiling all the way.

"*Scusi, scusi!*"

On the deck, he took the wine and stood by the railing, working the corkscrew into it with hard twists.

"Fucking kid. Why doesn't he just OD and stop torturing us?"

Now I understood—"Daveed," David.

There wasn't much to say to that. I had a flash of Pinto selling a bag to Davy in some dark alley, figuring out how much he could rip him off for. Lou would freak if he had any idea Pinto was prowling around Wildwood trying to figure out how to be a dope dealer.

"Hey, man, it's tough." I wasn't sure if I meant being Davy, or being Lou—either one was not easy.

"Fuck, that *stunad* Mrs. M is gonna get Concetta all fucked up about this again."

"Where is—?"

"How the fuck should I know? Wherever the junk is, sleeping in some piss-hole with his junkie friends until he wakes up and looks for more."

"Come on, man, drink the wine, have some dinner—you've done what you can."

I had no idea what he had or hadn't done; I was just trying to calm him down.

"It's fucked up," Lou said uncalmly.

Concetta came out, wearing an apron, quiet like she was leaving church. "We'll eat in half an hour."

"Okay." Lou said it like the doctor just told him he had cancer. He filled his wine glass and sat down, fidgeting with his sunglasses.

Concetta bunched the apron up, wiping her hands. "She's making her veal with pasta and prosciutto."

"Good." Lou answered like he wanted her to shut up.

"Like saltimbocca."

"Yeah, I know."

I got up. "Conci, I get you some wine or somethin'?"

"See if there's some white in the fridge."

I didn't know how much more of this I could take. Mrs. Minnucci looked over when I came in, then back to the stove. There was a bottle of white on the counter she had been using for cooking. I picked it up.

"Okay to use this?"

"Whaat?"

I held the bottle out, and she gave me a dismissive flutter of fingers from the hand that wasn't stirring the sauce. Out back, silence had set in, which I tried to fill with talk about how crazy the day was at the restaurant. Lou nodded and smiled, seeming to relax a little. Concetta drank her wine and stared at the rooftops.

I said, "I like Kevin, he's a good man. And Robert, what a great cook."

"How's Sheila holding up?" Lou asked.

Concetta sniffed, just a little.

Lou put his elbows on the table and twisted his wine glass back and forth. "She's had a lot to take care of with Arnie gone. You helping her out with the ordering and stuff?"

"She went through all her stuff with me—lets me handle some of the orders."

"That's good." Now he sounded paternal, like Sheila was one of his kids, or maybe it was me.

Concetta got up. "I'll go set the table."

When she had gone in, Lou shook his head. "This is so fucked up. We gotta—I don't know, come on."

He led me inside. All was forgotten, for me anyway, as the aroma from the food was unbelievable. Why wasn't I born Italian? This beat potatoes, meat loaf, and green beans up, down, and sideways. Mrs. Minnucci brought large plates over covered with the veal and pasta, and went back over to the kitchen area and sat on a stool with a bowl of noodles.

Lou called over, offended. "Sit, sit."

"No, no. I have a little, then I clean up."

"Come on."

"You, sit, *mangia tutti*, enjoy."

Concetta turned to face her. "Thank you, Mrs. Minnucci, it's wonderful."

I had never seen her do the Catholic schoolgirl thing so completely. Somehow, it was tied up with the problems with Davy. Lou was being polite, if a little stiff.

"Can you pass the parm, Concetta?"

She moved over the little dish with the grated parmesan.

"So, how was Cape May?" Lou asked, looking at his plate, making a job of shaking parm on it.

"Good."

"Sell anything?"

Concetta chewed slowly and dabbed at her mouth with a napkin. She swallowed, then answered.

"It was more of a...networking thing."

I wished she was better at this. Lou gave a little purse to his lips and rocked side to side, like he was considering what she said.

"Right."

"Yeah, Carol asked me to go."

"So you went down with Carol?"

"No, Carol couldn't go, she had a closing or something."

Now she was the Catholic schoolgirl who was no good at lying. Lou didn't say anything, just did a little more of the rocking. I tried to break up the conversation.

"This pasta is unbelievable. Hey, shoot me that bottle of red."

Lou passed the bottle and seemed to take my distraction as a challenge. "What, was this at Congress Hall or something?"

"No, we just went to a restaurant. You know, they had like a meeting room."

Lou shook out his napkin and wiped his mouth. He drank some wine with more energy. He was warming to the interrogation. "Yeah? We haven't been down there in years. We oughta go. What was this place?"

I looked at her thinking, don't fuck this up.

"It's called Randall's—Randall's on Broadway."

"Sounds good. Let's go this weekend, what do you say?"

"I don't know, the weekend is busy, we got a ton of rentals coming in on Saturday."

Lou looked at me. "What about you, you wanna go?"

I think he meant, you were supposed to be keeping an eye on her, so what the fuck was she doing in Cape May?

I laughed. "Hey, I'll be eating standing up at the Seabreeze—this'll be my first weekend, I gotta be there."

"Some other time." He pushed around the remains of his pasta. "I gotta write that down, Randall's, right? Maybe for our anniversary."

Mrs. Minnucci waddled over, her hands balled up in her apron. "How's it taste?"

"Fantastic." I held up my wine glass. "A toast to Mama Minnucci!"

Lou and Concetta raised their glasses and called out, "*Salute!*"

We all tucked in and worked our way through the meal. Lou finished first and pushed his plate forward with an exaggerated gasp of relief.

"Man, I'm stuffed!"

Concetta stood and collected plates, going back to the kitchen with Mrs. Minnucci. She put the plates on the counter, then went out to the deck, a cigarette raised in her hand in explanation. Lou sank back into his chair. He looked tired. He rubbed his eyes and shook his head like he was trying to wake up.

"What a fuckin' crazy day."

"You sell anything?"

He gave me a stony look. I held my hands up. "Hey, a joke, right?"

"Right." He played with a fork, scraping it across the tablecloth. "So, Cape May, huh?"

"That's what she told me. She stopped by the restaurant around five before she went down."

"Guess I could be a prick husband and call Carol, see what she says."

This was my night off, I guessed—being a witness to him interrogating his wife.

"I don't know, Lou, why don't you—talk to her, or something."

"That's what I was doing, right?"

"I mean—without me around."

"What, you're a marriage counselor now?"

"If I was a marriage counselor, we'd do it all together."

He stood up. "Come on, let's smoke those cigars."

Concetta was looking out at the neighboring rooftops, her arms folded, cigarette in her hand on top of her shoulder. As we came out, she stubbed the cigarette out and went past us back inside.

"I'll help clean up."

Lou gave me a "what did I do to deserve this" look. We stood by the railing, knocking ash from the cigars onto the concrete by the pool.

Lou said, "Seriously, how's it going?"

"It's good. Sheila can be a little—uptight, whatever. I think she figures she can handle everything. I try not to step on her toes."

"That's a plan. She's alright. Great with the waitresses."

I was getting dizzy from the smoke and let the cigar go out. "Arnie came in for a visit."

"That fuck. What, you were waiting for the right moment to tell me?"

I let that slide. "He didn't have much to say. Seemed to know who I was—that I was helping you out."

"He talk to anybody there?'

"He was talking to one of the older waitresses when he was leaving." I thought about Arnie's asking after Concetta, but thought that might really light his fuse. "I'll find out her name."

"Probably nothing there."

"So why did he come in?"

Lou stubbed out his cigar. "Cause he's a pain in the ass prick."

"You thinking about pressing charges or whatever?"

"You think the cops are gonna get me my money back? I'll deal with him."

It seemed to me that Arnie had a lot of balls showing up like he did, but clearly, there were a lot of things about running a restaurant that I did not understand.

Lou was stretched out, bent forward, resting his head on his arms on top of the railing. I thought of something else he probably should know.

"I called the State Police."

"What'd you do that for?"

I felt like Concetta now—I had to lie a little. It didn't seem like a good idea to tell him about the dope and everything. "I figured they'd run me down eventually. Anyway, the cop who saw us out there—on the Parkway—he came into the restaurant to see me." I leaned over the rail so I could see his face. "He was cool, thought it was funny. Figured it gave them an excuse to harass the junkie guy I bought it from. He said he knows you—said to say hi."

"I know a lot of cops."

"Name is Purcell. Tall guy, sort of good-looking, I guess." I chuckled. "Definitely looks like a cop."

Lou didn't look at me. "He's alright."

I tried to think what else I should tell him and decided that was enough for one night.

Chapter Eight

Lou was gone when I got up. Concetta was doing her office prep thing out on the deck. I joined her as it would have been too weird not to. She looked like she had had a rough night. She wasn't much of one for drinking, but I guessed either there had been a lot of talking, or none at all, when they went to bed, so maybe not a real restful night.

She was making a show of going through her notes, copying things from one piece of paper to another. I decided I had to say something.

"Hey, if you don't mind me asking—"

She looked up at me, bangs down to her sunglasses. I figured she was wondering which topic I would choose.

"How is he doing—Davy, I mean?" I asked.

She put her pen down, looking relieved. This was better than the other main topic.

"Ginty, we've tried everything."

The opening disclaimer, I'd kind of expected that. "Is he…does he have someplace to stay or what?"

She shrugged. "I don't know. He's been…I think he's got a girlfriend, back in Fishtown."

Good location, I thought, close to the dealers.

"If there's anything I can do…"

"You're a good man, Ginty."

Even through her sunglasses, her look made me squirm. I made a feeble gesture with my coffee cup. She kept up the look.

"No, really, you are. You are a good man. You care."

Unlike Lou, right? It's a lot easier to say you care when it's not your kid that's fucked up. I could feel she was still looking at me, all gooey, and searched for a seagull to stare at. She took her sunglasses off and put the big browns on me full bore, a little damp.

"You always tried with Davy. Maybe if…"

She stopped, her eyes getting damper and turning away.

"If what?"

She blinked a couple of times, then turned her eyes back to her papers, corralling them into her little notebook.

"I was serious, you know—about you doing better than the Seabreeze."

The Davy conversation was apparently over.

"I'm just helping Lou out—he needs it."

"Oh yeah, he needs help alright."

Everyone had their own script in this family drama, that was for sure.

* * *

By one o'clock, I remembered what a weekend afternoon behind a bar at the shore was like. Combine all the usual biddies and old guys who did lunch weekdays; the barely twenty crowd who ditched the beach (or never went there at all) and took up the whole bar and half a dozen tables getting shit-faced; the somewhat older guys and gals getting rid of their hangovers; and the married couples trying to stuff food in their sunburned, cranky kids. Then add an overworked, mostly hungover staff, and there you had it. I had been there in some of those roles, but had only dealt with it from the inside a few times back in my helping-out days. At least at McNabb's, it was a more consistent set of problems. There, you could usually see the trouble coming a mile away, even if it sometimes required the threat of a baseball bat to deal with.

But once you accepted that there was going to be a certain level of mess and hysteria, you could sort of join in the fun. 'Cause that's what everyone was looking for, fun, even if they were feeling miserable and at their wits' end trying to find it.

My job, as usual, was to figure out who was struggling and pitch in. Today it was running food. I figured out pretty quick which waitresses were falling behind, and which wouldn't bite my head off if I stepped in and carried their food out. I understood, the more touches they had with a table, the more likely they'd get a decent tip.

Around three, when things had died down and just a small group of serious drinkers remained at the bar, Lou showed up, in shorts and sandals, sunglasses, a very nice linen shirt, and a straw hat with a madras band, the kind they sell on the boardwalk. He went in the back where Sheila was taking a break and was there for ten minutes, getting up to speed I guess on how she felt it was going. He came out, and Ted poured a short vodka without being asked.

Lou looked around. "Pinto here?"

I thought, I hope to fuck not.

"He hasn't been around since Wednesday."

"He was supposed to be here."

Ted caught my eye and shook his head, then went back to his setup work. Lou sat on a stool.

"Maybe I should send someone to the Garden."

I put my hand up. "I can't go now, I gotta…"

"Don't worry, he'll show."

I went back in the kitchen before Lou could change his mind. Robert was sitting on a table in the back, still in his street clothes, talking to the prep cooks.

"Hey, say thanks to your mama again," I said.

"Sure, sure. What did you guys get her worked up about? She was all wound up when she came home."

I shook my head. "I don't know—it was a weird night."

"Yeah, from what she said, they're fighting about Davy again."

I wanted to say that it was his mom who started the whole thing. I grimaced.

"She was going at Concetta about it."

"Kid's got problems—I know, he worked for me for a while."

84

"Yeah?"

"In the kitchen, back last fall in Philly. He was alright for a while, then he disappeared...I'm trying to run a kitchen, you know? Then, some other scurvy creep shows up looking for him. Davy owed him a bunch of money."

I thought about Drew and wondered how small the junkie network was. Robert hopped off the table and went into a walk-in cupboard. I followed him in. He took a set of whites from the shelf and slipped off his loafers.

"I paid the guy off for him. But I had to let him go. He came back a couple of days later." He took off his jeans, then shook out the white pants and stepped into them. "He didn't look so good. And he was pissed I paid the guy off. Said 'I woulda fucking taken care of him.'" Robert shook his head. "Tough guy."

I picked a big can of tomatoes off the shelf and hefted it in one hand. "Conci says maybe he's in Fishtown now."

"Oh yeah?" He pulled the white shirt over his dark blue tee. "I heard he was down here somewhere."

"Really?" I tossed the can to my other hand, almost dropping it. Robert hung his jeans on a hook.

"But what the fuck do I know?" He grabbed the can from me in mid-toss. "Thanks, I can use that."

I heard a loud voice and went out to find Pinto at the bar with Lou. He was telling him something about his nephew. Anything was better than what he was really up to. Lou beckoned me over.

"You guys, listen to me a minute."

I stood waiting, hoping maybe for once a task involving me and Pinto might have a happy ending. Pinto sat up straight on his stool, acting serious, or as serious as a guy in a hot pink tank top with sunglasses on top of his head drinking a tequila sunrise through a straw, can.

"Ginty here had a visitor this week." Lou made a little motion with his hand, and Ted brought him a bottle of beer. "My good friend Arnold Goldbaum."

"Really?" Pinto gave me a hurt look. "You didn't tell me that."

Lou continued. "I'm gonna see if I can get him to come back. I'll get Sheila to tell him she screwed up his last pay or something."

Pinto looked skeptical. "You really think he'll fall for that?"

"Don't worry, I'll figure it out. I'll let you know when he's coming. Then I want you—" he tipped his beer at me, "to keep him here until he," now over to Pinto, "shows up."

"That's a lot of he's and him's for our friend here," I put my hand on Pinto's shoulder, "sure you don't want to draw a picture?"

Pinto shrugged my hand off and sucked at his orange-red drink. "I think I get the picture alright, smart guy." He put the drink on the bar. "So, is this a friendly talk, a little chit-chat about the old days? Or does he need a reminder that he don't work here no more?"

Pinto's eyes were turned to the ceiling as he thought through all the scenarios that might apply and that his training had prepared him for.

Lou said, "Just a reminder."

"So, maybe a little blood; that always makes it seem more real to them. But," Pinto stuck out his foot, "no need to put the boot in." He picked up his drink. "This time."

I looked at Pinto's flip-flops. "You'll break a toe if you kick anybody wearing those things."

Pinto smiled. "I could break your fucking ribs with my bare feet, podner." I felt like the real Pinto was starting to peep through.

Lou gave him a little jab on the biceps. "Hey, calm down, you may need his help."

"I don't need anybody's fucking help."

"Alright. But, yeah, that's about right, give him something to think about, but not too much."

Pinto nodded, his lips pushed together, thinking back into his professional mode. "Here? Or outside?"

"Well, you know, that depends. It's all situational."

"I know, I know, I just want to…do it how you want."

They could have been talking about where to set the chairs up for a backyard barbecue. Lou blew over the top of his beer, thinking.

"On the one hand, I'd like you to do it here."

Pinto rubbed his chin. "Definitely simpler. We don't gotta wait for him to leave or nothin'."

"I'm not so concerned about making your job easier."

Pinto put his drink down and folded his hands in his lap. "I understand."

"It's more…so others can see. So they don't get any bright ideas about following in his footsteps."

Pinto brightened, like a fourth-grader brown-nosing a teacher. "Right, like a lesson for them all!"

"Yeah, I think." Lou chewed it over. "I don't want to freak out the waitresses or anything. But, there may be someone who thinks Arnie got a raw deal."

"Or maybe they were even working with him." Pinto preened for approval.

"Yeah, could be why he was here, checking up on someone who helped him. Maybe they owe him. Who knows?" Lou looked at me. "Now, you, you gotta keep an eye out while this is going on, see how people react."

Fucking great, I thought. I wondered if this was how they did things at Randall's.

"Sure, no problem. Like if they cheer, then I put a few extra bucks in their pay packet?"

Lou took off his sunglasses. "You think this is a joke?"

It was official: I had a job now, the boss was pissed at me.

"Nah, I understand."

"This isn't that hard."

I looked around at the handful of oldsters at tables near the front. "What about the customers?"

Pinto shrugged, his chin tugging upward. "Fuck 'em."

Lou waved at a cute waitress as she walked by. "No, he's got a point. Let me think."

Pinto looked at me like I had fucked everything up. Lou was turning around, imagining the scene.

"I know. You take him in the back."

I frowned. "You mean in the office?" I didn't like the idea of him back there, in his old stomping grounds.

"I dunno, maybe the kitchen."

All I could see was sharp objects. "I'm not so sure…"

Pinto cut in. "Hey, boss, look, give us a little freedom here." Pinto turned to me with a collegial look. "We'll figure out the best…venue, right, for this *conversation.*"

What a great team we made. Lou nodded.

"Good, you guys understand, so…use your judgment."

So I not only had a job, but a job that required judgment. I was moving up in the world. And I judged that now was not the time to tell Lou that Arnie had asked after Concetta.

Pinto winked and elbowed me in the ribs.

"Okay, maestro, I will await your call."

I didn't rub my chest, but it definitely hurt.

* * *

Robert was explaining patiently to one of the dishwashers why he should never soak the huge cast-iron pan that lay on the table between them.

"This is seasoned. You don't want to let this get wet for too long—and definitely no soap. Got it?"

The kid picked the pan up. "Got it."

"Now wipe it out, use paper towels, then put it over there."

It had been a long night, but things had gone surprisingly smoothly. It was more like a regular restaurant after the drunks were all gone at dinner time, either home or to the real bars. We went out back where there were a couple of crates to sit on. Robert was still in his whites.

"I don't go out front in the whites while we're open. Not to the bar. Only if I'm visiting someone at a table."

We had a bottle of red and smoked, listening to the clatter of the kitchen being closed down. I asked him about Randall's.

"I been there." Robert pushed a stream of smoke out.

"You know the guys in the kitchen?"

"Everybody knows everybody, right?"

"How's the food?"

"Vertical." He flicked an ash on the ground. "A square white plate with a few scallops stacked up like building blocks, a sprig of looks like fucking pine needles on top, little carrots and sprouts artfully arranged below, sauce squirted in loops on the plate like it's fucking spin art."

I laughed. "But it's good, right?"

Robert didn't crack a smile. "They probably got a butane torch back there to do the glaze." He picked up the bottle and shook it. "It's really not bad, it's just you pay for all that artsy bullshit."

He poured out a glass and handed the bottle over. I finished it up and looked into my juice glass. There was a bug wiggling around on the surface of the wine, and I tried to get it out with my finger.

"Concetta was down there the other night. She had some kind of realtor thing, I guess."

Robert nodded, blowing smoke out, seeming to be deep in thought. "I'm sure she did."

We sat in silence for a minute. There was a sound of a spoon scraping against a pot. Someone in the kitchen said something, and then several people started laughing.

Robert said, "I met the guy who owns it."

"Really?"

"Yeah, Mark something. I talked to him, early in the summer, almost went to work there." He drained the last of his wine. "Don't tell Lou that."

"Don't worry."

"He knows Concetta."

"Yeah?" So she was not lying about going to Randall's.

"Said he met her...I don't know, maybe it was one of those real estate things."

"Maybe."

Robert stood up. "You should go down there."

"What, Cape May?"

"Yeah, go to Randall's, maybe a few other places, check out the competition." He took off his shirt and rolled it up. "I can't go, they know me."

"That's not a bad idea."

He picked up the empty bottle and went to the door. "I'm full of them."

Chapter Nine

She didn't have gloves on, but with the hat and sunglasses and the sleeveless shift, she reminded me of an Italian Jackie Kennedy. She stood next to the table where Lou and I were drinking coffee and reading the Sunday paper, holding a little white pocketbook by the strap in both hands. How many pocketbooks did she have?

"I just thought I'd go."

Lou spoke without looking up from the paper. "Long as you don't expect me to."

"No, that's fine. I just—I don't know, I just felt like it this morning."

"Say hi to the monsignor for me."

"Monsignor Hughes hasn't been there for years. He's probably eighty by now."

"Those guys live forever."

"It's probably good for business anyway."

"You're going to Mass so you can sell real estate?"

I got up and put my coffee cup in the sink. Lou looked at me.

"Don't tell me you're going?"

I headed to my bedroom. "No, no. I just want to get a smoke."

Concetta was backing her car out when I came down. She stopped it in the street. I went over and leaned in the passenger window.

"You okay?"

She flexed her hands on the steering wheel. "Yeah, I'm fine. Late for Mass."

I stepped back and tapped the car on the roof. "Just...forget it."

She put the car in gear. "See you boys later."

I supposed Concetta went to Mass every now and then, but I knew them well enough to know it wasn't a regular thing. Probably tied up with the Davy thing. Or she was meeting someone there. Or she wasn't going to Mass at all.

I walked around the block and had another cigarette. Now I was the jealous husband. When I went back up, Lou was in a good mood, like I had taken over the burden of worrying about her. He was done with the paper and had the television on, some old black and white show. I got the sports and sat down next to him on the sofa.

There was a guy being chased by aliens or something. They had big black rings around their eyes and medallions around their necks. The guy got caught by one and was rolling on the ground with him. He ripped the medallion off the alien's neck, and he vanished.

I leaned forward. "Is that Robert Culp?"

Lou was intent on the show. "Yeah, I think it is." He had a can of mixed nuts in his lap and was mechanically feeding them into his mouth. "You wanna go to AC?"

"Nah, day off, I just want to hang, maybe go to the beach."

Lou swiveled his head. "Who said you get today off?"

I looked at him and he kept a straight face for five seconds, then cracked up.

"I'll probably go in later for a while," I said.

"Hey, man, you're the boss, long as everything's running smooth."

I thought about bringing up his request to keep an eye on Concetta, and did he want me to keep doing it, but decided to let it lie. I thought about the plan with Pinto and realized that was what was really bugging me.

"Lou, this thing about Arnie."

"Yeah?" He was back into the nuts, pointing at the TV. "Hey, you see that? He's got a glass hand!"

"Right, but, man, I don't trust Pinto not to..."

"Not to what?"

"Not to go too far." I timed his feeding and got a grab into the can while his hand was moving up.

"That's Arnie's problem, right?"

"What if he—fucks him up bad, someone calls the cops?"

"Who's gonna do that?" Lou was starting to sound irritated.

"I don't know."

"So don't worry about it."

"Yeah, but..."

Lou pulled the can to the side so I couldn't reach it. "You know, I'm trying to watch this show." Robert Culp was looking at his hand, the glass or maybe plastic one. He was fitting a finger onto it. "If the cops come, let them do what they want. Take Pinto in, what the fuck? Wouldn't that make you happy?"

I got up. "I'm going to the beach."

Lou looked at his watch. "I might come down later. I wanna wait for Concetta."

I jammed a bucket hat on my head. "Ask her about the sermon."

"Yeah, that's what I was thinking."

* * *

I went right down to the water and sat in my little folding chair where the last ripple of waves would hit my trunks. I was glad that Lou didn't come with me. It was about the only place I could really relax and think. The Arnie and Pinto thing was a little too mob-like for me. I had to be careful about that word. I was sure Lou was connected, but basically, he was a legit businessman. At least that's what I kept telling myself.

But once I helped out with Arnie, I was in. And who knew what Arnie's deal was? If he was bounced for stealing, then he was a crook. What kind of folks might he hang out with? And clearly, he would see that Pinto was the dumb muscle and that I had set him up.

A pair of small, very white feet splashed in the water next to me, sending water up onto my lap.

"Hey!" I yelped.

I tried to wipe my trunks off which only made them wetter and squinted up at a lady in sunglasses and a big straw hat, violet-colored and a little floppy. She had on one of those white cover-ups. It took me a couple seconds to realize it was Sheila.

"Hey, what's up?"

She moved a foot back and forth in the shallow water. "My morning constitutional."

"Yeah, it's a nice day for it."

"You wanna walk?"

I carried my chair up and set it on the dry sand, pushing it down so it wouldn't blow away. We walked south on the wet sand, close to the water's edge. I looked at her skinny legs, even skinnier looking than in the black slacks she always wore at the restaurant. Her walk was completely different here. At work, she was always moving fast, quick strides from her stool to whatever needed her attention. Here, she sort of sashayed, moving from side to side, digging her toes into the sand and turning. She stopped sometimes and looked out at the water, her hands behind her back. She actually looked delicate.

I picked up a shell and scooted it out into the waves. "So if we're both here, who's minding the chickens?"

The breeze was blowing the brim of her hat back. "Sadie knows what she's doing in the kitchen." She put her hand on top of her hat to keep it from blowing off. "The girls on this morning can handle it until I get in."

We kept walking, down to where some kids were tossing a football, then turned around, the wind in our face now. Sheila had her hands behind her back, stepping deliberately.

"How was your fancy dinner?" she asked.

"Great. Robert's mom came over—surprised the hell out of us." I told her about Lou sneaking up on Mrs. Minnucci in the kitchen.

"Sounds like Lou." She stepped around a horseshoe crab. "Did he ask for your weekly report after dessert?"

"Sort of. He was a little distracted."

"Hard day at the dealership?"

"No." I looked at her, wondering, had she been married once? "No, it was…they were talking about Davy."

"Oh boy."

The way she said it made me think she had heard at least one side of the story many times—maybe both sides. We were back to where my chair was.

Sheila asked, "So what do you think Lou really wants from you?"

"I think…I think he just wants someone to…keep an eye on things. Help you guys out."

There was something about the way her head tilted that told me her eyes had tightened behind the sunglasses, and her morning mood was over. This was more like the Sheila I was used to.

"You've been there a week. Do you really think we need help?"

"Yeah, I do. You need someone to watch over the whole thing."

She didn't say anything, just kept her face pointed at mine. It made me nervous, so I kept talking.

"Hey, look, I'm sorry if I'm taking the job you thought maybe you'd get. I'll tell Lou you could run the place."

"I could." She took off her sunglasses and wiped them with the hem of her cover-up. "But I like my job the way it is. No, you're a big help." She looked at me for a few seconds, her blue eyes moving back and forth. "That's not why you're there, though."

I looked out at the ocean. A lifeguard was swimming back to the shore, a flotation device hooked around his arm, a practice exercise.

"It's about Arnie, right?" Her tone was flat. "Or whoever Arnie was working with."

I picked up the chair. "Something like that."

Sheila slid her sunglasses back on and walked away, giving me a wave.

* * *

The two of them were out by the pool reading, glasses of iced tea by their lounge chairs. I figured they had had another talk after Mass, while they knew I was gone to the beach, and now they were back in their corners.

I asked, "You coming in today?"

Lou waggled his hand like he wasn't sure, probably not. Concetta didn't look up, pretending to be engrossed in some novel with a shiny cover, the pages puffed out from the humidity.

I got cleaned up. It made me feel good to be going to work, to be honest. While I was combing my hair, looking in the mirror, I thought about getting my own place. Even just a rooming house or something. I went out to the pool. Lou was not there, and Concetta was sitting up, her real estate folder on her lap.

"Where's Lou?" I asked.

She didn't look up. "I have no idea."

I went back through the house. Lou was in the hallway on the phone, a garden trowel in one hand, phone in the other, looking out the open front door. I hung back while he finished his call.

"Yeah, it's great down here…No, I appreciate the call…no, it's cool, you don't need to…right, right…no, I'll take care of it…yeah, if you see him again, let me know."

He hung up and went out the front door. I waited a few seconds then followed him out. He lifted the lid off a small aluminum trash can and dropped a few weeds in it. I came down the steps, and he looked up.

"Hey, heading for the salt mines?"

"Somebody's got to." I walked out to the Caddy and called back to him. "So, you going back?"

"Nah, I'll go up tomorrow. I'll come in for lunch." He walked over as I got in and started the car. "How you likin' this baby?"

"It's great. If I had had this when I was eighteen, maybe I would have gotten laid."

"Never too late to start." He stuck his head in the car and looked around. "Shit, even an old mick like you should get laid at the shore."

"Fuck you." I turned on the radio. "Hey, I saw Sheila on the beach."

"Yeah? Hope she had an umbrella or something, she'd burn in a second."

"Yeah, she was pretty covered up. We took a walk."

"She's a little old for you, pal."

Music came on, some old rock and roll. "Lou, I…I don't like this thing with Pinto."

Lou looked away toward the street. "No?"

"It's just…" I turned the volume down. "Guess I'm just a pussy."

"Bullshit, I seen you…at the taproom…those guys wouldn't say you were."

"That's different. Guy causes trouble, you gotta deal with it."

"You think Arnie didn't cause trouble?"

"It ain't the same. Plus, I mean, Pinto."

Lou gave his head a little shake, his hair flopping around in the breeze. "Yeah, he's a fuck. That's what that call was about."

"What?"

"Guy I know in AC. Pit boss, used to be a dealer. Nicest guy in the world. That's why he called, just wanted to let me know."

I played with the radio and waited.

"Security guy there, he caught Pinto in a restroom."

I laughed unconvincingly. "What, he's peddlin' his ass?"

Lou put his hands on the roof of the Caddy and looked in at me.

"Dealin' H. Fucking drugs." It was like with Sheila and Concetta, he had his shades on, but his eyes burned right through them. "You seen any of that shit?"

"Fuck no. Jesus." I turned the radio down. "Is he in jail?"

"Nah, they just booted him. Hope they really did give him a boot. Fuckin' jackass."

I put the car in gear. "I gotta go."

Lou hung his head for a few seconds, then looked up. "Let me think about the…Arnie thing." He banged his hand on the roof and stepped back.

I drove off, thinking that lying to Lou wasn't a great career move.

* * *

Today I was behind the bar. Kevin had called in, his ulcer acting up. There was a couple, middle-aged, red-faced Irish types, sitting there. They wanted Bloody Marys. I hated the drink, more because I had made hundreds of them and cleaned tomato juice off bartops, carpets, and my clothes too many times, than the fact that I just didn't like the taste. I was no angel with the bottle, but I wasn't a big fan of the hair of the dog. The guy wanted to talk to me, which was a little challenging as I hadn't dealt with a rush like this in a while, in a bar that I wasn't used to.

He pointed with his drink at the TV over the bar. "Fucking Phillies. Every year it's the same."

I had lost track of them, but I knew you didn't tell your customers that. "Yeah, what're you gonna do?"

"You think they should trade the guy?"

I had no idea who he was talking about. A waitress, one of the older ones, came to the serving area and gave me an impatient look. I went over, and she pushed herself up on the rail.

"Two glasses of white. Remember?"

"I got it." I filled up a couple of glasses, a heavy pour to make up to her, and put them on her tray.

"Lou's here." She turned the glasses, settling them so she could carry them more easily. "He doesn't look happy."

"No? Is there a problem?"

Her expression was full of pity. "How should I know?" She picked up the tray. "Maybe you should go talk to him."

"Kinda busy here."

She raised her eyebrows and turned away. "Just thought I'd let you know."

I went over to where Sheila was sitting on a stool near the front, ready to seat people coming in.

"Can you cover for me for a few minutes—I want to talk to Lou."

She hopped down and turned the little sign around so the "Seat Yourself" side was facing the door. She went over to the bar without saying anything. Lou was at a table in the back by himself. He did seem a little morose, looking down at his crab salad and jabbing at the lettuce with a fork. When he saw me, he pointed with the fork at the chair across from him.

I sat and let the bad feelings move across the table and go into my stomach. Lou set his fork down and wiped his mouth with the cloth napkin. He folded the napkin and put it on the table.

"Why'd you fuckin' lie to me?"

"What?"

"Don't—" His neck muscles stuck out and he pressed his lips together, turning his head to the side, then back to face me. His voice got lower, under control, but he was fighting it. "Just don't."

He stared at me, waiting. I knew I had to talk.

"You talked to Pinto?" I ventured.

"Yeah, I talked to him."

"Alright, I'm sorry, I just...I knew you'd be pissed."

"You would be right. I don't need a fuckin' dope dealer on my payroll. Hey!" He called out to a waitress delivering sandwiches to a table nearby. He pointed at his wine glass. "Pinto made it out like you guys were partners."

Now I was pissed. "That asshole. I walked away when he started talking about keeping the dope."

"Now that I believe. So, what, you didn't tell me because you were protecting him?"

"Christ, Lou, after all that talk Friday...about Davy, you know...I just didn't want to bring it up."

Lou lifted his hands. "Sounds like this thing started way before that."

I shook my head. "Man, I'm fucking sick of this shit. I didn't do anything, except get sucked into trouble once you stuck me with Pinto."

Lou seemed to calm down a little. He knew Pinto was the root of all this. He held his head in his hands.

"Can you imagine what Concetta would say if Pinto got picked up for dealing? One of my guys?"

I wondered what Pinto had said about Drew. I decided this was not a time to hold back.

"So he told you about Drew, the guy I bought the car from?"

"Yeah, he told me about finding the dope and his bright idea to rip the junkie off."

"It's his dealer he's ripping off."

"Right, whatever."

The waitress had come back with a glass of wine. I waited until she left.

"The guy—Drew—he's still here."

"He didn't mention that."

"Yeah, I think Pinto figured the guy could help him."

"What, give him some on-the-job training?"

"Well…sort of. It's not like Pinto knows anything about dealing drugs."

"Apparently not. Getting caught trying to sell junk to some goomba who's never even smoked a joint."

"I wanted to let Drew keep the dope and send him back to Buena."

"So, what, he's rentin' him a room in his nephew's place?"

"He had him there during the week. I don't know what he did this weekend."

The waitress was back at the table. She leaned down.

"I'm sorry—Sheila said she needs you to come back."

"Alright, I'll be over in a minute." The girl walked away. "Why don't you make Pinto give it back to Drew, be done with it?"

"I don't trust that junkie to give it to his dealer. Shit, he may tell himself he's gonna, then do it all up anyway. You can't trust a junkie." His expression was pained. "I oughta know."

"What the fuck do you care?"

"Maybe this dealer decides to come after Pinto—he's sold some of it already."

I thought, what's the problem with that? Lou picked up his wine glass.

"Besides, Pinto don't got it anymore." Now, Lou had a little bit of a smile. "I got it."

I stood up. "I gotta—"

Lou flicked his fingers. I was dismissed. He had changed from a friend to my boss to…the Padrone. I didn't want to be in this movie.

Chapter Ten

Monday morning we had breakfast with Pinto at the Garden. I came in with Lou and Pinto gave me a hurt and angry look, like he wanted to blame me for this mess. He knew he couldn't, which just made him more pissed, which was just as well, because it wasn't going to get any better.

He started to talk as we sat down. Lou pointed me to the seat next to Pinto with a bored gesture that suggested this was a long-standing practice, to have his second pin the guy into the booth.

Pinto babbled. "Hey, look…"

Lou raised his hand. "Shut the fuck up."

We waited until the waitress had brought coffee, then Lou folded his arms on the table and put his head low.

"Where's the junkie?"

"What?" Now, Pinto had a reason to be mad at me, and jerked around to face me. Lou reached across and gave him a little slap on the cheek.

"You fucking moron. What, you're gonna get pissed at him now?"

Pinto's face got red. I hadn't seen that. He had been calm when he ripped off Ramon.

"He's at a rooming house. I got a friend there—"

"I don't want to hear about your fuckin' friends. The shit you gave me, how much is gone?"

"I don't know—maybe a gram."

Lou lifted his hand like he was going to slap Pinto again, but stopped. "You sold a gram?"

"I sold nine, ten, little bags—plus I gave some to the junkie."

"You *gave* it to him? What, you runnin' a clinic?"

"He's fuckin' sick, man."

Lou came forward in his seat. "I know all about sick junkies, you fuck. That shit's gotta be paid for."

"He'll pay."

"No, he's not payin'." Lou lifted his index finger and pointed it at Pinto. "You're payin'."

Pinto raised his arms in exasperation. "Why the fuck do you care?"

Lou almost came out of his seat, reaching over and grabbing Pinto's face, squeezing his cheeks. A fork flew off the table and rattled on the floor.

"Don't you fucking ask me why I care, you stupid fuck."

Pinto glared at him, but didn't lift a hand. Lou let go and settled back. The woman at the cash register was looking at us around the head of a customer paying up.

"Alright, Mr. Dealer. How much was it worth?"

Pinto's voice was low and flat. "I took in maybe two hundred—plus I gave Drew a half dozen bags—he was helping cut it, so figure that at cost, maybe a third of street—"

"Jesus Christ, enough with the cost accounting. Call it three hundred." Lou put his hand out. "Gimme it."

Pinto pulled back. "What?"

"Three hundred."

"I ain't got that..."

"Look, you stupid guinea, you don't go to buy a paper without a wad of C-notes in your pocket. Give me the fucking money."

Pinto looked at me as he got his wallet out and counted out hundreds. Of course, they were hundreds. Lou took the bills and got to his feet.

"Let's go get your friend."

It was one of those old places near the boardwalk. I remember staying in one when I was in my teens. The rooms were hot and cramped and everything smelled like piss. Lou parked in front of it and turned around to Pinto, who was in the back seat like a vagrant picked up by the cops.

"What room's he in?"

Pinto reached for the door. "I'll get him."

"The fuck you will." Lou turned to me. "You go."

Pinto slouched back. "203."

At least Lou didn't send Pinto in with me. I went up the rickety, grey, wooden stairs and into the vestibule. The guy behind the desk was on a high stool, reading a magazine. He looked at me for a couple of seconds and figured out I wasn't a customer. More likely a dad looking for his daughter. He went back to his magazine.

I went up the stairs and by a room with its purple-painted door open, a girl passed out in a bikini top and cut-off jeans, arm dangling off the bed, a bottle of schnapps on the bedside table. I knocked on 203 and opened the door.

Drew was sitting on a chair by the window, hugging himself and rocking back and forth. His eyes turned to me, then back to the window. The room smelled more like vomit than piss. There was a metal trash can beside Drew that I didn't plan to look in.

He had a little blue airline bag that said BOAC on it. I wondered how old that was. We went out to the car. Drew got in the back seat without saying anything. Pinto looked at him like he was a little brother that had gotten him into trouble.

Pinto asked, "So, what's the plan?"

Lou replied, "Just shut the fuck up."

He drove back to the Garden and stopped. He turned around and spoke to Pinto

"Get out."

"What...?"

"Just get out."

Pinto stood on the sidewalk and waved to me. I was not looking forward to seeing him again.

Lou drove to his house and parked in the driveway. He turned to me.

"Take him back to Buena. Find the dealer and give him the money and the dope." He took a sealed envelope from the glove compartment and handed it to me. He looked up into the rearview mirror. "You, I don't want to see you in Wildwood again."

I looked at the envelope but didn't pick it up. "Come on, Lou, I don't want…"

"You want me to send Pinto with you?"

"The guy's a fucking dealer, how do I know who…how he's gonna react?"

"Don't worry, it won't be a problem." Lou fiddled with the rear-view mirror. "You'll have a bigger problem if he comes looking for you."

I looked at Lou, who was staring straight ahead. He didn't look like your friendly neighborhood car dealer right now. He looked like somebody you didn't want to say no to, for all the wrong reasons.

Lou said, "I may need you to visit Ramon this week. I'll let you know."

Another assignment I would gladly forgo. I picked up the envelope, got out of the car, and walked to the Caddy. I called back over my shoulder.

"Come on, Junior, bus is leaving."

* * *

"Just a taste."

Drew had waited five minutes before he started begging me for a shot. I didn't answer him, and now he asked me again about every two minutes. I was trying to decide which was worse if I got stopped: having a strung-out junkie, a wacked-out junkie, or an actually fixing junkie in the passenger seat, with me holding a bag of heroin and a wad of cash.

I ignored him as I cut off Route 9 heading to Buena. I was thinking about Lou saying not to worry. My hunch was that he wasn't just trying to calm me down; that in fact he knew I shouldn't be worried—as long as I did what I was told

That worried the shit out of me.

When we got to Buena, Drew directed me to a little bungalow with a nice flower garden growing out front. There was a big Chevy Impala, well-maintained, mid-sixties in the driveway. Drew went inside and came back out in a few minutes.

"He says come on in."

I shook my head.

"Tell him to come to the produce store down the block."

Drew looked uncomfortable. "You can give me the…money and stuff, if you don't want to go in."

I laughed. "I need some tomatoes." I drove off. Maybe I had watched too many cop shows, but I wanted to meet this guy in a public place.

I parked on the street next to the store. It was like a little grocery store, mostly produce, but with a few shelves of cereal and crackers and stuff, and a refrigerated unit with eggs, milk, and cheese. I was squeezing the peaches when a guy came through the door. He was a young Mexican, a bit fat, wearing a black silk shirt with blue flowers on it, untucked, and blue khakis. He had on woven leather slip-ons that looked expensive. He waved to someone in the back, then came over to me.

"Hey, man, you Drew's friend?"

I looked past him to the door. There didn't seem to be anyone with him. I guessed this had to be Eduardo.

"Yeah." I picked up a few peaches. "Let me just finish up here."

"Cool."

I got the peaches and a jug of lemonade and took them to the counter. The woman there was Mexican, too. She gave me a smile and called out something in Spanish to him. He waved and left the store.

I paid and took my bag outside. I pointed to the car. "Want to take a little ride?"

"Sure."

I started the car up and looked over at Eduardo. He wasn't what I had expected. He seemed much cleaner than my image of a dealer, but what did I know? I reached over to the glove compartment. Eduardo put his hand on mine.

"Drive, okay?"

I started to get a little concerned. Eduardo sat back.

"Hey, man, it's cool. I'm not a…*loco cabrón, sí?*" He rolled down his window. "Just…not in front of the shop, *¿entiende?*"

I shifted into drive and started down the street. Eduardo pointed me through a few turns until we came to a diner.

"Here."

"Really? Looks pretty busy."

"That's better, *amigo.*"

I pulled in next to a pickup truck. A couple of guys were in it, drinking coffee and smoking.

I looked at Eduardo. "It's in the glove compartment."

He got the envelope out and folded it over, then lifted himself up on the seat a little and stuffed it in his pants pocket. He jerked his thumb toward the diner.

"Coffee?"

I looked at him. "I don't know."

He laughed. "You nervous?"

"Yeah, I am."

"Alright, take me home then."

We drove back to the house. He climbed out and shut the door, then leaned back in.

"Hey, man, thanks."

"I just do what I'm told."

"Yeah, I know. Look, let me buy you lunch, come on, eh?"

I thought, what the fuck? Maybe this was some courtesy thing. "Alright."

He tapped the door with his hand a couple of times. "Be right back."

I turned on the radio and waited, thinking for a minute about just driving off, then he was back out, coming down the walk.

We drove back into town and parked near the produce store again. It was a clean street with a half dozen modest little shops. Eduardo led me to a cantina with one of those big plastic signs hanging over the sidewalk, with the Mexican flag and a bunch of Mexican food words, half of which I recognized. It was a busy little shop. Eduardo went to a small table along the wall. The waitress brought us iced tea. Eduardo held out the laminated menu. I shrugged. He said something in Spanish and the girl went away, a little disappointed I thought, having spent the past week watching waitresses.

"You are a friend of Mr. Lou, yes?" Eduardo asked.

"How did you know—?"

"Drew tell me you work at his place."

"Yeah, he's a friend. You know him?"

His face scrunched up a little. "We have some…what…*mutual acquaintances.*" He said this with a little laugh, like he was repeating a phrase he had learned in school.

The girl came back with two plates, a couple of tacos on each. We ate and I thought how Lou had seemed so certain everything would be okay with Eduardo. I wasn't sure it was better that everything seemed so connected.

Eduardo finished his taco, then took his watch off and rolled the band around his fingers. It was thin and gold and real, I could tell.

"There was another guy, *correcto?*"

He looked at his watch, frowning. I didn't answer.

"Eh, it no matter." He slipped the watch back on. "Lou, he has a son?"

I nodded. "Yeah, he does."

Eduardo said, "The boy has…a problem?" His expression was serious. I didn't like it.

"Is that what you guys call it?"

He started to say something, then stopped. He took out his wallet and laid a bill on the table, then stood up. I followed him outside. He started walking slowly, his hands clasped behind his back.

I fell in beside him. He turned down a street away from the shops onto a stretch of sidewalk shaded by trees from the yards of the little bungalows. He stopped by a white picket fence and turned to face me. He held out a silver medal of Our Lady that hung around his neck.

"I sell jewelry."

"Do you?"

"I do—the other thing—a little."

I turned away to face the street. "You don't have to apologize to me."

"I hear a something."

"Yeah?"

"About Lou's boy."

I didn't know what to say—or whether I wanted to hear this.

"I'm sure it's not good."

He made the scrunched face expression again. "Maybe."

I turned back to face him. "Listen, is there something you want to tell me?"

He nodded. "I heard he left Philly-town."

"Okay. And went where?"

He shook his head. "I don't know. But I think somewhere down here."

"Like, in Buena?"

"No, no. At the shore."

"Who told you this?"

It was his turn not to answer. He said, "I tell you because you are good man."

"You want me to tell Lou?"

A woman walked by, dressed in overalls and high heels, pushing a carriage with an infant in it. Eduardo greeted her and bowed. He waited until she was near the corner to speak.

"The boy, he may need help."

I figured that meant it was up to me whether I told Lou. Mexican seemed a tricky language.

I left him there, playing with his watch, the healthiest, happiest drug dealer I ever met.

* * *

I hadn't planned to go to the Stone Jug, but once I got to Cape May, I thought, what the hell?

Concetta was surprised at first when I told her I was going to Randall's, though she tried to hide it. I let her twist in the wind for a few seconds, thinking no doubt about Lou going on about it the other night. Then I told her Robert said I should go and check out the competition. I couldn't tell if she believed me or not, but it was true in a way.

I did not think for two seconds that there had been a "networking thing" at Randall's. I did wonder why she had told the truth about going there, but figured it was one less lie to keep track of.

She finally recovered and then began to get on me for not taking a date. She was ironing a pair of khakis for me. I sat on the bed in my boxer shorts and t-shirt. Lou had gone up to the city before I got back from Buena, so the atmosphere was calmer.

"You're going by yourself?"

"Yeah, why not?"

"Going to such a nice place, why not…take somebody with you?"

"What, want me to take you?"

She gave me a fake flirty look and laughed. "Me? No, I don't think your boss would like that."

At least we agreed on something.

"You want me to ask Carol?" I suggested.

"God, no."

"Alright, so forget it. I'll be fine on my own."

"Here you go—ready for your big night." She set the iron on end and held up the pants, shaking them out. I put them on and hit her with the second barrel.

"Robert says you might know the guy who runs it—Mark somebody?"

She had her back to me, folding up the ironing board. She didn't say anything. I kept going.

"Robert talked to the guy once, I guess, almost went to work there. He mentioned he was working at the Seabreeze, and the guy told him he knew you."

She turned around. "Yeah—I do. He was…I met him at some real estate thing."

I didn't have the heart—or the nerve—to pin her to the wall on that. How many real estate "things" had there been down there that she had forgotten about, since Robert met the guy before the meeting last week that she said was her first visit to Cape May in a long time?

She looked up at me with a face too sincere to be anything but fake. "You want me to call him, let him know you're coming?"

I reached under the bed for my loafers. "Nah, it's better if you don't. I'll be like one of those restaurant reviewers, incognito."

Concetta carefully wrapped the cord around the handle of the still-hot iron. "You won't fool anyone by yourself. You'll stick out like a sore thumb."

I tucked my shirt in and stood in front of the mirror. "I'll go to the Jug first and pick up some floozy."

It didn't take half an hour to get down there, and I had time to kill before dinner, so I went into the Jug, which was about as I had remembered it, except that I don't think I ever went there so early in the evening. Still, there was plenty of action at the bar. I sat next to a couple of girls—young women, really, late twenties, early thirties, maybe. They were drinking white wine and looked bored out of their skulls.

I drank a beer quickly, then nursed another one, just enjoying the freedom of being alone. The bartender came down to check on the girls and bent over the bar, his ear cocked. The girl next to me, a tall brunette, had a pack of cigarettes in her hand.

"Is it okay…?" She held out the pack. She had a French accent.

The bartender nodded. "Sure, no problem."

He walked away. The girl picked a cigarette out and put it in her mouth. She turned to me with a look that made me feel impolite for not having any matches. I called out to the bartender.

"Excuse me—matches?"

He pointed at a glass on the bar a few feet down from me that had packs of matches. I got one out and turned back. The girl had the cigarette between her fingers expectantly.

Christ, I was bad at this shit. Brigitte Bardot, there waiting for a light, and I'm struggling a match out of the book and misfiring on the strikepad like a ten-year-old. But she made it easy, bending forward to catch the flame.

"*Merci.*"

Okay, she had me. I tried to think of something interesting to say.

"So, you're from France?"

She drew back and shook her head. "*Non, non. Je suis du…*" somewhere with "saint"—or "san" as she said it—in the middle. My high school French was barely keeping my head above water.

She pulled on the cigarette and blew out a dainty cloud. "It is in Quebec."

Great, not just uninteresting, but wrong.

"Oh." At least I didn't say "oui".

She seemed to be expecting me to keep trying. I turned in my stool.

"Cape May is great."

She shrugged. Maybe it wasn't so great to someone from *Something-Saint-Something*.

"You ever been to Wildwood?" I babbled.

She shook her head and repeated it as two words. "Wild wood?"

I pointed toward the door like I was pointing up the coast, which made no sense. "Yeah, it's the town just north of here."

"Oh." She tipped an ash into the ashtray in a way that indicated a complete lack of interest.

"It's got nice beaches, but it's not as...quaint...as here."

She made a face. "Quaint? You mean...pretty?"

"Sort of. Wildwood is more...honky-tonk, know what I'm saying?"

She frowned and shook her head. "No, I do not know what you are saying."

I didn't know about her, but this was maybe the most fantastic conversation I had had in a bar in my life. The other girl leaned over and said something then got off her stool and left. My girl, I mean BB, shrugged. She picked up her glass of wine and drained it, then tipped it in a way that I understood.

"Hey!" I called out to the bartender and gave him a little hand signal. He brought out a bottle of white and filled her glass. She never looked at him, just at me, her eyes narrowing a little.

"This...*honky-tonk*...you must explain."

I started talking, knowing I was being played, but loving every minute of it.

* * *

"This?"

The old Victorian house stood at the end of a long walkway and glowed in the twilight, electric candles lit in all the tall windows.

I pointed at the restaurant sign a few feet away. "This is it."

Pauline—that was BB's real name—gripped my arm tighter.

"Okay, Mister Ginty, we go?"

Our progress was slow, thanks to two hours in the Jug and her heels. I held the door for her and tried to stop marveling at her beauty and its unlikely closeness to me. We stopped at a podium that had one of those lights attached to it like a lectern in a church. The casually well-dressed maître d' did not seem to mind that we were an hour late or that I had brought a guest. He examined his little seating chart, then led us to a table by a window in the main dining room. I glimpsed a side room as we walked past, full of middle-aged folks.

It was a great table, in fact, it was the best table in the room, with a view of a garden lit by little flood lamps. We could see the entire room, and, I suspected, more importantly, everyone in the room could see us. That is, they could see Pauline.

The maître d' returned after a minute with two flutes on a tray.

"Champagne—our compliments."

I figured the shrimp scampi would have to be twice what we charged and I was not disappointed when the black-jacketed waiter—not waitress—handed us the large menus, printed on heavy paper that was not laminated.

We had a very nice dinner, a little frou-frou for my tastes, but then that was why I was here, I guessed, to open my horizons a little. I had been in some fancy restaurants in Philly, but they had all been Italian. This was French food—cuisine, as they say—and judging by Pauline's reaction, it was pretty good. I enjoyed it, though I did see what Robert meant about it being vertical.

Pauline had them from the start. A beautiful young woman, ordering in French, asking just the right questions about the preparation, but not seeming too impressed. They respected her.

It felt like an actual date, a first date, her telling me about her work as a paralegal and her family in a small town in Quebec. She laughed at my stories about growing up in the neighborhood and working in bars. As we drank coffee, she sat forward, her chin on her bunched fists.

"So, this is not…your kind of place, no?"

Why try to fool her? "No, it's not, it's…a research project."

"Oh, so you see how the others do it?"

"That's right."

She leaned forward a little more. "I like to see your place."

"You wouldn't want to do that."

"No? You are ashamed of it?"

"No, it's just…" A waiter came by and brushed crumbs off the tablecloth with a tiny comb, moving away quickly. "I don't know if it would be your kind of place."

She sat back, holding the coffee cup up to her lips. "That will be my… research project."

The waiter appeared with the check. He started to walk away, and I touched the little tray holding the bill.

"Wait."

I counted out enough cash to include a healthy tip. He took the tray and bowed.

"Thank you, *monsieur*." He turned to Pauline. "*Mademoiselle*."

I said, "Hold on."

He stood like a soldier at attention.

"Is Mark here?"

"I believe so, *monsieur*."

"Tell him a friend of Concetta's wants to say hello."

He whisked away. Pauline set her cup down.

"Is this when you…reveal?"

I shrugged. "I guess."

"Who is this Concetta?"

I hadn't told her about Concetta. Was she actually jealous? This was definitely a fairy tale night.

"That's Lou's wife—he's my boss."

"So this Seabreeze—her husband owns?"

113

"Yeah."

She smiled like she had discovered a secret. A tall man came across the room, stopping at a few tables before arriving at ours. I stood and extended my hand.

"John McGinty—a friend of Concetta's. She said I should say hello."

"Mark Taylor." He turned expectantly.

"And this is my friend Pauline." She had told me her last name, but I wasn't sure I would say it right.

"My pleasure." He took her hand, and for a moment, I thought he was going to kiss it.

Pauline said, "*Merci.*"

Mark put his hand on an empty chair at the next table. "May I?"

Pauline sat back with the last of a glass of wine, like she was watching an amusing theater production.

Mark said, "Concetta is such a sweet lady."

"Yeah, I've known her and Lou for years."

A waiter appeared with a bottle of wine and three glasses. Pauline and I needed this like a hole in the head.

Mark tilted his glass up. "Cheers." We clinked. "I haven't met Lou."

That I could have guessed. "No? He's actually my boss right now."

"Oh?" Mark smiled at Pauline, who returned it in a way that said nice try. I was beginning to understand the French—or French-Canadian—way of communicating. "At his car-dealership?" He tried to keep the disdain out of his voice, but I think he really wanted to keep it in for Pauline's benefit.

"No, at his restaurant."

"Oh!" He sat back and tilted his head to the side. "The place in… Wildwood?" He seemed to have trouble saying the word.

"That's right. The Seabreeze."

"I see."

Pauline said, "He is checking out the competition."

Mark nodded his head. Again, it was a tie between mocking me and not being sure how that would play with Pauline.

"And did you find everything to your liking?"

"What's not to like?" I raised my glass.

"*Les frites*," Pauline said. She put her glass on the table.

Mark was disconcerted. "The *frites*? What was…?"

"They were…*congelés*…"

"I'm sorry, what…?"

Pauline shook her head dismissively. "So I must translate also?" She banged her hand on the table. "Frozen."

Mark looked paralyzed. "I…I am sorry, but we prepare them fresh…"

"Frozen!" Her look was imperious. I guess this was what people meant about the French acting superior, but I liked it.

Mark was caught now. If he admitted they were frozen, then he looked like a phony. If he said they weren't, then he was calling her a liar or an idiot who couldn't tell the difference.

Pauline shrugged. "*Ça n'importe pas*."

I didn't need my high school French to know what she meant. She was done.

"I am so sorry. Please, let me…take care of your bill."

I shook my head. "It's alright. We serve them that way, too."

Mark smiled, which pained him a great deal. I guessed he wasn't going to hire me away. Pauline slid out of her seat.

"*Pardon, messieurs*."

Mark watched her walk away, more flustered than appreciative.

"Quite a lively lass." He was recapturing his cool; he knew he could deal with a nobody like me. "Is Robert still cooking for you?"

"Yes. He's a good man—great chef too."

"I know, I tried to hire him here." Mark seemed to have relaxed a little. "We do make those fries fresh."

It really did matter to him, especially with another restaurant guy.

"She's yanking your chain, man."

A busboy passed by, young, dark, and neat in a white shirt and black pants. Mark raised his hand, and the boy stopped by his side. He touched the boy's arm, and the kid lowered his ear, listening to some instruction, Mark tilting his head toward an elderly couple a few tables away. The kid straightened up, nodding, Mark's hand still holding his sleeve for a moment before letting him go. He watched the boy's progress across the room, the way I would have thought he would watch Pauline's.

He blew out a breath and turned back to me. "Concetta…did she tell you to come here?"

I figured a little lie was called for. "Yeah. She said maybe I should set my sights higher than Lou's place."

"Okay. If you're serious, we could talk."

"I don't know, I kind of like the Seabreeze. Anyway, it's just for a while."

My Junior Dick Tracy instincts told me there was something off about all this. I was pretty sure Concetta had called him—maybe told him to be nice if he had to talk to me. He did seem a little anxious about why I was at his place, but I suspected his tastes ran more toward the young, dark summer help he had just been pawing than a high-maintenance Madonna like Concetta. Pauline had clearly impressed him, but my guess was that was more the French angle than her beauty.

Pauline appeared at the table, interrupting the awkward silence. He stood and seated her a little too eagerly, easing the chair under her with a professional touch. He gave a little bow.

"I must be off." He smiled at Pauline, like he was surrendering, then turned to me. "Good luck with the restaurant."

I got up and extended my hand. "Thanks. And, you know," I gave him a sincere look, "maybe I will take you up on that talk."

He shook my hand and spoke with his own phony sincerity. "Absolutely. You know where to find me."

He threaded through the tables toward the kitchen, hoping, no doubt, that I wouldn't keep my promise. Pauline picked up her purse and held it in her lap. I wagged a finger at her.

"Those fries were fresh."

She gave a shrug that I supposed was Gallic. "*Naturellement.*"

Chapter Eleven

There was a tree outside the window, and when I finally got myself off the lumpy mattress and looked, I saw grass on the ground. These were pretty solid hints that I was not in Wildwood.

Also, the room smelled of cigarettes, and a flimsy nightgown was draped over a chair. I sat back down, as I felt like shit. I tried again after a minute and went out the door of the bedroom, which put me at the top of a staircase. There were voices coming from downstairs. I went back in the room and finally found my khakis crumbled up on the floor at the end of the bed.

Downstairs, there was a musty little sitting room and a kitchen, where Pauline was making toast. Her friend was sitting cross-legged on a chair with a bowl of cereal in her lap, which was either naked or covered by an extremely small pair of underpants. She pointed at me with her chin.

"*Ton copain.*" I wasn't sure what it meant, but from her tone, I didn't think it meant I was a long-lost friend.

Pauline gave me coffee, and I wondered how it was that she seemed so chipper. It had been her idea to return to the Jug, which was just a great fucking idea. Fortunately, there was no Garden State Parkway to deal with. And here I was, so as they say, I had no complaints.

Pauline asked, "We are going to the beach. Will you come?"

I looked around the room but could not find a clock. I decided it was a good day to take off.

"Do you have a phone here?"

The other girl shook her head. "*Non.* There is a..." she pointed out the window with her spoon, "a payphone, it is just down the street."

Pauline chewed her toast, then stopped suddenly. "You like some…
breakfast?"

"No, that's fine, I'll need to vomit first."

She pointed with the toast. "The commode is…"

"I'm kidding, right?"

The other girl stood up, revealing a skimpy bikini bottom, which was
good, as things were seeming all a little too French for me this early in the
morning. She left the room, and I looked at Pauline, thinking I needed to
say something.

She pushed the last of the toast in her mouth and licked her little finger.
"You are a good…" She rocked back and forth a little, looking for the word.

"A good man?" I was getting used to hearing that.

"Fuck. Right? You say, 'a good fuck', *non?*"

I went over and hugged her. "That's the nicest thing a girl's ever said to
me."

* * *

I wasn't sure if the dress code at Randall's allowed for wearing the exact
same clothes you had on the night before, but I didn't have much choice.
It was not crowded, which was not surprising, as even in Cape May, the
market for a fifteen-dollar lunch was limited. I opted for the tiny bar, tinier
even than ours. I asked the handsome bartender for a beer. When he set it
down, I asked about Mark.

He gestured with his head toward the door to the dining room, where
Mark was talking with a waiter. He finished up with the waiter and turned
in my direction. It took him a couple of seconds to register who I was, then
he came across with a big professional smile.

"I didn't know you were here."

"I ended up staying in town last night."

"Oh." He looked at the bartender as a way to not show me a knowing
smirk.

"It was easier to stop by than to call."

"Sure, sure." He gestured toward the door. "How about we...?"

We went through the main dining room, which was empty—they were doing lunch in the smaller room—and through a set of French doors out to a patio. There was a guy in kitchen whites at a table under an umbrella, sifting through a stack of papers. We went to a table at the other end of the patio, under a tree. A teenaged boy showed up almost immediately with a pitcher of iced tea and glasses with ice. When he left, Mark spoke

"So what can I do for you?"

I drank my beer, wishing I had paid more attention when my old man was watching Perry Mason. I pondered why a gay blade like Mark was spending time with Concetta and why it was such a big secret. Telling him the truth seemed like an easy out, but then at least it might be unexpected.

"I'm not looking for a job."

Mark nodded, which I took as a sign that he wasn't saying anything until I offered more.

"Lou asked me to keep an eye on Concetta. He thinks maybe she's fooling around."

That got a laugh, although a nervous one.

"What, with me? Do you believe that?"

I kept going with the honesty. "No, no, I kind of doubt it."

"She's a great lady, and, you know, quite attractive, but..."

I waved him to stop. "Understood. But you did see her last week?"

He shrugged. "Yeah, I did."

"Any particular reason for your get-together?"

"She came down for a real estate networking dinner."

"That's exactly what she said."

"There you go."

"But I don't believe it for a second."

Mark turned up his hands pleadingly. "What do you want me to say? It's the truth."

"Maybe I should ask her boss."

"Go ahead."

"Look, I know she's been down here before, and she lied to me about that, too. When did you first meet her?"

"Around Memorial Day. It was another real estate event—we host those all the time."

I gave him a fake puzzled look. "Then how'd you wind up with her outside a bar on the mall one romantic evening?" I paused. "A friend of Lou's saw you."

I didn't know it was him, but it seemed a reasonable guess.

Mark pushed his chair back and crossed his legs. "Are you some kind of PI? You know, I really..."

I smiled, figuring I could count that as confirmation. He looked like he wanted to just walk away, but was maybe more afraid to do that than to stay.

"No, I'm just a friend of Lou's."

His eyes told me that was not a comforting response. I felt instantly more confident. Is this how Pinto felt all the time? Who knew I could be intimidating? Mark seemed to retreat into his cream-colored jacket. I decided to shift gears. I spread my hands out.

"Look, Lou didn't send me. I found out that Concetta knew you from Robert."

"That was stupid of me." Mark's face sagged. "Keeping other people's secrets is a pain."

Now we were getting somewhere. Maybe some private investigator know-how had seeped into my skull from the TV without me knowing it.

"It was pretty obvious she was lying about her trips down here. So I figured I would come down and check it out—if there was something going on, maybe I'd talk to Lou."

He recovered a little. "So, will you?"

I put my hands back together on the table. "Is there something going on?"

Mark got up. "I think we're done."

I figured Mark must have watched the same detective shows, as he was channeling every crook who got pushed into a corner.

"Alright, I'll just let Lou know how it all went."

I was getting more comfortable in my role. Mark sat back down fast. I made a mental note to worry about whether Lou was more connected than

I had thought.

Mark spoke. "Don't tell Concetta I…"

My hand wave was more abbreviated this time. Mark would have to figure out if it meant don't worry, I won't tattle, or don't tell me what to do, punk.

His hands were folded like he was saying grace. "You know Davy, right?"

I instantly downgraded my PI rating to beginner status. I nodded with a look that said I wondered when he would get to that. I tried hard to put that lie over.

Mark looked away and then back at me.

"A friend put her in touch with me back in May. The kid was in some kind of trouble, drugs or something."

"A friend? Who was that?"

I kept my face as stony as I could.

He pressed his lips together. "I'd rather not…"

I figured we'd get there eventually, so tried out my wave again. Mark was happy to skip that question.

"So I got him a job."

"Really. Here?"

"No, no. It was like a hot-dog joint, a stand on the Promenade."

"The Promenade?"

"The boardwalk." He couldn't help sounding like he was translating into Wildwood-ese.

"Where is it?"

"Called Joe's Dogs. It's toward the south end. That's why your friend saw me on the mall. I took her there to meet the guy who owns the dog shack. But," he poured iced tea into his glass, "Davy's not there anymore."

"What, he quit?"

He shrugged. "I don't know. He was there maybe a week or two, then he just stopped showing up." He gestured toward the other glass with the pitcher. I held up my beer bottle. "The owner wasn't too happy. He was doing me a favor, now he's got one guy covering all the shifts."

"You think he's still around here?"

"I have no idea."

We sat for a minute as I digested all this. Mark leaned forward.

"Concetta doesn't want Lou to know about all this."

"Tell me something I don't know."

"She didn't tell me much, and of course," he twisted his glass around, "I didn't want to ask."

I couldn't blame him for not wanting to know.

"Why did she come to see you this week?"

He gave me something closer to an honest look. "She didn't. That was just her cover. She came to see her kid. She's worried about him, right?" Mark got up. "But, you know, I think the thing that scares her the most is Lou."

I put that comment in the back of my brain. "Where is the kid staying?"

"I really...why don't you talk to Concetta about that?"

I got up. Something told me it was time to let him go. For now.

"Hey, can you show me the kitchen?"

Mark smiled anxiously at this welcome change of topic. "You won't steal any ideas?"

I laughed. "I couldn't afford them."

Mark was a lot more relaxed leading me through his workplace. Even in the early afternoon, there were a dozen people doing prep work, professional-looking folks, guys and girls in neat whites, hair covered, like something in a magazine. Soup, vegetables, pastry. It all looked good. He showed me his *cave*, which was temperature-controlled. I guessed our approach of putting the reds next to the sacks of potatoes was at least a step in the right direction.

We passed through a hallway that had a doorway leading into the back of the bar. I looked through and saw a guy sitting there in a dapper sports jacket. We came back out into the vestibule, and Mark stood by the door, rising once up and down on his heels, rubbing his hands in a way that meant the tour was over.

I shook his hand. "Very impressive."

"You'll have to come back." He looked around like he was hoping I'd vanish while his gaze was elsewhere.

I still had the bottle of beer in my hand. "If I had a little more time, I'd go relax and have another."

"Well..."

I handed him the bottle. He blinked and accepted it.

"But I gotta go, so...you should stop in our place sometime."

"I'm sure..."

"We can show you the Frialators."

I tapped his arm with my fist. He flinched a little. After all, I worked for Lou, right?

As I walked down the front walk, I thought how relieved he must be that I didn't go in the bar and strike up a conversation with his and Concetta's mutual friend Arnie.

* * *

Pauline and the other girl, Lucie, were in sundresses, combing out their wet hair, legs up, on the tiny front porch of their rental.

"You take us to your Seabreeze?"

"How about a hot dog first?"

We took the Caddy down past the Mall and parked close to the boardwalk. I had a hard time calling it a promenade, despite my companions. The girls ducked into a t-shirt shop, and I asked the guy there about Joe's. He pointed me to a tiny kiosk a little further south, all the time watching the girls paw through the racks like we were a crew of grifters.

Mark wasn't exactly right about the name of the place. It was Joe's Famous Dogs, which no one would mistake for a pet museum. It was maybe ten feet wide with a red Formica counter sticking out and a sliding glass window to make your order. Inside was a young guy, hair sun-bleached, looked like a surfer. Behind him were both a hot dog steamer and a roller grill, and a pot that had to be filled with sauerkraut based on the odor that wafted out. The guy didn't look as miserable as he should have, but my guess was he was stoned morning, noon, and night. I was pretty sure he wasn't Joe.

I got a grilled dog, without the sauerkraut, and loaded on onions and relish from the stainless steel bins on the counter. I tipped the guy with a bill, which you could tell was outside the normal custom. I held the dog away from my body as I ate it, in true boardwalk fashion. I finished up and tossed the waxed paper into a wire trash can, then put my head up to the window.

The guy put his hands on the counter and leaned down. "Want another?"

"How 'bout a Sprite?"

He gave me a can and put his hand up when I slid a bill across.

"Hey, man, it's on me."

I took a big slug from the can, which I needed. "Joe around today?"

He gave a little chuckle. "Yeah, he's in the basement."

"Good one." I tilted the can in appreciation.

"There's no Joe, man." He said it like he was sharing a secret.

"No?"

He put his head down close to the window. "Guy named Rudy owns it. Pain in the ass."

"Slave driver?"

"Just a prick. Comes in late afternoon. Counts the buns against the register tape." He lifted a hand up, revealing an arm covered in tattoos. "Like I'm going to fucking steal them?"

I shook my head. "That's no way to treat your staff."

"Fucking right." He looked past me. "Hold on, got some customers."

The girls were behind me. Pauline was wearing a sailor's cap with an approximation of a lobster sewn into the turned-up brim; Lucie had on one of those gigantic pairs of plastic sunglasses. Pauline curled a hand around my arm while Lucie leaned forward on the counter in a way that got the full attention of my new friend.

It took a few minutes to sort out an order—a hot dog for Lucie and fries for Pauline. I peered in and located the tiny Frialator, which seemed a dangerous appliance in such a small hut. The girls ate with one elbow on the counter, swinging around, talking in French, and pretty much driving the guy crazy. I think he was just about ready to offer them a free dog, to hell with Rudy, when I asked if he knew Davy.

"No, man."

He pulled back from the window and got busy wiping the counter.

I tried to reassure him. "His dad's a friend of mine."

He turned around and took the lid off the pot of sauerkraut and stirred it with a big slotted spoon. The girls were still laughing and preening, but he wasn't having any of it now. He dropped the spoon in the little sink under the counter.

"You need anything else?" He wiped his hands on his apron and looked over my shoulder.

The girls linked arms and walked away slowly, glancing back and laughing.

I tried to reassure him. "I'm not a cop."

He put his head down to the window. "Listen, man, I don't know any Davy."

"But he did work here, right?"

He slid the window shut and turned around. He picked up a plastic bag of hot dogs and plucked them out, putting them on the roller.

If a guy with two horny French girls couldn't get him to talk, there was definitely something wrong.

* * *

The girls loved Kevin. I tried to get them to sit at a table for dinner, but they wouldn't leave the bar. Sheila gave me a look when I went outside to smoke.

"Hope he can keep up with the drink orders."

"What?"

Sheila shifted her eyes toward the bar. Lucie was standing up on the rail, fitting her fluorescent sunglasses onto Kevin's face.

"He's a little distracted," Sheila observed.

I pulled open the door. "I'll note that in his permanent record."

We had a little bench outside, and I sat on it, looking at the sky edging from gray to red over the rows of houses that spread back toward the bay. Concetta hadn't been home when I stopped to change, which was a good thing. I hadn't figured out what to say about Mark and Arnie. The truth didn't seem like the best way to start this time.

The door opened, and Pauline came out. I gave her a cigarette and she joined me. She didn't say anything for a few minutes; maybe she sensed my mood.

She stood and walked to the corner, twisting around, looking up and down the street. I had no business with a girl like her. I guess I amused her in some way.

She came back and stubbed her cigarette out in the ashtray beside the door.

"Your place, it is good."

I nodded. "Not exactly Randall's."

She made a hmph'ing sound I had heard a few times, which meant a disdain that I wasn't cultured enough to be capable of.

"I like your clams with the casino," she said.

"Clams casino."

"As I say."

She sat down and put her hand on my leg.

"So you think this place should be more like Mark's?"

"Nah. He's in a different league."

"League? That is like…a guild?"

"No, it's…it's slang, it just means Randall's is a fancy restaurant, you know. This is…like a mom and pop place."

"So, Lou is the pop? And this…Concetta?…. she is the mom?"

I squeezed her hand. "You're funny. No, I guess I'd say Sheila is the mom."

"So, Lou and Sheila…?" She scratched my crotch with a fingernail.

I wrapped her in my arms and pulled her to me, laughing. "Is that all you Frenchies think about?"

She struggled as I kissed her cheek. "I am not your Frenchie. *Je suis Québécois!*"

"Close enough."

She stopped struggling and fell against me. "Who is this Davy?"

I stopped mid-cuddle. "What are you talking about?"

She put an arm around my neck. "I hear you say the name to the hot dog boy."

"You were eavesdropping."

"What did I drop?"

"Forget it. It's nothing."

"*Non*? Then why did the blondie boy shut his...*fenêtre*?"

I disentangled myself and got up. "If you weren't so cute, I'd tell you to keep your nose out of other people's business."

"I guess I am just a curious girl."

"Yeah, you're curious all right."

The door opened, and Lucie stumbled out, Sheila's face appearing behind her for a moment with a pleading look. The sunglasses were backwards around her neck, and she was holding a glass filled with something green. She looked our way, though I don't think she really saw us, then turned and walked crookedly in the opposite direction. Pauline got up.

"I think she should go home now." She trotted after her.

I called out, "She's heading north, tell her to turn around."

Pauline corralled her, and I led them to the Caddy. Lucie curled up on the back seat. Pauline started in on Davy again.

"I think I can help you."

"No thanks, I don't need any help."

"Concetta...is Davy her son?"

"What makes you say that?"

"You say his papa is a friend. So I ask your Kevin if..."

"Oh, for Christ's sake."

"He say the boy is...always in the trouble."

"You should mind your own business."

She crunched down into the car seat and said something that I didn't understand but cut me to the bone anyway.

We took the Ocean Drive route, which was nicer than the Parkway. Pauline looked out the window and didn't talk. We got to their house and I helped her coax Lucie out of the car. She pushed us off and walked like a zombie up the steps. I reached into the car, where the sailor's hat was crushed between the seatback and the bench.

"Here." I popped it open and set it on Pauline's head. I kissed her and really meant it. I felt like I should tell her she was a swell dame, but figured I'd have to explain what that meant.

She played with my hair and said, "So, which one?"

"Which one what?"

"Mr. Mark or the blonde boy?"

"How about neither?"

"I want to help you."

"You can help by staying out of it."

"You do not think I can help?" She frowned like she was in a play. "I have seen many of these...investigations."

"What do you think, I'm Sam Spade?"

"Who is this Spade?"

"Forget..." I pulled back and cocked my eye at her. "Wait a second, don't tell me you're...you work for a prosecutor or whatever you call it up there?"

"*Au contraire.*" She lowered her head and gave me a bashful look that could have been professional. "I am with...*la défense.*"

"Jeez, doesn't that put you on the other side?"

Now her look was more impertinent. "Perhaps I know better how they think."

"Alright." I tapped the crown of the sailor's hat. "How long are you here, anyway?"

"You think you can just change the..." she struggled for the word, "*sujet?*"

"The subject?"

"Yes, the subject, you just change it like that?"

"Look, you take your pick. But don't..."

"'Fuck it up?'"

She said it like she was pronouncing the words phonetically with no idea of their meaning.

"That's right, don't fuck it up."

"Good, I will not fuck it up."

"Okay, that's enough. You didn't answer my question."

"Why does it matter?'

128

She was walking up the path.

"Because I want to see you again."

"*Très bon*. I just like to hear you say it."

"Well, I did."

"Then I guess you have not 'fucked it up'."

I followed her up to the door. She turned.

"We have two more weeks. So, you come to see me?"

"Yeah. I'll call first."

She opened the door. "Remember, no phone."

"Jesus Christ."

She went in and called back through the screen door. "So it will be a big surprise, *non?*"

Chapter Twelve

I had managed to avoid Concetta the night before, but she was lying in wait for me in the morning.

"I was a little worried about you Monday night."

It was a rainy day, so we were at the kitchen table.

"Sorry, Mom."

"Were you too drunk to drive?"

"Since when does that stop me?"

She was in a sweat suit today; I mean a nice running outfit—though I doubt she ever broke a sweat in it—not the kind with elastic around the ankles and a drawstring.

"But you must have stayed down there."

"I picked up a French girl at the Jug, took her to dinner, met that asshole friend of yours who runs the joint, then went back to her cruddy apartment, slept with her, then brought her and her friend both back up to visit the Seabreeze."

"You did not." She sounded like she was talking to one of her girlfriends.

"Okay, so I didn't."

"Why can't you just tell me the truth?"

"I did, you just don't want to believe it."

"A French girl."

"French Canadian, okay? I lied."

"What's her name?"

"Pauline."

"Is she nice?"

Now she sounded like my mother again. "Yeah. She did manage to insult your buddy Mark."

"How?"

"She said the *frites*—that's French for fries—were frozen."

"At Randall's? That's ridiculous."

I shrugged as Gallicly as I could. *"Mais, oui."*

"That's…"

"She was just giving Mark shit."

"Why?"

I stood and carried my cereal bowl to the sink. "Because he's a dick."

"Hey, that's…he's a good guy."

I rinsed the bowl. "Well, I don't think he'll be hiring me anytime soon."

Davy's unspoken name filled the silence. I put the bowl in the draining rack.

"Yeah, he's not really so bad. Just…seemed like a snob. But I went back for lunch yesterday—he showed me around the kitchen."

"You get any ideas?"

"Yeah, cut our portions in half and double the prices."

Concetta sheeshed me. I got my keys from the bowl on the kitchen counter.

"But I'll be going back. Maybe I'll learn a little more."

"Going back?" She sounded alarmed, which served her right.

"Yeah, you know," I paused at the top of the stairs, *"cherchez la femme."*

Concetta gave me a sad smile, though I couldn't tell if she was approving my romantic bent or conjuring an image of Davy floating in the air somewhere along the barrier islands.

* * *

Everyone gave me knowing looks while I walked around trying to act like I ran the place. It was like they had seen me at the holiday party with a lampshade on my head. I was enjoying the feeling of being an unpredictable man about town until someone tapped me on the shoulder while I was going over an order of lunch meats at the bar.

"Hey, boss."

It had only been two days since we had left Pinto steaming outside the Garden, but it felt longer. He looked different somehow, then I realized I had never seen him in a button-down shirt and khakis. He was even wearing socks. I had figured he would catch up with me on the street somewhere and threaten to kick my ass so I was a little apprehensive.

"What's up with you?" I responded.

"I'm going to work."

"What, back at Lou's?"

"Nah, he's got me coverin' a few shifts at this guy's dealership out in Cape May Courthouse."

"What, you running the cash register?" It seemed best to give him some grief.

"I don't know, moving cars around, some shit like that."

"Glad to hear you're gainfully employed."

"Yeah. Doing my penance."

I nodded, going over the sheet with a pencil. Did we really need two rolls of salami? I acted busy for another minute, then turned like I was surprised he was still there.

"So, what's up?"

He shifted from foot to foot, like a grammar school kid dressed up for his first day.

"You got time for lunch?"

"Sure, what do you want?"

"Not here."

We tooled over to the Garden in the Caddy without talking. We slid into the booth, Pinto playing his somber role to the limit. He was cordial to the waitress without any of the usual banter. It was getting painful to watch.

"Pinto, what the fuck is going on?"

He waited while the waitress came back with coffee, then waited some more while she walked away.

"How was Cape May?" he finally asked.

News travelled fast. "Cape May was great."

"Why were you down there?"

"I thought you had something to talk to me about."

"Concetta send you down there?"

I didn't see how this was going anywhere good. I got up. Pinto grabbed my arm.

"Hey, this is serious."

"That makes me feel better."

"Sit down, sit down."

The waitress returned and we ordered. Pinto had come to the point in the script where it was his turn to talk.

"I thought maybe she sent you down there to look for Davy."

"What?"

"Did she?"

"Fuck no. Will you just tell me what you...?"

"Alright, alright. When I was in AC..."

"Doing your dealer apprenticeship?"

He gave me a sour look. "Yeah, well, I didn't tell Lou everything that happened."

Why was I not surprised?

Pinto continued. "I met this dirtball who was looking for..."

I raised my hand. He nodded.

"Right, so this guy figures out that I work for Lou—I think the guy who hooked us up told him, I wouldn't have told him, fuck, I didn't even tell him my name."

I could see where this was headed. Pinto kept on in his low voice.

"This guy, what a dick, he laughs, says what a small world, maybe he'll end up selling some of the shit to my boss's son."

"Did you kick his ass?" It made me feel generous to say that.

Pinto breathed out heavily, then smiled a big fake smile at the unsmiling waitress as she set our sandwiches down.

"No, but I should have."

"So you sold this guy..."

Pinto cut me off, his hand moving in a short stroke that had more of the familiar Pinto feel to it. "After what he said? I didn't sell him nothin'. Fuckin' dick."

"Did he say where Davy was?"

"It took a little convincing, but yeah, he did."

"I thought you didn't kick his ass."

"I just scared him." He picked up his egg salad sandwich, trying to keep it from falling apart over the plate. "It didn't take much."

"So where is he?"

"He didn't say exactly. He said there was some problem at a hot dog joint in Cape May, kid was working there. Maybe he ripped it off or something."

I worked on my tuna salad, thinking Davy's whereabouts was a pretty badly kept secret.

"So you didn't say anything to Lou about this?"

Pinto shook his head. "When he was going apeshit about the other mook I tried to sell to?" He put the sandwich down and wiped his hands with a napkin. "It didn't seem like the right time to get him going about Davy. So when I heard you were in Cape May, I figured we should talk."

"Concetta was on him last weekend about Davy."

"You think she knows...?"

"Concetta said she thought he was with some girl in Fishtown."

Pinto was picking up dropped pieces of the egg salad with a fork. "Don't sound right."

"Yeah, you'd think his parents should know where he is." There wasn't much doubt that Concetta knew where Davy was, but I wasn't sure I needed to tell Pinto that.

"His mom, anyway. I don't believe her." Pinto looked thoughtful, something I hadn't seen before. "So she didn't send you down there?"

"No. Lou...he asked me to keep an eye on her. Someone told him they'd seen her down in Cape May. Then last week she had to go to some fancy restaurant down there—Randall's—for some real estate thing—so she said. Then she lied to me, said she hadn't been down there in ages."

Pinto's eyes widened. "What, he thinks she's...fooling around or something?"

"He didn't say that but...anyway, I mentioned the place to Robert—he said the guy who ran it knew Concetta. He was like, why don't you go down, check out the competition?"

"So, this restaurant guy...you talk to him?"

I peeled the bread back from my sandwich. "You think they put relish in this tuna?" I pressed the bread back. Pinto watched my misdirection with amusement.

"You're a sly motherfucker. Wanna play twenty questions?"

I knew once I brought him in, he was in for good. But I couldn't bear having Pinto do a Columbo routine on me. So much for my resolution to keep him in the dark. I told him all about my conversations with Mark and my visit to the hot dog shack. The waitress came and cleared our plates away.

I rubbed my face and tried to think. "So we both heard Davy's in Cape May—or has been, anyway. Lou acts like he doesn't know anything—could be true. Concetta's lying her ass off about it." I thought of something. "Christ, I forgot. That guy Eduardo mentioned him, too."

"Who's Eduardo?"

"He's the dealer in Buena, Drew's guy."

Pinto looked at his knuckles, which started turning white. He made an effort to pull himself back to the topic at hand.

"What'd he say?"

"He said Davy was down here somewhere. And he might need help."

"Don't all junkies need help?"

Pinto was starting to sound a little bit smart. He looked at his hands like they might have a message for him.

"So what do we do?" he asked.

I picked up the check and stood. "I don't know. I gotta get back to work."

We drove back to the Seabreeze in a thoughtful silence that would not have seemed possible a week ago. Pinto had a courtesy car from the dealer parked at the back of our lot, some crap subcompact that he was embarrassed to get in.

It wasn't clear what our mission was, but we had to do something. The notion that Pinto and I were a team again didn't make that any better.

* * *

I stayed as late as I could at the restaurant, partly to get my mind off the Davy mess and even more to avoid talking to Concetta. I thought about bagging the whole thing, but it didn't seem like a real option. If I left Pinto alone on this, somehow, he'd make me look bad for running off and not telling Lou anything, even if he didn't mean to.

So, Concetta wasn't having an affair. The trips were all about helping shield precious Davy from whatever trouble he had got himself into. And part of that shielding was not letting Lou know about it. No doubt, the real estate job was a misguided attempt to make some cash to give to Davy. Because she would never sell a house; she didn't have the killer instinct.

I didn't want to deal with any of this. I just wanted to go see Pauline again and let my head go all gooey like I was fifteen.

What I should do, I told myself, is tell Lou what I had found out. It would set his mind at ease about Concetta, at least as far as her cheating on him went. But it would set off fireworks, I had no doubt. He would confront Concetta—and why not?

Or I could talk to Concetta first, though to what end I wasn't sure. To let her know I was going to tell Lou? Because once I talked to her, I was going to have to talk to Lou. If he found out I was taking her side, that would not be good.

Then the big brother angle started creeping in. I had shielded Davy from any number of scrapes—shielded him from having his dad find out, mainly. And I had tried to talk sense into him. As a big brother, I had a pretty poor track record. How was I any better than Concetta—coddling him, bailing him out, and then watching as he said thanks, but fuck you sucker, now I can get on with my fucked up life the way I want to?

Maybe I could do better this time. If I went and talked to him, without his parents knowing, maybe I could figure out what was going on, maybe even really help him out of whatever the jam was. I thought about what Eduardo had said; I didn't doubt that he was in trouble, no doubt of his own making. Then, worst case, I'd have something concrete to come back to Lou with. Because it was Lou I had to talk to eventually.

Funny how you talk circles around your better instincts so you can take a path of least resistance.

Then there was Arnie. It gave me a weird feeling to see him hanging out in Mark's place. It seemed a good bet that he was the mutual friend that hooked Concetta up with Mark. So the guy who ripped off Lou is now helping Concetta with Davy?

I ended up out back of the kitchen again with Robert, who had the least history at the place and so was maybe the safest to talk with. I gave him the blow-by-blow of my visit to Randall's, leaving out the talk of Davy. He especially liked Pauline's little act.

"She got him good. But," he passed a bottle of white to me, "I know he's not using frozen."

I drank the wine and looked at the label, trying to memorize the name but knowing I would forget.

"So, guess who I saw there?"

"Margaret Trudeau?"

I lit a cigarette. "Our old friend Arnie."

Robert blew out a little breath through his nose. "Is he working there?"

"I don't think so. I saw him in the bar, but he didn't see me."

"Sure about that?"

I thought that over, but I had had enough wine that nothing came of it. "Did you know him well?"

"I had to deal with him, right, the first few months I was here. Before he got the boot."

"Was he...?"

"A pain in the ass sometimes. But what else is new? He doesn't really know the food end like I do, so he's gotta question stuff just to keep me honest. So, he really wasn't too bad."

"He close with anyone here?"

Robert poured the last few ounces of the wine in my glass and got off his milk crate. "You a detective now?"

I tilted my tumbler up and held the wine at the edge of my mouth, smelling it, then drinking it down. "Someone else said something like that not long ago."

Robert took off his apron and threw it over his shoulder. "'Course you're not. You're just Lou's friend." He went to the kitchen door and turned. "Or Concetta's."

"Can't I be both?"

Robert was standing in the doorway, calling out something to one of the dishwashers. A voice came over a clatter of china, and he laughed. He turned back to me.

"I take that back about being a detective, if you haven't figured that out."

Chapter Thirteen

There had to be one of those Greek myths that covered these breakfasts with Concetta, but I'm sure I slept through that class. The only way I could figure to avoid them was to move out, and that would just cause more problems. I talked about Pauline, which ordinarily I would have avoided, but under the circumstances, it was my version of talking about the weather.

Concetta went along with it, but as all roads in the discussion led to Cape May, it was hard not to feel like we were both dancing around the real issue. This morning she was wearing a knee-length skirt, a white blouse buttoned all the way up, and a little gold cross on a chain. It made her look like a Catholic school teacher.

"I guess you'll be getting back down there soon?" She said it like it was a homework assignment I had forgotten about. Concetta had always been at the top of the list of wives who wanted to see me fixed up.

"Yeah, I guess."

"Have you called her?"

"She doesn't have a phone."

"You think she's just gonna wait for you?"

"I have no idea."

"Doesn't that worry you?"

"Should it?"

"Maybe she'll get tired of waiting."

"She knows I've got to work."

She shook her head. Obviously, I was a dim student.

"You're half an hour away. How hard is it to take a break and go see her?"

I went to get my keys, which was like the two-minute warning. "Guess you're right. I'll go down this afternoon."

Concetta gave a tight little smile.

I went on. "I think we'll go back to Randall's, maybe we can see Mark again."

She kept the smile so perfectly even that I knew I had hit some kind of nerve. I moved to the door fast, so she was stuck with whatever she was thinking about. Like what did Mark really tell me, and how good was I at keeping secrets?

* * *

I told everyone I was going back to Cape May to visit my new friend Mark. That, and the nice shirt I was wearing, was like a public service announcement that I was going on a date.

Which I was. Or at least I was hoping to go on one if I could find Pauline. The lady prep cooks put together some sandwiches and things for me, all nestled nicely in a woven basket that must have been a prop for an Easter buffet. Thankfully, they didn't fill it with green plastic grass. Kevin put a bottle of wine and a couple of glasses in there. When Sheila came up to me as I was heading out, I thought she was going to give me a corsage and a flower for my lapel, which wouldn't have worked as I wasn't wearing a jacket.

"When's Lou coming down?"

I held up the basket. "You're ruining the mood, you know. I'm off work now."

"Seems like you're off a lot."

One week and now I was an absentee manager? "I don't know, Friday, I guess."

"Okay." She softened a bit and pinched my cheek. "Have fun with Mark."

"Yeah, wish I had some flowers for him."

"He'll understand." She moved off to the gaggle of waitresses hanging out

140

at a table near the bar.

I took the slow way down again, enjoying the drive in the early afternoon sun. I was disappointed that no one seemed nervous that I was going back to Cape May and maybe checking in on Arnie. But then, if someone should feel nervous, they would have acted the opposite. This detective stuff was pretty tedious.

I was the one who was nervous. I hadn't been on a real date in a long time, much less one where I ran the risk of not even having someone to go on it with. And while Pauline seemed eager to help with my Davy investigation, I was worried she'd think that was more important to me than seeing her.

Pauline was sitting on the front steps of the house like a girl in some fifties movie waiting for her beau. How did she know? She was dressed more like I expected a French girl to, black pedal pushers and a short sleeved striped shirt without a collar. I got a little fluttery, whether because she was just so attractive, or because I was lying to her about the purpose of our picnic.

We kissed, and she linked her arm around mine as we walked back to the car. She got in and noticed the hamper in the back.

"We have a pic-a-nic?"

"Yeah, just like Yogi Bear."

"Who?"

"Never mind." I started the car.

"So we go to find Davy?"

I pulled away from the curb, my maybe-not-so-fake romantic mood deflated. "Yeah, we go to find Davy."

* * *

But first, we needed to get a hot dog. I debated whether to take Pauline with me, but she made that decision.

"I talk to him. He will tell me."

There was a line today, and our boy didn't spot us until we were next behind a fat guy buying three dogs. He counted out the guy's change, one bill and then one coin at a time. I stepped up to the counter while the fat guy took a long time anointing his dogs with relish, mustard, and ketchup. Pauline squeezed in next to me in front of the window.

"What is your name?"

"Leo."

"Ah, Leo, I am Pauline."

He was looking over her head at the teenagers in line behind us.

"That's nice. You want something? 'Cause there's folks behind you who do."

"Fresca."

He dug a can out of the ice chest.

She counted money out of one of those plastic change purses that split down the middle when you squeeze them. She put the coins on the counter.

"Where can we find this Davy?"

"I can't help you." He lifted his head and called out, "Next!"

Pauline turned to the two girls behind us. "Please, you wait." She turned back to Leo. "Leo, we need to help Davy."

"I don't know where he is."

"I think you do."

I jumped in. "What happened here with Davy? He rip this place off?"

Leo stared at me for a few seconds. Then he reached his arm through the window and pointed at the side of the kiosk.

"You see that?"

The wall was made of wood slats and was white; a huge splotch in the middle was a brighter shade of white, like it had been painted over hastily. Leo talked in a low voice.

"About a month ago—came here to open up. Shit was spray-painted there. Like, 'we'll get you, junkie prick'. Davy saw that—he was gone."

We absorbed this in silence. Then Pauline spoke.

"He is in trouble—we want to help him."

Leo said, "Yeah, well, I'm staying the fuck out of it."

"Okay." Pauline took my hand. "We talk to Rudy."

Leo smirked. "You don't know Rudy."

"Oh?" She gave him a look that was a more high-class version of a smirk.

"He is not the fat man with the mermaid tattoo on his arm? And drinks that disgusting spicy rum?"

Leo looked a little sick. "Where'd you meet him?"

"You don't mind. He buy me a few drinks, want to—" she smacked the heels of her palms together with alarming force. "I say no, but I am sure he talk to me again."

"So talk to him."

The teenagers were crowding close to us, enjoying the dialogue.

"I tell him you look at my tits and say something rude."

"Bullshit."

"You take your chance. I think he love to be my..." Pauline looked at me, "what is it, a white knight?"

Leo rolled his eyes. "Oh, fuck me."

Pauline pressed up close to the window. "Maybe someday, since you are the cute beach guy. But now," her voice got hard, "just the address, *s'il vous plaît.*"

* * *

Leo pointed us to a Catholic retreat house in Cape May Point. On the road down there, I asked her about Rudy. She held her hand out the window, holding it against the breeze like it was a wing on an airplane.

She said, "I heard Leo say his name when you..."

"Of course you did."

"And I asked at that Jug. They tell me where he hang out—a piano bar."

"So, you..."

"I thought, maybe I can find out something."

"Did he really try to pick you up?"

She gave me a shocked look. "Of course. I wear the low-cut blouse."

It wasn't hard to find the place. It was an impressive building, or group of buildings really, the centerpiece being a huge white structure right on the beach, with two wings and a red roof. It looked like a first-class Victorian-era hotel, which was odd, given that it was a Catholic retreat house.

143

Or a convent or a monastery. Leo wasn't really sure exactly what it was, other than it had a chapel somewhere within the complex. And a bell that tolled with divine authority every hour, as we discovered. We parked a block away, which was plenty close enough to be impressed by the grandeur of it all. I wished I could get in on poverty like this, but I guess I'm just one of those ex-Catholics who smelled bullshit from the word go. Not that I didn't know and like a handful of clergy. But they were the exceptions who didn't seem to think that everyone in the world should subscribe to their version of the truth.

"Think they'll let us in?" I was nervous and not sure whether it was the thought of confronting Davy or the fear of disturbing the many ghosts of my grade school experiences.

Pauline reached into the backseat and grabbed the basket.

"I thought we have the picnic?"

I got the blanket from the trunk, and we set up on the beach just outside the invisible border projected by the looming building. We could see a handful of Adirondack chairs and rockers on the porches—first and second floor—of the building, some occupied and slowly rocking. As we ate, a few people wandered down to the beach, alone. One went to the water's edge, her white slacks rolled up over her ankles. Another, a man, sat on the sand, looking out at the water.

"Let's take a walk," I suggested.

We got to the sitting man first. He nodded and smiled with a faraway, communing-with-something-so-don't-disturb-me look. We nodded back, walking at a reverent pace, and approached the woman. She had a hand over her eyes and was searching the water.

She said, "We saw dolphins yesterday."

We watched with her for a minute, but didn't see anything. She wore a white blouse buttoned all the way up, her hair cut short and blunt. A simple cross hung on a chain around her neck. Her nails were trimmed short, and it didn't take much Catholic radar to figure she was a nun.

"Excuse me—Sister?"

She shifted toward me, her hand still over her eyes, giving me a look that set a few hairs going up before I recovered. Then her hand came down, and she extended it to me.

"Sister Louise—guess you can tell even without the habit." Her eyes flicked over to Pauline, who was crouched down and moving her hand through the water, as if to say, in comparison to that, I guess I'm easy to figure out.

We shook hands, and my grade school anxieties subsided, though I wouldn't say they completely went away. She looked me in the eye in that way religious people do, that says they know you probably won't be saved, but they're going to be polite and not mention it.

"I've got a friend—well, his son is staying with you. I was hoping to check in on him."

Wrong words, I thought; they made it sound like there was something wrong with him.

"There's a lot of people here now—sort of our peak season."

"His name is David—David Scolletta."

Sister Louise started walking back toward the sand. Something about the way she walked reminded me of Sheila. We fell in step.

"People come here to get away. Or, that's not quite right—I mean they come to spend time alone, to reflect and think." She gave me that professional, religious look again. "To pray."

Or to hide out. Maybe go cold turkey. Something told me that shooting up in your room wouldn't be tolerated. We came across the wet sand and stopped. Sister Louise gestured to the building.

"I have to go back. We have devotions in a few minutes."

"Can I—?"

"Not today." She started off, her hands clasped behind her. She turned back, as she sloughed through the sand. "There's visiting hours Sunday—one to three. I'll tell him you..."

"Tell him John McGinty stopped by."

The good sister waved and continued on her way. Pauline gripped my arm.

"Look!" She pointed out at the water.

Out about fifty yards a half dozen grey-black shapes looped in and out

145

of the water, moving south, splashing easily along. We watched them and heard a few cries. They looked like they were having fun.

As we walked back to our blanket, I looked at the retreat house, the chairs mostly empty now. I wondered if the devotions were just for the nuns. Then I saw a skinny figure leaning against the railing on the second floor, looking out at where the dolphins were playing. Even from the distance I could see that he was smoking a cigarette and that it was Davy.

Maybe the dolphins were his devotions. I could think of worse.

* * *

I didn't have to go back to work. I certainly didn't want to go back to work. I decided I had had enough of Cape May and not enough of Pauline.

"Let me show you a real boardwalk."

We drove back up the coast, and I took her to the busiest stretch of the Wildwood boardwalk. Tilt-a-Whirl, Skee-ball, pizza that burned the roof of your mouth, frozen custard, bumper cars. And then there were the people. Compared to Cape May, they talked more, yelled more, insulted each other more, laughed louder, and cat-called at women without shame.

We sat on a bench and ate pizza, while a group of teenage boys pushed each other around on the railings next to us, occasionally sending one of their group careening out into the path of girls wearing ripped t-shirts over their skimpy bathing suits.

I said, "We could go back to Cape May if this…"

A fat boy landed on his backside in front of us. He lolled there for a moment, making kissing sounds at Pauline, then jumped up and bounced back to his friends, who clapped and hooted.

Pauline acted like nothing had happened. "No, it is…nice."

I was glad she didn't insist on me defending her honor. We walked past the boys as we headed back to the car, and Pauline stopped in front of the fat kid. She gripped his cheeks hard and put her face close to his.

"Donne-moi un baiser, crapaud!"

She released him and cocked her head back, her eyebrows shooting up in a challenge. The kid looked terrified, and his friends laughed, but they were nervous as hell. I doubted they had won any French awards at Wildwood Catholic, but the message was clear. We kept walking, and no one yelled after us.

"What did you say?"

"I told Mr. Toad to give me a kiss." She looked perplexed. "I think he didn't really want to."

We got in the car and I headed to Pacific Avenue to go back to Cape May. Pauline put her hand on the steering wheel as we waited at a traffic light.

"No, you show me your home."

It was maybe seven o'clock. There was a good chance Concetta would be there.

"I don't know…"

"So I meet your friend…Concetta."

I crossed over Pacific Avenue. "Alright. But don't mention Davy."

"But of course."

I wasn't sure I liked her little smile, but like the fat kid, I was afraid to do anything about it.

* * *

Concetta was so happy gabbing with Pauline, sharing white wine on the deck, that I thought she might boot me out and ask her to stay on as favored guest. I went inside to get a beer, a revolt against the continental atmosphere that seemed to be enveloping the house. When I came out, they were chuckling and shaking their heads, Concetta watching me as I scraped a chair away from the table.

"Pauline told me you went on a picnic." Concetta said this with a tone that was approving and condescending at the same time, like it was totally out of character and maybe between the two of them, they could straighten me out.

"Yeah, I like my tuna fish with sand in it."

They talked about clothes and stuff, and I went back in and turned on the ball game. After a while, Concetta came through and went into her bedroom, then came out and hovered over me, patting me on the top of the head. She had something white and soft in her hand, which she laid on the sofa.

"She can use this. There's a new toothbrush in the cabinet over the sink."

I started to protest, but she shushed me and nodded to the door on the deck like I had missed my cue. For a strange moment, her eyes locked on mine, and I felt the same squirming shiver that had gone through me talking to Sister Louise on the beach.

They were a nation united, these women.

Chapter Fourteen

Concetta was gone by the time we emerged Friday morning. She had left a note letting us know she had bought sticky buns and there was orange juice in the fridge, which no one in the house ever drank. Pauline sat in her nightgown—it really was a nightgown, cotton, not a negligee—and I thought about how she looked a different kind of beautiful everywhere she showed up. There was something about the pale skin with the dark hair that was the opposite of the deeply-tanned, sharp-tongued women you met in bars in Wildwood, though I sensed there was a different kind of strength underneath.

"You must go to work." She took our dishes to the sink.

She was quiet during the drive to her apartment. Lucie was sitting on the porch steps, looking a little sulky. I waved to her. She took a drag on her cigarette.

"Do I need to find her a boyfriend?" I asked.

"She has too many already."

"Unlike you?"

Now I was the one seeking reassurance? How quickly it happens.

She spared me the pain of a response. "I like Concetta."

"She's a good lady."

"She worries about her boy."

"Did you talk about him?"

Pauline shook her head and walked along the path to the house, holding my hand. "No, but I can see. And I think she is doing the adding."

"Adding?"

"Yes, the two plus two."

"Meaning…?"

"That you are digging things up in Cape May."

"She could just say something to me."

"Maybe she talk to me when she comes down."

"What do you mean?"

We were at the steps. She picked the cigarette out of Lucie's fingers and took an alluring puff.

"We go to Mass—Saturday night."

I couldn't think of anything to say. She kissed me and handed the cigarette back to Lucie.

"Two good Catholic girls—so we must pray."

* * *

I called Pinto, which I found hard to believe I was doing, even as I dialed the number of his nephew's house. His niece said he was at the Garden with a note of relief. The woman at the Garden didn't say a word when I asked for him. I could hear the phone hit a hard surface with a clunk, then there were a few minutes of restaurant noise, which I admit I listened to with a professional interest—every joint had its own medley of sounds. Pinto came on the line.

"What's up, boss?"

He was at the Seabreeze in ten minutes. The bar was busy, but dinners were pretty much done. We took a table in a corner.

I sensed something out of kilter even before we started talking. It was the shirt: a red polo shirt with the name of the dealership. And a nametag. I reached over and pulled the tag out a little.

"Dominic?"

Pinto looked cross. "That's my name."

"Never heard anyone call you that."

"Just family."

"So you're part of the team over there now?"

150

The Pinto smile came back, his head tilting up. "I sold a car today."

"Really?"

"Yeah, I told him, look, I'll wear the shirt and the freaking name tag, but you gotta let me be a salesman."

"Just like that."

"The guy—he's a dick, but he's a friend of Lou's so you gotta cut him some slack—says, alright, you sell something today, I'll let you join the team."

"Good job, then."

"It was easy. I know one of the other sales guys—Marconi Plaza dude. Anyway, so I get him to pass me a sure thing—we split the commission, I make it up on the next deal."

I relaxed. This was more like the Pinto I knew. I let him bask for a minute in his success story while I considered whether I really wanted to bring him up to speed. Then I figured, who else could I talk to besides Pauline, who might head back to Quebec any day? But I wanted to make sure of something first.

"So you're done being a trainee dealer?"

He looked offended. "Are you kidding? A fuckin' mug's game. I mean, there's no shortage of customers, but they'd all rip you off or narc you out in a second if it meant getting a fix."

Or maybe Lou put the fear of God in him.

"We found Davy."

"Oh, really?" Pinto unpinned his nametag. "Hey, thanks for reminding me I was wearing this. Chicks would think I'm a schmuck."

"You might ditch the shirt, too."

He grimaced. "Thanks for the advice, Romeo."

"You won't believe this. He's at some retreat house in Cape May Point."

"You mean with priests and shit?"

"I think it's run by a bunch of nuns. We were there yesterday."

"We?"

"Me and Pauline." I regretted bringing her name up, but it would happen eventually.

"You got a girlfriend now?"

"I met her in Cape May. She's French-Canadian."

"Man." I didn't like the way he looked at the ceiling. "What's she like?"

"She's very nice. Look, forget her."

"What's Davy doing at a fucking convent?"

"Hiding out." I told him about the hot dog shack.

"Concetta must have put him there." He rocked his beer bottle back and forth on the table. "You tell her you know this?"

"No, I guess I'm waiting to see if she blinks first. I brought Pauline back to the house last night. We told Concetta about our picnic on the beach down there."

"So she didn't blink?"

I grabbed our beer bottles and stood up. "No. But Pauline and her got real chummy. She thinks Concetta knows we know. You want another?"

Pinto nodded, his face twitching a little. I guessed he was really thinking.

Ted set us out a couple more beers. It was almost ten. I took the bottles to the table. I told Pinto about Concetta and Pauline going to Mass together.

"Sounds like a smart cookie."

"Yeah, she's like a paralegal."

"She got a friend?"

I looked at him sideways. "What makes you think that?"

"On vacation, all the way from Canada," he took a cigarette pack from the pocket of his windbreaker, "she ain't likely here by herself."

"Yeah, she does."

"Well..." Pinto was sorting through the pack and pulled out a cigarette.

"Well, what?"

"Ain't you gonna fix me up?"

"Jesus."

He looked offended. "What, I'm not good enough?"

"Maybe not."

"Give me a chance." He held out the cigarette, which was not a cigarette. "Hey, you want to try this?"

I put my hand on his and pressed it to the table.

"Could you just be cool?"

152

"I wasn't gonna fire it up here. They call it Thai stick. Dude laid it on me."

"So you *are* still in the drug game."

Pinto gave me a pitying look. "Now you be cool. This is all peace and love and shit."

* * *

Driving aimlessly in a huge green Caddy while getting stoned may not have been the best decision we made that night.

We stopped at a traffic light, Pinto working the radio knobs like it was a crystal set behind the Iron Curtain. A car horn honked.

I looked up and saw the light was green. It may well have been green since the beginning of time. The radio announcer was speaking in some language I couldn't recognize, Pinto squinting as he tried to get the signal clearer.

I yelled to him like we were on a ship lost at sea. "Roll your window down!"

The smell from what we had smoked was overwhelming.

"It is down."

"Roll the back ones down."

Pinto leaned over the seat back, trying to roll down the back window.

"Fuck, this is fucking…"

We came to another light. I checked and rechecked the color. It was definitely red.

Pinto was having trouble, kneeling on the seat now.

"Fuck, this fucker is fuckin' stuck."

I looked across the intersection at a cop car facing us. I reached over and pulled on Pinto's khakis.

"Hey, sit down."

He gave up and flounced back on the seat. The cop car started forward. I verified the color of the light—green—and did the same. Of course, I looked over at him and grinned as we passed. Nothing wrong here, officer. As we got through the intersection, I saw the cop swing around and come up behind us, his lights flashing.

"Fuck, get that…"

Pinto slammed the ashtray shut, which did nothing for the smell or our own lack of any sense.

I pulled over, the cop easing in behind me. He sat there, taking his time. I looked at Pinto.

"Eat it."

"What?"

"Eat the joint, man. We're gonna get fucking busted." I checked the mirror. The cop—fuck, it was a trooper, I could tell by the hat—was out of the car and ambling toward us. He was at least seven feet tall.

Pinto had the joint in his hand. He stared at it like it was a canapé offered by a primitive culture.

"Just fucking eat it."

There was a knock on the window, the Texas Ranger's face looming. I mean the trooper's. I rolled the window down.

The trooper spoke. "Hey, Ginty, I thought that was you—Jesus, what are you guys smoking in there?"

Purcell. I turned to Pinto. He gave me a sickly smile, his lips clamped shut. My hands were locked on the steering wheel. I tried to talk.

"I—it's Lou's car, I'm not…" one hand came unstuck and moved to the glove box, "… sure where he keeps the…thing…" What did you call it? That piece of paper?

Purcell banged his hand on the sill of the door and laughed. "Hey, don't worry. I got a message from Lou to find you guys."

His statement lodged sideways in my brain, which was having a hard time grappling with its implications. Why was Purcell running errands for Lou?

Purcell peered across at Pinto. "Hello, there." His tone shifted to sarcasm.

"You remember Pinto?" I was recovering, though I was struggling to figure out what to do with my right hand, which was still attached to the glove compartment latch.

"Of course. The good Samaritan." He gave Pinto some special trooper eyeballs. "You guys going out to the Parkway to see if anybody needs help?"

For once, Pinto kept his mouth shut. His smile was starting to disturb me.

154

Purcell was enjoying himself. The radio was playing what sounded like a polka. I freed my right hand and turned it down.

"I guess we're going to see Lou now."

Purcell straightened up, directing a few cars to keep moving.

I kept talking, seeming unable to stop. "You coming with us?"

Purcell waved to someone passing by, then bent back down. "That was the plan. Hey," his voice lowered, "you got any more of that stuff?"

I looked at Pinto, his mouth still fixed in that awkward grin. "No, you see, we thought..."

Pinto reached up and pulled down the sun visor, the half-smoked joint rolling off into his hand. His teeth were showing now.

"That shit was too good to eat."

* * *

Cops always knew the best places to park. And what could be safer—or cooler—than smoking grass with a State Trooper in the parking lot of a seafood warehouse? Whether the fact that he was somehow a lackey of Lou's was a good or bad thing, I had no idea. A limitless capacity for not reaching conclusions seemed to be a dominant effect of Pinto's exotic herb.

We had figured out the radio now, and the oldies were flowing. Pinto and Purcell were singing along, Pinto surprisingly low and Purcell an amazing falsetto.

The song ended, and Purcell punched Pinto in the shoulder from the back seat, then stretched out.

"Man, we're like Buddy and the Citations."

Purcell had us stop at a bar on the way to get more wine. I was sure the guy never paid to eat or drink anything. The oldies station had Pinto in a trance. The rest of the Thai stick didn't hurt, either.

What better way to get ready to see the Big Guy?

Lou was on the sofa watching some black and white TV show, as we emerged from the stairwell. I came first, then Pinto bounded in like he had just gotten out of school.

"Hey, *Paisan!*" Pinto chortled, clapping Lou's face in his hands. Lou pushed him away.

"Keep it down, you stupid fuck—Concetta's asleep."

Pinto crouched, a finger to his pursed lips. "Shhhh!"

Purcell came from the top of the stairs. Lou stood, and the two of them went out on the deck.

Opening a bottle of wine was just the concentrated work I needed. I had leveled off from the smoke, but it was a pretty high level. Pinto was on his knees in front of the television set. Ernest Borgnine's sad face filled the screen.

"Marty." Pinto sounded close to tears.

I left him to it and joined the big boys on the terrace. That is, the deck. I offered a glass to Purcell, but he held up his hand.

"I gotta go."

He left abruptly, going down the stairs with his hat on, a special guest star exiting a teleplay none of us would ever be able to totally explain.

Lou was sitting on a lounge chair, looking distracted. He accepted a glass, and I filled it to the brim, thinking that the party was ending before it had begun.

For the next half hour, we drank without talking. Pinto joined us, posing against the backdrop of the deck's fencing, his features backlit by the security lights from the house next door, re-enacting a touching moment from Ernest Borgnine's Oscar-winning performance. Lou watched him, slumped in a chair, the same vacant look on his face as when he was watching television. The gigantic shadow of the departed Purcell persisted in my dim thoughts, a looming presence that I still could not explain.

I went into the kitchen, wondering how Concetta was sleeping through all this. I was rinsing out wine bottles when Pinto appeared beside me.

"I'm outta here."

"Need a ride?"

He looked frightened. "You're not getting me back in that thing."

As I washed wine glasses, I could see him through the window, shuffling up the block, hands in his pockets. I half-expected the credits to start rolling.

Lou came up beside me.

"I gave Purcell the Arnie assignment."

"Thanks." That was a load off my addled mind, though knowing that Purcell was another Lou flunky nearly put it back.

"But I got something else."

Lou held out a piece of paper, creased like it had been folded up a couple of times. "Maybe you gotta be stoned to figure this out."

The sheet had a message spelled in letters cut out of magazines and newspapers. "BEt THe COPS WoULD LiKe tO sEe THis mOVie!. MayBE YOU wAnt to buY thE oRIgiNAl? BE in TOuch. Yor pal Soupy."

"Okay, Sherlock, time's up," Lou said.

I handed the sheet back to Lou. "Soupy Sales?"

Lou folded the page and put it in his pocket. "What, so I'm White Fang?"

"Fucking weird. Where'd it come from? Was there a postmark?"

"Yeah, return address, Joe Blackmailer, East Bumfuck, New Jersey." Lou snorted. "Showed up on the service desk, no one knows who left it. I got it when I was walking out the door."

I had to ask. "What's this about a movie?"

Lou didn't say anything for a minute, staring at the sheet. Then his voice got real quiet.

"Come on."

I followed him into the living room, where he went to the safe, opened it, and took out a videotape. He put it into the VCR that was on a low shelf of the home entertainment center and beckoned to me with the remote for the device.

"We gotta keep this low."

It took him a minute to get the VCR synced up with the TV, then the video started to roll. There was a long shot of a garage that I recognized immediately as Ramon's. The camera panned around to the roadside, then moved toward the road and lingered on the mailbox that was on a post, adjusting focus so the numbers were clear. There was a date/time stamp in a corner of the screen, showing yesterday's date.

The image went dark for a moment, then the inside of the garage appeared.

There were scuffling noises, but the image was blurry and jumped around. A voice said something indistinguishable, then there was a loud "SHHHH!" There was an abrupt cut, and the camera focused on a big box, like one of the ones we had loaded, zooming in for a close-up.

A pair of hands with black gloves appeared and cut open the tape on the top of the box with a Stanley knife. Inside the box were nestled two car batteries in a bed of straw. The hands came in with a screwdriver and worked at the top of the battery, prying it off. The camera moved over top of the battery and looked inside.

I had never seen the inside of a battery, but I knew it was dangerous to fool with one, and also that it typically would not be filled with brown paper packages tied up with string. The hands took one of the parcels out and set it on top of another box. The whole scene was eerily quiet.

The hands were having a little trouble untying the parcel, given the gloves. They pulled back then reappeared with the Stanley knife and cut the string and unwrapped the paper. Inside were two plastic bags filled with something white, which as the hands picked up one bag and displayed it for the camera, was clearly a powder, like flour or…

The screen went blank for ten seconds, then suddenly a person appeared, sitting on a chair. His hands were pulled behind the back of the chair, and from the way he was straining, they must have been tied together there. His head drooped down, long hair hanging slackly. The camera moved in close, and a black-gloved hand pushed his head up, fingers pressing up on his chin.

Ramon.

I stepped away and grabbed the nearest chair, dragging it over and lowering myself onto it. I felt cold and nauseous, and dizzy like I was falling and couldn't keep my balance.

The hand held his face to the camera for a few seconds. He was conscious and clearly had been knocked about a bit. There were streams of dried blood descending from a cut on his temple as well as from his nose. The camera pulled back, and a piece of paper was thrust in front of it by a gloved hand. In big letters were scrawled the words: "WHAT'S IN THE BAGS?"

The hand then turned the sheet to Ramon, pushing it up close to his face, the camera zooming in, so nothing could be seen of the person holding the paper except the hand.

Ramon spat on the paper. There was an almost imperceptible blank screen, then Ramon's face was there again, bleeding freely from his nose. From the dazed look on his face, there had likely been more damage that could not be detected from the headshot.

"Heroin." He croaked the words.

Another sheet appeared in front of the camera. "WHO IS YOUR BUYER?"

The sheet was turned to Ramon. He shook his head. Another little gap in the tape, and Ramon's face came back, his mouth bleeding and working slowly like he had lost a tooth. He did not look good.

"Two guys last time…Pinto, little fuck…another guy…Gindy or some-thing…"

I was feeling real sick now, fighting an urge to vomit. I was way down from the weed. A black hand flashed into the screen, hitting Ramon's head with something hard. He yelped like an animal caught in a trap.

There was muttering off-screen, and a paper was thrust in front of his face. Ramon studied it, breathing hard. His eyes got a little brighter.

His voice was a croak. "You touch *mi familia*…"

The hand came in again, the hard object now clearly in vision, a small pistol. This time, the barrel moved under his chin, pointing up. The hand holding it was shaking.

An impatient voice hissed, "Give us the real name."

Ramon blinked, looking directly at the camera.

"Scolletta…Lou Scolletta." His voice got higher, his eyes widening.

The tape went blank. I dropped my head into my hands. I don't know how long I was sitting there. Next thing I remember was Lou holding my shoulder tight on the porch.

"I'm sorry, man. I wouldn't have shown you that except…"

I shook my head hard. I kept trying to figure a way that this wasn't happening.

Lou let go and stared out at nothing. "Fuck. We're both in this now."

There were no thoughts in my mind except an urge to deny it was true.

Then that battered face came back at me.

"What about Ramon?"

Lou shook his head. "I sent Purcell to check on him. He's gonna call."

Purcell graduated from flunky to henchman in my mind. Ten minutes later, the call came in. The ring shook me like an electric shock. Lou was on for half a minute.

I stood up. "Is he…?"

"Can't find him."

The knot in my stomach got worse. Lou looked like he was fighting his own. He went to the VCR and popped out the tape, putting it back in the safe. He looked at me for a moment and seemed to make a decision.

"I gotta go," he said.

Lou went to the top of the stairs, pausing and pointing at an ashtray. "Do something with that, okay?"

Three-quarters of the endless Thai Stick joint lay mocking in the ashtray. I stuffed it into a matchbox.

I didn't figure I'd be hitting it up again soon.

Chapter Fifteen

Saturday was busy as hell, which was good. There was no time to agonize over anything except keeping the kitchen and bar up to speed. Even Lou was pitching in, handling the seating duties so Sheila could deal with waitress drama.

Concetta had sort of told Lou the truth, saying she was going to Mass and then meeting some friends for dinner. He was glad to have her gone, you could tell; he had bigger problems on his mind now.

Around four-thirty, we settled at his table, and all the dread I had pushed into a corner of my mind rushed back. Whatever sleep I had managed last night had not been restful as I stewed over the horrible scenes of the video. And while I was worried about Ramon, my biggest fear was for myself, coward that I was.

Lou was picking at a salad in a way that just pissed me off.

"Why'd you have to drag me into this?" My voice cracked a little.

Lou lowered his head. "Keep your voice down. Alright, it's my fault—but you picking up that shipment—you had no exposure there. I mean, until…"

Bad, angry thoughts crowded in my head. "But you're…fuck, man, I had no idea you were…"

Lou's look got colder. He went back to his salad, and I slumped in my chair. After a minute, he put his fork down and got up.

"Let's take a walk."

The air, and just moving, helped. We went a block and turned down a street that headed back toward the bay, going past the last house to the edge of the water where an unused dock sat forlornly at the water's edge.

Lou faced me, putting his hands on my shoulders. "You gotta think. If someone gets the tape, I'll say I been getting parts from him for a couple of years. So he decides to get his buddy in Flint to include some extra cargo—what's that got to do with me? Ramon got scared and had to say something, so he pinned it on me. And you? You're just a friend who did me a favor."

I looked at the calm bay waters, trying to process what he was saying.

"But...the stuff was for you...right?"

Lou didn't answer. He seemed to be thinking about something else, staring at the rippling water of the bay.

"These stupid fucks. Messing with me is bad—but screwing with Ramon's boss, shit..."

The image of Ramon hefting a substantial wrench left little doubt in my mind that whoever his boss was, he had to be a bad hombre.

I kicked an unyielding piling on the dock. "Christ, Lou, why did you show me that tape?"

"Because I want your help."

The rest of his unspoken argument hung in the air: that if I didn't help him, the promise of keeping me out of the mess would go out the window. I forced myself to look at him, at the serious brown eyes that had a fear behind them that bound us together.

A skiff chugged by thirty yards out in the water, a sunburned guy wearing a military-style fatigue hat tending the tiller of the outboard motor. He had a beer in his other hand, which he lifted in a lazy greeting.

We both waved back. A black Vietnam POW flag flapped in the wind from its post at the bow of the little boat. I almost saluted, then stopped myself. Maybe I would have been better off going in the service and none of this bullshit with Lou would be happening. But given what a coward I was proving to be in the face of this duress, I no doubt would have been a terrible soldier.

* * *

Back at the restaurant, I was trying to calm myself down, pretending to review a seafood vendor's invoice, when Lou came over with a bottle of wine and two glasses. He filled them up and pushed one toward me.

His tone was concerned. "How's Concetta been?"

I looked at the guy who an hour ago was walking me through how to avoid being an accessory to his drug-dealing operation: my friend Lou, the glad-handing Cadillac salesman—or should I say, freaking drug dealer. His lack of interest in getting the cops involved with Arnie made a lot more sense now.

I said, "Busy—all that real estate shit."

"You keeping an eye on her, like I asked?"

I tried to hopscotch through a minefield of facts and half-facts.

"I went out to a bar with her and her friends one night. She wasn't..."

He stared at me, the glass halfway to his mouth. "Wasn't what?"

Maybe this was how it was when you thought your wife was cheating. You went back and forth from helpless sad sack to threatening prick. I guess even drug dealers could be pathetic victims.

"She was behaving herself."

"So where is she tonight?"

"At church, right?"

"Kevin was coming in from the Villas—said he saw her car heading out to the Parkway."

So I wasn't the only one in his network of informants. I had to give him something. "She's probably going to church in Cape May."

"Why do you say that?"

"'Cause she talked to Pauline about them going together."

"Who the fuck is Pauline?"

"She's my—this girl I been seeing, she's staying down there." Lou looked blank. "Didn't she tell you she was going with her?"

"No, no, she did not say that."

Why the fuck not, I was thinking. She was making things difficult.

"Well, you know...she's just..."

I had no idea what I meant, but the conversation was becoming impossible to continue.

"Tell me about Pauline."

"I met her in Cape May."

"What were you doing down there?"

It was my turn to stare while holding my glass of wine halfway to my mouth. "Trying to figure out what Concetta was doing there—like you asked."

"Okay, okay." Lou slumped a little. I poured him more wine, and he subsided onto his stool. "So, Pauline...?"

Now we were just talking about a girl. "She's French—I mean Canadian, right? I met her at the Jug."

"What, then you bring her back to our place?"

"Eventually."

"Eventually?" He laughed. "I like that. I meant, you must have brought her over, right? Unless Concetta was with you in Cape May, giving you pointers."

"Would you stop? Yeah, I brought her up for a day. Showed her the place." I waved my arm toward the dining room. "Then we went to the house. She and Concetta hit it off. And, you know, she's French, right, so she's Catholic. So now, they're going to Mass together."

Lou got up. He twirled his car keys, looking at me.

"I gotta go see someone." Lou jerked his head toward the door. "Why'n't you come with me?"

I thought about saying no, but I knew it wasn't really a request.

* * *

Lou talked casually as we drove, as if we were going to visit an old uncle.

"Guy's name is Cambro. Got a nice spread, maybe fifty acres. Always growing tomatoes." Lou shrugged and smiled, though it seemed a bit feigned. "He's alright. Sold him a few cars, you know?"

Cambro's place was an old farmhouse, with a lot of land, or at least there weren't any houses within half a mile of it. There was a barn at one end of the dirt and gravel driveway, in which I could just make out a tractor and some other bits of farming equipment. It was early evening now, but there was still a guy working on a very substantial flower garden in front of a picture window. He arose from his kneeling position, then waved us around toward the back of the house, returning to his work.

Cambro was in the middle of a tomato patch, maybe twenty yards long and ten yards wide. There was a cyclone fence ringing it, over six feet high, attached to tall metal poles, and another fence, a little more makeshift, chicken wire wound around green property stakes, a couple of yards outside it. He was staking up tomatoes. There were maybe a hundred plants in there from what I could figure.

He had to hear us coming up, but did not turn around. We stopped outside the fencing.

Lou called out, "Keeping the deer out?"

"I try." Cambro turned and pointed at the fences. "They do not like the two fences." He clapped his hands together to get rid of the dirt and opened a gate in the inside fence, then a corner of the chicken wire fence that was held in place by a bungee cord, a makeshift entrance. He came out and fastened it shut.

"Nice night, but the bugs…" He waved at a cloud of gnats. We followed him to a screened gazebo, the kind you stake out like a tent. He pulled back the flap for us. There were a few plastic chairs and a beat-up cooler, which he opened, clicked his tongue, then shut.

"Excuse me a minute."

Cambro walked to the back door, with a rolling gait. When he opened the door, a woman spoke sharply in Spanish. Lou and I sat down on either side of the cooler. The guy who had been working out front was now cleaning tools outside a little shed at the corner of the house.

I said, "So, this Cambro is…?"

Lou looked at me like I was a dim-witted child. "You want to ask him some questions, Mr. Detective?"

I shut up and tried to enjoy the balmy evening. The back door banged, and Cambro came across the yard with a half-dozen beers between his thick fingers. Lou held the flap open, and Cambro handed me one trio of bottles and jammed the others into the mostly melted ice in the cooler. He pointed at a rusty bottle opener tied to a string attached to one of the support poles.

Cambro pulled another chair close and lowered himself into it, the flimsy plastic legs splaying a little. He inclined his bottle toward us, and we clinked all around. He took a drink, foam sticking to his black moustache. We talked about tomatoes and the weather for a while before Cambro decided it was time to talk business.

"My *hombres* cleaned up the garage."

Lou nodded. "That's good."

"The…merchandise, it is, of course, all gone."

"Of course."

"Ramon's *familia*…they are worried. They have not heard from him." Cambro tapped his bottle on his leg. "I tell them we will find him, but…"

The alternative left unspoken was like a dark cloud that we had to accept and try to see through. We sat drinking our beers. After a few minutes, Cambro tossed his in the grass and pulled three more out of the tub, handing them around. He sat like a magistrate considering a messy case in his chambers. Then he spoke, the words careful and precise.

"Why did they not tell you what they want you to do? It is because they do not know how to do this. These *tough guys,*" he said the words in a disparaging tone, "they will find that it is not so easy. If a man say to me, I know who your mistress is, and I will tell your wife: I say, go ahead. Once he has done that, maybe he has fucked me, but he has nothing. And I am pissed off. Worse for him, maybe my wife is pissed off—it was much better for her not to know. This blackmail game is not a game for your lightweights.

"However, it is still a problem that the tape is out there. Maybe these people have other reasons to cause problems for us. Maybe they would be happy just to fuck our lives up. That is sad.

"So, we must find them and convince them that this game is not worth it. And they will find that getting their money—or selling the…merchandise—is a risky operation." Cambro smiled. "After all, it is we who are the professionals."

Lou was tapping his bottle against the leg of his chair. "And Ramon…?"

"My men...they are searching." Cambro lifted his bottle, catching a glint of the setting sun through it. "Is there anyone who...you think we should talk to? Maybe someone who is not such a friend of yours?"

Lou took a drink, in a way that told me he was deciding whether to say anything. He lowered the bottle from his lips and shook his head.

"I can't think of anybody."

Cambro looked at me, and I tried like hell to blank out my thoughts. He just smiled as if to say, I see what you're doing there, *amigo*. The back door opened, and a stream of Spanish issued. Cambro downed the rest of his beer.

"Eh, I must..."

He walked us around to the front, and we got into the car. Cambro put his hands on the roof, looking down at Lou.

"I keep you posted."

Lou put out his hand, and they shook. He pointed at a Lincoln parked near the house. "When you decide to upgrade that..."

Cambro banged his hand on the roof.

"*Absolutamente!*"

We drove in silence until we got past the Parkway and were driving through the marshlands toward Wildwood.

My mind kept going back to the image of Ramon with the gun to his frightened head. I was getting too skittish to manage my thoughts, so a question popped out.

"What about Arnie? Could he be...?"

Lou didn't say anything for half a minute, his knuckles gripping the steering wheel like it was somebody's neck. Finally, he spoke.

"Could be. But how would he know about that operation? And if you're wondering why I didn't mention him to Cambro, just think who the cops would want to talk to if something happened to Arnie."

I tried to smother my suspicions. "Seems out of his league."

"Yeah, well, like Cambro said, these guys don't seem like pros. And it's guys who aren't pros that you gotta worry about."

We were crossing the bridge into Wildwood. As Lou slowed down, he turned to me.

"I tell you, I wouldn't want to be whoever did this…you don't mess with Cambro. Don't let his country farmer act fool you."

I hadn't been fooled for a second.

Chapter Sixteen

"There's a lot of fags down here, right?"

Pinto said it like he was worried about bedbugs in a cheap hotel. It was Sunday afternoon, and we were just coming over the bridge into Cape May. I pulled the car into the lot of the first restaurant we came to.

Pinto fidgeted in the seat. "What, you hungry or something?"

"What did we talk about?"

"What?"

"I said, do me a favor and don't act like an asshole."

"What—did I say something?"

"Yeah—Jesus, Pinto—'fags'?"

"What, am I wrong? That's what I always heard."

"Is that important to you? You looking to meet someone? Maybe I can introduce you."

He gave me a serious look. "Don't you..."

I sat still for a minute, trying to figure out how to talk to him. I lowered my voice.

"Pinto, look. Yes, there are definitely some gay folks here."

He stared at me like he wasn't sure where this was heading. I went on.

"Just like in Wildwood."

His eyes shifted away. I continued.

"You know Sal? Guy who rents the chairs and umbrellas?"

"Yeah, I know Sallie. His dad had a bakery back in the neighborhood."

"Right. Sallie lives here all year, you know that?"

"No, I didn't, but so?"

"He's got a nice house. But no big surprise since the guy he lives with is a real estate agent."

"What, they share the house?"

"Yeah, they share it. They share everything. Armond, nicest guy you'd ever meet."

I had to let this sink in, as Pinto was slow picking up on it. Finally, he turned to me like I had told him there was no Santa Claus.

"Get the fuck. Sallie?"

I started the car and pulled back onto the main drag.

"These girls—they're from Quebec. They speak French. They're *sophisticated*."

I almost spelled the word out. Pinto looked hurt.

"I got it. Gay is good."

I nodded at his enlightened attitude. We stopped at a light close to the middle of town. I turned to say something and saw he had his troubled, thinking face on. He shook his head from side to side.

"Fuckin' Sallie."

* * *

"Yeah, I got it."

Pinto waved his hand at me from behind the wheel of the Caddy. He had on his sunglasses and was twisting and poking at the control buttons and knobs like he was a fighter pilot going through a pre-flight routine. A jet of washer fluid shot up onto the windshield. I was beginning to regret letting him take the car, but with Pinto, it was always regrets.

"Give me an hour and a half."

"Whatever you say, Chief."

The wheels chirped as he patched out, an impossible sound from that boat of a car. A joy ride in the Caddy was more than I should have had to pay, but it was a victory to have him not join me in visiting Davy.

They took me into a big room facing out to a veranda on the beach. It was hot, like a solarium, with glass doors and windows, floor to ceiling, and potted plants everywhere. At least there was a high ceiling with a bunch of fans hanging down. It didn't feel like a rehab place, and I guessed from what Sister Louise had said, it wasn't exactly that. But if you looked around, you could spot a few residents who had that itchy yet distant look that said they just wanted to get outside for a smoke.

"Hey."

I stood up and shook Davy's hand. Last time I had seen him was maybe two years ago, looking strung-out on the street outside a tough bar in South Philly. Now, he looked pretty good, in jeans and flip-flops, and a long-sleeve t-shirt. He sat down opposite me, and it did feel something like visiting a guy in prison.

"They say my dad asked you to check in on me." He shook his head. "I know that's a fucking lie."

A guy with white hair a few chairs down looked over.

Davy called out to him. "Sorry, man."

He jerked his thumb toward the veranda.

"Wanna go out?"

It was windy, but a lot more comfortable outside. We walked to the edge of the veranda and sat on the steps going down to the beach.

"So did my mom send you?"

"No."

I held out a pack of cigarettes. He took one and held it in front of him.

"You act like a cop."

I had to trust his judgment on that. I'm sure he'd had plenty of experience.

"They've been talking about you."

He lit his cigarette and snorted. "I can imagine."

"They're worried sick about you."

"And I should give a shit why?"

You little fuck, I thought. I smacked the cigarette out of his mouth.

"Why do you have to be such an asshole?"

He held his hand in front of his face like the cigarette was still there.

"Didn't you know, man? I'm a junkie." He picked the cigarette up and

171

brushed the sand off it. "How's things at the Seabreeze?"

"Guess your mom told you about that."

He laughed. "You trying to keep it a secret?"

I gave him the pack of matches. "You know a guy named Eduardo?"

"Lots of guys named Eduardo."

He was having trouble getting the cigarette lit. More than he should have, even with the wind.

"He's a dealer, lives in Buena. Mexican guy."

"Fuck." Davy threw the matchbook in the sand. I grabbed it and lit a match, cupping it in my hand. He leaned forward and sucked the flame in with a real hunger. He blew out the smoke with a relief that was uncomfortable to see. "Nah, I don't know him."

"He said he heard you were down here somewhere. Said you might be in trouble." I lit a cigarette for myself. "Then your pal Leo told us about what happened at the dog shack."

"That bullshit." He rocked back and forth, arms wrapped around his knees. "Glad to hear I'm such a celebrity."

He sounded more irritated than worried. I let him stew for a minute, and he twisted his head toward me.

"What are you doing talking to a fucking Mexican dealer in Buena?"

He had me there. "It's a long story."

"Everybody's got a fucking long story."

"Yeah, well, this one..."

I told him the whole fractured tale. That cheered him up a little.

He said, "Pinto. He's like a big kid."

He looked at the pack, and I nodded. He got another out and lit it off the one he had smoked down to the filter.

"I remember one Thanksgiving, Dad took me to the playground to play this turkey bowl game." He stood up and went down the steps to the beach. I followed him as he slipped out of his flip-flops and scuffed toward the water. "I was maybe thirteen. Most of the guys were older, twenties, thirties. Tackle." He gave me a rueful smile. "None of this touch shit. Guy was going after a pass, eyes up on the ball." He looked up, pointing with the cigarette.

"Then, Bam! Pinto blindsides the guy, just fucking levels him. Had to go to the hospital, broke a couple of ribs."

"Sounds like him."

"Yeah, an hour later, he's back in the alley, drinking homemade wine, laughing like he didn't do nothing."

We were at the edge of the water now. Davy seemed to have relaxed a little.

"So my mom really didn't send you?"

"No. She doesn't even know I know you're here."

He looked a little suspicious. Maybe he thought I was working for whoever he was in trouble with. Or maybe his dad. I thought, this kid needs truth.

"Your dad…he heard your mom was coming down here. He was worried she might be having an affair. He asked me to keep an eye on her while he was in the city."

"You must have loved that."

"Yeah. I mean…anything's possible, but I've known your mom a long time. So…one night she mentioned coming down here to Randall's—said it was for some real estate thing. Then a guy I work with said he knew Mark—the guy who owns it. And that Mark knew your mom. So I thought—maybe I should go see Mark, figure out if there was something going on with her and him."

"He must have been glad to see you."

I shrugged. "I figured out pretty quick he wasn't the right-type beau for Conci."

Davy shivered and gave a little chuckle. "Little light in the loafers."

"Right. So that got me wondering—why was she spending all this time down here? Then he told me about you, getting the job at the hot dog shack."

"Just like that?"

"I was straight with him—told him I was checking him out for Lou. I guess that scared him a little, and he opened up. Told me someone got your mom in touch with him."

He flinched. "That fuck Arnie."

No surprise there. "Guess you know he ripped off your dad."

"Once a crook, always a crook." Davy stabbed with his cigarette in the air. "Don't worry, smart guys like him always get wised up. His time will come." He huddled into himself, his shoulders seeming to vibrate. "I guess Leo told you where to find me."

"Eventually."

"Sure you're not a cop?"

I kicked at the slow ripples of foam. "Your mom says she's worried about you, but doesn't tell me—or your dad—that you're here. And people are telling me you're in trouble."

"And you work for my Dad but haven't told him anything?"

"Nope."

"Why the fuck not?"

Davy had a handful of pebbles and was throwing them into the water. I watched the little splashes.

"If I knew why your mom wasn't telling him…I don't know. I figured I'd talk to you first."

He had run out of pebbles. "She's always been a little scared of him."

"Are you?"

He dragged his foot over the foam as the tide sucked it back. "Fuck him."

I thought about Davy talking tough to Robert. One moment he's a lost child, the next he's a gangster wannabe. He started walking back to the retreat center. I followed along

"Who you in trouble with?"

He didn't answer. We went inside, and he put out his hand.

"I gotta go." He nodded toward a handful of people walking toward a smaller room off the lobby. "Group."

His hand was strong, and he held onto mine for a few seconds after I moved to drop mine.

"You're not gonna tell my dad you were here, right?"

"No." That was the answer he wanted. He sauntered off to his meeting, joking with a black girl in blue scrubs who laughed and tapped him on the arm.

I went outside and looked at my watch. Still ten minutes until Pinto would show up. That gave me enough time to sit on a concrete bench, smoke a cigarette, and try to shake off the sadness and anger that Davy had passed on like a bad cold.

* * *

"Ow!"

Pinto almost dropped the teapot as he tried to brace it with his left hand while pouring with his right. Brown tea splashed onto the white tablecloth. He pulled his hand back and wrung it in the air.

"Fucker's hot!"

He turned toward Lucie, who was reading a magazine.

"*Mademoiselle?*" He pronounced it *madame-moysel*. His pinkie wasn't quite extended, but he was heading in that direction.

Lucie nodded at her teacup and flicked a page in the magazine.

Pauline smiled and held out her cup. "Thank you, *monsieur*."

Fortunately, the girls had been willing to believe that Pinto was my friend when he knocked on their door. Now, Pauline was enjoying the show that was unfolding, in particular Lucie's dissatisfaction at being involved at all. She had picked this tea-room for our brunch with an unerring sense of Pinto's inability to fit in.

"So, *Monsieur* Pinto—" Pauline said.

"Please." A flourish with his hands. "Call me Dominic."

I poured myself some tea. "Okay, 'Dominic.'"

Pauline continued. "You are a colleague of John?" She said it like *"Jean"*, like Jean-Paul Belmondo.

"Yes, well," Pinto—sorry, Dominic—sat back and crossed his arms, "we're good friends."

"Oh? You seem—maybe a little older than he?"

Pinto waved his hand. "Hey, what's a few years? You're only as young as you feel, right?"

He directed this comment at Lucie. He seemed like he was going to clap her on the leg, and I was glad he did not.

"And you feel quite young?"

Pauline sure had a way of belittling someone behind her French girl façade.

Pinto looked around the room, I'm thinking the first tea-room he had ever been in: little old ladies, young women in small groups, a few couples, the men looking relaxed and well-dressed. His neck muscles loosened, and maybe he had snuck a little Thai stick during his drive, but he seemed to be softening before my eyes.

"You know, it's not about being young, right?"

Lucie looked up from her copy of *Elle*. "*Non?*"

"No, it's about…appreciating the beauty that's around you."

Lucie closed her magazine.

Pauline patted Pinto's hand. "*Vraiment, mon petit.*"

"*Vraiment.*" Pinto echoed the word back, mimicking her pronunciation.

I got up and led the group outdoors to stroll the pedestrian mall with its little shops. I had no idea how you did this so I just walked and joined in the peering into antique shops. I stopped at a bench and tugged Pauline aside. We sat as Pinto and Lucie continued to wander, Pinto the one who dallied longer in front of a shop window filled with old knick-knacks and jewelry.

"How was Saturday Mass?"

Pauline's face scrunched up. "They wore…flip-flops?"

"You mean the…attendees?"

"Yes, I do not mean the priest. Though that would not surprise me. Perhaps he had the surfing shorts under his cassock."

"Well, isn't it more important what people…"

She cut me short. "Do you go to the church?"

"I, well, not recently."

"Then you will shut your mouth."

I did as I was told. I went and bought some popcorn, and when I got back, she was ready to talk.

"After mass, she go to the little altar, put money in the slot and light a candle. I ask her what she prays for. Then she start."

"Starts what?"

"To cry. Then we talk, and she tells me about Davy. She put Davy in that

176

place. He was afraid of the…gangsters?…you would say?"

"Yeah, he didn't tell me she got him in there, but I figured that was how it worked."

"He went first to another…a *clinique*…to do the, how you say…*le retrait*…"

"Withdrawal?"

"Yes, he went the cold turkey. Now maybe he is better."

"He looked better than I expected."

"Yes, but it is every day he must do the same." She dipped her fingers in the popcorn which for some reason was very sexy. "That is how Concetta talked."

"Did she say what these…gangsters wanted?"

She sniffed. "You are not being the good detective today."

"He owes money, I would guess."

"That is the bull's eye."

I supposed it was a junkie's lot to owe money—or have stolen money—one way or another.

"So she's paying the retreat bill for him?"

She coaxed more popcorn from the box. Pinto was coming out of the shop. Lucie was sitting in the middle of the mall at the base of a tree, reading a book.

"She say she pays some. They are being…friends to her. There is a nun; she was a schoolgirl with Concetta. So she is…'cutting her slack'. That is what she said. What does it mean?"

"Doing her a favor."

"What is 'the slack'?"

A good question. "Is she paying off his debts, too?"

Pauline shrugged. Pinto was in front of us.

"Look at this."

It was some kind of image in a wooden frame, a wheel with eight points and a complicated design inside it, a whole lot of squares inside squares, and other ornate stuff. Pinto touched the surface with his hand.

"It's made out of sand."

Pinto sounded more like Leo the surfer dude than his usual street-tough self.

"The lady said it's a mandala." He looked up for Lucie. "Whatever the fuck that is."

That sounded more like the real Pinto.

"A path to enlightenment." This was Lucie talking, moving close beside Pinto, pressing closer to him than I ever imagined possible. She touched his chest. "Are you a Buddhist?"

"No." He said this in a tone that implied he would be willing to consider it.

I got up and started walking again with Pauline, as Pinto and Lucie considered paths to enlightenment.

"I wonder if that's why Concetta's gotten into this real estate thing."

Pauline turned her hand in the air. "She was not ready to talk about that. But, I think, yes."

"Christ. And I'm sure Lou knows nothing about this."

"That is for fucking sure."

I looked at her. She turned a little red.

"I am sorry. I try out your American slang."

We kept walking, away from the mall, into residential streets that were leafier than anything you would see in Wildwood. It was a very nice town, but I did feel like an intruder.

Pauline had her right hand wrapped around my left arm and held my right hand in her left hand. It seemed more like an Indian wrestling grip than any hand-holding method I knew. There was a bench in the middle of the block, just off the sidewalk on the edge of a well-maintained lawn next to a restored Victorian house. Again, unlike Wildwood. We sat and held hands some more. Lucie and Pinto were coming down the street towards us, not holding hands, but very close, Lucie gripping a book as she bent into him, reading aloud.

"Your friend, he is trying."

"Yeah, he's trying all right."

"No, he seems to change, a little."

I shook my head. They sat on the steps of a walkway leading up to a big house. Lucie was making Pinto read something. All this romance was great, but I was even more worried about Davy and Concetta than before.

"Why is Concetta being so secretive about all this? If Davy's in trouble, you'd think she would have to tell Lou at some point."

Pauline lit a cigarette. I didn't take the one she offered—it made me think too much of Davy.

"I guess it is not that point yet."

"I mean, I get that she thinks he'll blow up—but what would he really do?"

Pauline blew out a short puff of smoke. "Lou is perhaps a gangster, too?"

She was certainly a quick study. Pinto and Lucie were in front of us. I got off the bench.

"Come on. I need something to wash that tea out of my mouth."

* * *

Pauline gave me a reproving look as we walked in the door of Randall's.

"It is much too early for *le dîner.*"

"That's alright, I just want le drinkee." I led our group across to the entrance to the bar. "And I'm hoping to track down a guy named Arnie."

"A friend?"

"Kind of the opposite."

It was not even five yet, and there was no one at the bar. I was glad that Mark had not been there to greet us, although I was ready for that. The bartender seemed happy to have someone to distract him from his setup tasks. We sat with our wine, Pinto at one end, back straight and hands in his lap, like a good schoolboy on a class trip. The wine was good, I would give Mark that, my taste becoming more educated under Robert's guidance.

The bartender was the same one who had been there last time. He was talking French to the girls. I watched Pinto, concerned that hair would start growing out the back of his shirt and he'd pull a Lon Chaney Jr. But the bartender was a pro and didn't abuse his position. I picked a couple of salted almonds out of a pewter bowl.

"Nice spot. I'd think you might get a few folks stopping by for a drink."

Pauline chimed in. *"Oui, tout à fait charmant."*

"Merci." A modest bow from the bartender.

I continued. "Oh, Pauline, I forgot to mention. I was in here a week ago—stopped by to see Mark—and I saw Arnold. You remember him?"

"Certainement." She smiled at the bartender. *"Un bon homme."*

That was my girl. Didn't even need a cue card.

"I was in a rush, so I didn't stop to chat," I said.

The bartender had a wary look, which was good. That meant he probably knew Arnie and maybe didn't think he was so *bon* an *homme*. I turned back to him.

"Last time I saw him—I think maybe last summer—he was working at some little place in Wildwood." I pointed at my glass and our man—Gilbert, per his name tag—poured me out more of his excellent red.

I asked him, "Do you know if he's still working there?"

Gilbert shook his head. "No, he left there sometime this year." His English was good, with just the slightest hint of a French accent.

"Must have gotten a better offer. Then again," I winked at Pauline, "what wouldn't be a better offer, right?"

She sniffed as if the very thought of the Seabreeze gave her indigestion. Gilbert refilled her glass without being asked. She said a few words in French, saying his name with a soft "g"—okay, I was playing a dope, though I wouldn't have known anyway. He came back with the French as well. They went back and forth. Gilbert frowned and washed a glass over and over as he recounted a little tale to her.

I acted like I couldn't understand anything they were saying—which was true—and couldn't care less—which was not. Pinto and Lucie were talking quietly, Pinto sipping the wine as if it were the first vintage he had tasted that wasn't made in someone's basement, which was probably close to the truth. A waitress appeared at the end of the bar and Gilbert floated down to serve her. I nudged Pauline.

"So?"

She gave me a withering look. "Do you want to blow the covers?"

"How is the chardonnay?"

180

"Good. We can leave now."

Gilbert was back in front of us, the slightest of smiles going toward Pauline as he prepared drinks. I dropped a much-too-large bill on the bar and slid off the chair.

I raised my voice and spoke in a silly accent. "Come, my dear, we must away."

I wasn't sure what nationality I was imitating there, but I felt I had to do some sort of acting. Of course, Pinto left a grotesque tip as well, no doubt to impress Lucie. He hadn't changed that much. Gilbert gave us a sincerely enthusiastic wave, a spring in his step as he restored the zinc bartop to its former pristine state.

We walked hand-in-hand down the street. This double-date thing was nice, but now I was truly hungry.

Pauline smiled at me. "So now we have the dinner?"

"Definitely."

"And I know the where."

"Lead on, mistress."

She dropped my hand. "So I am your mistress now?"

I needed to stop being clever with the words. I hadn't meant that at all. "No, I'm sorry."

She folded her arms. "How can I be the mistress if you have no wife?"

Up ahead, Pinto and Lucie were arm-in-arm. I guess a few hours was not long enough to begin having fights. Pauline unloosed her arms and took my hand again.

"It is alright. It is all my little plan. We go to the bar with the piano." She poked my ribs with her elbow. "Gilbert told me there we find Arnie."

"Oh." The quick departure made sense now. "And maybe we'll see Rudy there too?"

"Mais, oui."

"Think you're pretty clever, don't you?"

She tilted her head. "So you must now tell me about Mr. Arnie."

I gave her the basics on Arnie as she led us back down to the mall to a tavern I had probably walked by dozens of times but never been in: "The

Hideaway", as it said in old English script above the door. I could just picture Concetta having a nervous smoke with Mark, watching the tourists stroll by.

Inside, it was dark and a nice change from the places that catered to twenty-year-olds and had rock and roll bands almost every night. I'm not sure I'd call it a piano bar, as the piano was not embedded in the bar, and there wasn't any singing going on right then. But there was a piano player, an older black guy who was playing jazz at a sedate pace. We got a table close to him that had a good view of the bar, and Arnie did us a favor by not showing up until we had a chance to order.

Maybe Arnie was just a misunderstood soul. After all, he helped Concetta out by introducing her to Mark. But I wondered whether Davy's opinion about his future well-being had anything to do with his visit to the Seabreeze and his message for Concetta.

Pinto and Lucie were sitting opposite us, facing away from the bar, which was good, as the sight of Arnie might have been enough to snap Pinto out of his good-behavior trance. And then there he was, coming through the door in the same classy jacket he had worn when I met him at the Seabreeze, looking like he had just come from the hair stylist. A few people at the bar waved from their posts, and Arnie slid in next to a burly guy who I guessed had a mermaid tattoo on his arm.

Pinto caught me looking toward the bar and turned around, the transformation beginning.

"Fuck." He jerked his head fast back to me. "That's fucking Arnie."

Larry Talbot to the Wolfman in ten seconds. For a second, I was glad to see the old Pinto, but then he started to get up. I grabbed his arm.

"Just sit down."

"That creep. I was pissed when Lou cut us out of that action."

"I'm sure Purcell will do a fine job."

"He ain't done it yet."

I had to agree. Arnie looked too spry to have been recently squashed. Pinto was crouched back now, his fingers thumping the table. Then his face lit up.

"Fuck. That's why we're here, right?"

Our food arrived, and I spent a few minutes with my hamburger before getting up, which prompted Pinto to attempt the same. I held up a finger.

"Give me a few minutes."

I nodded at Lucie, who put on a stage smile and held Pinto down with a firm grip on his thigh that was not entirely loving. I crossed the room and stopped behind the two miscreants.

"Mr. Goldbaum."

Arnie swiveled around on his stool. He didn't look that surprised to see me. No doubt, Mark and maybe even Gilbert had let him know I was prowling around town.

"Mr. McGinty." A fake-friendly greeting. "Let me get you a drink."

"That's okay." I gestured toward our table. Pinto and Lucie were still engrossed in their deepening relationship, though I knew his spidey-sense was on high alert. Pauline gave a little wave. "We just stopped in for a bite—wanted to say hi."

"Well, hi, then."

Arnie was watching Rudy staring at Pauline. I instantly loathed him. Rudy tapped Arnie on the arm.

"Hey, that chick was in here the other day. She was real..."

"Real what?" I cut him off.

Rudy looked at Arnie, his expression saying "who the fuck is this guy?" Arnie's look back told him to shut the fuck up. I felt pretty sure that Arnie had noticed Pinto seething at the table. I turned back to Arnie and pointed toward the door.

"You got a minute?"

"For you?" He slid off the stool. Rudy glanced over at the table where Pinto glared cheerily at us. I think Rudy wanted to come play with us, but Arnie gave him a signal to stay.

Outside the bar, Arnie took out a tin of some kind of imported tobacco product. I accepted a gold-filtered cigarette and a light from Arnie's gold-plated lighter. I came straight to the point.

"You talk to Mark?"

"Yeah." He scanned the walkers-by, avoiding my eyes. "You found out what you want, right? He's not fucking her. So what do you want from me?"

"Forget that. I'm trying to help Concetta—and Davy. I just talked to him."

"She ask you to help?"

"Maybe she's afraid to ask."

"And I'm supposed to help how?"

"You helped her once—with Mark."

"So now I gotta spend the rest of my life keeping her junkie kid out of trouble?"

I moved in front of him. "You don't act like much of a friend."

Arnie took a deep drag on his cigarette. "I know you're no cop, but you sure act like one."

"What kind of trouble is he in?"

"How the fuck should I know?"

"Didn't Concetta tell you?"

"She told me he needed a job."

I looked at the people strolling the mall, wondering if this was how a blackmailer and possible murderer acted. I looked back and he had tossed his butt on the pavement and was squashing it with a pointy-toed shoe. He started to move toward the door. I stepped in front of him.

"Why were you looking for Concetta that day at the Seabreeze?"

He lifted his chin up. "You're the chief inspector now? And you send your little French sidekick in ahead of you to waggle her tits and see what she can find out?"

My fist went into his stomach right below the button of his blazer. He bent over, but I didn't give him the follow-up shot to his chin that he deserved. I went back into the bar.

A happy voice greeted me. "Heyyyy!"

Pinto stood next to Rudy, beaming, Lucie curled into the crook of his elbow. Pauline was on Arnie's stool, and Rudy was doing his best not to look at her. Pinto beamed, lit from within by a weird combination of true love and a lucky meeting with a couple of punks who needed some education.

Arnie came in after a minute, still looking a little green. Pinto put his glass

184

on the bar and clapped his hands, then rubbed them together.

"Arnie, my friend—long time!"

Arnie's face went a little greener, making me wonder if their paths had crossed in some unfortunate way in the past. Rudy was being quiet; he had figured out pretty quick what kind of guy Pinto was, and that if he wanted him to sit and talk nice with the girls, that was what he was going to do.

"So, maestro, any news to report?"

Pauline handed me a bottle of beer. I winced a little as I took it, my hand not being in such great punching shape. Pinto put it all together quickly and tilted his glass toward me in a show of respect. Rudy looked like he had swallowed some bad clams. I figured Pinto had been so friendly to him while we were outside that he knew he was close to getting his ass kicked.

I swigged at the beer. "Unfortunately, I'm still in the dark on Davy's problems."

Rudy put up his hands. "That kid—walked off the fucking job on me."

"Shut the fuck up, Rudy." Arnie's resolve was coming back. He turned to me. "It's not that complicated. He got himself in trouble with some guys in Philly—dealers, right—owes a shitload of money, skipped out on it. Comes crying to mama. I got her in touch with Mark, figured he could help. He gets this fuck," Arnie jabbed a thumb at Rudy, "to give the junkie kid a job. Then the kid bolts from that, too."

I shot back. "Because he was scared out of his wits. Leo told me about the graffiti threat."

"Yeah, South Philly guys don't fuck around. But what the fuck do you want us to do about that?"

Pauline poked a fingernail at Arnie. "You—I think you are the lying fuck. You rip Lou off. How can Concetta trust you? You must know more."

"So I'm the bad guy?" Arnie laughed. "I don't think so. Listen, ask yourself this: why isn't she talking to hubby about all this?"

"How do you know she is not?" Good job, Pauline, keep this joker talking.

"How? First, she told Mark she didn't want to tell Lou, because she was afraid Lou would just cut the kid loose. Second, she's fucking wrong, because if she did tell Lou, he'd be down here in two seconds, ripping that kid out of his retreat house." Arnie was warming up. "Maybe the kid's even more scared of that."

Pinto set his glass delicately on the bar and spread his hands.

"Okay, enough. I just want to know one thing. Who are the fucks that are after this kid?"

Arnie shook his head. "No idea."

Pauline took my arm and started to pull me away, Lucie trying to do the same with Pinto, but now he was fully back into his true character. He put his face close to Arnie's.

"But you know they're from South Philly, huh? Don't worry. I'll find out. But you get any sudden memories, you let me know."

Davy's observation about Arnie being wise seemed spot on, but I didn't figure I had to let him know Davy's opinion about how soon he would get even smarter. We left them there and went out to the mall. It was a beautiful early evening. The girls went ahead of us, and Pinto put his arm through mine like we were a couple of swell guys on a boulevard in Paris. He took the hand that had been in Arnie's stomach and palpated the digits, which hurt.

"Ow!"

Pinto laughed. "I love you, man."

* * *

It was touching watching Pinto and Lucie say goodnight on the steps of the house. Pauline's knuckles ground into my stomach and brought me back to earth.

"What happens next?"

I wasn't sure. We had left Arnie and Rudy in the bar, looking like a couple of horse thieves that had escaped the Lone Ranger for the moment. Pauline unclenched her fist and rubbed my side.

I said, "Good job getting him going—calling him a liar."

"He is that."

"Yeah, I figured that out."

"But there is something more."

"Which is?"

"He ask us—why Concetta does not tell Lou about this? We must answer that question."

I thought about it. He had said that Concetta was worried about Lou cutting the kid loose. But then he said no way that would happen. Lou would get his kid out; not that he wouldn't personally kick the kid's ass once he got his hands on him.

Pauline stepped away and folded her arms. "He say that when I say that he had stolen from Lou."

"What would that mean?"

Pauline shrugged. "Maybe there is another part of this story that she does not want Lou to hear."

"Hey, big guy."

Pinto stood by the car, his hand on the door handle. He smiled at Pauline. "Nice job back there, madame."

Pauline gave a little click of the tongue. *"Mademoiselle, s'il vous plait."*

Pinto opened the door. "You French chicks got class."

We kissed, and I could feel she was crying just a little.

"I worry. We do not have time."

"Are you going back to Quebec?"

"No, no. It is Davy. I worry about *ces voyous.*"

"Uh…"

"Those bad men."

I held her back from me and looked in her eyes. "You stay away from them."

She stared right back. "I do what I have to."

As we drove back up toward Wildwood, I thought about Davy, his anger at his Dad, and what he said about Arnie getting his. I glanced over at Pinto.

"Never figured you for such a romantic."

His hand flipped out in a gesture of helplessness. I looked at the water and reeds as we passed through wetlands.

"You know I'm going to need your help, podner."

He put his hand on my shoulder. "I'm still on the job, Kemosabe."

Chapter Seventeen

I went into the restaurant Monday morning but could not stay focused. At lunchtime, I went back to Lou's place, just to have some time to think, or at least to worry without anyone noticing how scared I looked.

The place was quiet. Lou had gone back to South Philly, and Concetta was at work. I was making a sandwich when Concetta came up the stairs. She paused for a moment, looking around the room like I wasn't there, then went into her bedroom. She was making a lot of noise, banging things around. I took my sandwich and a Coke and sat at the kitchen table. The door to her room opened, and she came out with a suitcase.

I took a bite of my salami and cheese. "Going somewhere?"

She set the suitcase down. "I want to get away for a few days."

I thought for a second that maybe Lou had told her what was going on, maybe even said to get out of town. But I doubted she knew anything about this sideline of his.

She looked like she might fall down any second. I came over and took the suitcase out of her hand.

"Sit down. You want something to eat?"

She shook her head and sat at the table. She was crying, sniffing loudly. Something told me this wasn't about Lou and his dealings.

I pulled my chair close to hers and touched her shoulder. "Is this about Davy?"

She didn't say anything. Bringing this headache back on top of everything else pushed me to the brink. I pulled my hand away and spoke sharply.

"Why didn't you tell me about Davy?"

189

She shook her head, wiping her eye with a napkin. I kept at her.

"And you don't tell Lou? But you get Mark to help you?"

Then I thought of another point of pain

"And how the fuck does Arnie end up being your best pal?"

She sat in shock as it sank in that I knew all this. Then she stood up and went to the suitcase. I jumped up and grabbed her arms, and she struggled against me.

"Fucking let me go!"

I almost slapped her, but I figured that only worked in the movies. I just held her and moved her into the living room and pushed her onto the couch.

"You gotta talk. I've seen Davy. I've seen Arnie and the creep that gave Davy a job. So I want to know why the fuck you're sneaking around and not telling your fucking husband what's going on."

She took a couple of breaths and didn't look like she was going to bolt again. She pointed to the sink.

"Can I get some water?"

I filled a glass and gave it to her.

She talked in a quiet voice. "Sister Louise called. Some guy came to see Davy last night." She drank the water like it was medicine. "One of the girls said she could hear them shouting at each other. I tried to call him, but he wasn't in his room. I'm worried. I gotta go see him."

"You gotta talk to Lou."

"He'll kill him. I mean, he won't kill him, but—I don't know what he'd do."

I wasn't buying it.

"Okay, I'll tell Lou."

"You can't do that." Her voice was hysterical.

"No? Watch me."

I walked into the kitchen and picked up the phone. She was on her feet in a second, trying to get there first. I let her beat me.

"Come on. Arnie said to ask you why you hadn't told Lou." I held up my hand, which was yellow and purple around my knuckles. "I busted him a good one in the gut, so I owe him that."

"You can't tell Lou."

"Fine, go ahead, go see your boy. I'll wait until you leave, then I'll call him."

She put her hands up to her face, bent over. She wasn't making any noise, then I could see her body was shaking. I put my arm around her and moved her down onto a kitchen chair.

"Why can't I talk to Lou?'

She shivered a little. I could see she was really scared.

"It's Arnie…"

How did they do this? The cops, I mean. I pictured her with a blanket around her shoulders, a Styrofoam cup of coffee.

"What, what…?" I was wishing I had let Pinto operate on the well-dressed thief.

She shook her head. "No, I can't…"

"Stop this, you just gotta tell me."

I went and got her a water glass and gave it to her. She drank from it like an alcoholic with the shakes. I was afraid she would break it, the way she was gripping it.

"Davy…he was in deep with some people…said he owed a lot of money and needed help. I said only if he would go into treatment. He said he would, but he was afraid…like these guys were going to come after him. So I got him a little money so he could give them something, say the rest is coming. Then he took off down here—I got him into a rehab place in the sticks, back in the beginning of May, out past the Courthouse, he was there like three weeks. Then he got a job at this place on the boardwalk, and this nun—Sister Louise—she helped me get him into the retreat house."

"You never thought about telling Lou?"

"I couldn't tell him…"

"You keep saying that. Why?"

"I…at first I just didn't want to tell him. We just don't talk about it now. If I asked, he'd go off the handle. Maybe try to go after the…whoever he owed the money to…or find him and…I don't know. He's put him on the street already, once. I thought I could, you know…handle it myself."

"So that's why you got into the real estate thing?"

"Yeah. But I wasn't making hardly anything. Carol gave me some advances, but…that just turned into another debt. I needed cash for Davy's rehab, that was a lot, then just to keep him afloat. Plus we didn't know when the…dealers, the drug guys, would show up looking for their cash. So, I…" She blew out hard. "You gotta promise not to tell Lou."

"I can't promise anything right now."

"It started when I found out. About Arnie."

"You mean him dippin' in the till?"

"Yeah. He was out one day…there was a delivery, a big one, liquor. The account was overdue—Sheila couldn't write the check, she didn't have the, you know, signing authority. Plus she never handled that stuff. Lou was at the dealership, so she called me. I came in and paid the guy, then after he left, I figured I should look over the order."

I had a bad feeling, but I tried to avoid it. I waited for her to keep going.

"It was all wrong. I mean, the invoice was for stuff that wasn't in the order at all. It was way overbilled."

"When was this?"

"Like the first week of June."

I made a lame attempt to keep this from going off the skids. "Okay—so you told Lou and Arnie got fired, right?"

She shook her head. She tried to talk, and her mouth was dry. I refilled her glass.

"No, no, you see—I didn't tell Lou."

"Then how—?"

"I went to Arnie. I was through all the cash I had." She laughed. "I was pawning jewelry. Thank God Lou never remembers what he gives me. So I worked out a deal with Arnie."

Now my mouth was dry. "You were skimming along with him?"

"Yeah. Can you believe it? But I needed it." The tears were back in force.

"Did you tell Arnie why you needed the cash?"

"He knew I was dealing with Davy. He had put me in touch with Mark to get him the job."

Good neighbor Arnie. "So…?"

"Everything was good for a few weeks. Then something…somehow, right before the Fourth of July, Sheila figured out what was going on. I don't know, maybe Robert got suspicious, or Kevin, and they told her to look into it. So she went to Lou."

"So why didn't Arnie tell Lou about you?"

She shrugged. "He acted all noble about it—when we talked later."

This made sense, but then it didn't. "Maybe he figured he wasn't going to help himself by throwing you under the bus, too."

"Something like that." She sank into the chair like the weight of all this was taking her down. "Or he just figured this was something he had on me that he could...you know, use some day."

"Is that it?" I knew it wasn't.

"It's Arnie..." Her voice was a croak.

"What?" I felt like we were looking into a hole in a wall in a dark basement that had a bad smell coming from it.

"He's helping—with Davy."

Of course. That made perfect sense. As in no sense at all. I stood up.

"I need a cigarette."

I thought for a second about finding that bit of Thai stick to put me in another world, but I knew it would just make it worse. I found a crumpled pack on my bureau and went out on the porch. Concetta stayed in her chair, looking at her hands like a kid outside the principal's office.

I was into the second cigarette when she came out. I inhaled more nicotine than I was used to, just so I could feel it, and tried to keep my voice low and calm.

"I can't believe you're trusting Arnie, not Lou. It's his kid too, you know."

She came over and sat down. "Arnie's helping—"

Low and calm were out the window as I yelled at her. "Arnie ain't helping with shit!" Someone came out on their deck a couple of houses down, pretending to be looking at the sky. I lowered my voice. "So what the fuck is he doing?"

"He—he knows the guys who are—who Davy owes money to. He's helping..."

I cut her off. "Do not say the word 'help' again."

193

I got close to her where she stood, clutching the railing.

"Don't tell me you've given him money."

She didn't nod her head, but she didn't shake it either. She was crying again.

"Fuck." I yelled it loud. The person on the other porch came to the end of it and called over.

"Hey, can you keep it down?"

"Sorry," I called out. I took her hand, led her inside, and put her on the sofa. I had more questions than when I started. "Tell me about Arnie."

She exhaled like she was blowing out for a doctor. "I thought everything was okay when Davy got down here. No one bothered him. I mean, he still needed money, just to live. But nobody had come looking for him. He got that hot dog job—you know, that shack on the—"

"Yeah, I know about that, go on."

"You know about the graffiti?"

"Yeah."

"That got us both worried again. I saw Arnie at Randall's. He had heard about it from Rudy or Mark. He said maybe he could help—talk to these… dealers in South Philly. So, he did and said he worked out a deal. They'd lay off, he'd handle the payments, we had to come up with…well, it was less that what he owed. I was hoping I'd make a sale, pay it all off at once. But," she managed a broken smile, "it's not as easy as I thought."

"So you've been giving it to him bit by bit."

"He was taking it out of my cut—you know from the Seabreeze. Until that went south."

"So now you're paying him direct."

"When I can…"

I thought back to Arnie's visit to the Seabreeze. "Was that why he stopped in to the restaurant? To give you a reminder that he still needed to get paid."

"Yeah. I called him after that, told him I'd get him what I could. He told me then…don't even think about going to Lou and telling him…what Arnie was doing for us."

"Because…"

"Lou would think…he wouldn't believe Arnie was really helping me."

Which would have been a brilliant observation on his part.

"And if you did tell Lou?"

"He'd tell Lou about my…well, ripping him off."

This was all sorts of fucked-up.

I wanted to ask her if she thought it was Arnie visiting Davy in his room, but she didn't look like she could handle any more questions. Arnie seemed to be everywhere there was Scolletta money to be touched. But with his sharp clothes and weasel-like personality, he just came off as a grifter who liked soft targets to me.

I went into the kitchen and got a glass of water. This time the phone looked at me, like who are you going to call? But I had no answer. Maybe I was a coward, but as my thoughts turned back to Ramon and the impending blackmail, I doubted it was a good time to have a heart-to-heart with Lou about his wayward son.

Chapter Eighteen

It was a minor victory getting her to stay. At least I wouldn't have to call Lou to report her missing, or tell him where she was. At this point, I was living minute to minute, trying to avoid the multiple catastrophes waiting to happen. That night, I slept on the couch so I'd have a chance of seeing her if she tried to sneak out.

I was up early, worried Tuesday morning, and finally she came out for coffee around nine, looking like she either hadn't slept or had taken a huge dose of sleeping pills. I putzed around, cleaning up the kitchen and sorting through laundry until she appeared from her room dressed for work. She wasn't in any mood to talk and left in a hurry.

Driving in Lou's car to Lou's restaurant, I thought about how it was that I had not called Lou as soon as she left. It was like my mind was a glass of water already full, and some demon kept pouring troubles into it.

By lunchtime, I was behind the bar trying to remember how to make a Singapore Sling when Kevin showed up for his shift. As usual, he spread the Cape May County Herald out on the bar and drank coffee, ignoring the waitresses who were looking to get their orders filled. I had learned that this was how he worked—you had to give him this first fifteen minutes to finish the paper, which he read cover to cover, before he was willing to perform his duties.

I made a few drinks, and then Kevin flipped over the last page and pushed the paper aside, moving immediately into setup work. I dragged the newspaper over and leafed through it.

"Anybody you know die?" I asked.

Kevin was a big reader of the obituaries—the Irish Sweepstakes, he called it. Find yourself not there, and you've won for the day.

Kevin poured a bucket of ice into the bin. "Don't think so. Except maybe the guy they found in the water yesterday."

"What do you mean?"

"They found a body—they couldn't identify him, so who knows, maybe I know him." He put the bucket back below the bar. "But then, he looked like maybe he was a spic, so probably not."

I found the picture atop a short article. Body found. Gunshot wound. Police interested in anyone who can identify the man.

Even bloated by a couple of days in the water, the face was unmistakable. I felt cold and nauseous for a moment, and a fear went through me, like in a dream where you've done something horrible, or something horrible has happened, you're not sure which, but it's going to change everything and you can't get away from it.

"I need two glasses of white."

A waitress had her brown tray at the service bar, ticking a pen against one of the chrome rails that set it off. I turned the page over so I wouldn't have to see the face.

She tapped the pen on the tray. "C'mon, they're getting antsy."

I poured out two glasses of house white. She moved away, and I walked fast into the kitchen and through it to the back door. No one was out there, and I sat on a crate and wished to God I had a cigarette.

This was fucked up. I kept repeating that to myself, but it wouldn't go away. One of the dishwashers came out to toss some garbage in a bin. He looked for a second like he was going to join me, but wavered and went back inside.

I stayed outside until I realized I couldn't avoid reality. I went back behind the bar and thought about calling Lou. But I figured this type of news travelled fast in his circle.

* * *

Around two, I was helping out in the kitchen, cutting carrots and thinking about how to explain all this Concetta/Davy business to Lou, when Kevin came in from the bar.

"Hey," he said.

I beckoned him over with the knife, but he nodded at the prep cooks working next to me and shook his head. I followed him back to the office, where the phone handset was sitting on its side. Next to it was a bottle of whiskey and a glass. I knew he came in here to make calls to his bookie.

Kevin was nervous. "It's some lady." He looked around and used a whisper that was louder than his usual voice. "She says it's about Davy."

He looked like he wished he had not heard that. He put his hand on the door.

"I gotta get…"

I waited for the door to shut and picked up the phone.

"This is Ginty."

"Hello." The voice recalled the ocean and seagulls. "This is Sister Louise."

"Hi." Please, God, no bad news.

"Have you seen Concetta today?"

"In the morning." I hated when someone started with a question like that. It meant they had something they weren't looking forward to saying.

"I've been trying to reach her."

"She was heading into work when I last saw her."

"Really?"

Oh, Christ. "Yes."

"I called her at home and got no answer, so I called her real estate office. They said she didn't come in today. She called in sick."

"Maybe she's at home and just didn't answer." Was I trying to fool her or myself?

"I guess that's possible." A pause. "Can you check on that?"

This was too much. "Look, I'm at work. What's going on, do you need to talk to her now?"

If a throat could make a noise just tightening, hers made it. "Davy's gone."

I picked up the bottle, considered the glass, and decided it would be faster without it. She didn't speak right away, so I took another gulp.

"How long's he been gone?"

She gasped a little before she spoke, like maybe she had a bottle on her end, too. "He went out for a walk this morning—maybe around ten."

"He usually do that?"

"A lot of the time, yes. But he's always back within an hour or so."

"Anybody call him this morning?"

"Yes, he had a call right before he went out. A woman."

"Concetta?"

"Maybe."

"Have you called the police or anything?"

"Why would we do that? We're not a prison. He's free to go when he pleases."

"So why were you calling Concetta?"

"I'm concerned. He—you know he's had problems."

Really? "I know."

"He was doing so well. I'd hate to see him…start up again."

Sheila opened the door and stuck her head in. I waved her off pointing at the phone. She gave me a cross look then left. I squeezed my temples hard, but failed to feel the pain I wanted.

"Look, I'll check on Concetta at home and let you know."

I wished the problems would sit still for a moment so I could figure out what to do. The door opened again, and Sheila stepped inside.

"I got Lou on the line for you."

Why not?

* * *

Lou's voice was grim.

"You see the paper?"

I was at the phone behind the bar. Sheila was at the other end talking to a couple of waitresses, and Kevin was playing with bottles and glasses.

"Yeah. Can I call you right back?"

I hung up and walked past Sheila fast, trying to blank my mind so she couldn't use her female intuition on me. I got Lou back on the phone in the office.

He started in. "Jesus, these fucking guys…and I got a note from them…"

I cut him off. "Have you talked to Concetta today?"

"No, why the fuck—" he caught himself, and his voice slowed down, "no, not today, why, what's up?"

"It's Davy. He's in trouble."

"No shit, he's always in trouble."

I started talking, hoping I could figure out what to say and not say as I went along.

"He's been at a…like a retreat house in Cape May…trying to get straight, I guess."

"How do you know that?"

First lie. "Concetta told me."

"And you didn't fucking tell me?"

Second lie. "She just told me today."

"Didn't I tell you to keep an eye on her?"

I wasn't sure what that meant, so I didn't answer.

His voice got harsh. "Fuck me." There was a sharp noise—the headset being slammed on the table, I guessed—followed by a louder bang, definitely a door being shut. He came back on. "Do I have to come down there and straighten your fucking ass out?"

I hadn't even told him the good stuff yet. "Yeah, you might. Concetta told me he's in over his head with some dealers in South Philly. She knows some nun at this retreat place, so she got him in there."

"Jesus fucking Christ. This nun got a guy with a gun at the door to protect him?"

"I doubt it, but I think he's okay."

"You fucking seen him?"

I'd have to tell him that eventually, but for now, it was too soon. "No, no, Concetta told me that."

Lou's voice dropped a little, probably just exhaustion. "So, he's okay—but he's in trouble?"

"The nun called—called Concetta today, and said some guy came to see him Sunday night, then today he's taken off." I stopped counting the lies at this point.

A pause, then he spoke. "Alright, look, I'm coming down right now. You make sure Concetta's at the house and we're gonna have a talk."

"I don't know where she is."

"So fucking find her. She's either at home or at the office or…talk to that Mrs. Mussolini she works for."

"That's the thing—she's…she told me about Davy in the morning then said she was going to work. So I called to check in on her and they said she called in sick."

"Did you call the house?"

"I just got off the phone with…her office." I almost said "with the nun".

There was a pause. "She told you all this this morning, and you're just calling me now?"

"She asked me not to tell you."

"And you called to check in on her." His voice was quiet, which was even worse. He didn't believe me, which made sense, as my story was getting tangled. "Listen, check on her again, okay? At home and the office. I'll be down in an hour or two."

"Alright." What else could I say?

"And we'll have a talk." His voice got tight. "One way or another."

I went out to the bar and was greeted by a smiling face that I just wanted to smack.

"Hey, *Paisan!*"

I didn't need Pinto's goofy shtick right now. "Shut the fuck up, would you?"

Pinto went into his little-boy-hurt routine. "What? You got no love for your blood-brother?"

Kevin was looking at us as he put cherries in a couple of Manhattans. He didn't need a bad day to dislike Pinto. I grabbed Pinto by the arm.

"Let's get a smoke."

"Hey, great, I got some more of that…"

We moved to the door fast. Outside, Pinto pulled out a joint, and I whacked his chest with the back of my hand.

"Put that away, we got problems." I told him about Concetta and Davy. I told him exactly what I had told Lou. Pinto was practically moving his lips as he tried to follow what I had said and not said.

"Jesus," he said. "And on top of this shit with Ramon."

I stared at him. "How do you…?"

Pinto gave me a peeved look. "My name's on that tape too—so, by the way, thanks for clueing me in."

"I couldn't…"

"Forget it, Lou told me. What a fucked-up situation."

"You don't know how fucked up."

I told him about the body found in the bay. For once, Pinto was silent, hand gripping his forehead, staring at the sidewalk.

We went back inside, and I told Sheila I was leaving.

"What's up with Lou?"

I shook my head. "I don't know, he wants to get together."

She just stared at me. "Sure, fine."

She didn't need any special intuition to see that I was anything but fine.

* * *

We stopped by the agency first. A secretary showed me into Carol's office. Pinto elected to stay in the car.

"That bitch scares the shit out of me."

Carol's office looked like it could be either a brothel or a torture chamber, depending on which side of a deal you were on. Which fit Carol's personality to a T. She sat in her perfect suit with her perfect hair holding a gold-plated pen and pointed at a chair like I was an associate broker who had screwed up a deal.

I ignored her command. "Heard from Concetta today?"

She evaluated my question to determine how to best take advantage of it.

"You keeping tabs on her now?" She ticked the pen against the glass surface of her desk. "For Lou?"

"Yeah, that's right."

I wondered if this dragoness was somehow tied into the whole mess, or whether her normal business satisfied her desires for domination. She leaned back in her huge chair, her hands gripping its cushioned arms. It reminded me of a scary painting of the Pope I had seen on a museum field trip in high school.

She finished her plumbing of my soul's shallow depths. "She's home sick, right?" She looked at her pen, then at me. "But you should know that, shouldn't you?"

I really disliked this lady and could tell she liked that, and everything about the trouble she could smell happening under her nose. I didn't answer, figuring her predatory instincts would keep her talking.

"Maybe she's playing hooky? If that dyke friend of hers hadn't called, I would have thought maybe she went down there for some...companionship."

"She's a nun."

She gave me a look like I had to be pretending to be stupid.

"Really? Maybe Concetta should take her vows, too. She's about the worst fucking agent I've ever had in this office."

I had had enough. "She never was much good at being a lying cunt."

Carol coiled forward on her chair. "You know, I asked her why she wanted this job. Do you know what she said?"

"No."

"'I need the money.'"

I shrugged. "So?"

"What she meant was, I need money for something I don't want to tell my husband about."

"Is that so unusual?"

"No, no." She got out of the chair. I could see that the glass table made sense, as she came around it on her million-dollar legs perched on a gleaming black pair of high heels. "But I'm sure it's the reason you're here."

"That's not important."

She came very close to me. "I find it all very interesting. I've been very generous with advances—to help with…whatever is troubling her. But," she hooked a finger inside my shirt, a fingernail scraping my chest, "that debt may get called real soon."

She pulled her finger out, and I had maybe the angriest hard-on of my life.

* * *

The suitcase was gone. I guess it was too much to expect her to have left a note. I called the retreat house to let them know she was gone. Sister Louise was not available, which was just as well, as I had no idea what to tell her to do.

Pinto turned on the television, and I turned it off. He started to complain, then just went out onto the deck. I tried to get my story together for Lou, but realized what a joke that would be with Pinto trying—or not—to follow my lead.

There was a knock on the door below, then heavy footsteps coming up the stairs. In my bones, I knew who it had to be, maybe a flashback to last Friday night. Purcell was in uniform—did he sleep in it?—and had a grim expression on his face. Lou's personal strong arm of the law. I was beginning to realize that there wasn't likely any part of Lou's operation that Purcell wasn't wired into.

Pinto came back in, and the three of us sat around the kitchen table. I made coffee, which made me feel even more like a cut-rate private eye. Within half an hour, we heard a car pull up on the gravel outside. Lou came up and called the kitchen cabinet to order. He was calmer now, like a military officer in a crisis situation.

Lou spoke first. "What'd you find out about Davy?" The question was for Purcell.

Purcell responded. "Not much. I got the local guys to check out his room. It didn't look like he had packed or anything. But no wallet or money. So, probably he planned to take off."

"And Concetta?"

"Her car hasn't turned up anywhere. At least nobody's seen it on the Parkway or in Cape May—or Wildwood."

Lou took his watch off and twisted it around in his hands. He pointed a finger at Pinto.

"Why is he here?"

Pinto glared but kept still.

I said, "I thought we might need another body."

"What's he know about this?'

"Same's I told you." Not too far from the truth. I prayed he wouldn't start interrogating Pinto. It was maybe not my best decision to bring him on board. But at least I knew he would be on my side. I couldn't be sure about anybody else.

We sat there in silence. Lou got up and paced around the room. I thought about Arnie and Rudy. I couldn't figure out a way that it was going to be better if I waited.

"There's more."

Lou stopped in mid-pace and looked at the ceiling.

"I fucking knew it." He put his hands on his hips and blew out a scary breath. "You were fucking lying to me."

Purcell shifted in his seat, in case he needed to move fast to put his knee in the middle of my back. I didn't look at Pinto, but I was sure his mind was moving as fast as it could to figure out how to say what he knew and what he didn't. I let Lou come back to the table. He sat down and forced himself to be calm. His hands spread out on the surface like he was pressing them there instead of around my neck.

"Go ahead." One index finger lifted up. "The whole fucking truth this time."

Was there any part worth leaving out now? I started in.

"I went down to Cape May—to that fancy restaurant she was talking about."

"What'd you do that for?" It sounded like a threat.

I went right back at him. "You asked me to keep an eye on her."

"Go on." Lou said it like he was giving me one more chance.

"I had asked Robert about the place. Turned out he knows the guy who runs it—Mark Taylor. He interviewed there—and the guy said he knew Concetta. So I went there for dinner and met him. I told him I was a friend of Concetta's—and yours. And that I was checking him out because...you know."

Lou was getting pissed in a different way now, like he was being embarrassed. "What's this got—?"

I put up my hand. "I'm getting there. So, he's not—he's not involved with her. Not that kinda guy."

Pinto volunteered like a fifth-grade apple-polisher. "Guy's a fag."

I gave Pinto a shut-the-fuck-up look that I hoped would penetrate his skull, and plowed on.

"I wondered why Conci was spending time talking to this guy—and lying about it—and he still seemed real nervous, so I kept the pressure on—and that's when he brought up Davy."

"Davy." Lou got quiet, which was even scarier. You could feel the weight was coming down on him.

"He told me Davy was in Cape May. He helped him get a job—at a hot dog shack run by a guy named Rudy."

"How's she meet this guy?"

I looked at Pinto, who was making a big effort to clamp his jaws shut. I made sure I was out of Lou's reach.

"Arnie introduced her to him."

"Hold on. Stop." Lou made a settle-down gesture with his palms down, a slow up-and-down movement. I think it was more for himself. "Before we get to that—FUCK—Arnie...remind me about this debt bullshit." His palms went up. "Since you seem to know fucking everything."

"Best I understand, Davy got himself in hock big time to some dealers in South Philly. So he ran away to the shore, found a place—with some help from Mom. Got himself cleaned up, so I was told."

Lou grimaced. "Believe that when I fucking see it."

I kept going. "He thought he was okay—went maybe a month or so without anybody bothering him. Then when he was working at the dog shack, someone came in the night and painted a bunch of shit on the walls—like, you no good junkie welsher, we'll get you. So he freaked out and quit coming in."

Lou's look said I know there's fucking more, so I kept going.

"So when I heard this…I mean, I was already wondering about Davy. That guy Eduardo—the guy in Buena—he told me he had heard Davy was at the shore, and could be in trouble."

"And you didn't think that was worth telling me?"

Lou seemed to be inching toward me. I tried to keep cool. "I figured I'd try to find out more—you know, vet his story—before getting you…"

"All worked up?" He was definitely worked up now.

I grimaced. "Yeah, let me…"

He made an impatient rolling motion with two fingers. I went on.

"I found out from the kid working at the dog shack that Davy was staying at this retreat house down there. I went there and talked to him."

"When?"

"Just this Sunday."

"Which you lied to me about two hours ago." He flipped his hands up. "Just for the record."

"Well, yeah…"

"Never mind. So he was okay?" Lou was sincere now.

"Yeah, he seemed to be doing good. He looked clean."

"You tell Concetta about this?"

"No, no—I mean, I was—I wasn't sure how to handle it, since she hadn't told me anything about him. So I figured I would wait and see where it went."

"Did he say he was in trouble?"

"In so many words."

"And you didn't tell me fucking that either." A statement, not a question. "Who the fuck are you working for?"

"Conci's not telling you a thing. You say let the kid die in the streets. The kid tells me not to tell either of you that I saw him." I gave him back his hard stare. "My job is running a restaurant. And you can fire me from that whenever you want."

Lou stood and went into the dining room. He came back with a bottle of vodka and a few glasses.

"So maybe she went down to get him? Christ, they could be headed to fucking Canada."

Pinto was looking at his fingernails. My eyes shifted to Purcell, who was staring at me. He got up abruptly.

"We need to get on this now, Lou."

He seemed to be in a hurry. I raised my hand. "I'm not done."

Purcell sat back down. Lou set the glasses on the table and poured out one for himself. He looked around the group, but no one responded. He downed the shot and sat down, motioning for me to continue.

"When I went to Mark's restaurant, I saw an old friend there hanging out at the bar." I looked at Purcell, then Lou. "Arnie." I avoided looking at Pinto, hoping he was following me. "I thought he might know more about all this, so after I talked to Davy, I found him. We had a drink."

I got up and brought the coffee pot over to the table. I stood next to Purcell and gestured with the pot. He nodded, and I filled his cup. I talked as I went around the table.

"He knew about Davy's troubles."

"Of course, he knew. Everybody fucking knows but me." Lou's face went red. "How'd he look?"

"Fine, dapper as ever."

Lou turned to Purcell. "Did you get to him?"

Purcell shook his head. "I've been on a detail since Saturday."

Lou held Purcell's gaze for a solid five seconds of uncomfortable silence. "You're giving out speeding tickets and my wife and son are on the lam from…the fuck knows who?" Lou looked at me with a sarcastic, yet pained expression. "I do you a favor and give him the Arnie assignment. Lot of fucking good it did me."

Purcell didn't look at me, but I could feel all seventy-six inches and two hundred twenty pounds of State Trooper resisting the urge to take me behind the nearest official building and make me recite some kind of loyalty oath with a lot less teeth. Pinto interrupted the silence.

"Ginty's not telling the truth, boss."

We all looked at him like he had lost his fucking mind, for different reasons. Pinto lifted his hands.

"I'll tell you, Mr. Arnie didn't look so fine after this mick pasted him one in the gut." He smiled at Purcell. "Softened him up for you, big guy."

Lou blinked. I blinked. Purcell didn't blink because troopers have that muscle frozen when they join the force.

"You were there, too?"

"Yeah." Pinto crossed his legs and sat back in a relaxed manner that made no sense. "We were on a date. Double date."

Lou gripped his head. "I must be losing my fucking mind."

I dropped my hand on the table, giving it a little bang with my fist to break the trance. "Don't worry about that."

Lou curled up a little in his chair, hands still on his head. I focused on him. I had to, because I was terrified of looking at Purcell. There was dead silence. I kept talking.

"Then Arnie said something interesting. He said 'ask Concetta why she hasn't told Lou about all this.'"

Lou's voice was a monotone. "Why'd he say that?"

"Knowing what I know now—I think he was scared we were getting close to the truth, and wanted to pull her in, too."

"What…the fuck…does that mean?"

"So I asked her—when I caught her packing her suitcase to go…see Davy."

Lou's hands opened, and he peered out. "You didn't tell me that already, right? That you caught her getting ready to go?"

"No, I didn't. That was last night. I stopped her—at least right then."

"Good, good." His hands closed over his face. Pinto leaned forward like a kid at story time in the school library. I drank some coffee, which failed to prevent my mouth from getting dry.

"I asked her what Arnie meant. She told me she'd been giving Davy cash for a while, helping him get out of Philly, deal with his rehab, stay afloat. I guess she had some…"

Lou interrupted me. "Get to the point."

"She found out about Arnie's scam at the Seabreeze. Before you did." I hoped this wouldn't get Sheila in dutch. "She had to sign some checks one day…anyway, she figured out something was wrong. So she…she went in with him."

"What do you mean, 'went in'?" Lou's voice was flat.

"I mean she took a piece of what he was getting—in return for letting it go on." I couldn't read Lou's mood anymore—he seemed catatonic. "So she'd have money for Davy."

"Until Sheila got wind of—" Lou stopped. "Was Sheila in on this, too?"

"No. And she didn't know about Conci."

"Why didn't Arnie take her down?"

I shrugged—more of a shiver. "Maybe he couldn't see how it was going to help. Maybe he felt sorry for her—and Davy."

Lou jumped up, knocking over his glass. He screamed, "He's my fucking son! I'm the one who gets to feel sorry!" He started pacing again. "I'm confused. What's her being in on Arnie's scam got to do with Davy?"

"According to her, things were quiet for a while with Davy. Nobody was showing up looking for him. Then the hot dog shack got targeted. So Arnie offered to help—said he got to the dealers in South Philly who were after him, and—so he was gonna be like a go-between with them."

"She told you that?"

"Yeah. And he said if she told you about all this—his helping her out—that he'd tell you about how she was in with him on scamming the Seabreeze. 'Cause you wouldn't believe he was really helping her and would come after him."

"No fucking shit! He got that right. Jesus fucking Christ. So, you were gonna…what, never tell me about this? Until both of them end up…?" Lou walked in circles, bumping into a chair. "You…you're like fucking Dick Tracy here." He stopped and laughed. "You're a fucking bartender. Holy jeez."

He sat down again. We all sat quiet. I figured Lou was now grappling with the available puzzle pieces of Arnie's thuggery and trying to figure if the missing piece had a picture of Ramon's face with a gun jammed into it. Lou stabbed a finger at Purcell.

"You. Find fucking Arnie." Purcell's eyes shifted up, like he wanted to challenge Lou, but knew that wouldn't work out well. "Dollars to donuts it was him that came to see Davy." Lou turned to Pinto and me. "You two come with me."

Purcell sat still. Lou put his face close to him and said very quietly.

"What the fuck are you waiting for?"

There was just the tiniest feel of mutiny in the two seconds that elapsed before Purcell stood and headed out. I followed him with my eyes and was not disappointed. Just before his head disappeared below the staircase wall, he looked at me. It was a scary look. What made it even scarier was that I could see that he was scared, too.

* * *

I read and re-read the note Lou gave me as we headed to Buena. It had the classic letters-cut-out-of-magazines look and gave instructions for dropping off a big bundle of cash—$20,000—and how Lou was supposed to get the tape. Pinto reached over from the back seat.

"C'mon, let me see."

I tossed it back to him. After a minute, he handed it back like it was an old comic book he had already read a hundred times.

"These guys. So we hand them the cash, then just trust they'll give us the tape?"

Pinto hadn't seen the tape, but Lou had given him the high points. Pinto continued his musing, Lou driving in grim silence.

Pinto said, "And put the cash in a life guard stand? What if some bum just picks it up?"

Lou broke his silence. "They'll be close by, so that won't happen."

Pinto kept at him. "So how do they know we won't just swoop in and catch them?"

Lou lifted his hand off the wheel and said in a bored tone, "They have the spot covered, they pick us off if we try to interfere. Says it right in the note."

"So we just follow them—"

"Then we don't get the tape." Lou stopped for a red light and turned around. "Now just shut the fuck up. And don't tell Cambro any of your bright ideas, alright?"

When we got to Buena, we pulled up at the cantina where I had met Eduardo. The sign on the door said it was closed, which seemed odd given the hour. Inside, all the booths were empty except one in the back, occupied by Eduardo and Cambro, and another on the other side of the room where a couple of hefty guys were eating methodically like they were on a lunch break.

We sat down, Lou and I in the booth, and Pinto on a chair he pulled over. Cambro folded his hands together, signaling that the meeting could begin.

"You want to pay these...*desperados*?" Cambro said the word with contemptuous irony. "I am not so sure they understand...what they are doing."

Lou nodded, adopting the folded hands pose, as if in deference to Cambro. "If we get the tape, it will be worth it."

Cambro tapped his thumbs together. "And how do we know there is no...other tape?"

"We don't," Lou admitted.

"Or that we get the tape at all?"

Lou shook his head. "I know. It's fucked up."

Cambro unfolded his hands and laid them flat on the table. "I think, these men, they do not know what they are doing. They are not...professionals. The police—they call Ramon's family. They identified him from his fingerprints. A pro...there would have been no fingers. Maybe no teeth, either, eh?"

He gave a little chuckle that Eduardo nervously joined in on. Cambro's calmness at the murder of Ramon was alarming, at least to a criminal-in-training like me.

Pinto leaned into the table with an elbow, his head turned toward the opposite wall. He pointed with a finger, speaking to Cambro.

"Hey, I'd like to try that tamale thing." He was pointing at the yellowed white plastic menu on the wall, with the items and prices on it, and a red Coke clock in the middle. The menu was right above the booth with the two big guys. They made a point of not looking up as Pinto leaned back and called out to the woman who was behind the counter, studiously not listening to our conversation.

"Hey!"

Eduardo stood. "I get her."

I got out to let Eduardo go up to the counter. I glanced over to the other booth and one of the guys looked up and leveled a stare at me for a few seconds, chewing all the while, then went back to the pile of beans on his plate. I had a flash of what it must feel like in the mess hall at the state pen.

Eduardo came back. "She take care of it."

I slid over so Eduardo could sit.

"Excellent." Pinto relaxed back into his seat.

Lou stared at him like he wanted to strangle him, but Cambro laughed and called out to the big boys.

"Sleepy."

The larger of the two shuffled over. His eyes were droopy, but I wasn't about to question his lack of awareness. The other guy went to the counter and talked with the girl, his head turning to watch us. Cambro said a few words in Spanish. The guy looked at us and said a few words back. Cambro flicked his fingers out, and the guy looked at us again, then over at his partner. The two of them left the store.

Lou said, "You were saying?"

Cambro continued his musings. "I think...we can get to them. If we can catch them, then we can show them that...they cannot win at this game. That is important, so they do not try again."

Pinto interjected. "So we ambush them?"

Lou tightened his mouth, like he wanted to smack Pinto, but figured he'd let Cambro handle him. Cambro's right hand rose from the table and fluttered delicately.

"Not so...blunt...but we follow them and when the time is right, we can do what is needed."

Lou put his hands on the table now. "They want to do the drop tomorrow."

Cambro lifted his head in assent. "That can work. My friends there...they will help."

The girl was at the booth with a plate. Pinto patted the table in front of him. She put it down, and Pinto looked confused.

"That's the tamale?"

"*Sí.*" The girl went back to the counter.

Cambro smiled a real smile, letting Pinto feel helpless for a minute, then put his hand out.

"I show you, okay?"

Cambro unwrapped the tamale, sliding the corn husk off to the side of the plate. Then he moved a bottle of hot sauce in front of Pinto. He held it there, tipping it questioningly on its edge.

"You want I ask for the *gringo* sauce?"

Pinto took the bottle and shook it up, then splashed what was surely too much on the tamale. Cambro's chin went down in appreciation.

"*Un hombre de verdad.*"

We all sat and watched Pinto devour the tamale. The girl brought over a big glass of water, which Pinto sipped, no doubt avoiding a gulp that would give away his pain. When he finished, he pushed the plate into the center of the table.

Cambro considered him with what looked like affectionate curiosity. "Not too hot, *amigo?*"

Pinto allowed himself a big drink of water and a bigger burp. "Just right, *senor.*"

Cambro laughed and clapped Pinto on the back. He looked at Lou. "I hope this caballero is on our team tomorrow."

Lou's smile was thin. "Oh, yeah, he'll be there." The smile disappeared. "There's something else...sort of personal." Lou turned to Pinto. "Can you give us a minute?"

Pinto sat still for a few seconds, then stood, clearly hurt. "Okay, boss."

Eduardo got up. "Come on, we take a walk."

They left. Cambro looked at Lou and me in turn, "So we talk?"

Lou spoke. "It's about my son, Davy."

Cambro's eyes softened a little, a look of sympathy. "Yes. And I have heard of his troubles."

Lou's tone was anxious. "Eduardo told Ginty he had heard Davy might be hiding out down here." He stared at the table. "We know now that's true. And somebody visited him Sunday, they had an argument, then he disappeared. So if you could keep an eye out…"

Cambro frowned. "After we talk Saturday, I see Eduardo and tell him you have been here, and he tell me about your son. So I make calls. The guys—the *traficantes*, in your South Philly—I find who they are, little people. They give your son…the credit, eh? Maybe they give him enough *droga* to be a little dealer himself. Back in early spring. But," he swept his arms apart, "he do not make the good job of it. So he owe them." He rubbed the fingers of his right hand together. "Mucho, right?"

Lou took all this pretty calmly. He looked up like he was talking the price of a used Chevy. "How much?"

Cambro shrugged "Ah…it not matter. It is all done."

"Done?" Lou tilted his head.

"Yes, it was all forgiven. They find out…who he is," a wide smile, "so, they no longer try, sí?"

"So…" Lou mused aloud, "when…?"

"When I call, I talk to the boss of these little low-lifes. He tell me that two, maybe three months ago, when your boy could not pay, he ran away. This boss did not know who he was. And after a few weeks his men…they are making the noise about a…search party, sí? So, he bring them in to explain about their problem. Then he find out that it is your Davy. He was not happy." Cambro laughed, then put his hand to his mouth. "I…do not mean to laugh…at your misfortune. The boss, he put an end to it. He knows who you are. And he has business to run, *sabes?*"

"But Eduardo heard he was in trouble." I focused on Cambro, hoping Lou wouldn't smack me later for asking too many questions.

Cambro lifted his hands. "Maybe that was before they were…instructed."

He moved his hands farther apart. "Or maybe they did not spread the word that their boss sat on them. It maybe would make them look weak."

Things were starting to become more clear. Cambro picked up his glass of iced tea.

"Your son, he is troubled and has fallen in with…a bad bunch." The bottom of the glass tilted up questioningly. "I tell you, we can give a lesson to these men who try to…enlist him in their service."

"No need." Lou waved his hand. "So, he called them off…sometime in May?"

Cambro nodded. "Yes. Before Memorial Day, that is sure."

Lou looked up at the ceiling, thinking. Then he looked at me.

"And this graffiti thing at that hot dog stand?"

I struggled to get the timeline straight. "I think…had to be mid-June—after Memorial Day, definitely. Davy didn't start there until after that."

I could read Lou's thoughts like they were in a thought balloon. This had Arnie written all over it. Another scam of someone who couldn't see through him. But a grey cloud of uncertainty still surrounded Arnie's possible role in the blackmail.

Cambro said, "Your tall hombre, the police, he is…helping you?"

Lou's response was quick. "Yeah, we were just with him."

"Of course." Cambro folded his hands together. "It is good to have someone…on the inside, yes? But we must always watch."

"Agreed." Lou nodded. "Ginty, go find Pinto, make sure he's not disturbing the locals."

I left them and went outside, where Eduardo was leaning against the rail of the little porch. He extended his hand.

"Good luck."

I shook his hand. "Will you be there…?"

Eduardo shook his head ruefully. "No, that is not…my expertise, as they say." I watched him walk away. I walked toward Lou's car and saw Pinto standing in the middle of the sidewalk, acting like he owned it. I caught up to him and we continued towards the Bronco past a lime-green Charger, with one of the guys from the cantina behind the wheel, the other—

Sleepy—sitting on the hood. He looked like he had grown since last I saw him.

Pinto called out to him. "Nice ride, *vato.*"

Sleepy took a drag on his cigarette, but didn't say anything. I continued on, resisting the urge to look back. We loitered next to the Bronco, and I grabbed Pinto's shoulder.

"What the fuck was that?"

He took a toothpick out of his mouth. "What, you don't think that was a nice car?"

"Maybe he thought you were being a wise guy."

"Maybe if we say nothing, we look like a couple of scared gringos. Anyway," he shook my hand off, "we're gonna be working together."

I shook my head and kicked at the curb. "Why'd you get that tamale?"

"I was just being polite. A show of respect, you know?"

"You ready for another?"

He put his thumb up. "Just give me the sign."

Chapter Nineteen

On Wednesday, I went to work. The drop wasn't until the evening, so there wasn't much point just sitting around watching Lou worry. Purcell hadn't turned up anything. Arnie seemed to have disappeared. Lou figured maybe he had taken off for his place in Jupiter. Purcell had even been inside his house, but didn't see any signs of a sudden flight.

Around seven, I told Sheila I had to go back to the house to meet with Lou to go through our numbers for the past week. She gave me a big take-out container of chicken parm as I left.

"Have fun." She could see how worked up I was, which she found amusing.

Lou went through the plan while we ate. They had picked a beach at the far south end of the island. The lifeguard stand was supposed to be between two streets. I would drive with Pinto to the street to the north of the stand. Pinto would take the cash in a small duffel bag and put it in the stand at exactly 9 PM. Then he would come back to the car. We were supposed to leave and come back in a half hour. The cash would have been picked up, and the video placed in the stand.

I played Pinto's role now, poking holes in the plan.

"How do we know they're going to give us the video? And how do we know they don't have another copy?"

Lou's expression was serious and worried. "We don't know. And they don't know that we won't try to ambush them. But if we do ambush them, we may never get the tape. And if they stiff us, we'll be after them in spades."

"How are they going to know we've left?"

"I guess they'll be watching us somehow. Look, there's guys on the other side having these same conversations right now. And our bet is they are even more scared than we are. If these were real players," Lou's hands turned over, supplicating, "they wouldn't be doing it like this. Someone with real juice would be talking to Cambro directly and cutting a deal."

"I guess."

A little after seven thirty, we headed out. We picked up Pinto at the Garden and parked on a lonely street out by the bay. It was barely eight o'clock. Lou ran down Pinto's job.

"You take the bag. Make sure there's no one out there. Put it in the stand. Then just come back."

Pinto was in the back seat with a bag of peanuts, popping them in his mouth and tossing the shells out the window.

"Great. So they decide to take me out, I'm shit out of luck?"

Lou spoke calmly. "They're not going to do that."

"No? They fuckin' killed Ramon."

"That was different."

"Yeah?"

"Yeah." Lou was getting exasperated. "They go after you, we'll rush in and get the cash, Anyway, look, that's why you're gettin' combat pay."

"What, a grand? I get that when I sell a car."

Lou turned around, poking a finger at Pinto. "We get the tape, I'll give you two G's, alright? Now shut the fuck up."

Pinto rattled the peanut bag and offered it to me. He chuckled. "I been learning how to negotiate at the dealership."

Lou put his hand up. "Alright, enough. When you go in, we'll be watching from the steps."

"And what—you got Mr. Bottle-Washer here armed with a bazooka?"

"Don't worry." Lou edged the car away from the curb.

It was starting to worry me the number of times Lou said not to worry. I hoped he wasn't going to hand me a gun at the last minute. It had been a long time since I had been to a range with one of the friendly neighborhood cops.

Lou drove slowly, killing time. "We got your friends—Cambro's guys—they'll be there." He looked up and caught Pinto's eye in the rear-view mirror. "They don't fuck around."

We drove to the end of the street where we were supposed to wait. We still had a half hour. Lou took a flashlight from the glove compartment and got out of the car, heading to the walkway that led to the beach. Pinto and I followed him. He went a little ways down the walk and gave a signal with the flashlight, five quick bursts of light. He was looking south; after about fifteen seconds, a winking light returned the signal.

Pinto was peering south.

"What, we the fucking Coast Guard or something?"

Lou came back. "That's our boys."

There was nothing to do now but wait. Pinto finished up his peanuts and tossed the bag into the dunes. Lou looked at his watch and went to the back of the Bronco, opening the hatch and bringing out a leather bag. He handed it to Pinto.

Pinto took it, dropping it on the street. He reached behind his shell jacket in the back and pulled out a sizable pistol. He gave Lou an inquiring look. Lou nodded.

Pinto took the bag and went toward the beach like he was taking his an after-dinner stroll. It was dark and we couldn't see the stand. Pinto disappeared from sight after about forty yards.

There were lights from a few fishing boats far out to sea, and we could see the light from the houses and hotels up near the boardwalk. But down here, it was dead quiet.

After five minutes, we could hear the sound of movement through the sand, and then Pinto appeared. He came onto the street and wiped his hands together, brushing off sand. We all got in the car, and Lou drove off.

Pinto shook his head. "Can't believe we're just leaving that cash there."

Lou responded, "Don't forget, Cambro's guys are still down there."

Pinto countered, "Yeah, but how they gonna know if they really drop the tape?"

Lou pulled to a stop a few blocks away. "Just...let it play out."

We were waiting, me nervously, Pinto nonchalant, Lou…it was hard to tell…when the sound of a police siren jolted me out of my seat.

"Fuck!" I yelled, the stress of the day coming out in one word.

Lou threw the car into gear and made a screeching U-turn, racing back to our drop-off spot.

I was panicked. "What are you doing?"

I could hear gunshots as the Bronco rocketed up the street and skidded to a halt in front of the bulwark. Pinto was between the seats, pressing forward, almost up between us.

"Holy fuck!" he exclaimed.

There were flashing lights on the beach, and we tumbled out of the car, following Lou toward the beach. I was scared as I ran behind him, but not as scared as I would have been if I'd hung back. I had to be part of the team now, even though we were heading straight toward a cop car, which didn't seem to be where we should be going at all.

As we got close, I could hear shouting and saw there were two cars, both jeeps, one with a blue flashing light strapped atop. There was a tall cop with a Smokey the Bear hat leaning over a figure prone on the ground, that was writhing and calling out in pain. The cop had a big boot on the small of the guy's back. Two large figures stood about ten feet away, which I could tell from their girth had to be Sleepy and his partner.

Lou went right up to the cop, who looked up, his face illuminated in the cone of light from Lou's flashlight.

It was Purcell. He pointed at a bag next to the guy on the ground. Lou nodded to Pinto, who came over and grabbed it.

Lou came close to Purcell, and they exchanged a few words. Then Lou turned and kicked the guy on the ground hard in the ribs. The guy cried out and tried to lift his head. Lou knelt next to him and shone the flashlight in his face.

Rudy.

Lou grabbed his hair. "You miserable fuck."

I looked up and Purcell was staring at me, a hard smile on his face, a box the size of a videotape in his hand.

221

Chapter Twenty

Rudy had been bundled into Purcell's jeep. Sleepy and the *otro vato*, whose name I didn't know and hoped to keep that way, were assigned to ditch Rudy's jeep somewhere appropriately out of the way. Lou instructed Purcell to bring Rudy to his house. You could tell Sleepy and The Other Mexican were miffed at not being invited to this soiree.

I asked Lou to drop me off at the restaurant, saying I needed to check in on things. As he drove, Lou explained that Purcell had come up with the idea of the surprise raid just that morning.

"And you didn't think of letting me and Pinto in on the plan?" I asked.

"I treated that strictly on a need-to-know basis." Lou shrugged. "And you didn't need to know."

"I'm getting a bit paranoid about how that mug keeps showing up unexpectedly. Like, how was it that he just happened to come by us at my wreck on the Parkway?" I squinted at Lou. "Did you have him tailing us?"

"Fuck no."

Pinto chimed in from the back seat. "He's a shifty copper."

Lou didn't say anything more. Maybe he was wondering how shifty Purcell really was. But even though Lou hadn't said it directly, there was no doubt now in my mind that Purcell was involved in the drug operation.

When he pulled up at the restaurant, Lou gave me a disappointed look, like I was leaving just as the party was getting started. "Just...don't stay long." He put the car back in drive. Pinto gave me a smirking wave from the back seat.

I got out and watched him drive off. How things were going in the restaurant was the last thing on my mind.

There was just a handful of diners, a slow night. Sheila was sitting on a barstool, making notes on a sheet of paper, probably the waitress's schedule.

"Everything okay with Lou?" She didn't look up.

"Fine." I went behind the bar, got a bottle of wine, and went to the kitchen. The dishwashers were busy wiping down counters and equipment, hoping to get out early. Robert was out back with his own bottle of wine. We drank without talking for a few minutes, Robert tossing pebbles into a trash can.

"Typical Wednesday." Robert rubbed his hands on his whites.

I was grateful for the normal conversation. "How many we do?"

"Fifty-sixty." He laughed. "That girl, Sherri, you know her?"

"What, she started last week, right?"

"Yeah, that's the one. She sold a bottle of that Barolo."

"You're kidding."

Robert lit a cigarette. "She played it perfect. Guy in his forties, dressed to impress—a date, girl's maybe twenty-five. Guy's married, doesn't even bother to ditch the ring. He wanted to order a Barbera—not a bad wine—she says, oh, you sound like you know Italian wine."

"Of course, he's flattered."

"Right, so she says, we don't have a fancy list, but we have this fantastic Barolo—only reason we have it is for the boss, so he can drink it and charge it to the house. And really, it's just a little more," he blew out smoke, chuckling, "like twenty bucks more—but it is out of this world. So, the guy is stuck. He doesn't want to look like a cheapskate. He doesn't even want to take much time to think about it, 'cause he's only thinking one thing, which is how fast he can get this chippie between the sheets." Robert held out his bottle so I could see the label. "Only drank half of it—the girl had a couple of stingers, he left the rest."

I tossed out the dregs in my glass, and Robert splashed a bit in it. I took a sip, holding it in my mouth for a moment, just to focus on something else.

"That's even better than I remember."

"Had a chance to breathe a little." Robert tilted the bottle and poured the last few ounces in his glass. "See, your palate is improving."

"Maybe I could get a job as a...what do you call it?"

"Sommelier." Robert drained his glass and turned it upside down, watching a drop slide along its curved surface. "Thinking you need a change of scenery?"

"Desperately."

The drop of red fell onto the concrete. I stared at the spot like it was one of those ink-blot tests. It was a confusing splash, turning black, with tendrils stretching out like a killer amoeba in an Outer Limits episode.

"Hey." Robert set the bottle against the wall and stepped toward the kitchen door. "You okay?"

I didn't answer. We went back in the kitchen. I rinsed my glass in one of the big metal sinks and set it down.

"Thanks for the Barolo."

"Anytime." Robert picked up a chopping knife that had been left out on a prep table.

I got cold all of a sudden. I had a flash of the wine blotch, spreading like a stain that wouldn't stop.

* * *

Rudy was on a chair in Lou's kitchen. His hands were tied behind his back just like in the movies. His nose was still dripping blood, and there were black and yellow splotches on his golf shirt that reminded me of the wine stains that had had me in a trance just a half hour before. I guessed from the awkward way he sat and breathed that his ribcage and stomach were on the sore side.

It was like in those plays where the bad stuff happens off-stage, except you could still see and smell enough to make you sick if you were someone not cut out for this kind of stuff. Like me. Fortunately, I had taken my time walking over from the restaurant and missed the first act.

Pinto, on the other hand, was as chipper as could be, cutting up cheese and pepperoni like he was getting ready for the guys to show up and play poker. Purcell was sitting in a chair in the corner, with his hat, tie, and gun all off. As much as he undoubtedly was used to this type of scenario, I was guessing that there was some indelible part of his soul that knew it wasn't so cool for a trooper to be in a private residence with at least one questionable accomplice and an uncharged citizen looking like he had fallen down the proverbial flight of stairs.

Lou came out of his bedroom and strode over to Rudy. He stepped on Rudy's feet—which I saw now were bare—with his boots, leaning over him and holding onto the back of the chair, so he could get all his weight on them. He backed off, then slammed his heel down onto the toes of one foot, then the other.

Rudy screamed, and Pinto dropped his knife and came over and grabbed the bottom of Rudy's jaw with one hand and the top of his head with the other, clamping his mouth shut. Rudy eeked out grunts and whines, his face getting red, then purple.

Lou picked up a piece of pepperoni and popped it into his mouth. He crouched over so his face was right in front of Rudy's.

"You're going to talk to us."

Pinto let go, and Rudy slumped forward. Lou tilted his chin up with a finger.

"You don't, the officer will take you to Buena. Those Chicanos were really disappointed they weren't invited to this party." He let Rudy's head drop back. "And they're not like us. They do this kind of shit every day."

I looked at Pinto. "He talk about…Ramon?"

Pinto shook his head. "Nah, we ain't got to that yet. We just been beatin' the shit out of him mostly."

Lou dragged a chair over in front of Rudy. He sat on it backwards, his arms folded on its metal back.

He called out, keeping his eyes on Rudy. "Get me a glass of water."

Pinto was back to preparing hors d'oeuvres, and Purcell was staring at his hands in the corner. I filled a glass from the tap and handed it to Lou, who held it to Rudy's lips. Rudy drank sloppily. You could tell it hurt him to do anything. It occurred to me that Lou seemed comfortable in his role, like he had been in this play before.

When Rudy had finished slobbering, Lou pulled the glass away and spoke.

"So you were there, right? When Ramon was robbed?"

Rudy didn't say anything, his head dangling. Lou grabbed his chin and jerked his head up.

"Were you there? I fucking know you were. I wanna hear you say it."

Rudy clamped his lips together.

Lou yelled. "Pinto!"

"Hold on." Pinto wiped the knife he was using to cut the cheese into cubes with a dishtowel and set it down. He went over to a tool chest I had never seen in the house, and took out a cable-cutting tool. He held it up to the light for a second and gave it a few snips. It had a hole that could easily handle a finger and possibly other body parts if necessary.

He came over behind Rudy and knelt down, grabbing one of his hands

"I like to start with the pinky, that okay with you, Lou?"

Words spurted out of Rudy's mouth. "Yeah, I was there, Jesus fuck!"

Pinto craned his head around Rudy's fat, struggling body. "Just give me the word, boss."

"And Arnie?" Lou pressed on.

"Yeah, Arnie."

Rudy kept trying to look behind himself. Pinto rapped him sharply on the side of his forehead with the hard metal of the tool.

"Pay attention, numbskull!"

Lou scooted the chair closer with his heels, his face right in front of Rudy's.

"Did you kill Ramon?"

Rudy yelped. "No!"

Pinto was sitting on the floor, looking bored. "What'd you expect him to say?"

Lou ignored him. He held Rudy's chin hard and twisted his face. "So it was Arnie?"

Rudy's mouth opened and shut like a fish deciding whether to strike a purple worm he knew was fake, but was damned alluring.

Lou let go of his face and slapped him hard. "What're you protecting him for?"

Rudy moved his head around loosely. There was a new cut on his cheek from a heavy ring on Lou's finger. Lou nodded to Pinto, who scrambled back into finger-removal position. Rudy's face strained forward, turning redder.

"It wasn't Arnie."

Pinto was fitting the tool over his finger. He looked at Lou for a signal.

An image from the video flashed into my mind. Two hands at Ramon's face, from either side, one holding his head by the hair, the other pointing a gun under his neck, the camera moving in.

I jumped away from the kitchen counter toward Pinto, grabbing his arm. "Hold on!"

Pinto's face turned sour. "Hey, you're spoiling the party!"

"No, no, wait." I stood and went by Lou's side, his gaze intent on Rudy, whose eyes were alive and wild. "There were three guys there, right?"

Lou shifted in the chair and looked up at me. "You sure?"

"Yeah, I mean, we can check the tape. But when they put the gun to his head, there were two hands—from different sides, it couldn't be the same person. And the camera was moving in. So somebody was operating the camera—it couldn't have been, like, on a tripod."

"That was me." Rudy was staring at Lou.

Lou turned back to Rudy. He seemed uncertain now, like the balance had somehow shifted to Rudy in some way.

Lou stood up, hands on his hips. "Who was the third, you piece of shit?"

Rudy's head sank for a moment. Then he raised it up, a weird grin on his face.

"Your fuckin' boy. Yeah, and he's the one..."

Lou's arm pulled back like he was Jim Bunning, then windmilled his fist hard into the middle of Rudy's face, toppling him over in the chair. He crashed on top of Pinto, who came up hopping mad.

"Jesus Christ, Lou, what the fuck!"

Purcell jumped to his feet like a prizefighter when the bell rings. Pinto played the part of the trainer for the other palooka, hauling Rudy back up and settling him in his chair. Lou was bent over, breathing in rough gasps, holding his right hand gingerly with his left, palpating possibly broken digits. His face was red and getting redder as he struggled to breathe normally. He limped over to the sliding doors, pushing them open and stumbling out onto the porch.

We all looked at each other, but no one wanted to be the first to follow him out.

* * *

Rudy kept massaging the rope burn on his wrists and touching the many tender spots on his face and skull. This was another lesson for me in the art of interrogation. Rudy needed to be a little more comfortable if we wanted him to talk.

And Lou really wanted him to talk.

Lou had turned his chair around the normal way, which I guess was another friendly gesture. Pinto and I sat on either side of him, like the members of an interview panel. Purcell stood sentry at the door, which I guessed was just one of his default postures.

Lou started with an obvious question.

"How do I know you're not lying? Maybe it was you that did it?"

Rudy answered, "You don't know. But it was a stupid thing to do. And I'm not that stupid."

Lou half-started out of his chair, then checked himself. "Tell me about this plan."

Rudy said, "I get a drink of water?"

Lou nodded to Pinto, who went to a kitchen cabinet and sorted through cups until he found a green plastic one, like you would put in your bathroom. He filled it and brought it over to Rudy.

Pinto explained, "Figured don't give him glass, know what I'm saying?"

I was learning so much hanging with this bunch. Rudy took a drink and handed the cup back to Pinto.

Rudy spoke, gaining energy as he went along. "I came in kind of late to the plan but from what I could figure, it was Davy's idea. He said he found out about what you were doing with Ramon from someone in South Philly."

"Who was that?" Lou's tone was sharp.

"You gotta talk to him about that. So he'd been watching Ramon's garage and knew when a shipment came in. He got with Arnie, and at first, they just were going to heist the stuff. But then Davy got the idea of the video and squeezing…"

Rudy stopped. He looked at the floor, then at Lou. He seemed to be gauging how Lou was going to react. Lou, in turn, folded his arms and spoke in a calm voice.

"Go on."

Rudy continued. "I guess Arnie liked that idea, too. I know you and him had some…history." He watched for Lou's reaction, but there was none. "They wanted another hand, and I got enlisted." Rudy shook his head. "Not my kind of action, but…I owed Arnie a few favors. I figured we could get in and out quick, not get made by the spic. Which, the way it went, didn't matter."

Rudy was trembling, his resolve breaking down. Lou leaned forward, putting a hand on Rudy's beefy shoulder.

"You gotta tell me what happened."

Rudy nodded. "The plan was to scare him. And we did that." A nervous chuckle changed into a painful cough. "Fuck."

Pinto handed the cup back, and Rudy drained it. He went on.

"We were just gonna leave him there—I mean he was alive, right, we had just threatened him to get…what was on the tape. Then Arnie said we ought to move him, just, I don't know, drop him off somewhere. He was worried someone would come to the garage, his family, or something. We could get a little more time if we dropped him in the woods or a salt marsh or something.

"We wore ski masks when we were in the garage, but had to take them off once we started driving. So we blindfolded him so he couldn't see the car or where we were going. We tried not to talk in the car, just in case he could…describe our voices or something. His hands and legs were still bound up. We took him out to some woods on a back road, got him out of the car. I led him maybe thirty yards into the trees, then came back. Arnie was in the driver's seat. I got back in, and Davy jumped out, said hang on a second. He sprinted in and then…he fucking shot him, three-four times.

"Davy comes back, hops in the car, says, come on let's go. Arnie's looking at him like he's lost his fucking mind. Says, what the fuck? Davy's all jittery, excited, he's like, man, that's how you do it, that's how we do it in South Philly, he can't talk now, right?"

Lou was struggling to look calm, his fists clenched into balls. Rudy rushed on.

"Arnie went after Davy, hysterical, pummeling him—I was scared the gun would go off again. I had to pry him off from the back seat. We all sat there, felt like forever, probably thirty seconds, then Arnie says, we can't leave him there, we gotta do something with him. So we loaded him in the trunk, and took him down to this old dock—West Cape May. We—Arnie and me—Davy was a basket case now—took a fucking row boat and got him out a couple hundred yards and dumped him."

He stopped. He was crying.

"What a fucking stupid thing."

Lou got up and went to the glass doors, staring outside.

He asked, "And you were the schmuck that had to do the pickup? Probably delivered the note, too, huh?"

Rudy sniffed loudly, and Pinto handed him a box of tissues. He blew his nose, then answered.

"Yeah, I was at the bottom of the totem pole. Arnie—well, you're not the only one being blackmailed here. You see, back in the…"

Lou turned and put up his hand. "I don't give a shit about whatever Arnie's got on you. But I'm wondering—you came in all by yourself? Or was there someone hiding in the dunes that left you dangling?"

Rudy was looking exhausted. "I don't know. Arnie was supposed to be covering me. Yesterday, I went to meet him at the bar to get the tape, and he's not there. But the bartender has a package—the video—and a note for me, says to call Davy. So I do, and Davy says Arnie'll be at the drop, but they talked, and it's better if we're not seen together again. Said Arnie's going to split for Florida as soon as he gets the cash. So, I don't know, maybe Arnie was there covering me—and got freaked out when he saw the cop car."

"Maybe. Where were you calling Davy at?"

"I don't know. It wasn't that retreat place. Maybe a phone booth somewhere."

Pinto said, "I still ain't sure I believe this guy."

Rudy responded, "You asked me to tell you what happened, I did. And if Davy tries to finger me, I'm telling the same story to the cops. But," he looked at Lou, "I'm guessing the plan is for that not to happen."

Lou said, "Pinto, you watch him." He gestured to me and Purcell. "You guys—come on."

He led us into his bedroom, like we were charades partners. I sat on the bed, Purcell stood by the window looking out, and Lou paced.

Lou stopped in front of Purcell. "What do you think?"

Purcell was silent for ten seconds, then said, "I believe him."

Lou stared for a moment, then turned on his heel, walking to the other wall. "So do I."

Lou looked at his reflection in the wardrobe mirror.

"How does this go?" he asked. "The cops got a body. His family's gonna be too freaked out to say much of anything." He turned around. "What should we be worried about?"

Purcell spoke. "They're going to figure out—eventually—that you were buying parts from him. They'll look at phone records, that sort of thing. So, I think they'll want to talk to you."

I could see how it was handy to have a State Trooper as a personal advisor.

Lou picked up the thread. "Okay. I bought parts. But I can say I never touched the drugs. I was just the cover. So, it'll be a big surprise to me if they figure out that Ramon was bringing stuff in for Cambro. I'll say he must have taken the drugs out before he gave me anything."

Purcell mulled this over. "But maybe there could be other reasons why you and Ramon could have fallen out. He gave you a bad shipment, fucked-up parts or something."

Lou waved his hand. "That's weak. Besides, I can get an alibi for when this happened. I was with a bunch of people in Philly that day." He tugged at his chin. "I think Cambro's got more to worry about than I—we—do. Someone's likely to know he had dealings with Ramon."

Purcell replied, "But why would he go after one of his own guys?"

"Easy—Ramon was skimming something somewhere."

There was a nerve-wracking stillness as we all tried to work out the many paths in this fucked-up trail.

Purcell broke the silence. "They got nothing now but a body. Cambro will have to be careful, because they may come poking into his business. But I think you're clean. As long as none of these..." he jerked his elbow at the door, "idiots lose their nerve and start to talk."

I didn't like the sound of that. Silencing witnesses was something I didn't want to hear about. I was only one step away from the idiots in question. And maybe the possible silencers weren't just the folks in this room.

"What about Cambro?" I asked.

Purcell looked at me like I was a kid in detention asking for a cigarette break.

"What about him?" Purcell's shoulders went back, making him look even more threatening. I guess they teach that in Trooper 101.

"What's he gonna do when he finds out it was Davy that popped Ramon?" The gangster slang felt ludicrous coming out of my ex-altar boy's mouth.

"How's he gonna find out?" Purcell was thinking hard. "Maybe we say Rudy told us Arnie did it."

Lou considered the idea. "Okay, let's say we do. But what happens if he gets his guys to talk to Rudy?" Lou put up both hands. "And don't even suggest we whack this moron. We don't need any more bodies floating in the bay."

There was a knock at the door. Pinto opened it a crack.

"Boss, we got..."

Lou yelled out. "You watching that guy?"

Pinto turned around for a second and said something to Rudy. He put his head back in the room.

"He's fine. But, there's this big Lincoln outside, and a bunch of guys getting out..."

"Fuck!" Lou exclaimed. He pointed at me and Purcell in turn. "Let me take the lead here."

That was a directive I could easily comply with.

* * *

Our guests came up the stairs all smiles; or at least Cambro was smiling. Sleepy and the other *vato* looked kind of pissed off, like Cambro had told them they had to behave. Cambro raised his eyes at Rudy, perched uncertainly on his chair in the corner like a busted piñata.

Cambro said, "I see you have been having the chat with this unfortunate man."

Lou beckoned to Cambro. "How about we...?"

He nodded toward the bedroom. Cambro shrugged.

"Okay, if you like." He waved his hand at the big Mexicans. "I hope you do not mind that I bring my friends. They will be nice guys."

Lou waved Cambro into the bedroom and shut the door. I looked at the *vatos*.

"You guys want something to drink?"

Sleepy shifted toward me. "You have...*cerveza?*"

I was ecstatic to find a few bottles of Miller High Life in the fridge. Somehow, I managed to get Sleepy and his friend to sit on the sofa. Purcell took up a position between them and Rudy. I sat opposite them and tried to convey friendliness.

Pinto talked with the other *vato*, Ernesto, about the green Charger. He was an expert now that he had worked at a dealership for a week. Sleepy asked if Pinto had had any tamales recently. Everybody laughed—except Purcell, who kept trying to project the image of being the Real Tough Guy in the room.

It was getting to be a nice little tea party when the bedroom door opened. Cambro came out and gave a little signal with one hand, and the big boys stood.

Cambro gave Lou a nod. "We talk again soon."

They all left, Sleepy giving me a nod that seemed comradely and foreboding at the same time, as if he respected me but had to let me know that wouldn't get in the way of whatever duty he was assigned.

Rudy was lying in the corner now, a beach blanket over him. We didn't bother going into the bedroom to talk. It was after midnight.

Lou sat on the sofa. Purcell got his assignment first. Lou told him to use his cop connections to search for Concetta and Davy. Then he turned to Pinto and me.

"You guys take this mug back to Cape May and see if you can find Arnie and bring him back here—maybe he knows where Davy is."

I was beyond tired. "Can we just sack for a few hours?"

Lou reached across the coffee table and gripped my biceps, pressing down to the bone.

"We got just a couple of days to get Davy...before Cambro sets his dogs loose."

So he had told Cambro. His voice had a desperation in it that I wasn't used to hearing. He let go of my arm, looking at the floor, shaking his folded hands between his knees.

Now his voice was quiet. "Maybe he'll talk to you...Christ, you're the only one who's seen him besides Concetta. So listen careful. You tell him I'm gonna give him the cash—the twenty grand...but," one fist came up, marking his words, "we're getting him out...out of the country..."

Pinto asked, "Where you gonna send him?"

Lou's voice was quiet but seething. "What the fuck do you got to know for? I'm working on it, alright, just get that piece of garbage out of here and do what I told you." Lou turned to me. "Tell him we'll meet him...wherever he wants."

Purcell left, and Pinto knelt beside Rudy.

"Hey, wakey-wakey." Pinto nudged Rudy onto his side like he was an injured soldier in a bunker. Lou came over and stared at the floor.

"Fuck, the asshole's bled on the carpet."

There were a half dozen red splotches on the grey fiber rug. I didn't look at them too long, figuring I'd go into a trance again. Lou got a roll of paper towels and started rubbing them.

Pinto said, "You gotta use cold water." He filled a glass with water and bent down, pouring a little on the blood. "And you gotta blot, not rub."

Lou watched him work at it. "Concetta will fucking kill me."

Pinto called up from his work, "Hey, man, if she shows up, you'll be so happy, you…"

Lou stared at him, then went into the living room and dropped onto the sofa. We all waited, Pinto blotting away. When he was satisfied with his work, he got Rudy to his feet and led him to the kitchen sink.

Lou breathed out a big, unhappy breath and muttered to himself. "That fucking Arnie. Rips me off at the restaurant and still has to scam Concetta and Davy for the fake drug dealer payoff."

A deep laugh interrupted his complaint. It was Rudy, his face dripping with water he had splashed on himself from the tap. He accepted a dishtowel from Pinto, wiping himself off.

Rudy said, "I got news for you, man…your boy was in on that drug payoff deal. Yeah," Rudy laughed again, "him and Arnie had a lot in common."

Pinto grabbed his arm roughly and gave me an urgent look. We hustled Rudy out of the house, leaving Lou with his head pressed against his clenched fists.

Chapter Twenty-One

When we got to Cape May, Rudy led us to Arnie's house. His car was gone, at least according to Rudy. There was no answer at the door. We peered in the windows. It was posh enough, in a tacky way, to be Arnie's, and there were a few lights left on, like you might do if you were going away. We decided not to break in, disappointing as that was to Pinto.

Our next stop was The Hideaway. Pinto wanted to take Rudy in.

"Scare them into saying something, right?"

I vetoed that idea and went in by myself. There was the usual mix you would expect in a joint like that half an hour before closing time: professional drunks, guys avoiding going home to either empty houses or hectoring wives, women who had given up trying to attract anyone. The bartender hadn't seen Arnie since Sunday. But then, would he really have said anything?

We went back to Arnie's place and parked down the block where we could keep an eye out. We moved Rudy up front and took turns crapping out in the back seat. I took the first shift and sat behind the steering wheel, thinking about all the ways things could go south. Even if we convinced Davy to get out of town, was a Ramon investigation going to touch any of us? It seemed sure the cops would want to talk to both Cambro and Lou. Could they both deflect attention? And if one of them felt any heat, were they going to keep the other guy out of it? And of course, my biggest worry was that somehow I would get pulled in. I didn't know how good a liar I would be faced with the threat of time in the joint.

Then there was Purcell. Was he keeping an eye on us? Maybe wondering who these clowns were that Lou had brought into his operation?

I was asleep behind the wheel when Pinto banged on the window.

"Hey, you can go in the back for a while."

I stretched out and tossed and turned, thinking I couldn't sleep, but then suddenly I was awakened by early morning sunlight. I got out of the car and found an empty house to piss behind. When I came back, Pinto was smoking a cigarette, leaning against the hood. Rudy was asleep or in a coma, the top half of his head lolling out the window.

I let some of my musing float out. "Wonder if Purcell's found anything out?"

Pinto fumed. "I don't trust that big dick."

I looked at his disgusted face. "You were just singing doo-wop harmony with him last week."

"He's a sneaky fuck. Even for a cop." Pinto shook his head. "An Italian named Purcell? That's fuckin' Purcelli in the old country."

"Guess they sold out to the soup line."

"What's that mean?"

"It's an Irish thing."

He threw the butt on the ground. "Gotta be something open by now."

I got in the driver's seat. It was quarter to seven. "Maybe a 7-11." Pinto clapped his hands and went around to the other side of the car, leaning in the window. "You hear that? We're getting Slurpees!"

* * *

The 7-11 was open. I pulled around back, behind a dumpster, and got out. I bent down to the back seat window. "Any special requests?"

Pinto gave me a thoughtful look. "I'm thinking blueberry." He turned to Rudy, whose eyes were open but maybe not really seeing anything. "Hey, what flavor you want?"

Rudy's eyes shifted without his head moving, like he was the mummy. He didn't seem to care what flavor he got.

Pinto said, "Get him cherry. And take your time. Me and Rudes got plenty to talk about."

At least someone was happy. I went into the store and got two Slurpees and a coffee.

As I came back to the car, I heard a conversation floating out. I handed a Slurpee through the window, which Pinto immediately handed over to Rudy, who had a little more color in his cheeks, which offered a nice contrast to the dried black blood crusted under his nose and chin. I gave Pinto the other cup. He took a noisy slug through the straw and beamed.

"Hey, guess what, this mug went to Bartram."

I looked at Rudy, who was staring straight ahead. He turned and looked at me. His eyes said, "Is this guy for real?"

I sipped at my coffee. "No shit. Small world, huh? What, you go to Bartram, too?"

Pinto shook his head as if I were a fool. "What, you kidding me? I went to Southeast Catholic."

"So, what's the...?"

"Hey, there's all sorts of Bartram guys hung out with us...at Pop's, you know, the luncheonette." Pinto drifted into a reverie. "Morty and Sol...those guys were funny."

"Really, that's great. You ask him what parish he's from?"

Pinto turned like he was shifting on a barstool. "Hey, right, what...?"

Rudy looked at him like he was...well, a stupid fucking dago. "I'm a *Jew*."

Pinto pulled back, then turned to me. "Yeah, what kind of a fucking question is that...?"

Rudy grunted a little laugh, which I took as an acknowledgment that he knew I wasn't a stupid fucking dago. I got behind the wheel, started the car, and turned around.

"I hate to interrupt the corner-boy reunion, but...we making any progress in locating Arnie?"

It was like the principal had asked if anyone knew who had thrown the stink bomb in the gym. They both looked out opposite windows. Rudy was the guy who maybe knew who did it but couldn't violate the unwritten rule

238

not to rat anyone out. Pinto was the teacher who was failing to control the class. I wasn't very convincing as a hard-ass principal, but I had to give it a try. I nudged Rudy's shoulder.

"Maybe we should get Purcell down here."

That was a bull's-eye. Rudy got a little mad. "Yeah, you candy-asses could definitely use some help."

I started to say that wasn't such a smart remark when Pinto beat me to it. Or, rather, Pinto beat the side of Rudy's head with a beer can that happened to be lying conveniently on the floor. Several times. He threw the crushed can out the window, and I wondered if Lou cared how much blood ended up on the car's upholstery.

I considered Rudy's lolling head. "Jesus Christ."

There was a new gash on his temple that was going to need a doctor. I got out of the car and went back into the 7-11. I got some gauze, tape, and a box of Band-Aids. I came back and tossed them in the back seat. Pinto had calmed down and began patching Rudy up.

"Shit, man, sorry, I lost it."

I asked Rudy, "So where might Arnie have gone?"

I was beginning to worry that Arnie really had fled to Florida. Rudy muttered something inaudible. He had drifted away again. I got in the car and banged the steering wheel.

"Pinto, you fucking moron."

Pinto threw the roll of tape against the dashboard. "Fuck you. I'm done dealing with this hebe."

He got out of the car and stomped off toward the store. I listened to Rudy moan for a few minutes, then pulled the car around front. Pinto was on the curb in front of the 7-11, smoking a cigarette. He got in the back without saying anything.

We drove around town, looking for Arnie's car for an hour. Then we headed south to Cape May Point.

I parked in a corner of the lot at the retreat house. The peacefulness that emanated from the environment seemed phony to me now. Just a few nights ago, Davy and Arnie were having an argument here about…how to cover up a murder?…who was going to take the fall?…who was going to get out of town first…? Yet nobody could interrupt their navel-gazing to see if something was wrong.

Pinto accepted his duty to stay in the car stoically. It was after nine now, and people were moving about. The girl at reception—a novice, I guessed from her age and the simplicity of her garb—wasn't keen on finding Sister Louise. But I kept mentioning Davy's name loudly until I was brought into a small waiting room that felt like a holding pen for incoming penitents.

I was looking at the binding of a red-leather-bound copy of The Lives of the Saints—which was about as deeply as I was interested in delving—when Sister Louise came in and sat down.

She was as worried as I was and twice as clueless. I asked if I could see Davy's room, having no idea what I would look for, but thinking it's the kind of thing a flatfoot would do.

Sister Louise recoiled just a tiny bit. "I'm sorry…we can't…"

She kneaded the fingers of her left hand with those of her right. I didn't need to be Colombo to figure out that she was hiding something.

I pressed her. "Hey, this kid…he could be OD'd…or in trouble…"

Her hands went to her knees, gripping them. "It's…the police were here… and…"

"Police? Do you remember who it was?"

She was staring at a picture of the Blessed Virgin on the wall, which was not difficult as there were several to choose from. "He was a tall man…"

"Dark? With a Smokey the Bear hat?"

"Yes. He checked the room…and told me not to let anyone in there."

It wasn't a huge surprise that Purcell had been here. I told her to call the Seabreeze if she heard anything.

I got back in the car with my two bored, surly charges. Suddenly, I was insanely hungry. I started the car up and we headed back north. When I got into town, I made my way to a familiar leafy street. I parked the car and got out.

"You guys hungry?"

There were folks going in, which was good, as I hadn't been sure if

Randall's did a brunch. Pinto looked at me like I was nuts.

"What the fuck?"

"Come on, get him out."

We stood Rudy up against the car. He was still woozy, and the sloppy bandaging on his head was soaked through with blood. Pinto reached back in the car and started unrolling the gauze.

"Let me clean that up…."

I grabbed the roll out of his hand and threw it back in the car. "He's perfect."

We frog-marched Rudy up to the door between us. We stood in the vestibule for a second, then plunged forward into the dining room. Things were pretty busy, but a big table in the middle of the room under a chandelier was empty. It lacked the privacy that would appeal to all the well-dressed couples with their mimosas and smoked salmon, but it was just the thing for our grouping.

The maître d' was not at his podium, but he showed up soon enough as we settled in.

"*Pardon, messieurs*, but that table is reserved."

He said this like I was Cary Grant with a couple of pals. I had to admire the guy's Gallic poise. Pinto had his arm around Rudy's shoulders, preventing him from nose-diving onto the blindingly white tablecloth. He gave the guy a big smile.

"We hate to impose, gar-con, but my friend here," he shook Rudy roughly, "he had kind of a tough night. So, if you don't mind…keep it simple, three burgers, three fries, and three beers." The guy did not move, but Pinto put up his hand as if to call him back. "Oh, and my friend will need a straw."

The maître d' looked at me as if I were the reasonable member of the party.

I said, "Make mine medium rare."

He gave me a look that summed up what the French thought of asshole Americans.

"I am sorry, but we have no tables available." He pulled himself up an inch or two taller. "I will have to ask you to leave."

"But we're friends of Mark's," I responded.

That news didn't seem to surprise him too much. "Nevertheless."

I made a mental note to see if we could lure this guy to work at the Seabreeze. He had style and balls.

Pinto, on the other hand, was getting hungry. He banged the table, causing the silverware to rattle and all the guys with grey temples and women with pearl necklaces to look over.

"Listen you faggot frog. I want my french fries. Now!" He hit the table again. A fork hit the floor. Rudy's head, unsupported for a few seconds, hovered over the table and delivered a few drops of blood.

The maître d' said, "Very well." He took one step, then turned back. "And would *monsieur* like the...*ketchup*...with his *pomme frites*?"

He didn't wait for an answer, just strode away in a manner that made me think he had been a military officer. I really did admire these French dudes. Pinto turned to a couple at a table close by. The woman was giving us a look like Margaret Dumont would give Groucho when he propositioned her. The guy was trying not to look at us at all.

Pinto said, "Is the service here always this bad?"

A handsome busboy came and poured water into our glasses. I watched the door to the kitchen and could see through the porthole window the maître d' talking with great urgency to someone.

The door pushed open, and Mark came out. He stopped at a few tables on his way to us, chatting amiably like nothing had happened. He must have studied at some school for fancy French restaurant owners. I stood and shook his hand, which seemed to calm the nerves of the couple closest to us. Mark gestured with his head toward the door leading to the bar.

"Can we...move this discussion somewhere...more private?"

I sat back down. "I don't think so."

Mark looked around. Several couples were moving hastily from their tables, shooting dirty glances our way. I pointed at one of them, the guy practically dragging his high-heeled 1940s debutante wife across the floor.

"Whoa, bolting the check?"

Mark gave me a sour look. I brightened.

"Hey, maybe I can learn something. How do you handle that? You got a bouncer or something? Or does André," the maître d' was watching us from the kitchen door, hands behind his back, "get the old service revolver out and execute them at dawn?"

Mark tried to get tough. "What's this all about?"

Pinto pointed a butter knife at him. "Shut the fuck up and sit down." He rocked his chair back on its rear legs and shouted toward the kitchen. "And where are my fucking French Fries?"

Mark hissed at me. "What are you trying to do?"

Pinto stood and walked fast across the room. André—or whatever his name was—stepped aside as he banged through the double doors into the kitchen. André looked pointedly at Mark, then marched toward the entry arch where we had come in, a silent reprimand to his spineless superior officer.

Rudy was awake now and had removed the sodden gauze and tossed it on the table. He made extravagant red marks on a napkin as he tried to stanch the flow from the triangular cut next to his eye.

I pointed at Rudy. "He's looking for his friend."

Mark replied, "What friend?"

That made me mad. I grabbed one of the three forks in my setting— no doubt the wrong one—and jabbed it against Mark's stomach, just hard enough to get him to jump.

"Shit!"

The maître d' was back at the table. He gave my fork a dismissive glance, focusing his eyes on Mark with an only slightly less dismissive expression.

"Would *monsieur* like me to call...?"

The constabulary, I thought? Just a guess. I had a flash of Claude Rains. Mark looked down at the fork, which I withdrew.

"No, Didier, that won't be necessary."

He'd always be André to me. He bowed.

"As you wish."

He went back to the front. I expected maybe we could find him at the Hideaway later, enjoying a well-deserved Pernod. Pinto was back with a big aluminum charger laden with wads of french fries.

"Voila!" He dropped it on the table. "Hold on." He reached into his coat pocket and produced a bottle of Heinz ketchup.

I grabbed a few fries. Pinto was leaning over the table, banging glops of ketchup onto the charger. It was a different red than the bloodstains that marked out Rudy's territory. I bit into a fry, then held the uneaten half out in front of Mark's face.

"Pauline was wrong. These are real." I twisted it around. "Or did you just start doing this after she embarrassed you?"

"I don't know what the fuck you're on about…"

Pinto turned the charger upside down and dumped the fries on the table.

"Easier this way." He threw the charger over his shoulder. It banged against the floor and rolled around on its edge, ending up next to the table of the couple next to us. The guy got to his feet, his face red and scared. I watched them leave, then turned back to Mark.

"We're looking for Arnie."

Pinto was off again to the kitchen. Mark was realizing he couldn't control the assault on two fronts.

"I don't know where he is."

"Bullshit."

"Can we…" his eyes were on the kitchen door, "… go in the back?"

I shook my head. The kitchen doors swung open, and Pinto came out triumphantly. He held up a bottle of champagne.

"Hey, what the fuck…they were all out of Ortlieb's." He shook the bottle up as he got to the table. He peeled off the foil and untwisted the wire cap. "Hey," he grabbed a busboy hurrying by, "get some glasses, would ya?"

I gave Mark another reminder with the fork. "Davy's gone. So is Concetta. This weasel said he doesn't know where Arnie is." I pulled Rudy's head off the table. He was out. "That didn't go so well."

"Why are you looking for Arnie?"

Mark looked perplexed. Maybe he was sincere, but I really didn't care.

Pinto shot the cork up at the chandelier and poured champagne for us all. He plunked a glass in front of Mark, who ignored it.

Mark muttered, "Someone's gonna call the cops."

I watched a few more couples leaving the room. He was probably right. André—I mean, Didier—would rather see Mark suffer, but some gallant from the grey-temple ranks might decide he needed to save everyone else. I got up and tried to tug Rudy to his feet.

"Need some help."

Pinto was at another table, scaring the shit out of a couple by demanding that they join him in a drink. I yelled at him.

"*Paisan!*"

He left the champagne with the lucky couple and helped me lever Rudy's corpulent form upright. He was a lot heavier, fully passed out. We followed Mark to an office in the back and dumped Rudy onto a leather couch there. Mark went behind his desk. Pinto and I took the two chairs in front like we were meeting with our lawyer.

Mark asked, "What's this about Davy?"

I figured I'd give him part of the truth.

"Arnie's been squeezing Concetta for cash—saying he's paying off the kid's debts, but just keeping the money. Now Davy's run off."

He stared at me. Was he astonished, pretending to be astonished?

Mark said, "I don't what you're talking about, but it's got nothing to do with me."

"I saw Arnie in the bar here the day we met. You hooked Davy up with Rudy to get a job." I looked at Rudy's slovenly form. "Should we wake him up and ask him what you know? I'll bet he's looking for someone to share his pain."

"I don't ask Arnie about his business." Mark was feeling more in control behind his desk. "I run a clean operation."

Pinto started to jump up. I put my hand on his arm.

"When's the last time you saw him?"

Mark looked at the ceiling. "Sunday—he had lunch at the bar."

"By himself?"

"Yeah."

Pinto broke free from my hand and was on his feet. "He's a lying fuck."

245

Mark rolled back in his office chair and put his hands up. "Hey, it's the truth. Look, I did you guys a favor, not calling the cops on this bullshit."

"Bullshit?" Pinto grabbed a glass tchotchke dolphin and threw it against the wall. It bounced off and landed on the carpet, unbroken. Fuming, he scrambled over and picked it up and was looking for a hard surface to crash it against when the door opened.

"*Mon dieu!*"

Pauline stepped in, her hands crossed in front of her face.

"Do not hurt me with the glass fish!"

Pinto lowered his hands, so the figurine was in front of his crotch like a Flipper-shaped fig-leaf. He was looking past Pauline, no doubt wondering if Lucie was lurking there. Pauline eyed the scenario with an imperious glance a lot like André's. I mean Didier's.

Pauline looked at me. "I call to find you and talk to Mr. Lou. He says you are in search of Arnie. It is a good guess you come here." She walked across and bent down next to Rudy. "You boys have been busy with your tough-guy labors. He is the easy target." She touched his forehead lightly and stood. "You should be ashamed."

Pinto stepped forward, his arms-wide gesture made somewhat ludicrous by the glass fish. "Hey, we're trying to find Davy." He was clearly worried that word might get back to Lucie about what a big bully he was.

Pauline made a French-sounding scoffing noise, blowing air out through her lips. "Pfff! I know where the Davy boy is."

I got to my feet. "Where?"

She went to Pinto and took Flipper from his hand and ran her hands over its curved back. "He is safe."

"But where is he?" I approached her.

She set the dolphin on Mark's desk. "That I do not tell you."

"Why?"

"Maybe then, he is not so safe."

I looked at Mark, who seemed uncertain whether to flee his own office, or stay put for the lover's quarrel.

I said, "I need to talk to him."

Pauline made her scoffing noise again, with a slight change in intonation. She could probably sing a scale in scoffs.

"Then you have the same thought. Davy ask me to find you for the chat." She went to the door. "Come, time is in the waste basket."

I looked at Pinto, who could see his assignment coming and didn't like it.

I pointed at Rudy. "Keep an eye on him until we…"

Pinto flopped into a chair and raised his arms in surrender. "Whatever you say, boss."

I turned to Mark. "Let me talk to Davy, then we'll figure out what to do with this guy."

He wasn't happy, but he didn't argue.

Pinto called out to Mark as Pauline and I left. "Hey, any chance of that burger now?"

* * *

Pauline and I drove to her apartment in silence. I parked the car, and she started to get out. I grabbed her arm.

"We should talk here." I was thinking about Lucie. "So you spoke to Davy?"

"No." Pauline pulled the door shut. "I talk to Concetta."

"Are they together?"

"Not now." She shook her head. "Davy was in much trouble. A lot of money. Arnie said he would help make the payoff to these gangsters."

I started to interrupt her, to tell her she was on an older version of the script. But I stopped myself so I could hear what Concetta thought was happening.

"Go on," I prodded.

"Just last weekend, Davy was thinking maybe he could go back to your South Philly when enough is paid off. He call a friend to check his temperature."

"You mean the temperature."

"Do not interrupt. And his friend say he is still in big trouble. That no one has paid off his debts, what is he talking about? But that he hears some

247

folks now think they know where he is."

I sorted through the half-truths and outright lies, then nodded so she would keep talking.

Pauline continued. "Davy understood then that Arnie was doing the rip-off. So he calls Arnie."

"So that was who came to see him on Sunday?"

"Yes. Davy tells Arnie he will tell Lou what Arnie has done if he does not pay back."

"And Arnie says...?"

"Arnie says he will tell Lou about Concetta's..."

Her face held a question for me, which was—did I know? And anyone else? I gave her a nod.

"Lou already knows."

"And Davy tells Arnie that he does not care. He must pay back. Then Arnie laugh at him...says if he tells Lou about this scam, Arnie will make Davy meet the dogs."

My Pauline translator repeated back the corrected phrase. "Throw him to the dogs, you mean."

"Yes. And now, Concetta says Davy wants to talk with you...as the talk-between to his father. He tells her to step to a side and let him do the cleanup with his father."

I had to bite my bottom lip and then my top one to keep from laughing at what a load of baloney Davy had fed his mother. I couldn't think of a good reason to tell Pauline this. Her ignorance was important to me.

It seemed like a good time to find a phone booth for a call that I both wanted and feared.

* * *

I was sweating in the booth as I put a dime in the phone and spread the rest of the change out on the shelf. I knew what Lou wanted me to say, but I was still working through what Davy had apparently told Concetta. Maybe it all made sense as a way for him to keep her out of the real trouble. And I guessed it was not easy to tell your mom that her husband was a drug dealer and her son had ripped both of them off and killed a more-or-less innocent bystander to boot.

And Davy had killed the guy. I believed it. And this wasn't another dust-up with Officer O'Toole that I could smooth over and give him a stern talking-to about. We were out of Dead-End Kids territory.

I thought how odd it was that each higher level of danger buried the anxiety that went before it. Just a few days ago, I was freaked out that I could end up in prison as an accomplice to Lou's drug-running, and now that was pushed out of my mind as I took on the assignment to negotiate a separation package for a psychotic would-be gangster.

But something inside me said Davy wasn't a psycho. Deluded, certainly; convinced he was a victim and aspiring to a stupid life that he was too lazy to realize would be a disaster, no doubt. But not a psycho. So what was Davy's problem, really? Was he just a kid who believed the gangster bravado? That being a working stiff was for mugs who didn't have the balls to go after the easy life?

Was he junk-sick—did that somehow lead to his trigger-happy behavior? He had seemed clean when I saw him. I was no expert on addiction, but I knew it could be a never-ending battle. But if he was still on the needle, I didn't think cold-blooded impulsive murder was that likely for a junkie who had just heisted enough heroin to obliterate his feelings for a decade.

Davy and Lou never had a warm relationship, though they both would fake it on occasion. I always felt that his dad confused him. Lou knew a lot of "the guys" in South Philly, and no doubt was in some minor scrapes and larceny when he was a kid, but he really had been pretty straight. He had toyed with the idea of being a doctor like his dad, but that ended after one year of college. Then he said he was pre-law for two years, but what did that really mean? The fact is, Lou was a born salesman, and he made a good choice going into the car business. He kept his South Philly connections, and sure, he sold cars to a lot of questionable characters, and if customers weren't candidates for a normal car loan, he would hook them up with the local back-of-the-barber-shop lenders.

So Davy saw the mob guys eat pasta with the old man, heard their shtick, and watched Lou laugh with them. And Lou maybe never told Davy that he wasn't one of them. Like a lot of dads, he was so wrapped up in his own psycho-drama, like my film teacher used to say about Bergman's heroes, that he expected Davy to figure everything out for himself. And the kid tried, but he took so many wrong turns, eventually it became impossible to retrace his steps to a solid starting point. Finding out that his dad had taken up drug-dealing as a hobby also did not help.

Pauline said she didn't know where they were hiding out. I was supposed to call at a specific time, so I figured he was waiting at a phone booth in some fleabag motel.

The phone picked up after more than twenty rings, but no one spoke for thirty seconds. Then a dead monotone responded.

"Yo."

"Davy?"

Another ten seconds. The voice was a little more alive. "Yeah, it's me."

I thought for a second about whose call this was. While I was figuring that out, Davy spoke again.

"The fucking old man needs to step up."

"Meaning what?" I wanted to reach through the phone and push his scrawny neck up against a wall like I had done just a few years ago.

"Meaning I want my money."

"You got bigger things to worry about, my friend."

"Yeah, so does he. You think I don't got a copy of that tape?"

Jesus Christ, I thought. "You shot a guy in cold blood, you fucking idiot."

"I don't know what you're talking about."

"We got Rudy. He told us the whole story."

Davy laughed. There was no happiness in the sound. "Bullshit. That was Arnie, man."

"Really? Good luck convincing anyone of that. Besides," I pushed a quarter around in circles, "it's not the cops you gotta worry about."

"So the old man's put out a posse on his only begotten son?"

Now I was mad. "Listen, you stupid fuck, we're trying to save your ass.

Ramon's boss is itching to let his crew loose on you. You may be hoping the cops pull you in then."

His voice went dead again. "I want my cash."

"Don't be stupid. You'll get your cash. And a ticket to get your ass out of the country. It's your only option."

"I don't need your stupid ticket."

"Yes, you do. Don't be an idiot. You tell us where to meet and we'll bring what you need."

"How do I know you're not gonna bust me?"

Jesus Christ, I thought, this is like the fucking blackmail discussions all over. I tried a little psychology.

"Because you're right, Lou needs to play your game and give you the cash. But he's…thought this through, and he's right, you've got to get where the cops can't get you."

There was silence, which I took as a good sign. Then his voice came back, wary.

"Okay, go to Higbee Beach, on the west side of the Cape…then head south. Tomorrow night, eight o'clock."

"Where will you…?"

"I'll see you coming."

"Right." I thought of something else. "What about the tape?"

"If I get the cash, he'll get the tape."

"How do we know there's not yet another copy?"

"Guess you'll just have to trust me."

I figured we were finished, but questions kept springing up. "Why'd you have to rip off your mom?"

"You mean that shit with Arnie—the drug debts? Guess Rudy told you about that. What the hell, she's enabled the old man enough."

"Enabled him? Glad to see you picked up some lingo from your treatment. So she's just getting what she deserved?"

"Something like that."

"I guess I did my share of enabling you—and I fucking regret it now."

"Say three Hail Mary's and call me in the morning."

I was getting exhausted. An automated operator voice came on and insisted I put in more coins. I slammed a quarter into the slot.

"So where is Arnie?"

I didn't like the laugh that came back down the line. "Don't worry about that piece of shit."

"I heard you guys had a big argument at the retreat house."

"He was scared. Like I said, he popped Ramon, now he's shitting bricks. He punked out on the drop; wanted me and Rudy to handle the whole thing, then give him his share. I told him fine. But since the thing got botched, he hasn't shown his face." Davy laughed, a sharp sound that made me sad. "I figure he split. He's got his share of the H. He was going to take it to Florida and unload it there."

It all sounded a bit too neat. I forced myself to return to my mission.

"Look, we gotta do this right. You have to be out of here in another day."

"Sure, sure...don't want to screw up the old man's story."

"This isn't about him now—it's about you."

"Yeah, sure. How about I go tell the cops right now that the old man came to me with a big box and said hold this for a while, it's just...don't worry, no one will ever think of bothering you at your retreat? And that I read in the paper about Ramon dying, and, thought, isn't that the guy my dad used to buy parts from? So, Christ, I didn't know what to do...and I shouldn't have done it, but I opened the box. And I'm an addict, so I knew right away what it was. And jeez, I never thought he was a murdering gangster drug-dealer, but...I had to do the right thing. I did do the right thing, right, officer?"

"The cops won't believe that once they hear Rudy talk."

"Guess he decided he's more scared of Arnie than me." His laugh came from an even deeper blackness. "Wrong fucking guess. Anyway, it's his word against mine."

This kid was twisted. "You got clean. You had a chance to straighten yourself out. Why are you fixed on fucking your old man?"

"You want chapter and verse? Or the Cliff Notes Version?"

"Not to mention what this is doing to your mom?"

"She made her bed. Hey, you know, I got started in this drug game selling

252

nickel bags to kids at Neumann. One of Dad's poker buddies was my supplier. After a while, the guy got worried that Lou would find out and get pissed. So he told him. You know what he said?"

I waited. I felt like I was on one of the rings of hell, and the heat in the phone booth didn't help.

Davy's voice rose. "He told the guy, 'I don't want to know. As long as he's not using."

I didn't know what to say. Davy pressed on.

"Then I did start using." That empty laugh came up from the depths again. "And he didn't want to know about that either."

I was getting tired of this bullshit. "It's always somebody else's fault, right?"

"Oh, fuck me...it's all about the guilt with you Irishmen."

Another face flashed into my mind. "Is Concetta...?"

Davy sounded annoyed. "Don't worry about her."

"When you say don't worry, I get fucking worried."

His annoyance edged into anger. "She's fucking fine, just...she's fine."

"Is she with you?"

"No. I gave her a story she could accept and got her out of the way."

I had one last question. "What'd you have to do it for, Davy? I mean, Christ, Ramon..."

Davy's voice was quiet. "What, now I'm supposed to spill my guts to you? Whatever happened to Ramon, he was in the game."

"So it's a game?"

"That it is, Uncle Ginty. And you better be asking yourself whether you're in or out. 'Cause there ain't no halfway."

The line went dead.

Chapter Twenty-Two

Friday morning, Pinto and I sat on the front porch, enjoying our coffee like a couple of husbands on vacation. The girls had taken over the bathroom, which just made it seem even more like a domestic situation. I had a feeling like when you cut school. You know you're going to get in trouble eventually. You may even feel like you're being an idiot long-term by not learning whatever they're dishing out that day. But you say, what the fuck—we're having fun now, right? I had talked to Lou; he was pulling together his plan for Davy's exit. I didn't ask where he was sending him. We agreed that Pinto and I would take Rudy to his house and tell him to stay there for the next couple of days. And then to go about his business as usual, with the understanding that he was the next candidate for a visit from Sleepy & Co. if he started gabbing.

When I mentioned that Purcell had been to the retreat house and searched Davy's room, Lou acted surprised.

"He didn't say anything about that to me."

"Sounds like normal cop stuff."

"Maybe. But we don't want Sister Whoever to start calling the cops asking for an update, right? This is supposed to be just Purcell and the guys he can trust doing what they can on the QT."

We left it at that. So here we were with our Chock Full O' Nuts and cigarettes, when up rolls a State Trooper's car. I didn't need to check its number to know who it was.

Pinto yelled, "Hey, *Paisan!*"

I was beginning to understand how Pinto's standard greeting could accommodate any situation, depending on the intonation and shared history of the target—sort of like Pauline's mouth scolds. In this case, he was telling Purcell that he was a disgrace to all Italian-Americans for changing his name.

I grabbed Pinto's arm. "Don't say anything about my call with Davy."

Purcell had gotten out and was standing on the sidewalk like he was Marshal Dillon. Or The Thing. One of those James Arness roles.

He came up the walk and gave us the cop-stare.

"Aren't you guys supposed to be finding Arnie?"

"He's disappeared." I came off the porch and sat down on the steps. "No one's seen him for a couple of days."

Purcell took a few steps and put his big black boot up on the step next to me. "I had a guy down in Jupiter check out his place there. He hasn't shown there either."

Pinto came off the porch, ignoring Purcell. He picked up a handful of pebbles and began tossing them at a no-parking sign next to Purcell's cruiser.

Pinto called out. "How 'bout Lou's missus?" A rock dinged against the sign. "Anything to report there, Mr. Super Trooper?"

Purcell's head rotated toward Pinto like it was on a hydraulic hinge. "No."

Pinto flung another pebble at the sign. It bounced off the metal at a sharp angle, then hit the hood of the patrol car with a loud thunk. Pinto chortled.

"Bank shot!" He gave Purcell his best phony sales-guy smile. "Hey, no worry, bring it in the shop and we'll buff that right out."

I offered innocently, "We went to the retreat house, but they couldn't tell us anything more than what we'd already heard."

Purcell made an effort to move his gaze back to me and nodded seriously. "We haven't found any trace of either of them. Maybe they went back to Philly."

At least Purcell was being consistent in not telling me about his visit to the retreat house. And either Lou hadn't talked to him at all or had decided not to tell him about my call with Davy.

Pinto had bigger rocks now and was throwing them at a telephone pole at least thirty yards away. Purcell pulled his foot off the porch, his boots creaking as he stood up tall. I was really getting tired of his *Gunsmoke* reenactments.

"Why are you here, anyway?" I asked. "I didn't hear Lou tell you to tail us."

"I was hoping to talk to the young ladies here. Just normal police work. Lou told me one of them had gotten close to Concetta." He laughed. "Guess I'll call Lou now, tell him you guys were taking a little poontang break, but you'll be back to work soon."

Pinto threw a rock backhanded against the fender of the cruiser and was in front of Purcell before the hollow bang had stopped reverberating. By "in front of", I mean his head was tilted up right under Purcell's chin, and his hand had grabbed the leather strap that ran across the trooper's torso.

"You got a mouth, you know that, you big dick?" He pressed his fist into Purcell's stomach. "Now you're gonna tell those ladies you're sorry."

Pauline was on the porch, on cue, and Lucie was edging out through the screen door. Purcell turned his eyes down, his chin doubling against his neck. He reached a hand up and grabbed Pinto by the shirt, lifting him up on his toes.

"Watch it, you little piece of shit or I'll..."

Pinto was totally relaxed in Purcell's grip, smiling. He said, "Looking forward to it, big guy."

Purcell let go of him. Pinto didn't release his grip, nodding toward the girls.

"Do the right thing, my friend."

Pinto released his hold and stepped back. Purcell shifted toward the girls. "My apologies, ladies. Just a school-yard misunderstanding."

Lucie sashayed down the steps, turning her nose up at Purcell. A hound like him couldn't help but be bamboozled by her alluring figure, and by her nuzzling up to a little guy like Pinto. I considered Purcell ogling her.

"Guess she doesn't have a thing for a man in a uniform," I said.

A sarcastic voice brought our attention back to the porch.

"This is the infamous *gendarme* Purcell?"

Pauline came down the steps.

"You are wanting to question me?"

Purcell's manner turned all charming. "Ma'am, I'm just trying to..."

"Mademoiselle, mon chum."

She gave him a frosty look. I was beginning to catch on to these niceties, but it went right over his head.

"Must I get my lawyer?" she asked mockingly.

Purcell took his hat off and held the brim in his hands like Gary Cooper.

"This is a serious matter." His voice lowered. "We're trying to locate Concetta Scolletta…"

Pauline put her thumb and index finger into her mouth and produced a whistle that my high school basketball coach would have been proud of.

"Lucie! *Alors, ici!*"

Lucie held up her hand, put her head on top of Pinto's for a moment—she was taller in her high heel sandals—and left him there musing on the street corner. She ignored us men and came up to Pauline. They talked in French, Lucie giving Purcell a disparaging look.

Purcell tried his strong and silent shtick again. "I'm just trying to…"

Pauline flicked her fingers, which was a different way to scoff, apparently. "Please to talk to my *avocat.*"

Purcell looked at Lucie. You would think he had never seen an attorney with breasts before. He put his hat back on and walked to the car. Lucie made a little noise that meant a sarcastic "big man," if I understood her.

I followed him over. He opened his door and looked at me.

I said, "We'll let you know if we find anything."

It was a lie, but one the situation demanded. Purcell pulled away without a word. I felt for the guy. It wasn't every day that a State Trooper got bested by a small-time thug from South Philly and a barely clothed lawyer from Quebec.

And aside from that, he really did have something to worry about. One thing I had learned in years working behind a bar was you never called a guy like Pinto "little".

* * *

I wanted it all to go away. Of course I did. Pinto seemed more able to compartmentalize what was coming tonight, keep it away from the humid yet relaxed atmosphere in the apartment. He went for a walk with Lucie, who borrowed two cigarettes from Pauline on her way out. They spoke in French, and for once, Lucie seemed genuinely concerned about Pauline's mood. Pauline had been quiet since Purcell left, but that ended quickly once Lucie and Pinto were gone.

We were in the cramped little kitchen. I was pretending to read a newspaper that was yellow with age. It could have been from the Nixon administration for all I could tell, as my eyes ignored the words on the page.

Pauline flicked the page with an angry finger.

"It is all the bullshit."

I set the paper down. "Yeah, they're talking about the Tet offensive here, and it was bullshit even back then."

"Don't be the smart-ass. You know what she told me was not true. But you do not say anything." She smoldered over her coffee, which was not unattractive, but alarming still. "You like me in the dark."

I didn't disagree with that last statement, but I was smart enough not to get smart right now.

"It's better this way." I sounded like I was placating her, but I believed it.

"I know that Davy is in trouble." Pauline held her mug in two hands, looking into the liquid. "Concetta has been lied to. Maybe she is lying too, I do not know. But I know her little boy is in trouble."

"He's not a little boy. He's…"

"He is still hers, even if he is now a nasty big guy." She held the mug to her mouth but did not drink. "This Purcell, I do not like. Why is he coming here if Davy's problem is with Arnie? That is a stupid problem. I have met this Arnie and he has a lightweight."

I reached across and touched her arm. "Pauline…"

"And this Purcell…he does not act like the police I know."

My hand was on her arm, but she wasn't responding to my touch. "Purcell is tight with Lou."

She snorted in disgust. "If I am Lou, I look at my back."

I gave up on her arm and stood. "Come with me."

She followed me like I was a social worker leading her to a cubicle for a depressing discussion. We went out on the porch, and I tugged her arm.

"Let's walk."

We went in the direction of the beach. It had clouded over, and the humidity made your shirt stick to your back. She let me hold her hand, and we walked without talking until we came to the edge of the beach. We climbed the steps and went down to the water.

There were scatterings of people on chairs and blankets. It was likely to rain soon. I kept moving toward the water, and when we got to the wet sand, Pauline stopped.

"My jeans will get wet."

I looked down at the khakis I was wearing, which were already damp and sandy at the bottom. I rolled them up to my calves. Pauline laughed.

"You look like…"

"A beachcomber?" I reached down and dug a cracked shell out of the sand. "You always see pictures like that, right. Even Robinson Crusoe rolled his pants up."

"Yes?" She sounded doubtful, but she tugged at the cuffs of her jeans, trying to fold them up, holding on to my arm for balance. She stood on one leg and was not making much progress.

"*Merde!*" She yelped and plopped down on the sand. "Now, I can do."

She got her jeans rolled precisely. I helped her back up and pulled her into me. I kissed her like…like I wanted it to be the only thing I would do for the rest of my life. She dropped her head and pushed it into my chest.

"I hear you and Pinto talk…about tonight."

I hoped she had not heard much. I tried to sound business-like. "We just need to take care of something. Don't worry."

She pulled her head back. "I am allowed to worry. I have paid the price of the mission. Now," she linked arms with me and tugged me along, "feel the water with me. Then you can go do your performance."

I let her guide me, and I wished that she could do that for a long time, with the salt air wrapping us inside its shroud.

* * *

Pinto brought pizza, but he was the only one who ate it. Lou couldn't stop moving, getting the cash together, talking on the phone to someone who was making arrangements for wherever Davy was supposed to land. He zipped up a leather gym bag and stood staring at the kitchen table.

"We'll drive him to the airport." Lou spoke as if convincing himself that Davy would just jump in the back seat.

I didn't say anything. Nothing about this felt like it was going to work, other than Davy taking the money. Davy would be stupid not to follow the plan, but being smart wasn't that high on his list of priorities.

Pinto paused with a slice halfway to his mouth. "I'll get him in the car. Shit, I'll stuff him in a suitcase if you want."

Lou ignored him. The phone rang and he almost fell over a chair picking it up. He didn't say hello, just listened, pinching the bridge of his nose, his eyes closed.

The hand dropped from his face, and he held it out emphatically. "Yeah, yeah…" His hand clenched. "You work on finding my wife, right? Call me if you find anything. Right."

I didn't need to ask who that was. "Someone's feeling left out?"

Lou sat down. "He doesn't need to know about this."

"That's good. He gives me the heebie-jeebies. Goes to the retreat house, but doesn't tell either of us. Comes by Pauline's apartment…finds us, says he was really hoping to get Pauline by herself. Always just turning up.

Lou responded unconvincingly. "Sounds like good police work."

I replied, "I said the same thing yesterday, remember?"

Pinto interjected, "He ain't good police." He picked a piece of pepperoni off a slice. "'Course you know that. If he was good, he wouldn't be working for you."

It was a sign of Lou's distress that he let this dig go. His hands kept moving, drumming on the table, then clenched together, then gripping the seat of his chair.

"I don't want to spook the kid any more than he already is." The hands came to his face, massaging his temples. "He sees cops again..."

I nodded and looked at the clock. Then I got up to pee for maybe the tenth time in the last two hours. When I came back, Pinto was trying to fit the pizza box in the refrigerator. He gave up and turned to Lou.

"You got any tin foil to wrap this up with?"

Lou ignored him for the third time. He grabbed the bag and headed for the stairs.

Pinto started to say something, then tossed the pizza box on top of the stove and fell in step behind me.

* * *

It turned out that none of us had ever been to Higbee Beach. We followed signs to a parking lot at the end of a lonely road. The sun was just beginning to set. There were a handful of cars. We walked on a winding path through trees and unruly vegetation, passing several folks bundled in sweatshirts and windbreakers coming the other way. They all smiled that way that people do who are just glad to be able to do nothing.

When we reached the beach, we looked south and could see maybe a dozen people idling around, looking out at the bay or picking up shells. It occurred to me that for this meeting, maybe Davy preferred somewhere more public.

Pinto was ten yards ahead of us. Lou tugged at my sleeve, holding me back. I fell in step with him. He talked without looking at me.

"This is the right thing. It's been...everything this kid has done, it's been a fucking disaster. How many times do I got to bail him out? This is it. He's on his own after this."

I wondered how many times he had said the same thing before.

Lou kept going. "I mean, what the fuck am I supposed to do? The kid's got no respect for anything. Not even for himself."

I realized Lou was expecting me to tell him he was right. But that wasn't what came out of my mouth.

"Maybe you've been too tough on the kid."

Lou stopped and grabbed my arm. "Too tough?"

Pinto had stopped up ahead and was pointedly not looking at us.

Lou lowered his voice, but the tone was even harder. "He been crying on your shoulder? What a bad dad I was?"

I knocked his hand off my arm. "Maybe he wishes you didn't have friends who were so ready to take him on as a street dealer."

Lou pulled back. "Oh? So that's my fault?" The sarcasm was bitter.

"What did you do when you found out?"

Both of us were surprised I said it. Lou took a step back, a step that would separate us forever.

"So you're on his side now?"

I started walking. When I caught up to Pinto, I stopped and looked back. Lou was looking at the bay. Maybe he was figuring out how he was going to deal with me. I didn't care.

Lou started walking toward us at a fast pace and didn't stop or look at us. We followed him along, going another half a mile. The beach was deserted down here. Then we saw a guy sitting in the sand in front of a driftwood fire, halfway up to the dunes.

Davy stood up and waved. As we approached, he was poking the fire with a stick.

"I got into this shit at the retreat house." He held up the stick, its end glowing. "I woulda made a hell of a Boy Scout."

He had on shorts and a Tony Mart's sweatshirt. Pinto gave the bag to Lou, who dropped it in the sand in front of Davy.

Lou turned to Pinto and me. "Give us a minute here."

Pinto put his hand in the air, saluting with two fingers, and walked off, trying to light a cigarette in the wind. Davy stepped forward.

"No, Unka Ginty, why don't you stay?"

Lou didn't even look at me. He touched the bag with his shoe.

"Here it is. Cash, plane tickets. There's some…foreign currency there…for when you land." It was like he was sending him off to camp. "There's a note, tells you what train to take. When you get to the town, there's a café, you ask for Phillip, he'll take care of you." He flipped his hand out. "It's all in the note. Flight's early tomorrow. We'll drive you to the airport now."

Davy knelt and unzipped the bag, pulling out a stack of bills. He riffled them with his thumb. He gave his dad a look that he'd probably used a thousand times.

"So that's it, huh? Then I'm outta your hair."

Lou kept up the dad act. "Davy, this is the only way."

Davy smirked. "Yeah, well, fuck you, old man. And thanks for the cash."

Lou was as close to a breaking point as I'd ever seen. He asked, "Where's the tape?"

Davy put the bills back in the bag and zipped it up. "I gave it to the old lady."

Lou reached down fast like he was going to grab Davy. I stepped between them, and he stopped.

"So she's seen it?" Lou's face was down close to Davy's.

Davy looked up casually. "No. I fed her a whole lot of bullshit about what's going on—just ask your junior partner there." He gave me a head-nod. "So she has no idea. The tape's in a box. She doesn't even know what's in there. I told her you'd be real interested in what's in it. And I said don't open it, just use it to get whatever you want from the old man."

Lou straightened up and stood back. "So the bullshit never stops."

Davy's answer was matter-of-fact. "Well, you know that."

There was a moment of silence. I looked south and far away, I saw a blinking light that was getting closer. Within ten seconds, it was a lot closer, and I could see it was a blue light and it was bright, turning atop a jeep that was rocketing toward us.

"GET DOWN!"

The words came from the dunes. I froze as another command came, amplified through a bullhorn.

"GET ON THE FUCKING GROUND! NOW!"

The three of us dropped to our knees. I looked toward the dunes and saw two figures moving toward us. One had a bullhorn and both had their arms outstretched. The sun was setting, and it was hard to make out if they were pointing guns at us, but it wasn't a bet I wanted to take.

263

Pinto was halfway between us and the guys with the guns, and was moving to his knees nonchalantly, like he was following instructions at five o'clock mass. Lou and Davy were both on the ground like me, but unlike me, suddenly had pistols in their hands.

The jeep screeched up ten feet away, spraying wet sand everywhere. A big cop got out, and I didn't need a program to know that Purcell was entering the scene.

One of the cops was standing over Pinto, and the other was standing over us.

"Drop the weapons!" he shouted.

The cop—was he a cop?—wore a dark hooded sweatshirt pulled tight around his head, his face partially obscured by a pair of safety goggles. Lou dropped his gun. Davy did not.

Davy craned his neck around to Lou. "What, is this an instant replay?"

Lou stared at Purcell. I knew right away that this was not a repeat of the last beach rendezvous.

Purcell strode over and tapped Lou and me on our heads. "Come with me."

We followed him twenty yards down the beach, out of earshot of the others.

Purcell spoke as if he had no idea who we were. "I don't know what you gentlemen are doing here, but this is a police operation." He pointed at Davy, who still had not dropped his gun. "That's a dangerous criminal over there."

Lou said, "What the fuck..."

Purcell cut him off. "I shouldn't tell you this, but he's got a kilo of an illegal substance with him in that pack."

He pointed at Davy. A small green backpack had magically appeared in the sand next to him.

Purcell continued. "And we know that he's here to make a sale. We already have his buyer."

Purcell nodded to yet another hooded possible-cop, who was frog-marching a scrawny figure across the sand toward us.

Purcell said, "We tailed this second gentleman all the way from Buena...

264

and he's a known trafficker…"

I interrupted. "That guy couldn't buy a dime bag without pawning all his Brewer and Shipley records."

Of course, it was my old friend Drew. Of course. Purcell's façade dropped for a moment.

"Your operation was getting too hot." He stared at Lou. "I've been looking for a way to shut it down and get out. Which I knew you and Cambro wouldn't be too keen on." He turned his intimidation act to me. "Then Ramon told me someone new just did a pickup. That's why I tailed you and your big-mouth friend out to the Parkway; no problem spotting that old Caddy. Figured maybe you could be the fall guys. Lucky for you, this fell in my lap." He laughed humorlessly. "It was child's play tracking Davy down. Didn't know we'd find you here too." His look went back to Lou. "Kid'll take this rap in a heartbeat. And no one will want to talk about Ramon. Or our little venture."

He slipped back into his role.

"I suggest you gentlemen vacate this location immediately. For your own safety."

Lou's voice was like ice. "You take him in—you take me, too."

Purcell said, "I don't think so."

He beckoned to the guy with Drew. "Get these guys out of here."

The cop parked Drew on the sand next to Davy, then pointed with a very convincing firearm toward the dunes. As we walked past Pinto, who was still on his knees, the guy with us turned to the also-hooded henchman guarding Pinto.

He gestured at Pinto. "Bring that guy too."

The man over Pinto turned to look at his partner, and in that split second, Pinto sprinted away toward the dunes. With a curse, the man started to chase him. The one guarding Davy turned and fired a shot toward Pinto, who was zig-zagging across the sand like he was Gale Sayers eluding tacklers.

Then Davy grabbed the bag with the money and took off in the opposite direction. The guy wheeled around and fired a shot after Davy, who stumbled, then turned in a crouch and fired back at him.

At the first shot I dove onto the sand and was flat out, hoping nobody—especially me—was getting hit in this mess. Then I saw a big pair of boots moving past me and looked up to see Purcell raising his gun with both hands like he was on the firing range. Three shots rang out in rapid succession.

I had never seen a gunfight except in the movies or TV, but I knew this was not a gunfight.

This was an execution.

* * *

One of the hooded guys had dragged Lou off of Davy's lifeless body and deposited him by the smoldering remains of the driftwood fire. Then he left without talking to Purcell. The others were already gone, along with Drew. Maybe they were trying to chase down Pinto. Maybe they had gone back to their Beagle Boys' lair, where they could grin and throw knives against the wall. Or maybe they really were cops or troopers or whatever: Purcell had certainly shown that having a badge didn't exactly make you eligible for canonization.

Lou was trembling, his head buried between his knees. Purcell talked to me as Lou would either have collapsed or tried to kill him with his bare hands if he came near him.

"Take him and get out of here." He looked up and down the beach. "Before the ambulance shows up."

"You mean the hearse."

I hadn't inspected the body, but it hadn't moved in ten minutes. Purcell got very close to me and took the fabric of my shirt between two fingers and pulled me even closer.

"This was a drug bust. He drew on me. If he wasn't so stupid, he'd still be alive." His grip tightened. "I don't need another witness. And you don't want to explain why you were here. Because you were either in on the drug deal, or you were having a bon voyage party for a murder suspect."

I pulled away from him, and he let go. "It would almost be worth it to have the whole fucking crew of you put away."

Purcell laughed, a disgusting sound. "You want to put a target on your back? It'd be a contest to see who gets you first, your good buddy Lou or that fat fuck Mexican."

"Or you."

Now, Purcell smiled, which was even uglier than his laugh. "Smart guy, aren't you?"

My insides were churning with fear, but hatred would not let me stop talking.

"I guess you're lucky the kid actually drew on you. 'Cause I'm guessing that was going to happen one way or another."

Purcell was done. "Get him out."

I got Lou to his feet and we began the long walk back to the car. I kept us close to the water so Lou wouldn't have to see Davy. I don't think he was seeing anything. When we got close to Davy's body, I left Lou staring out at the dark water and forced myself to approach him. He was half on his side, his body curled up, arms splayed out. His forehead was in the sand. I knelt next to him and tried to think of a prayer, but even if I still believed in praying, I couldn't bring any words into my mind. I touched his back and just held my hand there with my eyes closed. After a minute, I opened them and noticed that there was a tattoo on the back of his neck, barely visible in the moonlight. I flicked on my cigarette lighter and held it close, and read the words: *"Non Dimenticarmi"*. I didn't know what it meant, but it had to be something sad.

* * *

We waited at Lou's house until the call came to tell us of the tragic shooting. I offered to drive Lou to identify the body, but he wouldn't let me. He hadn't talked on the drive home. I told him what Purcell had told me. He just shook his head, but my guess was he was going along with the story.

Lou had been gone for a couple of hours, and it was around two o'clock when I heard someone coming in the door. I got upright on the couch and saw Pinto's head appear in the stairwell. He went to the sink, washed his hands, and splashed water on his face. Then he sat at the kitchen table. His tracksuit had grass stains and mud on it. He was inspecting some scrape marks on his hands.

"Where's Lou?"

I gave him the story. For once, he had no comic come-backs. He sat back in the chair. He looked very tired.

"I heard the shots. But I figured...I don't know, I wasn't thinking anything except I wasn't letting that bozo take me in."

I got two beers out of the fridge and handed him one. "That's the last thing he wanted to do."

"Yeah, I can see it now." He took a long drink. "Lou's gotta be..."

"He's in shock, or something like that." I looked at my bottle, which was half-empty, although I had no memory of drinking anything. "Maybe I am, too. How'd you get here?"

"I ran through more fucking dune grass and shit than you could believe. I don't think those guys really wanted to catch me. I hunkered down for an hour, then took a chance on the road. Walked until I found a phone booth and called a guy...owes me a favor, right? He picked me up."

I was getting tired of the favor culture. We sat in silence for fifteen minutes, then Pinto spoke.

"Is Lou really gonna let that *giamoke* get away with this?"

"What can he do? It'll be his word against four cops."

"You think they were cops?"

"I don't know. I didn't see any badges."

Pinto had that thinking face again. "Yeah...undercover, probably. Purcell needed witnesses. Not that they weren't the kind of cops who would say whatever he told them to. Especially if the victim is a degenerate drug dealer."

Pinto had clearly spent more time thinking about these types of things than I had.

I asked, "So how can Lou fight that story?"

Pinto picked at a scab on his hand. "Suppose Lou says we were there. Davy was in trouble with some guys in South Philly. Sort of true, and easy enough to back it up. Lou was trying to get him out of the country."

"Yeah, but Purcell's got Davy with the drugs—even if he did plant them. And I figure he got it from Davy's room. Davy said Arnie was going to take the H but I don't think that happened. Even without getting Drew to agree to be the buyer, that's enough to justify the bust. Then Davy drew on him—which he really did, but even if he hadn't, the other guys would back Purcell up."

"How do you know Purcell found dope at Davy's?"

"I know he was there. Sister Louise told me."

"You didn't tell me that." Pinto sounded hurt.

I shook my head. "Sorry. It was…just tough to figure out who to tell what."

Pinto waved a hand. "Forget it. Makes sense, though. Purcell was tailing Davy. And us for that matter. But, yeah, I'm thinking now it's not going to be easy to pin a murder rap on Purcell. And Lou can't rat him out for running protection on his own drug-running scheme."

I thought of my first conversation with Lou about the blackmail. "He could say he didn't know anything about it. Ramon was using him."

"What, give the cops the video and say he had nothing to do with it? Best case, the cops believe him, and trace Ramon back to Cambro." Pinto swallowed the last of his beer. "Wouldn't be good news for Lou. Cambro wouldn't be looking for the cops to solve his problems." He set the bottle on the table. "And my guess is neither would Lou."

That last guess pressed down on my spirit like a life sentence. Pinto looked morose.

"Fucking Davy," he said. "Seen it a million times. Young punks want to prove they've got cojones so they whack somebody. Very unprofessional."

I had to laugh, but it turned into a sob.

Pinto stood up, then reached down and put his hand on my shoulder.

"Want me to stay?"

I looked at his concerned brown eyes and started to cry. He pulled me in and gave me a hug. I laughed while the tears still streamed down my face, thinking maybe Lucie wasn't all that crazy for taking a shine to this crazy mug.

* * *

Saturday morning I was alone in the house; but not as alone as Lou must have felt returning to the police morgue to find out when he could get Davy's body moved to South Philadelphia for the funeral. Purcell's story must have been hanging together because no one had shown up looking to ask me what I had been doing in West Cape May last night.

I couldn't call Pauline because she did not have a phone, which was a good thing, because I was afraid I wouldn't be able to keep telling her lies. She'd read about Davy soon enough in the newspaper.

Lou had called the retreat house late last night, hoping that Concetta might have fetched up there. The girl on night duty roused Sister Louise. Lou couldn't bring himself to tell her what had happened, so he just left an urgent message in case she turned up.

I was making more coffee when I heard the door open downstairs, followed by footsteps. Then a head appeared above the floor beside the stairs.

The head was followed by a body, and the body looked familiar even if the head seemed…not right. At first, I thought maybe someone from the Seabreeze had come to check on us, but then realized that the short-haired—shorn-haired—woman was Concetta.

She looked like a teenage boy who had been sent to an evil barber to get rid of a mangy Beatles mop. She still looked beautiful, but in an alarming way, the bones of her forehead and cheeks framing her dark brown eyes. Those eyes looked like they had seen, and were still seeing, things that had pushed her past the brink of the maelstrom that her husband and son had brought her to. Concetta stopped on the edge of the living room area, turning toward the kitchen by instinct, the tendons on her neck stretched taut. She saw me but there was no sense of a greeting in her eyes. She moved to the table and sat, her back erect. As she sat, I saw she had a box wrapped in brown paper in one hand.

I was lost. "Concetta, I don't…I'm so sorry."

She answered, her voice so controlled it was scary. "Lou called this morning from the police station. Guess he's still there."

I answered, "Yes." I tried to push down my anger at having to lie to Concetta, maybe even before her husband had. "He called the retreat house last night…"

"I was there. I told Sister Louise to lie to him." She said it like it was a lie she knew she would have to confess. "Now I know why he called."

"Do you want some coffee?" The words sounded inane.

She stood. "I'm going to lie down."

She took the box with her. I had another cup of coffee on the deck and was considering whether I could just leave when I heard a car pull up. I went in, and Lou was coming up the steps. His eyes still looked horrible, but he moved with a manic energy.

I pointed toward his bedroom. "Concetta's…"

She appeared in the doorway like a hypnotized victim in an old vampire movie. Lou stopped in his tracks as he took in her gaunt visage.

Lou went to her and pulled her in. She did that not-raising-her-arms-to-touch-him thing. Lou tensed for a second, then pulled her closer. But it didn't matter how close he held her. He would never touch her again.

Lou let go, and Concetta stood still.

She asked, "He needed your help. Did you help him?"

I didn't know whether she meant the bullshit story Davy had told her about his falling out with Arnie, or some deeper need that Lou had ignored for a long time.

Lou spread his arms. "We were out looking for him…"

And so the lies continued. I felt as horrible as it seemed possible to feel.

Concetta spoke without moving or looking at her husband. "Now, I need your help."

She turned and went to the bedroom, then returned with the box.

Her voice was distant. "I tried to help him. Even when he was lying to me. I've heard so many lies…" She walked to the sliding doors, touching the glass as if to confirm that it was real. "I took that job to get money. And it wasn't enough. Carol…" she choked on the name, "she could be one of your friends. Happy to lend me whatever I needed to get myself in too deep…"

271

She turned. "So it's simple. I only want one thing from you…before you take me to see my son."

She walked toward the stairs, where she paused and turned, a faint glimmer of the old Concetta showing in her eyes. "We're going to see Carol. And bring your friend. We may need a witness."

* * *

The girl at the front desk had a dozen sets of keys laid out and was putting them on keychains. She didn't want to lose track of her work, you could tell, but when she saw Concetta, she got up quick and led us to Carol's office.

Carol wasn't at her desk—instead, she was sitting on the sofa. Concetta sat at the other end of the sofa, the box on her lap. There was one chair across the glass coffee table from the sofa. It felt like a set for some TV crime drama, one that Carol had starred in a hundred times.

Lou took his assigned seat. I had to ad lib quickly, grabbing a chair from next to her desk and dragging it over. There was no way I was sitting on the sofa between those two. Carol's polite nod indicated she agreed with my choice.

She offered us coffee and a concerned look that was scarier than even her normal smile.

"I was so sorry to hear about your son."

Lou tried to stay cool.

"Thanks."

I decided that coffee sounded great. I made a mess pouring myself a cup, spilling coffee on the table and rug. There was a part of Carol that was pissed, but she had more high-level evil to work.

"I know it's difficult, but…" Carol touched a folder on the table with her hand, "we have business to discuss."

Lou tried to cut to the chase. "How much?"

Carol gestured to Concetta. "Your wife borrowed a lot of money from me. Advances, we called them." She took her hand from the folder, having drawn attention to it. "All she'd have to do is get the listings for a couple beachfront properties and sell them."

Lou didn't say anything. He was looking at Concetta, who was staring straight ahead like she was in a trance, which maybe she was. Carol kept talking.

"Which will be a challenge since I fired her yesterday. And no one else will hire her, I can assure you."

I looked away from Concetta and found Carol smiling at me, in a glad-you-came? kind of way. She turned the smile to Lou. I never realized how vicious a smile could be.

"I understand Concetta has something you want." Carol pointed a finger with a long, crimson nail at the box. "What it is...is no concern of mine. But if you want it...I have a proposal."

She picked up the folder on the table and took out a sheaf of papers, several documents, some legal size, clipped together. She passed them to Lou.

"Your restaurant. A very interesting property."

Lou ran his finger down the page, stopping at what was undoubtedly a number.

"No fucking way."

Carol inched forward. "We'll pay you in cash. Today."

Lou tossed the papers on the table like he actually was in a negotiation. "It's worth twice that."

Carol played along with the negotiation charade. "We'll forget about the five grand Concetta owes me."

"That's a fucking hill of beans compared to this...bullshit." Lou pushed back in his chair.

Carol gave me that smile again. I think she liked having an audience. She and I both knew Lou was fucked. Carol dragged the papers toward her with a long fingernail.

"You have a choice. Do you want what's in the box? And by the way, if that's not enough incentive—whatever it is—I'm sure that there are plenty of things you'd like to keep quiet." She straightened the papers out. "Like your business arrangements with a certain pillar of the Mexican community down here."

Lou scoffed. "I don't know what you're talking about."

"Please. You think I don't make it my business to do...risk assessment... when I've got money on the line? And there's plenty of retired...fellows... down here who like to parlay their deep investigative experience into some pocket money...helps to pay the dues at the yacht club, that sort of thing."

Carol uncapped an expensive-looking fountain pen and handed it to Lou.

Lou took the pen and spoke in a hoarse voice. "I loved that fucking place."

Carol couldn't resist one last shot. "I know. Concetta said that's why this is the perfect deal."

Lou signed the papers. Carol took the pen back and stood.

I asked, "I thought you needed me to witness those."

Carol's head swiveled to me like I was a bug she had forgotten to squash. "No, we just needed someone who can attest that this was not done under duress."

I watched Carol walk out and promised myself that somehow I'd make sure she got the reward she deserved. In this life.

Chapter Twenty-Three

The black bow tie was hanging on the frame that held the mirror, one of those big oval ones attached to the chiffonier. The mirror had seen better days—and better mugs than mine, for sure. But I liked it—I liked the pale green color of the frame, and the blurry blotch in the upper right corner of the glass. The room was always dark, even with the lights on, except for the spot near the one window, where I had stationed a chair so I could look out across the street and see the surf through a space between the beachfront properties. Sometimes I spent a couple hours there in the early afternoon before my shift, drinking coffee and reading the sports section.

I got the clean white shirt from where it was hanging off the edge of the closet door. I put it on and buttoned it all the way up. Then the bow tie—it was the pre-tied type, with an elastic band so you just snapped it around your neck. Then the black vest.

It was a healthy little walk to work, but I didn't mind at all, not even in the late August heat. A few blocks from the boarding house, I was under trees and clipped along past folks coming back from the beach.

Gilbert gave me a nod as I came behind the bar. With these French guys, it was a profession being a bartender or waiter, not just a dead-end job for a dropout. I had learned a lot in just a few weeks working with him, especially how to interact with customers. There was a way he did it that was not just respectful, but also demanding of respect.

The sale of The Seabreeze had gone down within a couple of days of Davy's death, and I told Carol I was done. Within a week, I was doing shifts at The Jug, where the summer staff was already beginning to wander off. On my third day there, I was surprised to see Mark at the bar. But then I guess if he wanted to have a drink and relax, he couldn't go to his own place. He didn't act surprised at seeing me. He probably knew I was working there; maybe that's even why he stopped in. I put a cardboard coaster in front of him.

"We've got both kinds of wine here." I swept my hand toward the bottles behind me. "Sorry, I mean all three—red, white, rosé."

"Give me a Heineken."

I plunked the bottle down. We didn't give you a glass unless you asked for it. He didn't. It was a quiet late afternoon. It wasn't easy to avoid talking to him, but I waited for him to start.

"Shame about Lou—his son, I mean. I can understand why he wouldn't want to keep the place after that."

He sounded sincere. Maybe he didn't know how the sale went down, though he probably could figure there was a bad story behind it. I was cutting up lemons and limes.

I said, "Think Lou's had enough of Wildwood."

In fact, Lou had had enough of South Philly from what I was hearing. Pinto got it on the grapevine from guys at work that Lou was looking to unload his dealership. Apparently, he was already in Florida, which isn't a place folks typically run off to in August.

Mark slugged at the beer. "You seen Concetta?"

"Yeah." I pushed a bunch of lemon wedges into a bowl off the cutting board. "She's doing alright—as good as you can expect."

He shifted around on the stool, looking the place over with a professional eye. "She hasn't been in since…"

I shrugged. "Not a surprise." I thought about my last visit to Mark's place. "Hey, sorry about all that mess we made." I really was sorry. Mark was about the least guilty party in the whole fiasco. His problem really had been being friends with a couple of scumbags.

"Forget it." He paused a few seconds. "You ever see Arnie in here?"

"No."

"I haven't seen him in a while. Guess he must have gone to his place in Jupiter."

As far as I knew, nobody had seen Arnie. But then, it wasn't like I was asking after him. I could think of a few people who might have known what had happened to him, but one of them was dead, and the others would certainly not have been happy to hear his name brought up.

Mark turned back to me. "How much they paying you here?"

Trading a green t-shirt for the bow-tie and vest was an easy decision. I suspect it worked to have a mick behind the bar with all the French guys. It was a nice change, advising silver-templed guys in blazers on wine, versus slinging six beers for a dollar on Wednesday nights. Pinto said it was "karma" for all the bad shit Arnie had caused, but then he was all about the karma these days.

I was busy icing a few good bottles of white for what we called the dinner rush (what a joke) when Gilbert came over. He nodded toward the far end of the bar, where a very big Mexican guy waved to me.

Sleepy shined up pretty good. In fact, he was a commanding presence, wearing a spread-collar shirt that was a flowery pattern of purple and silver, pressed white linen slacks, shoes with a military shine. With him was a girl who would have given Pauline a run for her money as the one who was going to most light up the room.

I had read about Ramon's murder investigation in the papers…a focus on family members…allegations of domestic abuse…Green Card violations. After a few weeks, the story sank from view. Lou had expressed to the police his shock at the violent end that Ramon had met. He had been happy to give some business to such a hard-working minority business-owner and would be sure to make a contribution to the fund set up to help his family.

The whole thing made me sick and didn't exactly restore my faith in the criminal justice system. Davy's death caused even fewer ripples. There would be a proforma review of Purcell's actions, but I felt sure that would yield the expected result. It made me hate myself to know that I didn't want the truth to win in either case.

I served *cerveza* and tequila to Sleepy and his date. We joked about Pinto.

When their table was called, Sleepy put a much too big bill on the bar and lowered his head.

"His wife and *chavos*. They are all gone now."

I asked, "Who?"

His eyes locked on mine for a moment. *"El mecánico.* They go back to Mexico."

The girl was pulling his hand.

He lifted a finger to her and turned back to me. "Why stay?"

Chapter Twenty-Four

The sun was just about blinding me in my little room. I had dragged the chair right up to the window and had my bare feet propped up on the sill. The wind was blowing hard, even through the crack I had left at the bottom, propped up by a piece of driftwood I used to deal with the broken sash cord. I had a sheet of paper clipped to the checkerboard I had borrowed from the basket of old games on the porch—it was that kind of place.

I had just finished explaining to Pauline about finally stopping back at the Seabreeze, which in just a month was about fifty percent of the way to becoming a fern bar, a transformation that seemed to always follow my departure from a place of employment. I told myself that I wanted to see the people. But I knew that I also thought staying away was an admission of guilt.

Kevin was still there—I guess he could be grumpy working for anyone, what did it matter, but Sheila and Robert were both gone.

Sheila was doing nothing—she talked about opening a gift shop with a friend of hers, but she was glad to have a few summer weeks off after many years. Robert—I practically begged him to talk to Mark, but there was something there that wasn't right, maybe an old tiff with the current chef. He was going to Florida once it got cold and, in the meantime, was working here or there, subbing for friends who ran kitchens at golf clubs at the shore.

Carol showed up at the bar one evening, awaiting the arrival of her dinner date. She sat like a spider in her black dress, emanating the usual dangerous, muscular sexuality. I poured her drink and accepted the generous tip without comment.

She had gotten a new listing that week: Arnie's house. His attorney had contacted her. Apparently, Arnie was out of the country indefinitely. Gilbert, his unerring radar detecting my distress, came from the other end of the bar to refill her Lillet, allowing me to escape into the back.

Pinto—Pauline would get a kick out of this—was taking a French conversation course at a community college. That way, he could handle any mishaps with the gendarmes in our little road trip to Quebec after the summer was over. When I visited him in the tiny attic apartment he had found in Cape May—he was done with the nephews and cousins—he was serene, his hair now getting long in the back and lacking Vitalis, a wooden pipe with whatever he was smoking in an ashtray, the sun glinting off the mandala hanging in the window. The old Pinto was still there, I was sure, but reconfigured by whatever galaxy he was moving through now.

One of the bartenders at the Jug, where I occasionally dropped in for sentimental reasons, told me there was a story going around that there had been a fight at a biker bar out in the Pinelands, where a State Trooper got pretty banged up by some little guy wearing a black t-shirt and a lot of gold chains. When I saw Pinto a few days later wearing sunglasses and an uncharacteristic bucket hat inside a bar at midnight, I was too much of a gentleman to ask if he was trying to hide anything.

I wrote words that I didn't think I knew how to say to close the letter, and sealed it up in the envelope before I could change my mind. I still had a few hours until my shift. I slipped on my sandals and grabbed a little plastic cooler. I drove the Caddy to the post office, then up to the boardwalk. Lou never talked to me about the car, so I just found the guy he had borrowed it from and bought it for cash.

"Yo, Leo."

I looked over the counter of the hot dog shack. Leo was stretched out on a chaise lounge that just about filled the entire space. He got to his feet and turned the lounge on its side in a single, practiced motion.

I held the cooler up. He got two buns out, plunked dogs into them, then did them up as usual—one plain, one with kraut. He squirted mustard on them and wrapped them up in double sheets of waxed paper. A Sprite and a Dr. Pepper went in the cooler first, then the dogs in a cardboard tray.

Leo looked down at the half-smoked joint in an ashtray and back to me. I shook my head, although if you ever wanted to smoke a joint, he was the guy to do it with. I gave him a few bills and went back to the Caddy.

It was a short drive down to the Point. I liked to park just a few blocks south of the State Park where the lighthouse is, and walk down the beach from there.

As I got close to the retreat house, I saw a woman at the water's edge, her white slacks rolled up almost to her knees. She was shading her eyes from the sun, looking out at the waves. I called out and held up the cooler. When I got up to her, she spoke.

"I saw a dolphin—just now."

I stood there with her and looked, but didn't see anything. Her white blouse was buttoned all the way up. I had gotten used to the short, blunt haircut. Maybe she had grown into it, or maybe I had. I guess she could never really be a nun, but in my mind, she was there.

We sat on the sand and ate the hot dogs. I left her there with her Sprite. I walked up toward the building and stopped when I got to the veranda, sitting down on the concrete edge. I cracked open my Dr. Pepper and watched Concetta walking back and forth on the shore, and searched like hell for a dolphin in the sea.

Acknowledgments

I would like to thank Jon McGoran for his editorial advice; the following folks who read and provided comments on the ms— Nick Sweeney, Nick Wardigo, the late Mike Burke, Tim O'Neill, Bob Stapleton, Joe Mancano, Jeff Markowitz, Jane Kelly and Tara Tomczyk; the people at *Ambit* magazine, especially J. G. Ballard, Martin Bax and Geoff Nicholson (all, sadly, no longer with us), who gave me my start; the Liars Club of Philadelphia for support and encouragement (especially Gregory Frost, Merry Jones and Kelly Simmons); and Anne Dubuisson for contract and literary advice. Also, thanks to the folks at Level Best Books for their excellent work—Shawn Simmons, Verena Rose and Deb Well. Finally, the work could not be done without the support and advice of my wife Anne, always my first reader and believer.

About the Author

Joel E. Turner has combined his writing work with a career as a consultant in business analytics to banks in the US and Europe. His fiction has appeared in many US and UK journals. He also writes about Soul Music, film, and books at joeleturnerauthor.com. *Wildwood Exit* draws on his extensive work experience at some of the finer dining establishments at the Jersey Shore. He knows how to operate a Frialator.

Mr. Turner splits his time between Philadelphia and White Cloud, Michigan.

AUTHOR WEBSITE:
  joeleturnerauthor.com

SOCIAL MEDIA HANDLES (live links):
  Facebook: Facebook.com/joeleturner2
  Twitter/X: @JoelETurner1
  Bluesky: @joeleturner.bsky.social

www.ingramcontent.com/pod-product-compliance
Lightning Source LLC
Chambersburg PA
CBHW020603110726
47899CB00002B/356